Praise for *The Love of a Lawman*

"Real characters come to life in this heart-wrenching tale littered with imperfect characters readers come to love and root for."　　　　　　—*Rendezvous*

"Engaging . . . the story line is loaded with action and the cast is a strong ensemble. . . . A warm romantic tale."　　　　　　—The Best Reviews

"If you like well-written, character-driven romances . . . with engaging characters and lots of internal conflict, I highly recommend *The Love of a Lawman*."
　　　　　　—Romance Reviews Today

"A very good read! This was a very strong character-driven read which will take the reader on an emotional journey. I highly recommend Ms. Jeffrey and suggest that you not miss her latest effort."
　　　　　　—Romance Designs

"This book definitely worked as a stand-alone novel in this trilogy, and this reviewer will be reading more by Anna Jeffrey in the future, including the rest of this series. *The Love of a Lawman* is highly recommended."
　　　　　　—Love Romances

Praise for *The Love of a Stranger*

"Delicious . . . a riveting read." —*Publishers Weekly*

"Fun . . . a delightful, solid novel."

　　　　　　—Harriet Klausner

continued

Other Books by Anna Jeffrey

The Love of a Lawman
The Love of a Stranger
The Love of a Cowboy

Sweet Water

Anna Jeffrey

A SIGNET ECLIPSE BOOK

SIGNET ECLIPSE
Published by New American Library, a division of
Penguin Group (USA) Inc., 375 Hudson Street,
New York, New York 10014, U.S.A.
Penguin Group (Canada), 90 Eglinton Avenue East, Suite 700, Toronto,
Ontario M4P 2Y3, Canada (a division of Pearson Penguin Canada Inc.)
Penguin Books Ltd., 80 Strand, London WC2R 0RL, England
Penguin Ireland, 25 St. Stephen's Green, Dublin 2,
Ireland (a division of Penguin Books Ltd.)
Penguin Group (Australia), 250 Camberwell Road, Camberwell, Victoria 3124,
Australia (a division of Pearson Australia Group Pty. Ltd.)
Penguin Books India Pvt. Ltd., 11 Community Centre, Panchsheel Park,
New Delhi - 110 017, India
Penguin Group (NZ), cnr Airborne and Rosedale Roads, Albany,
Auckland 1310, New Zealand (a division of Pearson New Zealand Ltd.)
Penguin Books (South Africa) (Pty.) Ltd., 24 Sturdee Avenue,
Rosebank, Johannesburg 2196, South Africa

Penguin Books Ltd., Registered Offices:
80 Strand, London WC2R 0RL, England

First published by Signet Eclipse, an imprint of New American Library,
a division of Penguin Group (USA) Inc.

First Printing, January 2006
10   9   8   7   6   5   4   3   2   1

ACKNOWLEDGMENTS

In spite of my nagging and nit picking, Kristin Gibson came up with the beautiful song lyrics that tell Ben's story. Thank you, Kristin.

Good critique partners are like gold and I have two who fit into that category, authors Mary Jane Meier and Laura Renken.

As always, I thank my husband, George, for his unwavering support and faith in me, and my daughter, Adrienne, for being my relentless, cheerleading fan.

Chapter 1

Marisa Rutherford was elbow-deep, sweating and cleaning and cussing the only espresso machine in Agua Dulce, Texas, when Mr. Patel came into Pecos Belle's Emporium & Eats and reported that the whole damn town had been sold on eBay.

The news brought Marisa up from her task so abruptly she jammed her finger against the side of the espresso machine. She yowled and rubbed the injury and cussed some more. "You're kidding," she said through her pain.

"No. I am not." The East India native's dark eyes glistened as if he might break into tears. "He is going to construct a monster petrol station."

For a fleeting second Marisa wished for an Internet connection so she could personally check that information. Though all of the Agua Dulce citizens knew the embittered widow of the town's owner had posted the village on the Internet auction a month earlier, no one had believed it would be sold. Who in their right mind would pay a million dollars for a town of ten residents in the most sparsely populated county in Texas? And in *West* Texas, at that?

Without a good-bye, Mr. Patel turned and headed for the front door, weaving through tables of antiques and flea market wares, dodging aged oxen yokes and weathered hames that hung from the ceiling. As he went, he muttered in a language Marisa didn't even know the name of, much less understand.

From where she stood in the back of the building—the location of the "Eats" part of Pecos Belle's Emporium & Eats—she had a clear view of the Patels' dumpy service station on the opposite side of the highway. The setting sun cast the stucco building in gold, which made it look twice its fifty-year-old age. Mr. Patel sold gasoline outside, but inside, he and his wife and two daughters operated an overcrowded convenience store that peddled everything from quarts of milk to T-shirts with Spider-Man logos on the front.

As Marisa watched him wait for a passing car, then dash across the highway, fear gripped her. How the hell would she support herself and her mother if Agua Dulce's new owner built one of those mega service stations right next door? Or worse yet, right on top if them. Marisa's thoughts careened into each other as she considered the consequences if the old brick structure her mother had leased for more than thirty years suddenly fell into the hands and under the control of a new owner.

By the time she reassembled the espresso machine, she had worked herself into a full-blown panic. Pecos Belle's balance sheet showed the combined value of goods for sale and functioning restaurant equipment to be close to a quarter million dollars, an investment accrued over the years by her mother. If the new owner demanded that they vacate, what would she do with Mama's stuff? All she could think of was screeching at her mother. Why had she done business in a leased building, in a privately owned town, in the middle of nowhere, for most of her life?

But Marisa already knew the answer, and it was too late for recriminations. The chance of a rational discussion of the problem was forever shut out of Mama's brain. A brutal bastard was steadily sucking the intelligence and the very life from the mother who had once been witty, wise and loving. The scourge had a name Marisa had come to equate with hell: Alzheimer's disease.

The wall clock that shrieked and chugged like a locomotive at twelve and six every day—only God knew where Mama had gotten it—blasted Marisa from her thoughts. Suppertime. Time to get a meal together for Mama.

She locked the plate-glass front door, hung up the CLOSED sign and turned off all but the night-lights. Then she went to the kitchen. A gas-flame griddle and a short counter with a stainless-steel cabinet hanging above it filled one wall of the galley-style room. A huge refrigerator and freezer, a commercial dishwasher and a stainless-steel triple sink covered the opposite wall. Marisa could stand between the appliances and touch the refrigerator door with one hand and the hanging cabinet with the other. She couldn't imagine sixty square feet of space being used more efficiently anywhere in the world.

After spending most of the afternoon cleaning the espresso machine, she felt fatigue weighing heavily, but she pulled a ground beef patty from the refrigerator, placed it on the hot griddle and seasoned it. Pecos Belle's served hamburgers made of lean sirloin, ground and molded into patties by Marisa herself. She hated that preformed, frozen-cardboard product that too many cafés—including the one where she had last cooked, in Arlington, Texas—touted and served up as "fresh, home-style hamburgers."

She constructed a hamburger with all the trimmings, then sliced it in half and tucked it into a parchment-lined plastic basket with a few French fries. Not the healthiest meal, but Mama loved hamburgers and Marisa indulged her. Her mother was dying. At this point what difference did it make what she ate?

She turned off the flame under the griddle and spent a few more minutes wiping down and straightening the kitchen. On the way out the back door, she stopped off at the bathroom medicine cabinet in the apartment that butted up to the café's kitchen and dining area. There, under lock and key, Marisa kept Mama's assortment of pills. She stored them in the building separate from where she and Mama lived because it was too risky leaving them where they were easily accessible. Mama, in her addled state of mind, might swallow all of them at one time. Marisa bumped one tiny tablet onto her palm and slid it into her pocket.

Carrying the hamburger, she exited through the back door. A Fleetwood singlewide mobile home was set up behind the building where Mama had operated Pecos Belle's flea market/antiques store and café/coffee bar since before Marisa was born. Oh, and there was a museum of sorts. It boasted reproductions of dinosaur footprints cast in plaster, a stuffed and mounted rattlesnake more than fifteen feet long and a giant papier-mâché gorilla statue. There was also a real, full-sized covered wagon dating back to the post–Civil War migration west. Anything to drag a motorist off the highway. If Mr. Patel hadn't already cornered the market on gasoline, Mama surely would have tried selling that, too.

Marisa followed a rock pathway two hundred feet to the mobile home's front deck. When she entered the singlewide, she saw her mother sitting in front of TV watching a sitcom. Mama had put her blouse on backward and some strings of pink yarn hung in her white hair—not tied, just sort of draped.

Marisa felt a little ping in her heart. Mama had been so pretty when she was young. Marisa could vaguely remember her blue eyes, complexion like porcelain and long blond hair. Instinct caused a woman who had once been so attractive to still attempt makeup and hairdos, Marisa guessed, but more often than not, the effort came off with Mama looking like a clown. Seeing it broke Marisa's heart, but she didn't interfere. Her mother didn't know the difference, and these days it was rare for anyone but Marisa to see her. What little family they had seldom came and Mama's friends in Agua Dulce, out of respect, were reluctant to gawk at her decline.

"What's happening on TV?" Marisa asked, setting the burger on the table in a cramped dining area that was squeezed between the kitchen and the living room.

As Marisa took ice cubes from a tray, Mama answered her question by summarizing the TV show she had been watching, clearly mixing in a few scenes from other TV shows from who knew when.

Marisa pulled a pitcher of tea from the refrigerator and poured it over the ice, stirred in a teaspoonful of sugar and set the glass on the table beside the hamburger. Then, still listening to her mother's prattle, she urged her up from her recliner and guided her to a chair at the dining table. She wrapped a warm hamburger half in a napkin and placed it in her mother's wizened hands. "There, now. Eat."

Mama lifted the burger and obediently took a bite. "I saw your daddy today," she said, chewing robotically and looking into space, the vacancy in her eyes magnified by thick glasses.

To Marisa's knowledge, her mother hadn't set eyes on Marisa's father since before her birth. She once heard from her aunt Rosemary that her parents had lived together for a time. "Hec, the Sperm Donor," Aunt Rosemary called him. Hector Espinosa. He was from Arizona, half Apache and half Mexican, which accounted for Marisa's olive coloring and straight black hair. And possibly her sometimes hot temper. Her ancestry did not, however, explain her amber eyes.

"Really, Mama? Where was that?"

"I was at a dance in Odessa. I tried to get his attention, but he had his back to me."

Even now, Mama loved to dance. Marisa had no trouble believing she had once tripped lightly with the best of them. "Awww. That's too bad."

"I'm not going over there again," Mama said. "Nothing but a bunch of drunks. I got so mad I just walked home."

Odessa was a hundred miles east, but that fact meant nothing. These days she and Mama had many nonsensical conversations. Marisa always played along, not knowing what else to do. "I don't blame you," she said.

"Marisa, if he's found somebody else, you can tell me, you know."

A burning sensation flew to Marisa's eyes and she

turned away. *Goddamn it!* Hadn't fate been cruel enough to her gentle, caring mother? Hadn't it been enough that some sonofabitch she had obviously never been able to put out of her mind left her pregnant and stuck in this West Texas sinkhole of a place for her whole life? No, apparently all of that hadn't been enough. Now, a disease from hell was taking her mind.

"Why, Mama," she said, "he could never find someone else like you. Go ahead now and finish your supper."

Marisa had tamped down and dammed up so many emotions, sometimes she thought her skull might explode, yet, as she did a dozen times a day, she fought back her grief and frustration and took her time helping her mother eat, chatting along about this and that.

Changing the subject from Mama's past wasn't hard, as her ability to concentrate on anything for longer than a couple of minutes had been gone for a while. Lately, even companionship meant little to her. None of that mattered now. No one had given more love or care to her friends and acquaintances, or to Marisa, than her mother. Nothing, not even eviction from Pecos Belle's, would keep Raylene Rutherford's daughter from making sure her beloved parent spent her last days with a roof over her head, good food in her belly and love surrounding her.

After supper Marisa removed the yarn from her mother's hair, helped her bathe and get into her nightgown. She had her swallow the pill she had brought from the medicine cabinet in Pecos Belle's. What good the drug did Marisa couldn't tell. She didn't know its exact purpose in the first place, but it always put Mama down for the night. According to the doctor, that was good. The last thing anyone wanted was for

Mama to be up wandering during the night. Science's best solution appeared to be to zonk her with drugs.

Marisa waited for her charge to grow drowsy, then helped her to the bed. The crinkly eyelids fluttered shut and Mama's breathing became deep and even. Marisa held her mother's hand for a time, studying the papery skin, the distinct blue veins that carried her lifeblood. Her hand looked like an elderly woman's hand. Raylene Rutherford was sixty-six years old. Marisa had been born a bastard when her mother was thirty-two, old enough to know how to avoid an unwanted pregnancy. Marisa longed to know her mother's story, but no one had ever told her. Through the years, only bits and pieces had been dropped by her aunts.

Once again, so as not to be immobilized by her emotions, Marisa pushed them to a dark place deep in her psyche.

Chapter 2

The black of night was fading to daylight's soft gray as Terry Ledger plugged his key into the front door of his twelfth-floor condominium in the Tower in downtown Fort Worth. He hated dragging in at this hour. He should have come home last night after dinner, shouldn't have stayed the night at Michelle's.

As he stepped into the entry, the clean smell of lemon oil met him, proof that his housekeeper, Irene Mendoza, had been on the scene. To his left the muted glow of streetlights beaming through bare windows dimly lit the rectangle that was the living room. Its bare maple floors and stark white walls reminded him of a racquetball court. He dropped his truck keys in a heavy art glass bowl on a massive oak harvest table in the entryway, made a right turn into the high-ceilinged white kitchen and put coffee on to drip.

While waiting for the eye-opening brew, he walked back to the living room, his footsteps echoing through the almost-empty space. His few pieces of living room furniture were mostly mismatched castoffs from dozens of model home showings across the Fort Worth/Dallas area. His plants were artificial. His only window treatments—they had come from the shelves of Wal-

Mart—didn't hang in the living room, but served to provide privacy in his bedroom.

To a successful home builder with his schedule, his condo decor meant next to nothing. He was asleep most of the time he spent here. His only requirement was that it be meticulously clean, kept that way by Irene, who came in every day except on weekends. For as long as he could remember he had been a stickler for cleanliness, but he had become a regular martinet after a six-year hitch in the army.

Despite the lack of furniture and decor, his digs weren't shabby. The condo was located in what had been the Bank One building before a tornado crashed through downtown Fort Worth, took out more than half the skyscraper's glass and devastated the interior. What had once been luxury offices was now luxury living spaces. Downtown living wasn't his style, but getting in on the ground floor when the Tower opened for occupancy made the condo an outstanding investment.

He liked owning a little part of downtown Fort Worth. The city was in the midst of a revival, and he liked being on the scene to watch the transformation. As much as he loved everything about the construction of something new, he loved the reconstruction of something old. He loved progress. He was filled with awe and admiration at everything the wealthy Bass and Tandy families had accomplished. They had methodically restored the old areas that had fallen into decay after the flight to the suburbs of businesses and retail stores. They had built a concert hall and a mega movie theater and remodeled any number of historic buildings. Other entrepreneurs had followed, adding shopping and museums, opening high-caliber restaurants and trendy nightclubs. Downtown Fort Worth now surpassed Dallas as a happening place for a fun night out.

Now, as he gazed out his wall-to-wall windows over the awakening city, the lights still visible were mostly streetlights, casting the streets and buildings in a dull pinkish glow. Few human beings were awake at this hour, much less walking the sidewalks, so the only sign of life was a pair of private cops on bicycles. A stillness hung in the air, as if the city waited to burst into action at the first pink shard of daylight.

Last night's awkward conversation with Michelle intruded into his thoughts. It had been all about commitment and his lack thereof. They had eaten a delicious quail dinner and downed a bottle of good wine at Reata, then gone to her apartment in West Fort Worth for dessert—a session of blood-boiling sex.

Afterward, as they shared yet another glass of wine, she laid out a plan for a four-three-two house in a bedroom community within commuting distance to her downtown office. Her scenario included a nanny to care for the two kids they would have while she worked toward a partnership in the firm where she practiced personal-injury law.

Knowing her lofty ambitions, Terry was surprised that institutions as mundane as matrimony and motherhood interested her. Unfortunately, sharing those two life steps with Michelle didn't interest *him*. Her true loyalty lay with whoever could do the most for her, and too often her sharp tongue or her self-centered attitude reminded him too much of his mother. Terry couldn't wrap his mind around playing the role with any woman he had now watched four men play with his mom.

Still, he didn't mind Michelle's company. Oh, sure, she was argumentative and did have to have the last word in any conversation, but she was witty and quick with a quip, thus entertaining. And she was a head-turner in the looks department. And she was an animal in bed, as was he. Before knowing her, he thought he knew most of what there was to know about sex, but she had taught him a few new tricks. He had never asked where she learned them—didn't care. From the beginning of their affair he had suspected he wasn't her only sex partner, though he was certain she would deny it.

For the six months they had been seeing each other, he thought sex was what their relationship was about. The L-word had never been uttered, nor had the C-word. Then, *wham!* Last night, after more Merlot than either of them needed, she brought up children and family and insisted on a discussion. He felt as if he had been ambushed. Marriage was the farthest thing from his mind. And living in a suburb, even in a subdivision he had designed and developed, held less appeal than watching a freight truck unload.

He tried to be kind, tried to say gently that if and when he chose a woman with whom he would spend the rest of his life, one who would be the mother of his children, the same woman would most likely be a stay-at-home mom. If he ever had a family—and at age thirty-six, he had begun to wonder—no nanny or babysitter would raise his kids.

Chauvinistic? Perhaps. He had been labeled as such by the fairer sex more times than he could count, and he had no intention of changing. He had been reared by babysitters himself while his parents pursued their respective careers. His mother was a trial attorney who had usually shown more concern for her cases than her family. His dad, a consulting petroleum engineer, traveled the world.

He remembered the loneliness of being the only kid with no parent present at a Pop Warner game, the embarrassment of parent-teacher conference week with no parent available to participate, being handed a hundred-dollar bill and told to choose his own athletic shoes because no one had time to take him shopping.

Even now, he didn't know exactly where on the planet his parents might be. His dad could be somewhere in the Middle East, or perhaps Indonesia. His mother, the last he had heard, was in California, honeymooning with her fourth husband, no doubt already arguing talking points with the poor bastard, just as she had done with her first husband and her succeeding husbands. And her son.

The previous evening still on his mind and his conscience, he returned to the kitchen, poured a cup of joe and made his way to the master suite. Michelle had ended up in tears, which was why *he* ended up spending the night at her apartment. Leaving with her so upset felt too callous. No question, he was a soft touch for a woman in tears.

He stayed over, then got the hell out early this morning while she slept. Not the most chivalrous move he had ever made, but, under the circumstances, the easiest and most surgical. With a busy and exciting day ahead of him, he did not—repeat, *did not*—want to be distracted by another session of her weeping and him tactfully trying to explain that as far as he was concerned, the feminist idea of a woman "having it all" was hogwash.

He clicked the TV on as he strode through the huge master bedroom on his way to the bathroom. The news came on with headlines. Mortgage interest low, new home starts up. Good news for a man who owed more than a million dollars in mortgage debt and had fifty spec homes on the ground in various stages of completion.

In the bathroom, as he brushed his teeth and shaved, he planned his day. This morning he would meet his engineer, Brad England, at a new subdivision site he had bought at a distress price fifty miles southwest of Fort Worth. The roughly two thousand acres were incredibly beautiful, with gently rolling hills, groves of hundred-year-old live oak trees and a huge stock tank with the potential to be expanded into a small lake.

He and Brad were in the process of carving and shaping the old ranch into ten-to-twenty-acre parcels. It would become Rancho Casero, a subdivision and gated horse community. There would be stables and an arena for playdays and cutting-horse events, a clubhouse and pool and a restaurant that would be planned and operated by a chef well known for his Tex-Mex cuisine. Buyers were already migrating out of Fort Worth and Dallas and laying down premium prices to own an elegant little piece of Western-style country living.

His construction company, Terry Ledger Homes, had already begun construction of upscale Santa Fe–style houses in which commuters and still more retiring baby boomers would live. The population of well-heeled retirees would patronize his restaurant. His profit would be enormous. He knew all of this from having already done it several times.

He entered his marble walk-in shower and turned on the radio he kept on a shelf in the shower. He shampooed his hair while one part of his brain listened to local news and weather and another part thought beyond the meeting with his engineer.

He would be finished by noon, then he would head west to the most exciting real estate buy he had ever made. His pragmatic persona shuddered at the gamble he had taken; his risk-taker side, the one that lived to skydive or hang glide or jet-ski at daylight across a Texas lake at full throttle, the one that usually won out, cheered him on.

It was the risk-taker side that had made him rich.

It was the risk-taker side that had been in charge when, just four days ago, he had purchased a town in West Texas, sight unseen, on eBay.

Now, as he soaped and rinsed his body, an exhilaration thrummed within him. He could hardly wait to get to his town. He had wanted to return to West Texas since his discharge from the army. For several years, Ledger Ranches, a retirement community on the order of Sun City, had been on the drawing board, waiting for him to find just the right location. He believed his quest had ended. Both desires could now be met. A hamlet with good water and two hundred acres adjoining a cattle ranch on one side, which, he had learned from one of his fellow Realtors in Odessa, could be bought.

He stepped out of the shower less than fifteen minutes later. Time was money. He rarely wasted it. As he finger-combed and dried his hair in front of the vanity mirror, something caught his eye. When had the hair at his temples turned silver?

He stopped for a few seconds and looked closer, noting the creases in his forehead, the crow's-feet fanning from the corners of his eyes, the lines framing his mouth. He clenched his jaw against one of his deepest dreads—growing old or dying before he completed his many plans.

He shook his head, driving away the disquieting thought.

He carried an extra toothbrush and toothpaste, shampoo and shaving gear back to the bedroom and stuffed them into a small nylon duffel. He pulled on clean jeans, a long-sleeved knit shirt and his heavy biker boots, then crammed half a dozen changes of socks and boxers, jeans and shirts, sweats, his cowboy boots and his Nikes into the duffel. He was packed.

By the time the sky turned lavender, he stood perusing the nearly bare shelves of his refrigerator. He pulled out a Styrofoam take-out box and found half of a beef-and-bean burrito, which he zapped for thirty seconds in the microwave. It tasted like plywood, but he didn't worry over little things like taste and texture. Food was sustenance, nothing more. During survival training in the army, he had eaten the unthinkable. He washed the burrito down with coffee, quelling the empty feeling left in his gut by too much vino last night.

As wine entered his thoughts for a second time, another wave of conscience passed over him. On a sigh, he called his favorite downtown florist and ordered a spring bouquet—roses would send the wrong message—to be delivered today to Michelle at her office. He told the florist to include a note saying, "Sorry I'm not the one. Terry."

Then he was out the door. In the parking garage, he donned his leathers and helmet, backed his Harley out of its closeted slot, mounted up and roared out onto the street. By sundown, he would be five hundred miles away in Agua Dulce, Texas.

Chapter 3

Marisa came awake to a bedroom bright with sunlight. The aroma of something cooking teased and tempted her. A jolt of fear popped her eyes wide and she sprang from bed, nearly falling from being not quite awake.

She stumbled to the kitchen in her sleeping costume— boxer shorts and a Dallas Cowboys T-shirt—and saw Mama sitting at the dining table. At least a dozen slices of toasted bread, sans plate, stood in a stack on the tabletop. The remaining untoasted slices from the loaf were scattered across the kitchen counter.

"I didn't mean to wake you," Mama said, munching on a toast slice.

Marisa suppressed a groan. "That's okay, Mama. I'm sorry I didn't wake up."

Last night, unable to shut out the endless parade of varying disasters that could result from the sale of Agua Dulce, Marisa had lain awake for hours. "I didn't drop off until late. Is everything all right?"

"Oh, yes. I just made some toast."

Having Mama in the kitchen alone cooking *any-thing*, even toast, was an unacceptable risk. Every day Marisa pondered if she should remove all cooking utensils from the kitchen and disconnect the stove.

Her brow arched as she whipped herself into wakefulness. A pain throbbed behind her eyes. "Lord, I'm late. I hope no one's showed up for breakfast." She went to the coffee grinder and fumbled through grinding beans, wincing at the noise the grinder made. "Listen, Mama, I'm gonna get a shower, then run over to the café and heat up the griddle. You'll be okay here 'til I can get back, right?"

"Oh, yes. I'll get dressed and take a little walk."

"No!" The thought of Mama alone outside was another of Marisa's nightmares. In the vast expanse of unpopulated desert that lay outside the singlewide's walls, Mama could get lost in nothing flat. Marisa switched on the coffeepot and lowered her voice. "No, don't walk, Mama. I'll come back after breakfast and we'll take a walk together, okay?"

Her mother's eyes teared and her chin trembled. "If you say so, Marisa. I hope you don't forget. I do need my exercise."

Shit. Now Marisa felt like a heel. Emotion so close to the surface was part of Mama's disease. It had taken some getting used to, because such displays were so out of character for the mother Marisa used to know. "Look, you need to eat something besides toast." She pulled Cheerios from an upper cabinet. As the coffee dripped, she prepared a bowl of cereal with canned peach slices and set it in front of her mother. "Eat some cereal while I take a quick shower, okay?" The coffee gurgled to a finish and Marisa poured Mama a cup, then poured one for herself.

Carrying the coffee, Marisa padded to the hall bathroom, which was barely big enough for a tub/shower combo, a commode and a sink. The mobile home had a master suite of sorts on one end, but Mama used that.

Marisa hurried through a shower and shampoo, bumping her elbows on the fiberglass walls and vowing that when she got rich, one of the first things she would have was a decent-sized bathtub and shower.

She dried off quickly and styled her hair. Cut to a shoulder-length bob, it required nothing more than a hairbrush and a few minutes with the dryer. She didn't wear makeup, but this morning, she rubbed a bit of cream from every jar on the bathroom counter under her eyes. None of it seemed to lighten the dark circles or shrink the puffy pouches.

She pulled on a Western-style shirt—white, with embroidered red roses and silky fringe hanging from arching yokes across the front and back—and stuffed herself into clean Rockies jeans. Through the belt loops, she slipped a Mexican tooled-leather belt with conchos and a silver buckle the size of a saucer. She pulled on cowboy boots and added some silver jewelry to her earlobes and wrists. Marisa, Queen of the Cowgirls.

Though she could ride a horse and had been around livestock growers most of her youth, she wasn't a real cowgirl. Not even close. But it was important to look like a Westerner. In this part of Texas, near Langtry, where the legend of Judge Roy Bean flourished and not too far from Billy the Kid's haunt in New Mexico, the Wild West was what tourists expected to see. Since those roaming visitors were her and Mama's bread and butter, Marisa would climb aboard a bucking bronc before she would disappoint them. She even laughed at their lame jokes about her being "Pecos Belle."

When she returned to the kitchen, Mama had finished eating and, thank God, had forgotten about walking. Marisa seated her in front of the TV, then consumed another cup of coffee and slid all of the bread and toast slices into a Ziploc bag.

She reminded her mother that she would be back soon, then headed for Pecos Belle's, carrying the toast slices with her. *When life hands you lemons, make lemonade,* she told herself. Only today, she would use the toast to make bread pudding. Waste not, want not.

As she made a tour through the flea market, turning on lights, straightening displays, brushing away a speck of dust here and there, unlocking the front door, the sunrise began to brighten the large room. Early morning was the most peaceful part of her day. She enjoyed being alone in the café with its silence and its mix of spices and good food smells left over from the day before.

She put two flavors of coffee on to brew in the Bunn on the back counter across from the lunch counter, drew a large empty pickle jar full of water, added two giant teabags and set it just outside the front door to steep.

Ready to begin work, she turned on the radio to keep her company and heard a new tune with a good dancing beat. She loved dancing—in that way she was like Mama—but how long had it been since she had dressed up and hit a honky-tonk?

In the tiny café kitchen, she turned on the flame under the griddle, then set about measuring ingredients for bread pudding. Back when she'd had a job as a professional cook, her recipe for bread pudding had always been a favorite. She usually used sourdough bread she baked herself, but today toasted store-bought white bread would have to do.

Soon, the delicious aroma of the baking pudding surrounded her. Savoring the smells of butter and vanilla, she hummed along with the radio as she cleaned and straightened the back counter. A car engine sounded out front, then died. She glanced across the flea market, out the display windows that took up the whole front of the building, at a state trooper's black-and-white. She smiled inside. Two minutes later the front door chimed and the best part of her life strolled in. Keith Wood, or just Woody to his friends. He had probably come for breakfast.

In his taupe-colored uniform and gray Stetson, he looked good enough to *be* breakfast. She had a weakness for a man in uniform, especially one who was lean and tanned, with mysterious dark eyes and a come-hither smile. She and Woody had been an item for about a year and he still came by several times a week. The good-looking son of a gun had touched every one of her secret places and she usually couldn't wait for him to do it again.

"Hiya, copper," she said, eager to tell him about the sale of Agua Dulce. Just a few weeks ago they had laughed about the widow posting the town for sale and the odds against someone ever being dumb enough to buy something like a town on eBay.

He took a seat on one of the round stools that fronted the lunch counter and she leaned across to kiss her favorite Texas DPS trooper. He kissed back, but without the usual enthusiasm. "Uh-oh," she said, deferring her own news to listen to what could be bothering him. "Don't tell me. You've had a run-in with some real bad guys."

He shook his head and looked up at her with serious eyes.

She braced herself on her forearms just inches from his delicious lips. "Tell you what," she said softly. "I could lock the front door for a while. There's clean sheets on the bed and I know all sorts of remedies to take your mind off your troubles."

Growing up, she and her mother had lived in the two-bedroom apartment in the back of the building. Mama hadn't bought the singlewide mobile home until after Marisa left home. Many times, Marisa and Woody had heated up the apartment bedroom that had been Mama's.

"Don't I know it," he said with a crooked grin.

She could see in his eyes he wanted to follow her back there. But she could also see it wasn't going to happen today. Something was *really* bothering him. She touched his lower lip with her finger. "What is it, sugar?"

He lifted off his hat and set it on the counter. "You got just a plain old-fashioned cup of coffee?"

She tucked back her chin and widened her eyes in a display of mock surprise. "What, no French-Colombian-Traditional-Campfire blend flavored with vanilla?"

He snickered and she stepped away and poured him a cup from the carafe labeled REGULAR.

"Smells good in here," he said. "What's cooking?"

"Bread pudding. Comfort food. Be done in a few minutes. Want some?"

He shook his head and lifted the mug to his lips.

After a long sip, he set the mug back on the counter. "I need to talk to you, Marisa."

She heard a solemnity in his tone and felt a chill that had nothing to do with the air-conditioning. "You know me, sugar. I'm always up for good conversation." She set the coffee carafe back on its heating element, the news of the sale of the town forgotten for now.

He stared into his mug without saying anything, but in her head, Marisa heard Santa Anna's trumpet blowing at the Alamo.

Finally he looked toward the front door. "I guess I'm getting married, Marisa."

Marisa's heart dropped to her shoes. On scattered occasions she and Woody Wood had skirted the edges of taking their relationship to the matrimony stage. She hadn't imagined that the union would include him but not her. She swallowed, but it didn't help. Her tongue seemed to have stopped working. "Oh?" was all she could push from her mouth.

He looked up with an expression so aggrieved that uncertainty vanished. She had to glance away to keep from bursting into tears. "Well, uh," she said, fighting for dignity when the very breath had been knocked from her lungs, "anybody I know?"

"You know Nikki Warner over at Wink?"

Wink, Texas. If God ever decided to give the earth an enema, if he missed Agua Dulce, he would stop at Wink, Texas. Until she had graduated from high school, twice a day, five days a week, from September through May, for twelve long years, Marisa had ridden the school bus an hour between Agua Dulce and Wink.

But somehow she had never met Nikki Warner. "Uh, no. Can't say that I do."

"She's, uh . . . preg—expecting."

Santa Anna's trumpet blew louder in Marisa's head. She stared at Woody, her eyeballs straining and gluing themselves to his. He was starting to seem more like a stranger with every passing minute. "And that's *your* fault?"

He dodged her stare by looking at the front door again.

As his non-answer sawed its way through her heart, hot anger zoomed through her whole body. She wanted to slap his face, she wanted to grab up the carafe of hot coffee and dump it on his head, she wanted to dash into the kitchen, grab her sharpest knife and whack off his dick. "So? What?" she said, failing to control the tremble in her voice. "All this time you've been traveling up and down the highway providing stud service? Nikki in Wink on Tuesday, Marisa in Agua Dulce on Wednesday? Someone in Pecos on Thursday?"

"No! It's not like that. I—"

"Really, Woody? If it's not like that, then how the hell did Nikki in Wink get knocked up?"

"I don't know."

Marisa planted a fist on her hip. "Now *that,* trooper, I don't believe."

"You know how I feel about you, Marisa."

"No, I don't think I do."

He rubbed his eyes with his hand. "I have to do my duty in this. We're both Catholic. I don't know what else to say."

Catholic? Okay, she would give him that. With a

Mexican mother, maybe he had been raised in that religion, but he hadn't been in a church since she met him. Her innate good sense finally overcame paralyzing shock. "Well, if you don't know what to say, I do. I think the word is good-bye."

His eyes locked on hers with an anguished expression. "Marisa—"

She stopped him by raising her palm and turning her head. "Don't 'Marisa' me. You're right. There's nothing more to say." She spun on her heel, intending to walk away from the counter, needing to remove him from her sight before she sank into a hair-tearing, chest-beating fit.

"Marisa, I don't want to lose our . . . our friendship."

His voice, soft and deep, halted her. God, the afternoons and nights she had lain in bed and listened to that voice speaking of the future, of feelings, whispering lusty intentions in her ear . . .

He stood up. "I—I need our friendship, Marisa. It means a lot to me. I thought we could—"

She leveled a glare of incredulity at him. "No! The answer is no. Get out of my sight, Woody."

Before her former lover could reply, the front door chimed again and a couple strolled in. Unmistakable tourists—tanned older man wearing a polo shirt, cargo shorts and deck shoes, tanned older woman in Bermuda shorts, a tank top and Keds. They stopped and looked at a display Marisa had created using some vintage 1940s cooking utensils. She walked away from Woody and struck up a conversation with the total strangers about where they had come from and where they were going.

Woody soon walked out, setting his hat on his head

and throwing a "Be seeing you" over his shoulder. Marisa ignored him.

The couple, JimandMariefromOhio, on their way to Roswell to visit the UFO museum, sauntered to the lunch counter as if they had nothing to do but kill time. Inwardly, Marisa sighed.

As they took a seat and plucked the yellow laminated menu from between the napkin holder and the salt and pepper shakers, Marisa glanced at Woody's mug on the counter. He had left a dollar beside it. *Bastard*. She charged $1.25 for a cup of regular coffee and he knew it. She caught a breath to halt her tears and stuffed the dollar into her pocket, then carried the mug to the kitchen and set it in the sink with a sharp *clunk*. She opened the oven door and found the bread pudding overcooked and curdled. *Shit*. She pulled it from the oven and set it in the sink also, to be flushed down the garbage disposal after it cooled. Drawing a deep breath, she returned to the lunch counter and gave her undivided attention to JimandMarie.

The retired couple put their heads together and decided to try the homemade chicken salad sandwich. Marisa had poached the chicken herself in a mixture of white wine and herbs, then shredded it and added white grapes and pecans to the traditional ingredients, along with her special dressing. It was her own recipe and, like most customers who tried it, JimandMarie thought it delicious. They stayed and talked for more than an hour, for which she was grateful. If they hadn't been present to keep her mind and mouth busy, she might have broken down.

As they left, the locomotive clock began to chug and whistle. She locked the front door, hung up the

CLOSED sign and tramped back to the singlewide, wishing for a girlfriend who would lend a dry shoulder. But besides herself and Mama, only one other female resided in Agua Dulce. Tanya Shepherd ran a beauty salon and gift shop in the space next door to Pecos Belle's. Unfortunately, Tanya was out of town.

Chapter 4

When Marisa reached the trailer, Mama was waiting for her, wearing her walking shoes and sitting primly in a chair at the dining table. Her blue eyes glinted with life. Her voice sounded stronger as she described something funny she had seen on TV and she laughed at the appropriate time. Her mind seemed clearer than it had been earlier.

Mama's illness was such a puzzle. Sometimes she would be so lucid Marisa and she could have an almost normal conversation. Marisa often thought that if she could just recognize the thing that triggered the spurt of normalcy, she could pass it on to the doctor and maybe he could invent a solution.

As they talked about the need to get Mama into Tanya's shop for a hairdo, they ate a simple lunch of leftovers—reheated baked chicken and steamed broccoli. After a hamburger for supper and Cheerios for breakfast, Marisa wanted to provide her mother with something healthy.

Marisa herself ate healthier these days. Back when she was cooking in various fast-food joints, convenience drove her to sample all that fried food and thus she had put on weight. In the year that had passed since she came back to take care of Mama, she had lost thirty pounds.

She had also been walking and jogging, more to fight a deep-seated anger straining to escape than out of any fierce dedication to physical fitness. Sometimes she trekked as far as five miles, thinking and talking to herself about the mysteries of life, before she realized how far she had traveled and then she still had to turn around and walk back. She had worn out three pairs of name-brand running shoes, but her legs and butt muscles had become as firm as when she was a kid. Her thirty-four-year-old body looked better than when it was twenty.

"I'm going to change clothes and we'll take that walk," she told Mama after they finished lunch. She had her mother swallow the handful of vitamins she fed her every day, having read somewhere that some vitamins showed promise in halting the progress of Alzheimer's disease.

Marisa changed from her cowgirl clothes to sweats and Reeboks, covered Mama's head with a bonnet and her own head with a bill cap. Then they strolled up the driveway toward Lanny Winegardner's XO Ranch, engaged in a discussion of Lanny's cows. It would be nice to be able to discuss Agua Dulce's uncertain future or to cry her heart out to Mama about Woody. But neither of those conversations was possible. Lanny's cows was the best they could do.

Less than a mile later, they returned home, with Mama hot and exhausted. The spring sun and the low-eighties temperature were too much for her. In another month, the temperature would be in the nineties and Mama's walking days would be over until winter came again.

Marisa poured her mother a glass of tea over ice, helped her to the chair in front of the TV, then went to the bedroom to change clothes again. The jeans and cowboy boots she had been wearing earlier held no appeal. Role-playing called for an enthusiasm she couldn't muster. She put on loose cotton slacks and a gray T-shirt with bold white script saying, I'LL TRY TO BE NICER IF YOU TRY TO BE SMARTER. The cranky statement matched her mood.

She stamped to Pecos Belle's, pissed off again, at life, at men. She couldn't deny she had felt that way about men for years. Most of the time she fought it off, but since returning to Agua Dulce and being reminded of her mother's lonely past, she felt an anger hovering just under her skin like a mad dog waiting to lunge and she couldn't shake it. A good part of the time she didn't try. The emotion was a dichotomy she didn't understand because, in truth, she preferred the company of men to that of women.

Back in the Pecos Belle's kitchen, as her focus zeroed in on Woody's mug sitting in the sink and the bread pudding she had let burn, the truth hit. In all likelihood, unless she got arrested, she would never see Keith Wood again. Tears welled up as she flushed the bread pudding down the disposal, but she was forced to suppress them because three people showed up to eat.

She kept her composure and ended up feeding sandwiches and hamburgers to a dozen customers. They complimented her on the food, and after eating they lingered, buying souvenirs and some small antique pieces, ogling the dinosaur footprints and the gorilla statue, petting the stuffed rattlesnake and fondling every artifact and piece of junk in the flea market.

She was glad to see them go so she could get down to some serious self-pity.

If no more customers came in, she would have several hours to think and grieve over love lost.

He's not worth a minute of your unhappiness, an inner voice told her. *In thirty-four years, haven't you learned a thing or two about men?*

You bet, another voice answered. What she had learned was that all it took to replace one was another one. Before that unlikely occurrence, the best distraction was to throw herself into challenging chores.

By six o'clock, she had cleaned the soft-serve ice cream machine and polished the gray Formica back counter and every object on it until everything shone. With the heavy string mop, she had mopped the black-and-white-checkered floor all around the lunch counter and the eating area, filling the whole place with the fresh smell of Pine-Sol.

Finished with all of that, she had pinned new, unfaded posters of giant hamburgers and sandwiches on the wall above the back counter. After her neighbor Tanya, who was an artist, said the wall looked blah, Marisa had painted it hot pink. Now she routinely put up new posters and photographs the Pepsi-Cola truck driver seemed only too happy to supply for her, especially if she wore a revealing shirt when she asked him.

As it had turned out, the hot-pink walls complemented the gray countertops and the black-and-white-floor tiles in the eating area. Together they gave the appearance of a decor that had been planned rather than achieved accidentally. Baby boomer Elvis and James Dean fans loved it.

The dying sun beamed amber through the front win-

dows into the flea market, the rays reaching all the
way back to the café. Marisa called it a day and began
wiping down the tables, thinking about a soothing bath
after Mama had eaten and after every chore was done.

In Mama's more coherent days, she used to say
there was always a blessing. Marisa just had to remember to look for it.

Marisa had just finished cleaning the lunch counter
when the front door opened and a lone guy came in,
a motorcycle helmet tucked under one arm. He halted
just inside the doorway and peeled off his sunglasses,
the black aviator type with mirrored lenses. She glanced
through the plate-glass display window into the dark-
ening color of late afternoon and saw a black Harley-
Davidson parked out front. She hoped he hadn't come
for supper.

The newcomer stood for a moment, surveying the
room, wall to wall, ceiling to floor. Was he casing the
joint? Though she tried not to let robbery enter her
mind, the possibility was ever present in the back of
her consciousness. With no agent of law enforcement
stationed closer than Wink, Pecos Belle's was a good
bet for a thief who had no way of knowing how sorely
disappointed he would be with the loot.

After a few seconds, the stranger in heavy boots
clumped over to the jukebox standing against the wall.
The thing was a Seeburg, manufactured in 1954, the
kind that had once been placed in restaurants and
diners. It wasn't a cherry, but whoever had refurbished
it did a decent job. It had a $3,000 price tag and if
this guy wanted to buy it, Marisa would figure out a
way to strap it onto that Harley.

She dropped her dish towel on the drainboard under the lunch counter and dried her hands. "Help you with something?"

He was now bent over the jukebox, engaged in a more thorough examination. "This thing work?"

His baritone voice carried across the room, as rich as if it came from the jukebox speakers.

"Sure," she answered. "I play it all the time."

Thinking about what she could do with $3,000 generated a spike of energy. She made her way through an assortment of vintage name-brand signs and a set of turquoise plastic patio chairs and finally reached the jukebox. She pushed its plug into the wall outlet behind it and, to her relief, the old thing lit up like it was brand-new.

She straightened, but still had to tilt back her head to look the stranger in the face. Being five feet eight, she could look many men in the eye, so this stranger was taller than average. He looked like Mel Gibson, his eyes long-lashed and blue as the desert sky. The eyes held an intensity, as if they could penetrate concrete, but with the fan of laugh lines at the corners they looked friendly. Mel Gibson eyes. No doubt about it. "Uh, you have to put quarters in it," she said.

A slow smile eased across his mouth as he looked right back at her and dug in the pocket of his tight Levi's. S-E-X lit up like an aura around him. He had it, that mysterious allure she had always been able to spot in a man the instant she met him. He liked who he was and was comfortable in the fit of his skin. A feeling she couldn't describe slithered through her.

He came up with a quarter and dropped it into the coin slot. As he made a selection she noticed his hands. Agile fingers and clean, short nails. Masculine hands, but not those of a laborer. After a whir and a series of clicks, orchestra music swelled as if Pecos Belle's were a concert hall. Frank Sinatra broke into "All the Way."

"What's on the menu?" he asked.

"Uh, anything you want, I guess, so long as it's a sandwich or a burger. The daily special's all gone. We've got a menu you can look at. Oh, and breakfast. I serve breakfast all day. You know, bacon or sausage and eggs—and toast."

"Coffee?"

She smiled, feeling like an empty-headed loon. "Now, that we've always got plenty of. Better'n Starbucks."

He smiled, too, and it warmed her to the soles of her running shoes. He had well-defined lips and perfect teeth.

"Great," he said. "Let's have some. Where's that menu?"

She led him back to the lunch counter, his boots *clump-clump-clump*ing on the tile floor. She plucked a menu from between a napkin holder and a sugar dispenser and handed it over. "You can have anything on it. Only takes me a few minutes to cook a fresh hamburger. We're well known around the area for our burgers. We use real meat."

He smiled again. Those intense eyes continued to bore into her. "Great. As opposed to what?"

"That artificial stuff," she answered, resisting the urge to straighten her clothing. "I grind it myself, out of sirloin. No fillers, no enrichers."

He placed his helmet and sunglasses on the counter, then removed his leather jacket, folded it and laid it on a stool. He was wearing a henley waffle-weave shirt in a color that almost matched his blue eyes. He pushed up the sleeves, showing sinewy forearms, then combed his fingers through his short brown hair that had been disheveled by his helmet. She found herself looking for a wedding band, but she didn't see one.

Dope, she chided herself. Just because a guy wore no wedding ring didn't mean he wasn't married. On the other hand, a married man didn't usually look like a movie star and roar around an isolated part of Texas on a big Harley. She turned her back on all that animal magnetism and reached for a mug and the coffee carafe. "Which kind do you want?"

"A burger'll be great."

Jeez, was everything *great* with this guy? Even as sexy as he was, her earlier encounter with Woody still had her short on patience with men, especially when what she really wanted was to just go home and wallow in her misery. She set the mug on the counter in front of him and poured it full, then tapped her fingernail on the menu that listed eight different styles of hamburgers. "Which kind?"

He scanned the menu. "Bacon cheeseburger sounds good."

"You got it." She whisked back to the kitchen. Miss Competence.

Hearing his footsteps again, she peeked through the kitchen doorway. He had gone back to the front of the flea market and was looking out the display windows. Was someone chasing him or what? He seemed to be staring at Mr. Patel's service station across the highway.

Well, whatever he was doing, was it any of *her* business?

With a mental sigh, she plopped a hamburger patty onto the hot griddle along with three slices of pepper bacon. As everything sizzled, she began opening doors, dragging out foodstuffs. She found a slice of apple pie she had wrapped and saved for Woody but hadn't given to him. The sight of it triggered emotion she had suppressed all day. Suddenly powerless to keep the tears locked inside, she began to cry in great, hiccuping gulps and couldn't stop. The next thing she knew, the customer was beside her in the shoe box of a kitchen. "Hey, hey," he said softly, "it can't be as bad as all that."

"Yes, it can," she blurted out on a sob. Then, remembering the sputtering hamburger patty, she flipped it over and wiped her eyes on her wrist. "I'm okay now. Something just got the best of me for a minute."

"Nice kitchen," he said, looking around. "It's . . . well, tiny."

He stood so close she could see the pulse at the base of his throat. "It's not my dream kitchen," she said on a sniffle, "but I've cooked in worse. At least it's easy to keep clean. Look, you shouldn't be in here. I'd appreciate it if you went back to the other side of the counter."

"Come with me?" he said.

She frowned. "Where? To the lunch counter?"

His white smile lit up the kitchen like a bright light. "Keep me company while I eat?"

"Look, I'm okay. You don't have to—"

"I hate eating alone."

She didn't believe him. This guy had lone wolf written all over him. Eating alone had to be the norm for him. On the other hand, she couldn't imagine that anyone who looked so delectable ever *had* to eat alone. Still, she wiped her eyes on the back of her wrist and said, "Let me finish up. I'll bring it out and sit for a minute, okay?"

Holding her gaze, he pointed a finger at her nose. "I'll be waiting."

She would bet her last nickel few women kept him waiting.

After he left the kitchen, she sneaked into the apartment bathroom and splashed cold water on her face. As she looked into the notebook-sized mirror on the front of the medicine cabinet, she was sure she had seen herself looking worse, but couldn't remember when. "To hell with it," she mumbled at her image. "He's just a man, right?" She blew her nose, ran a brush through her hair, then washed her hands and returned to the kitchen.

Though there wasn't much to be done for her appearance after the day she'd had, she did put extra effort into making his hamburger as good as she knew how—meat cooked to a perfect medium rare, bacon fried to just the right degree of doneness, vegetables clean and crisp. She added an extra slice of cheese and a side dish of special dressing, which was a modified Thousand Island she made from scratch. She even placed the finished burger on a white crockery plate rather than in a plastic basket and added a handful of potato chips, showing gratitude for the care he had shown her.

On the way to where he sat at the counter, she picked up the coffee carafe and an extra mug for herself and forced a smile.

"Like your shirt," he said, flashing a grin. "How smart does a man have to be?"

"What?" Having forgotten what she was wearing, she glanced down and saw the declaration across her boobs: I'LL TRY TO BE NICER IF YOU TRY TO BE SMARTER. She couldn't help but smile.

His eyes held a teasing glint as he patted the stool beside him. She filled her mug, uncertain if she *wanted* to be teased into cheeriness or if she wanted to keep her pity party going for a while. Still, she couldn't tell him no. She skirted the end of the lunch counter and sat down beside him. Feeling a new tear coming, she touched the inside corner of her eye with her fingertip.

He lifted the top half of the bun off his burger and spooned on the dressing, behaving as if he didn't notice her wipe away a tear. But she knew he saw. This dude wouldn't miss *anything*.

"So what's making a pretty girl like you cry?" he asked without looking at her.

Unused to discussing her problems with the café's customers, she hesitated. But then, what difference would it make if she told him? She had no one else to talk to and she would never see this character again, which might have caused her some regret if she had been in better spirits.

"Sometimes your world just falls apart, you know? Yesterday, I hear somebody's bought this building and even the whole damn town and I have no clue who." She lifted the mug and sipped. "Then today I find out my man's done me wrong."

She would have added, *And my mother's dying,* but she hadn't yet been able to say those words aloud.

He didn't remark right away, but bit into his burger. "Lovers' quarrel?" he asked, chewing.

"Goes a little further than a quarrel. I think it's more a scorched-earth retreat."

He swallowed and sipped his coffee. "Good hamburger."

"Thanks."

"So he cheated a little, huh?" He set down his cup and took another bite.

"Understatement."

"Cheated a lot?"

She puffed out a sarcastic laugh. "He got another woman pregnant. I think that qualifies as a lot."

He stopped chewing and those blue, blue eyes shot her a sober look across his shoulder. "You don't say."

Speaking the truth was almost more than she could bear and the tears came double time, so many she couldn't catch them before they fell. She turned her head and stood up, intending to escape into the kitchen.

His hand wrapped around her forearm and she could feel the strength in his grip. "Wait," he said, and stood up, too. "C'mon." The jukebox had stopped playing, but he tugged her to the front of it, dropped in another quarter and played the same Sinatra song. "You dance?"

She managed a don't-be-dumb look. He smiled that killer smile, drew her into a dance position and began to maneuver her around the floor. With his heavy biker boots, his feet moved like concrete blocks, but his arm around her waist felt like the most natural thing in the world and she fought herself to resist wrapping both arms around his neck.

"Listen to the words in this song," he murmured, "especially the first part."

She knew the words. The song may have been popular before she was born, but in the hours of solitude that sometimes dragged by in Pecos Belle's, she tired of the radio, so she played the old jukebox. The poetic words reminded her that Woody had never loved her all the way and in the deepest part of her, she had known that all along. Maybe she hadn't loved him that way, either. "This is an old song," she said with a big sniff. "How do *you* know the words?"

"I like music. And I dig Sinatra."

She sniffed again.

"It's okay," he said, pulling her closer. "Everybody needs a good cry sometimes. Just go ahead."

"But your shirt," she blubbered.

"Just go ahead and cry," he repeated.

So she did, dampening the front of his shirt and his handkerchief. Unusual that he had a handkerchief. With the exception of Lanny Winegardner, most men didn't carry them these days.

As she took comfort in the strength of his arms and body, the firmness of his muscled chest, his cheek against her hair, soon her tears subsided. Even with her stuffy nose, she couldn't miss his scent. The masculine mix of soap and water and musky cologne seeped clear into the marrow of her bones. She had read somewhere once that smell was the oldest and most profound of the senses. She knew she would never forget how this stranger felt and smelled at this moment.

After a while, she told him she had to lock up and check on her mother. He said he would take the burger with him, and she wrapped it in a to-go package. When he started to pay, she refused his money. The price of a hamburger was cheap therapy.

He roared away on his big black bike without telling her his name and she hadn't told him hers. She didn't even feel embarrassed for breaking down in his presence. He was just a stranger she would never see again.

Chapter 5

By nine o'clock, Marisa had finished the nightly ritual of helping her mother bathe, swallow her pills and get into bed. The nighttime silence hung around her like a heavy black cape. With no one to talk to, it was easy to feel restless and down in the dumps. She could think of no one to call for a time-consuming chat. In the world she left behind when she came here, she had acquaintances, but few friends. She had lost touch with them months ago.

If she went to bed now, she wouldn't sleep. Lying alone in the dark would only give rise to dark thoughts, to match the ones that were already blacker than the bottom of a mine shaft.

She kept a stack of crossword puzzle books in the dining-area hutch, but tonight she couldn't make herself sit in the quiet and play with words. TV's offerings promised to only depress her more. The walls of the fourteen-foot-wide mobile home seemed to be closing in on her, so she opted for the great outdoors.

A wooden deck spanned half the length of the trailer, and a pair of aged oak rocking chairs sat near the front door. Before going out, she switched on the front porch light and checked for rattlesnakes. April might be early for them to be out, but it wasn't impossible. With her luck, one could be passing by and seeking heat on the planks of the wooden deck that had been warmed by the sun all day.

Satisfied that no viper awaited her, she slipped into a coat, turned off the porch light and went outside, into the night's embrace. Technically it was spring, but Agua Dulce lay on the eastern shoulders of the Rocky Mountains at an elevation of three thousand feet. The nighttime temperatures dropped into the low fifties and would for a few more weeks.

A zillion stars hung against the clear velvet-black sky and a three-quarter moon washed the landscape with silver. Marisa plopped into one of the rocking chairs, staring up at the moon's oval shape and ethereal color and thinking that nothing but that lunar surface could be more silent than this part of Texas at night. In a town of ten people, clustered in the western reaches of a huge county with a total population of ninety-seven, only coyotes and a few desperate crickets made night noises. Even the highway was quiet and dark after nine o'clock.

As a child, she had been frightened by the vastness of the silence and the density of the utter darkness. As a teenager, she had been bored by the ambience. Tonight, even with her heart heavy and her future bleak, she wondered how she had lived away from Agua Dulce for fifteen years. This arid, remote corner of Texas was the only place that felt like home. And, God help her, she found comfort in the isolation that had shaped her childhood.

She clicked on the radio that anchored a TV tray beside the chair and tuned in on a Vince Gill song. "Someday." A song of loneliness, yet hope that someday the right one would come along. Boy, could she relate. Vince's fine tenor voice in the chilly dark air seemed to crystallize all the wretchedness that simmered inside her and she pondered why had she never been able to hang on to a long-lasting relationship with the opposite sex. Woody was just one more example of her rotten history with men.

A couple of years before coming back to Agua Dulce she had been engaged. Her intended's company had worn thin as he became increasingly content to let her pay the bills. The last straw had come when he used her MasterCard without her knowledge and bought a Jet Ski. She had faithfully sent a money order every month for two years to pay off the balance.

And it was a good thing the payoff had taken no more time than that, because she sure couldn't afford to make payments on a credit card balance now.

She had not once anticipated her present circumstances. At eighteen, she left home for Dallas, full of ambition to earn a degree in culinary arts. Her dream was to be hired as a sous-chef in an upscale metropolitan restaurant or one of the big hotels in Dallas or Fort Worth and eventually work her way up to executive chef. She had even considered becoming a master baker. She was good.

Then things happened. Plans failed to gain traction. Out of money, she dropped out of school and drifted from cooking in one fried-food joint to the next, going nowhere, accomplishing nothing, barely making ends meet.

And now she had returned to where she began.

Agua Dulce. English translation: Sweet Water. This place's reason to exist was a single water well of unknown depth and volume that produced cold, sweet drinking water, a rarity in West Texas.

Not far from where she sat, visible in silhouette,

stood the flat-roofed, pumice-stone building that protected the precious well. And not far from that stood the huge round tank that stored water for the use of all Agua Dulcians. Just after World War II, so the story went, a promoter from the East had the well drilled at great cost, hoping to establish a real town and make a fortune in a land sales scheme. She wondered if he knew he had drilled for the wrong commodity. In those days the fortune to be made from holes in the ground in West Texas was from crude oil. The modern-day testimony to that fact was more than six hundred oil wells in Cabell County.

She stopped her mental wandering. What was she doing musing over geology and geography? She had enough that was closer to home to worry about.

As Vince finished on a blue note, she heard the crunch of footsteps and peered out into the night. She recognized Bob Nichols approaching, bundled up in a safari coat, his bushy white hair and beard appearing to glow fluorescent in the moonlight.

"Good evening, Marisa," he said softly as he stepped up onto the deck.

Bob always spoke formally and barely above a whisper, as if he feared he might disturb the measureless desert quiet. He had lived in Agua Dulce for at least twenty years. She remembered when he came. He owned and operated the Starlight Inn, a ten-unit motel that was a hodgepodge of mobile homes and concrete-block buildings ranging from ten to fifty years old.

"Hi, Bob," was all she answered, not really wanting to encourage conversation or a visit.

"How is your mother this evening?"

"She had a good day, I think. Her mind seemed to be working better."

He nodded. "Ah." He came over to where she sat, carrying an Albertson's bakery sack. "I brought her a treat. I went in today." He handed her the white paper sack.

He meant he had gone to Odessa or maybe Midland, where all Agua Dulce citizens went for shopping or doctor visits or other necessities. To Marisa, the trip to Odessa or Midland, where she had lived and worked at Denny's for a time, was a chance to mingle with other human beings—to see the bright lights, so to speak. To a recluse like Bob Nichols, the trip was a trauma. She looked into the sack. Doughnuts and sweet rolls. "Hey, thanks. She loves these." She set the sack on the TV tray and turned down the radio's volume. "Did you have a good trip?"

He shook his head and sank into the other rocking chair.

"Do you have customers tonight?" She asked mostly because his having guests in the motel usually meant breakfast business in Pecos Belle's. He raised seven fingers. "Seven? Hey, that's good for April, right?"

The months between tourist seasons were lean, April being one of the leanest. With school still in session, no families traveled the highway and the snowbirds who had come south to escape the snow and ice of the northern climes were heading home.

He nodded and sighed.

"Where they from?"

"The North mostly." In Bob-speak, that meant anywhere north of Amarillo. "Except for a biker. He came from Fort Worth, I believe he said."

So the guy on whose shoulder she had cried was

spending the night. An inexplicable flicker of interest flared. "A biker?"

"Not a real biker. Not a Hell's Angel or anything. He does have a very nice Harley-Davidson, though."

This time, it was Marisa who nodded and said, "Ah," wondering if he would show up for breakfast in the café.

"Marisa," Bob said, and she could hear an almost indiscernible tremor in the way he said her name. "Have you heard the news?"

Here it comes, she thought. A conversation she wasn't up for. "You mean about the town selling?"

"I'm very worried. If things start happening here, I fear they won't come."

They were visitors from outer space. Marisa couldn't see Bob's eyes in the dark, but she had seen them light up often enough in the daylight when he talked about *They* and *Them.* In a different way, he was as far out of touch with reality as Mama. To his credit, she believed him to be just as harmless. "Before we get all excited and worried, Bob, let's wait and see what happens."

"I've worked so hard, and for so long, Marisa. We shouldn't discourage them. There are signs. Very positive signs. Sounds. Coded messages. I know they want to come, but I suspect they fear they won't be welcomed."

Marisa couldn't imagine what kind of communication he had going on with *Them.* He had never said exactly from where *They* beamed in, but in the doublewide mobile home where he lived, it appeared to her he had radio equipment sophisticated enough to communicate with Pluto.

He looked toward something neither of them could see in the dark, but both knew was there—a level, football field–sized concrete slab, surrounded by boulders as big as a car, and on one side, several tiers of seating made from slabs of limestone.

The thing was located in Lanny Winegardner's pasture that butted up to the far side of Bob's motel. Lanny had often said that when he gave permission for the construction of the UFO landing pad, he had no idea what a monstrosity Bob would create. With the occasional help of a hired backhoe or a CAT out of Pecos or Kermit, but mostly single-handedly, Bob had toiled at building the landing pad ever since he came to Agua Dulce. He had even built a chain-link fence around it, shutting out Winegardner cattle.

Just as the rancher hadn't anticipated the size of Bob's endeavor, he hadn't counted on the groups as outlandish in dress and behavior as Bob who came and sat on the limestone seats for meetings. Even so, none of it appeared to be of great concern to Lanny. When a man owned as much land as his XO Ranch encompassed, losing the use of a little square of it wasn't that big a deal. If she had ever met a man who truly championed a "live and let live" philosophy, it was Lanny.

Marisa couldn't imagine how much the landing pad had cost. Tonight as she and Bob stared toward it together, she wondered again about the source of his seemingly unlimited supply of money. To this day, his background was a mystery. All she really knew about him was that he was kind to her mother.

"Ben's drinking," he said.

Ho-hum. What else was new? At least now she knew why Ben Seagrave hadn't been in to have coffee and pass on words of wisdom in recent days. Ben, a binge drinker, was Agua Dulce's very own alcoholic sage. He had traveled between Nashville and Agua Dulce for as long as Marisa could remember. He leased a mobile home in the Sweet Water RV & Mobile Home Village, within walking distance of Pecos Belle's. Marisa was constantly amazed that he had written the lyrics and composed the music to many beautiful and well-known ballads. The royalties provided his income.

"How long?" she asked.

"Several days now, maybe a week. I spoke to him about stopping, but he gets so testy when I try to counsel him. I tried to make him understand that in light of what's happened, all of us need to be clearheaded."

If Marisa hadn't felt so sad, she might have laughed aloud at *that* statement. As far as she knew, there wasn't a clearheaded human being in town. Including herself.

"I suggested he wean himself off whiskey and go to beer," Bob went on. "He'd sober up faster that way, you know."

No, she didn't know. She rarely drank hard liquor. What she did know was that it took almost nothing to set Ben off on a drinking spree, and as he had gotten older he had gotten worse. No doubt hearing about the sale of the town and the home where he lived totally unbothered and unpressured had been enough. And as for Bob persuading him to do anything, he'd might as well forget it. Except to a few people, Ben was downright rude. "That was probably a waste of your time, Bob."

"I know, but I felt obligated. He *is* one of us. He

says tangential influences drove him to whiskey this time. He's waiting for the click in his head. He says he'll stop when he hears it."

Marisa had no idea what Bob had just said, but she refused to give credence to a conversation with a man awaiting the arrival of aliens from outer space.

She felt helpless as a babe to deal with the Agua Dulce citizens who surrounded her. How had her mother done it for so many years, shepherded this odd collection of eccentrics? Dropouts were all she could think to call them, people who weren't dumb, but for some reason couldn't quite make it in the big world. Like children, they had looked to Mama for wisdom, for guidance. Now, with their captain losing her mind, every time Marisa turned around, they were looking to her to replace her mother and right their ship.

"Hm. Well, for his sake, I hope it's soon."

"Marisa, will you be speaking to the new owner?"

"I don't know. I hope so. I'm sure he'll contact us sooner or later."

He nodded. "You will speak for our interests?"

Leaning on her elbow, she put her thumb in her mouth and bit down on the nail. What did *he* have to worry about? Unlike her and Mama, he *owned* his motel. Pecos Belle's Emporium & Eats, however, was a tenant of the town's owner, whoever it might be. If the new landlord told her and Mama to pack up and move, there would be no choice. That thought brought her an onslaught of problems and decisions she was in no shape to face tonight. "Of course I will, Bob."

He nodded again.

They sat in silence for a while, rocking and looking toward the heavens. In Bob's company, she couldn't keep from wondering if *They* really were up there somewhere, looking back.

Eventually Bob stood up and said good night. He walked off into the moonlight, weaving through the cacti, sparse desert shrubs and fragile range grass that struggled to grow in the sand and rocks. She called after him to watch out for snakes.

Chapter 6

The digital clock showed 4:45 in neon red. Marisa had survived another night. With a silent groan she rolled over in bed and buried her face in her pillow. In the fog of half-sleep, the name Nikki Warner, the *pregnant* Nikki Warner, rose in her mind. How long had Woody been seeing her, and was she the only one? As much as Marisa hated losing Woody, she hated being made a fool even more.

She flopped to her back and lay staring at the still ceiling fan in the gray morning light, considering the cruelty of fate. She and Woody had never discussed kids and what might happen if one came along unexpectedly. His priority had always been his career and moving up in the Department of Public Safety. For him, she had been so cautious to avoid pregnancy.

The irony was as painful as a hard kick. Most of her life she had wanted a family. And friends. Growing up, the loneliness of being an only child, of living in an isolated place with no other children of any age, no parent except her mother and no more than infrequent contacts with her two aunts, had almost overwhelmed her at times. She had told herself that *someday* she would meet a wonderful man and have a dozen kids who would never be lonely because they would have each other.

Sheer fantasy.

Now she was thirty-four, her biological clock was ticking off time faster than an Olympian sprinter and *someday* wasn't even on the horizon.

Wide awake now, she sat up on the edge of the mattress and pushed the hair out of her face. She shifted her thoughts and ran through a mental list of things to look forward to, forcing her attention to the most important one—staying strong for her mother, who desperately needed her.

And *would* need her and need her and need her, for an unknown span of time. Amen. The duration of Mama's illness was an unknown. The doctors had said she could linger another ten or twelve years. . . .

Another ten or twelve years . . . *where*? . . . And with Marisa doing *what* to support them?

Until a few days ago, Marisa had assumed that she would live here in Agua Dulce for the rest of her mother's life, eking out a meager living for the two of them from the flea market and café. Now the sale of the town could change everything in such a dramatic way Marisa couldn't channel her thoughts toward what to do next.

She heard no shuffling footsteps, no clattering dishes, so Mama was still in bed. Since Marisa didn't open the café until seven o'clock at this time of year, there was time for a short run before the heat rose. She forced herself to her feet and went to the bathroom, where she got into knit pants and running shoes. Forty-five minutes and a quart of sweat later, she had showered and was selecting clothing. Another day, another cowgirl suit. Today it was Rockies jeans and a pink T-shirt with a Cruel Girl logo accented with silver nail heads across the front.

Then she was in the kitchen, cooking bacon and eggs. Mama came in wearing her nightgown.

"Morning," Marisa said, glancing at her mother's feet. She was wearing two different shoes. Shoes were always an issue with Mama. More than once Marisa had discovered her wearing them in bed. "Want some coffee?"

Her mother didn't answer. Instead, she went to a cabinet drawer, yanked it open, rummaged inside it with jerky movements and came up with an apron. "I have to clean today." She tied the apron on, her teeth clenched, her lips drawn tight. "Rosemary's coming and you know how she is. She'll *inspect* . . . everything."

Mama might work at cleaning, but it would be with nothing more than clear water. Months back, Marisa had transferred all cleaning products out of the mobile home to the café apartment. Walking in and seeing her mother eating something sprinkled with Comet cleanser was more than Marisa wanted to deal with.

The emphasis on the word "inspect" told Marisa Mama was angry. She and her older sister hadn't gotten along for years. For as long as Marisa could remember, Aunt Rosemary had never failed to remind her younger sister how foolishly she lived her life. Now that Mama could no longer think or argue, Aunt Rosemary rarely even came to visit, let alone squabble, with her dying sister.

Hearing Mama make such positive, rational statements always threw Marisa a curve. She never could be sure if her mother and her aunt had had a real conversation or if another of those errant figments of Mama's broken imagination had taken over. "Who told you she was coming?"

"Lanny. Yesterday at his house we talked about it."

They hadn't seen Lanny Winegardner yesterday, nor had they gone to his house. All they had done was walk on his road and talk to each other about his cows. Marisa dismissed the possibility of her aunt Rosemary's visit.

Mama closed her eyes and the corners of her mouth tipped up in a dreamy smile. "That Lanny. He's sweet on me. Clyde's sooo jealous."

One more fleeting figment of broken imagination. Lanny had never been sweet on Mama. Indeed they had been friends, just as Mama had been friends with Bob and Ben and Mr. Patel. Clyde Campbell, oilman from Midland and Agua Dulce's former owner, was another story. Her mother's relationship with that arrogant asshole was a subject Marisa didn't discuss. Where Clyde Campbell was concerned, she felt the same as her aunt Rosemary. The jerk had dropped dead from a heart attack five years earlier. "Well, we won't worry about Clyde. I heard he's out of town and won't be back for a while."

"He'd better be careful going off without telling me. I just might take up with Lanny."

With that, Mama left the kitchen. Marisa exhaled a great breath. Today was going to be another one of those days.

Marisa followed her charge into the bedroom. It made her too sad to return from the café and see Mama with her clothes on backward, so she said, "Let me help you get dressed."

She took a pair of clean slacks and a blouse from the closet and helped Mama out of her nightgown, exposing her pale skin and shriveled breasts. "Bob had guests in the motel last night," Marisa said, stretching underpants for her mother to step into. "Soon as we eat, I need to get over to the café to be ready for breakfast." She picked up her mother's bra.

"Have They come yet?" Mama held out her arms so Marisa could slide the bra on.

They again. There was no telling how many hundred off-the-wall conversations Mama and Bob Nichols had had over the years about Area 51 and government secrets and aliens from outer space.

"Any day now," Marisa said, turning her mother around and hooking the bra.

"That Bob. He's sweet on me. He's going to take me to meet *Them* when they come. He's been on one of *Their* ships."

Marisa rolled her eyes to the ceiling. God, she needed to get away, just for a few hours, an afternoon. What she wouldn't give for an afternoon at the mall in Midland, where people seemed to be rational and function normally.

"Things always happen when I'm out of town." Tanya Shepherd sat the lunch counter, a beringed finger hooked in the handle of a mug of Cowboy Breakfast Blend. "If Jake hadn't run into Gordon Tubbs, I wouldn't even have known the town got sold."

"Goes to show you should stay home."

"I wonder what it'll mean to my shops."

"Hell if I know." The question resounded like an echo of the one that had been going around in Marisa's head for nearly a week.

Tanya's shops—a beauty salon, Tanya's Tangles, and a gift shop, the Art of the West Museum—shared the building with Pecos Belle's. The beauty shop did a decent business during vacation season when campers stopped off at Sweet Water RV & Mobile Home Village. In addition to the traveling drop-ins, Tanya advertised herself as a "color specialist" and a few patrons drove all the way from Odessa to have her color and cut their hair.

In the Art of the West Museum Tanya sold beautiful Southwest-style jewelry she designed and made herself from semiprecious stones. She also displayed her own drawings and oil paintings of the area landscape.

Now Marisa examined a pair of beaded leather mules Tanya had brought Mama from Ruidoso. The hairdresser never failed to think of Mama. "These should fit," Marisa said.

Tanya took a drag off a long, slim cigarette and blew out a stream of smoke. "How's Raylene doing?"

"About the same," Marisa said. "A few days ago, I overslept and she toasted a whole loaf of bread."

"That's not good." Tanya's head slowly shook as she tapped ash from the end of her cigarette. "I miss how Raylene used to be. She was always there for me. She always helped me a lot." Tanya and Mama had had a relationship for years before Marisa's return. Knowing Mama, she had treated Tanya like a daughter.

"I know. That's the way she was before . . ." Marisa

stopped herself. Nothing more needed to be said to someone who had watched Mama's mind drift away for years. "Did y'all win any money at the casino?"

"Nah. I mostly went shopping and toured the art galleries."

"Oh? You took some paintings to show them?" Marisa thought her neighbor was a wonderful artist. Until she'd seen Tanya's paintings, Marisa hadn't appreciated how much true beauty existed in Agua Dulce's desert landscape.

"I'm almost afraid to. They've got work from some big-name artists and I'm nobody. Jake says my paintings look as good as theirs, but what does he know? He's a cowboy."

Marisa glanced at Tanya's profile, her eyes landing on the tiny diamond stud in the side of her nose. She had a number of body piercings in places Marisa had heard about, but hadn't seen. The last thing she appeared to be was a cowboy's wife. She was taller than Marisa, but wore high heels every day, the higher the better. At some point she'd had a boob job and on her rail-thin frame her breasts appeared globelike. She had huge green eyes, usually made up with a kaleidoscope of eye shadow and a pound of black mascara. Her straight brown hair hung to her waist and she wore it cut in layers, with a center part. The top layer was streaked in stripes of half a dozen colors ranging from near white to burgundy. Marisa thought she looked "arty." Ben Seagrave said she looked like a confused zebra.

"Count on Jake to be supportive," Marisa said.

Tanya swallowed a sip from her mug, a frown creasing her brow. "You know, if push comes to shove and I have to move my shops to Pecos or somewhere, I guess Jake and I can live in one of those old ranch hands' houses out at Lanny's and I can commute."

Her attention settled on the wall in front of her, where Marisa had pinned Pepsi-Cola's newest over-sized poster. Alongside a large paper cup showing a red-white-and-blue Pepsi-Cola logo, it showed French fries and a hamburger with ruffly pastel green lettuce poking out the sides. "Hey, you got new posters," she said and took another drag off her cigarette.

Marisa glanced at the wall. "The Pepsi delivery guy gave them to me."

Tanya giggled. "He'd probably give you his whole truck if you pumped him up a little."

"Hunh. Not interested."

"You know, it'd be easier on Jake living out there at that ranch," Tanya said. "He only stays here in town because of me and my business."

Marisa gave her neighbor another look. She had said "in town" as if there were a difference in living here in Agua Dulce and living in the country. Though Lanny had offered living quarters to Jake and Tanya many times, the hairdresser refused to live at the XO. She and Jake lived in the largest doublewide mobile home in Sweet Water RV & Mobile Home Village and paid no-telling-what in rent to Clyde Campbell's estate. Every day except Sunday Jake made the twenty-mile drive to his job cowboying for the XO Ranch.

The mention of the Pepsi truck driver and his blatant attraction to Marisa reminded her of Woody and she couldn't hold back any longer. Her former lover and Tanya had gone to school together in Pecos. Marisa told Tanya about him and some woman in Wink named Nikki Warner.

"I know her," Tanya said without registering surprise. "She's a hair stylist. . . . And she's a kid. I think she's only, like, twenty or twenty-one."

A pain of deep origin began to press under Marisa's ribs. "Don't BS me."

"I mean it. She's a kid."

A picture of Woody mushroomed in Marisa's mind. At forty, he was starting to lose his hair on top. "Good grief," Marisa mumbled. "I wonder how he got mixed up with someone half his age?"

Tanya glanced toward the far end of the lunch counter where Gordon Tubbs sat, not quite within earshot. As he often did, the manager of Sweet Water RV & Mobile Home Village had come in to have a salad for lunch.

Tanya tamped out her smoke, then lowered her voice to a conspiratorial level. "I hate to tell you this, Marisa, but Woody was like that when we were teenagers. Even then he went after younger girls." She pushed a sheaf of long hair behind her ear, revealing silver hoops the diameter of a Coke can. "He always wanted to, you know, do it, which was probably easier with the younger girls. I mean, they were dumber. He could talk them into it easier."

Tanya set her mug down and went on. "In high school we used to joke about it, but none of us went out with him. Nowadays, if he did some of the stuff he used to, he'd get arrested." The hairdresser scrunched up her shoulders and giggled. "Or shot."

Marisa cringed at this new information about her former lover. She had talked to Tanya about him many times over the past year. If he was such a cad, how could a friend and neighbor not have warned her away from him? Marisa's memory zoomed backward and she recalled that Woody had made a pass at her the very first time they met. She felt heat rise to her cheeks because she also remembered how flattered she had been at his attention. *Dummy,* she called herself.

Woody did have an appetite for hot sex, all right, but that wasn't a crime. "Tanya, for god's sake," she said in an equally low tone, "he's a cop. And a special cop at that. He wants to be a Texas Ranger." *The epitome of heroism,* Marisa didn't add, doubting that Tanya knew the meaning of the word "epitome."

The hairdresser shrugged. "Can I help it how he is?" She gave a knowing but humorless chuckle. "Girl, I could name you a dozen places he's dipped his wick." She leaned closer to Marisa, touching her shoulder. "You want to know something weird? Even with all the stuff I knew about him from school, I did it with him myself a couple of times. I mean, he's hot, you know? And he's good."

A blast of fury exploded within Marisa.

From the corner of Tanya's eye, a sly look passed Marisa's way. The woman seemed to be oblivious to the fact that Marisa was on the verge of screaming. "A lot better'n Jake," she said, "if you know what I mean. Jake's never made me come half a dozen times in one screwing." She drew in a deep breath Marisa could only define as wistful and lifted her mug. "Yessir, that Woody can go and go." Tanya's hips shifted on the stool.

Marisa felt like a voyeur. Good grief. She stared at the woman who appeared to be enjoying something sexual right before her eyes. The last afternoon she and Woody had spent in the tiny apartment bedroom flashed in her memory. The sex had been . . . well, lengthy.

"It's funny," Tanya went on, "that everybody calls him Woody? Get it? I know it's tied to his name, but when I first heard it, I thought I'd die laughing."

Marisa hated herself for wanting to know, but she schooled the anger out of her voice and asked, "And when did you and Woody, um, get together?"

"Oh, it was over ten years ago. Before I hooked up with Jake."

A feeling of relief almost overcame Marisa's anger, followed by disgust with herself for being so naive.

A little smirk lifted the corner of Tanya's mouth. "I always wanted to tell you so we could, you know, compare notes, sort of. I've been curious if Woody's still got it. I mean, he *is* forty, right?"

As if she read Marisa's thoughts, Tanya said, "But I decided not to mention it because it wasn't important, really. I mean, it was just was one of those things that started with a few beers, on a picnic table over at the sandhills in Monahans one night. Then another night in the front seat of his pickup out in the parking lot at Rustler's Rest. It didn't mean anything, you know? All we did was fuck. Either time, I didn't even take off all my clothes." She took another swallow of coffee. "Besides, I thought knowing about it might hurt your feelings."

From what Marisa had seen in the short time she had known her, Tanya rarely concerned herself with anyone else's feelings.

"You think I'm not hurt now," Marisa said in a stage whisper, "finding out all of a sudden that he's a, a . . . a damn Roto-Rooter? That he screwed around with my neighbor? I didn't have a clue."

"Hey, don't blame *me*. Until you started dating him, I hadn't seen him in years."

"Dammit, even if it *was* ten years ago, I can't believe you didn't tell me. How would you like it if I told you I fooled around with Jake ten years ago?"

Tanya shrugged. "I'd say, 'No big deal. That was then, this is now.' "

Marisa could only blink. The words that fell from Tanya's mouth often left her dumbfounded.

Marisa set her jaw, trying to shut out the image of Woody and Tanya doing it on a picnic table and thinking about something she had read once about character being formed by the time people are six years old. Or something like that. The voice of another expert. Her head was filled with incomplete snatches of trivia that came back at unpredictable moments. As she took a sip of her Colombian Roast, she concluded she would be happier if she stopped reading.

"Well, gotta go," Tanya said. "Gotta do a perm. Bring Raylene over this afternoon and I'll do her hair."

"Sure," Marisa said, refusing to let her annoyance at Tanya affect something Mama enjoyed. Tanya always fussed over her hair and, if there was time, they even played with makeup.

"When you come over," the hairdresser added, "I'll show you the new stuff I made. I took those pieces of raw amethyst those rock hounds from Arizona gave me and mixed them with some turquoise and made this cross thing out of hammered silver. I only had enough stones for a pair of earrings and a pendant, but they look pretty."

"Sure," Marisa said. At the moment, she didn't care if she never saw Tanya Shepherd again.

And she was damn glad she hadn't mentioned the sexy stranger who had come into the café and how they had danced to Frank Sinatra's music from the old jukebox.

Chapter 7

After Tanya left, Marisa let go of her anger. Hanging on to it accomplished nothing. The very first day she met the cowboy's wife, Marisa had pegged her as being empty-headed and self-centered. Yet she was generous to a fault and never failed to show concern and compassion for Mama. Marisa excused her more bizarre behavior and ignored her blunt remarks. After all, Tanya was an artist, and weren't artists supposed to live in a realm apart from the rest of the population?

Marisa picked up a pitcher of tea and moved down the counter to where Gordon Tubbs sat, his bald pate gleaming under the fluorescent light mounted above the lunch counter. Marisa suspected he had been straining to hear the conversation between her and Tanya, but he gave no indication that he knew what they had said. "Want some more tea?" she asked him.

He shook his head, keeping his eyes on his salad. He forked a tomato wedge. "Guess I'll soon be leaving, Marisa."

Gordon was a gentle man, but usually morose about something. Marisa steeled herself against letting his pessimism affect her. God knew she had enough depressing thoughts of her own; she didn't need his, too. She set the tea pitcher on the back counter and pulled a two-quart plastic pitcher of sugar from a shelf under the drainboard and began topping off the sugar dispensers. "Where you going?"

He didn't look up and didn't answer right away. "I'm out of a job," he said finally.

Hearing a quiver in his voice, she glanced up and saw him spear a lettuce leaf. His fork tines tinked against his plate. Gordon Tubbs was the only person in Agua Dulce directly employed by the owner of the town. Marisa hadn't thought of it before now, but obviously Gordon's employment either transferred from Clyde Campbell's estate to the new owner or disappeared altogether.

"Really? Have you gotten some kind of word from the new owner?"

"I've talked to him on the phone. I don't think there's gonna be a place for me in his plans." Gordon shook his head slowly.

The splinter of fear that had harried Marisa for more than a week grew into a two-by-four. She set the pitcher of sugar on the counter and walked back to where Gordon sat. "Did he say so?"

The trailer park manager looked up, his brows tented. "He's closing the RV park."

Marisa felt a cold wind waft through Pecos Belle's. "But why would he close it? It isn't in his way. You have tenants. And campers. I thought the trailer park made money."

Gordon's shoulders lifted in a shrug. He dropped his fork on the counter with a clatter and covered his doughy face with soft-looking hands. "I don't know what I'm gonna do." He picked up a napkin, wiped his eyes and blew his nose.

Marisa looked away. She didn't often see men cry.

This week, she had seen almost everyone in Agua Dulce on the verge of tears.

"I don't know what I *can* do." Gordon seemed to be in control again and Marisa turned back to face him. "I've been here for so many years," he said. "Clyde always took care of me. What I mean is, he paid me a wage and gave me health insurance through his company."

He shook his head again and fanned a hand in front of his face. "A man my age ain't gonna get a job that amounts to diddly. And nowadays, a diabetic who's had two heart attacks not only ain't gonna get a job, he ain't gonna get health insurance anywhere on this earth."

She didn't know Gordon's exact heart problem, but she knew it was expensive. After his last heart attack, he had been in ICU in a Midland hospital for days, his life saved by a highly skilled cardiologist. He now swallowed a handful of medications every day that couldn't be cheap. And he was too young for Medicare. "No, I guess not."

What he said about health insurance might be true. Marisa had fought the health insurance battle on her mother's behalf before Mama became eligible for Medicare. Even now, Marisa didn't have health insurance for herself and hadn't had it since she left the IHOP company.

She felt her brow tug into a frown as she tried to calculate how many years Gordon had been the manager of the RV village. "Surely you've got some savings, Gordon."

"Savings? Clyde Campbell was the stingiest man I ever met. Do you think he paid me enough money for me to have any left to save?"

Marisa's jaw clenched involuntarily. Hell, yes, Clyde Campbell was a skinflint, along with being a thoughtless asshole. Look at how he had treated Mama. Of course, Mama had let him take advantage of her, but that was beside the point.

What *was* Gordon going to do? What was he qualified to do? As far as Marisa could tell, the answer was a resounding *nothing*. Without the Sweet Water RV & Mobile Home Village, he wouldn't even have a place to live. "So the new guy's going to just close up the trailer park"—Marisa snapped her fingers—"just like that?"

The middle-aged man nodded.

"But what about Ben? What about Tanya and Jake? Where will they go?"

A new spark of indignation burst within Marisa. The big guy kicking the little guy. She had never been able to keep quiet when she saw it happen. She had also never been able to *do* anything about it, but she had always been vocal. "He can't just put people out of their homes. That isn't fair. He has to—"

Shit, what *did* he have to do? He wasn't obligated to a single citizen of Agua Dulce. "He has to give them time to make plans," she said, putting an effort into making a firm statement.

"He's coming here for a few days," Gordon said. "He plans to start using one of the mobiles. He ordered me to have a phone installed and buy some groceries. Even gave me a shopping list. He sounds like he's used to giving orders."

Gordon wadded the napkin and dropped it on top of his salad. "He sounds like a real piece of work, Marisa. He told me to make sure the trailer's ready for occupancy when he gets here. Said to make sure there's no roaches. He wants everything clean as new. The small doublewide's the newest trailer, so I got Rosia to come up from Pecos and we're cleaning it now. He even wants the walls scrubbed and the carpet replaced."

"No kidding?" Marisa muttered, shocked. "New carpet?"

Gordon nodded. "I've already gone to Odessa and bought it. Rosia's washing and ironing all the curtains. The carpet'll go down tomorrow."

"Hunh," Marisa said. The new owner sounded like an arrogant nut. Okay, fine. No problem. Marisa could hardly wait to meet him. She had experience with nuts.

Terry returned to Fort Worth on Monday. He spent Tuesday morning with Brad England in the offices of England Engineering, the firm he usually hired to design, survey and lay out a new project. After spending the weekend in West Texas and confirming the potential he believed was there, he was so excited he could hardly wait to get started.

In the afternoon, he caught up with his best friend and construction foreman, Chick Featherston. Chick was overseeing the building of a two-story cut limestone with three fireplaces, four bedrooms and five baths. It was all crammed into 4,500 square feet in a gated subdivision west of Fort Worth.

They reviewed the progress; then Terry led Chick to his truck and unrolled a large plat of Agua Dulce. "Want to go back to West Texas?"

Chick's chin dropped and his head slowly shook. "Aww, no, man. You didn't really do it."

Terry grinned as he spread the plat across the

truck's hood. "I won the bid. I closed on the deal yesterday. Just got the town so far, but the ranch is next. I have to do a little more research and get a loan in place."

Chick looked at the plat with him. The blueline drawing showed the perimeter of the town's 199.4 acres, with the principal structures drawn in—water well, flea market/café, adjoining building leased for business, RV village consisting of eight permanent mobile homes, a separate office building and fifty RV spaces.

The foreman shook his head again. "Ledger, that last time you jumped out of an airplane, you must have landed on your head."

Chick knew Terry's passion for skydiving. The cowboy engineer was one of Terry's few friends who went all the way back to the first time Terry had parachuted from a plane.

Chick was more like a brother than a friend. They had met as kids in boot camp. Both being from West Texas, they had become friends almost automatically. Terry had served as an Army Ranger and, among other things, had learned to parachute, and Chick had been a combat engineer. Different duties and different assignments, but their paths had crossed in unexpected places in various parts of the world. Together they had partied hard in Germany, chased women in Italy, liberated Kuwait.

Chick had been the construction foreman at Terry Ledger Homes ever since the company had grown large enough to need one. He was now surfacing from his second divorce and starting a new life at age thirty-seven. He had handed well over a million dollars' worth of real and personal property to two women. These facts only added fuel to the notorious Ledger distrust of the female of the species.

"After the smoke cleared, which place did you finally buy?" Terry wanted to know.

"The one with a few acres in Weatherford. Gotta have grazing for my horses. And a place for Clay to come. His mother's gonna fuck up one time too many and God as my witness, I'm gonna end up with custody of that kid."

Clay. Chick's eight-year-old son. To hear Chick tell it, the only good thing that had come of his first marriage.

"What's it look like out in the Wild West?" Chick asked. "As if I didn't know."

"Looks good. That's why I want you to come on out and be a part of this. It's gonna be great, Chick. Honest. Hell, I may even build a golf course."

"Out of what, Astroturf? You couldn't grow a blade of real grass in Cabell County if you needed it to eat."

"I'm spending some time out there, Chick, starting the end of the week. If everything comes together, I want to get homes on the ground before the year's out. I want the houses to take on the flavor of the area, like what we're doing in Rancho Casero, only smaller."

His good friend nodded and stared at his boot toes. "Well, what the hell. Those are easy houses to build. Yeah, I'll go. But not permanent-like. I don't want to get that far away from the kid." Chick pointed at a blueline square on the plat across the state highway from a cluster of other blueline squares. "What's this?"

"An old service station."

"And you don't own it. Well, a Larson's will put him out of business in a hurry."

Terry had confided in Chick months back that he had his eye on a Larson's Truck & Travel Stop. The Oklahoma company had yet to make any inroads into Texas, but it was excited at the prospect of building a discount gasoline and diesel full-service station and convenience store on one of the few north/south routes in West Texas. Inside its convenience stores, Larson's usually placed at least one nationally known fast-food restaurant. Nothing like a Larson's Truck & Travel Stop existed between Odessa and El Paso.

"Kim's been researching all the properties and the ownerships," Terry said. "I wouldn't be surprised if the service station's already in trouble. It was built in the forties. The state's bound to be after it for storage tank cleanup."

Chick dragged his finger across the highway to a smaller cluster of squares on property that had a common boundary with the town of Agua Dulce. "And this is?"

"A motel. Ten units. I slept there a couple of nights while I was scoping out the area."

"But you don't own it, either?"

"Right. The owner's some strange little character who believes in flying saucers."

Chick looked up from under an arched brow. "For real?"

Terry answered with a shrug. "That's what he told me."

"Hm. Takes all kinds, I guess. With a new motel opening, I doubt he'll stay in business."

"That's up to him."

"And the water?" Chick tapped a finger on the blueline square labeled WELL.

"Good water and plenty of it, as far as I know now. Looks like it has a good storage tank. Too small for my plans, but that's not a problem. I'll have to put in a water system to state standards anyway."

"When I go out, is the motel fit to stay in?"

"Sure, but half the mobiles in the trailer park are vacant. You know you're welcome to stay in one. They're furnished. You just need to take some bedding. If you don't want to cook, I'll foot the bill for you to eat at the café. Not bad food."

Terry reached inside his truck for a notepad and wrote down the name Gordon Tubbs. He tore off the page and handed it to his foreman. "Keep this name. This guy's the manager of the trailer park. He's an employee who came along with the town. When you're ready, I'll call him and tell him you're coming."

"I haven't been to West Texas in years," Chick said, his eyes taking on a distant look. He had grown up in the small town of Andrews, thirty miles from Terry's hometown of Odessa. "What about the ranch?"

"It appears to be what I'm looking for. It's big and has history. Goes back to the days of the cattle drives north. It's been owned by one family since the twenties."

"Well, that's not a bad thing. And you're sure he'll sell."

Terry grinned. "If the deal's right, *anyone* will sell."

"Okay." The engineer puffed his cheeks and blew out a long breath, continuing to study the plat. "Big job."

"When you come out, I'll rent a plane and a pilot and we'll fly the whole area. I want your input. I've got some old aerial maps, but I'd like to eyeball the landscape."

Chick laughed. "Uh-oh. I don't have to jump out, do I?"

Terry laughed, too. "I might, but you don't have to."

"Mind a little *input* right now?"

"Not from you."

"You're going out on a real skimpy limb on this one, Terry. Especially if you're going in debt to buy that ranch. You could lose your ass. West Texas is known for three things these days. Oil, cows, and unemployment. Not retirement."

Terry laughed. "It's only money, Chick. Hell, I didn't have any when I started. If the subdivision doesn't work out, I can always be a cowboy."

"But it doesn't make sense, Terry. We've already got houses to build in Rancho Casero. Soon they'll be selling faster than I can stand 'em up. The whole subdivision will be sold out in a year or two, max. You'll make so damn much money you could retire."

"I'm too young to retire."

"Maybe so, but this thing in West Texas is more of a long shot than a crippled racehorse. My God, man, if you could get your hands on the mineral rights, you'd be better off drilling for oil."

"My business is real estate. Wildcatting's too big a gamble."

Chick laughed. "Hell, it's all gambling, pal. Whether it's oil wells or houses and lots."

Terry laughed, too. "Maybe that's what makes it fun."

Chapter 8

Barely awake, Terry basked in his queen-sized bed, floating through nebulous memories of his youth— spelunking in Balmorhea's water caves, climbing the steep walls of El Capitan, kayaking the Pecos River at flood stage. God, he loved West Texas. He loved the shifting sand and the ever-present wind touching his face. Even the sulphur gas smell that frequently pervaded the air was more pleasant than the North Central Texas swamp odor, to which he had never grown accustomed.

He had returned to Agua Dulce late last night, picked up the key to this mobile home from his RV park manager and opened every window before falling into bed, worn out after the five-hundred-mile trip from Fort Worth.

The little mobile home wasn't bad. Probably eleven-hundred square feet. Solid-feeling floor. Big enough kitchen. Two bedrooms, the master with a queen-sized bed. Like a calculator, figures rippled through his head. The mobile home had probably cost a quarter what he would spend putting up a stick-built house the same size.

Insistent knocking on the front door brought him full awake. He could think of no one who should be banging on his door, especially so early in the morning. He pushed himself out of bed, pulled on jeans and padded to the door. Through the peephole, he saw . . .

. . . a woman standing on his deck.

Oh, yeah. The good-looking chick from the café. And she was dressed up like Dale Evans, fancy shirt, fringe and all. His memory flashed on the first time he had seen her, when she had been wearing loose slacks and a T-shirt.

He combed his fingers through his hair, ran his tongue over his teeth and opened the door. She looked at him with an odd expression.

"Hi," he said cautiously, rubbing a hand down his bare chest and subtly checking his fly. Sure enough, his top button was undone, but too late to worry about it now.

"I, uh, uh, want to speak to you," she said.

Her eyes settled on his hand at his fly, setting off a little stir in his jeans. "Um, you got me out of bed. Can it wait a while?"

She looked up and stared him in the eye. Her fists went to her hips, her breasts shifting beneath her snug cowgirl shirt. Among other things, he could see a big "no, it can't wait" in the gesture.

"I don't have a lot of time," she said.

Uh-oh. This woman on his deck was a different personality from the weepy one he had danced with that evening in the café. All he had on was a pair of jeans and he didn't usually invite women he didn't know into his quarters when he was half naked and only half awake, but there didn't seem to be a better choice. Having met her before and having let her cry in his arms, he felt as if he did know her. "Okay. You want to talk standing on the porch or you want to come inside?"

She looked away, then looked back, jaw tight, red lips pursed. "I'll come in."

He stepped back from the doorway and allowed her to enter. "Want to sit down?" He gestured toward both the dining table and the sofa a few feet away in the living room area.

She looked around. "Well. This place looks like new."

It did. The manager had apparently followed orders. New vinyl in the kitchen and the two baths, and new carpeting on the floors in the living room and the two bedrooms. The odor of "new" and some kind of cleaning product filled the whole mobile home.

She crossed in front of him, adding yet another scent to the mix, something musky and appealing. He felt that little stir in his jeans again. She took a seat at the dining table and crossed her forearms on the tabletop. Whatever she had to say, she meant business.

"You know," he said, seeking to lessen both the tension that seemed to be coming off her in waves and the uneasiness he felt himself, "I talk better after I've had a cup of coffee."

He had already spotted a new coffeemaker on the kitchen counter. He went to the cupboard and began opening doors, searching for a can of coffee and hoping the park manager had also followed his instructions to get some food into the place. "Now it probably won't be as good as *your* coffee, but—"

"You came into my café. Why didn't you identify yourself? Why didn't you say you had bought our town?"

His ears pricked. *Our town?*

His assistant, Kim, had done a cursory profile on all of the citizens of Agua Dulce. This one had to be Raylene Rutherford, who had run the flea market and café for more than thirty years. Kim must have made an error. The woman sitting at his table would have been a little kid thirty years ago.

He found a new can of Maxwell House and a small jar of phony cream on a cupboard shelf and filled the coffeepot with tap water. Lifting it to eye level, he looked into it and found it clear. "I hear there's good water here. Guess you'd know about that, huh?"

A safe topic. Why he was concerned about calming her and why her attitude was making him nervous he didn't know, because this real estate belonged to him. He had just walked into a Fort Worth lawyer's office a week earlier and handed over a check for a million dollars.

"It's fresh well water," she said. "Untreated with chemicals. And it doesn't have a lot of minerals."

Good news. And different from much of the water in West Texas. Though saturated with oil, this part of Texas, the great Permian Basin, was almost without potable water. As he filled the coffeepot's reservoir, he decided to take advantage of the opportunity to learn more from someone who might know the answers to some of his questions. He braced a hand on the counter while he waited for the coffee to brew. "I understand everyone in town uses the well water. Right?"

Her brow knit into a frown. "Of course. Where else would we get water?"

"What about the motel and the service station across the highway? Do they pay for the water?" He thought he already knew the answer to this—Kim, in her research, had found that they did use the water, but she had been unable to find that they paid for it.

"I don't know. Clyde Campbell owned the well. He didn't discuss his business with me. What difference does it make?"

"Their property isn't part of the town. They really don't have any right to the water unless the well's owner gives it to them, either for free or for a fee."

"Clyde had the first nickel he ever made. Knowing him, if there was a buck to be made by selling water, he probably made it. But I don't recall hearing of anyone paying him for water."

"You saying Campbell was stingy?" He couldn't keep from giving her a look. "Ma'am, if those two property owners have been using the well water gratis all these years, I'd say that was pretty generous of Mr. Campbell. Maybe the guy wasn't as stingy as you think."

She huffed and looked away, obviously annoyed. "I'd be amazed to hear he was generous when it came to money. The water system was set up a long time ago, even before he owned the town. It was probably cheaper for him to just leave it alone than to try and change it."

"In any event, the system's in violation of state regulations. With so many families using it, it's subject to being monitored by the state."

"We don't need the state. We've never had a problem with the water."

In the heat of her bristling attitude, this conversation was turning into something Terry felt a need to take control of. Being half dressed weakened the possibility of that happening and his bladder was full to boot. He preferred conducting power conversations standing, fully clothed and without the urgent need to pee. "Listen, do you mind if I step back into the bedroom and put on a shirt?"

"Please do."

He made for the bathroom. Soon he returned to the kitchen and saw the coffee finished. He pulled two ceramic mugs from the cupboard. "I'm sure the well isn't what you came to talk about so early in the morning."

"It isn't early. It's nine o'clock. I came to speak to you about Gordon."

Belligerent, for sure. "Who?"

"Gordon Tubbs. The manager of this trailer park. Your employee. Or hadn't you noticed him?"

Yep, definite hostility. A side of her he hadn't seen the first time they met. He looked at her with a wary squint. "And?"

"He's afraid he's going to be laid off from his job."

Terry hesitated, wondering what can of worms was about to be opened regarding his only known Agua Dulce employee. "That's possible. If I don't have an operating RV park, I won't be needing an RV park manager." He offered her the jar of cream. "Uh, cream? Sugar?"

The heat in her eye said she wasn't interested in hospitality. "I don't suppose you've thought about, or care, how losing his job will affect him."

"And how is this your business, Miss—what's your name again?"

"Gordon's been a friend of mine for years. And I have other friends living in the trailer park."

"That would be who?"

"Jake Shepherd and his wife, Tanya. And Ben Seagrave. They lease mobile homes here."

"Ah. The cowboy and the drunk." He carried the two mugs of coffee to the dining table.

She ignored the coffee. "You shouldn't belittle them. Ben's lived here since I was a little kid. And Jake and his wife and Gordon are all good people. Gordon can't help it if he's sick."

"What's wrong with him?"

"Heart trouble. Serious heart trouble. But he's always done a good job. He's honest and conscientious."

Terry sat down opposite her at the dining table. "Are you here as Mr. Tubbs' representative?" *Or your own?* he wondered.

For the first time, her demeanor softened. She looked down at the mug of coffee, hooked her finger in the handle and pulled the mug toward her. "No, I'm just Gordon's friend." She said it almost affectionately and he realized the simple admission had deep meaning for her.

His own attitude softened, a reaction that rarely happened when someone approached him aggressively. He had to admire her loyalty to this Gordon fellow. And her chutzpah. Terry drank from his mug, watching her over the rim. And with her expressive eyes and fine features, she was worth watching. "Something tells me you want me to do something. What is it?"

"The trailer park makes money. It always has."

"And you know this how?"

"The former owner, Clyde Campbell, was friends with my mother before he died. Good friends."

Terry almost grinned. Just a few minutes earlier she had declared she knew nothing about Campbell's business. So this was *not* Raylene Rutherford; it was her daughter.

Human beings fascinated Terry and this one was starting to interest him more than he wanted her to. Golden brown eyes, heart-shaped lips and a small mole at the corner of her mouth. Her features were almost perfect. What could a woman this good-looking be doing in this remote place and how had Kim missed her in her research?

"Gordon's been living on borrowed time for a couple of years," she said. "He was on Clyde's group insurance. Since the trailer park's profitable, maybe it wouldn't interfere with your plans to let him stay on. He needs a job and he's desperate for health insurance. Besides that, having the RV park open is good for all of our businesses. We depend on tourists." She looked him sharply in the eye. "Of course, if you plan to close us all down, that's another story."

Terry sat back in his chair, emotions conflicting. Something about her had driven straight to the male part of him and that part wanted to get to know her better, but his pragmatic side warned him she would be a handful. She definitely had ideas of her own about the town he had just bought and they probably clashed with his. His business sense nudged him, pointing out the folly of discussing his plans with her or any other stranger.

But for the most part she was right. The RV park wasn't in his way. The thing did make a small profit. Terry was reluctant to start his venture with pissing off everyone in the town. The public relations persona that had served him well in his real estate career stepped up. "Tell you what I'll do. I'll leave the RV park as is for the moment. I've got other things to take care of right now anyway. Since Mr. Tubbs is already on the payroll I've got no problem adding him to my company's group insurance plan. Would that make you happy?"

But I can't promise how long I can do that, he refrained from saying.

For the first time since she knocked on his door, she smiled. And what a smile. Dancing eyes, red lips and straight white teeth. The little mole moved with her mouth.

"Gordon will be so relieved," she said. "I'm relieved, too. I was worried about him." As she picked up the mug and sipped, Terry felt a mysterious weight lift from his chest.

"Well, I've got to get going." She stood up. "I haven't opened the café yet and I may be losing business."

Terry didn't want her to just leave. He stood, too. "Look, I'll be having some people come and go, doing some work. They'll need a place to eat and I'll be paying their expenses. For that matter, I'm going to be around here quite a bit myself. Can I start a tab in your café? I can write you a check when I leave or if you'd rather, I can give you a credit card number."

"Sure. Either one's okay. I do serve three meals a day if I've got customers. And the food's always fresh."

With the stridency of anger removed, her voice had a soft alto tone that made him think of phone sex. Her eyes had turned warm and friendly and for some damn reason, he didn't want to relinquish the moment. "Great," he said.

"You say that a lot, don't you?"

"What?"

" 'Great.' That's one of the things I remember about that day you came into the café. You thought everything was *great*."

He shrugged and grinned. "What can I say? I'm an optimist."

She gave a partial smile. "Why didn't you tell me who you are? I was shocked and a little upset when you opened the door this morning and I realized you're the town's new owner."

He lifted a shoulder. "You were so unhappy that day. I didn't want to make things, whatever they were, worse." He shrugged. "I don't like seeing a pretty girl cry."

"Well . . . " She looked down, almost shy. "I don't cry very often." She started for the door.

"Listen," he said, and she stopped. "What happened to . . . you know, the guy?"

A little frown of puzzlement formed between her brows. "Guy? . . . Oh, *that* guy. His name's Woody." She toyed with a ring on her finger. "By now he's probably a bridegroom. Probably the best thing that ever happened to me." She smiled again. "Well, I gotta go."

Terry stood in the doorway and watched her cross his deck, jog down his steps and walk out into the sunny morning. She made her way through the sparse bunchgrass and brush, toward a singlewide mobile home parked behind the flea market. A confusing mix of emotions stirred within him. Instead of wading into the confusion, he focused on the fact that there wasn't a damn thing wrong with how she looked in a pair of tight jeans. He did like a woman with a fine ass. Woody, whoever he was, must be a damn fool.

A pesky question niggled at him. She had picked

up the standard for Gordon Tubbs, so why hadn't she asked him about his plans for the flea market and café? If any building in town was in his way, it was the one *she* and the adjacent beauty shop occupied.

Not once had Marisa suspected that Agua Dulce's buyer would be young and good looking. Or that vitality would leap from his pores. Weren't rich guys supposed to be old and fat?

She kept her steps even and her chin level as she hiked toward her mother's singlewide. She had barely sat through the meeting with Mr. Ledger without crawling under the furniture in humiliation. How could he have let her open herself up so completely that day in the café and not reveal his identity?

She felt his eyes on her back all the way to the singlewide's door and was glad to reach home. Her heart hammered as she closed the door and leaned against it.

A sense of doom hung on her shoulders like a heavy cloak. He may have said he would leave the RV park alone, but she had enough common sense to know it was a temporary commitment. In time, he would leave nothing alone, including Pecos Belle's Emporium & Eats. Unless she could pull a rabbit out of a hat and find a job and a home in another town, she and her mother were as good as homeless. She shut her eyes and pressed her forehead against the door for a moment.

When she opened her eyes and turned, Mama was standing at the kitchen counter, holding the phone receiver, her brow knit in a frown and a distant look in her eyes. "Who's on the phone?" Marisa asked her.

Mama looked at the receiver, then at Marisa. Tears

welled in her eyes and she began to cry. "I don't know."

Marisa went to her and hugged her close. At the same time, she put the receiver to her ear and said, "Hello?" She heard only a dial tone, so she would never know if someone had called, if Mama had made a call or if she had simply picked up the receiver.

Her mother's body shook with sobs and Marisa cooed to her and rubbed her back. When Marisa had first returned, Mama cried often, knowing she was losing touch with the world and grieving over it. In those days Marisa heard her say things like her body was going to outlast her mind or that she was becoming a prisoner in her own skin, and Marisa had even feared she might do something drastic, like take her own life.

Lately the fleeting moments of awareness occurred less often. Now it was Marisa who grieved, functioning in a constant state of stress and debating in the deepest recesses of her heart whether Mama was better off alive and crazy or dead and at peace.

"I don't know, Marisa," Mama said again, sobbing. "Oh, Lord, I don't know."

Chapter 9

Marisa headed for Pecos Belle's too late to catch any breakfast customers who had spent the night in the motel. Sessions like the one she had just had with her mother always left her drained. It had taken one of the knockout pills to calm Mama and now she would be out for the rest of the day.

Marisa entered Pecos Belle's through the apartment's back door and made her way to the café, then through the flea market to the front door, sidling past and stepping over this and that. Mr. Patel, Bob Nichols and Ben Seagrave were standing on the sidewalk waiting for her. Knowing, and dreading, that an impromptu meeting of some kind loomed, she unlocked the front door and let them in.

The three men passed in front of her single file and silent, with Ben bringing up the rear. She hadn't seen him in nearly two weeks. He wore a silly grin and reeked of whiskey. His gray T-shirt and knee-length khakis looked as if he had been wearing them for days. Both were covered with stains, the origin of which Marisa dared not speculate. Bob had been right. Ben was drinking.

"Hello, Marisssa," he said. In his cups, he always

pronounced her name as if it were spelled with three *S*'s.

"Hi, Ben," she answered, unsmiling.

As she dragged mugs off the shelf, the men sat down on the padded vinyl stools at the lunch counter. These guys made an odd trio if she had ever seen one. Ben, tall and skinny with leathery skin tanned to the color of toasted almonds; Bob, short and pale, his face and tiny eyes almost hidden by a bush of white hair and beard; Mr. Patel, short, thin, dark and intense.

Ben declined coffee. He had brought something over ice with him. She allowed him to drink liquor in the café if he brought it, but refused to serve him. She had no license to sell or serve alcohol.

The men sat grim-faced and silent, sipping their respective beverages. When no one said anything, she threw some crushed ice in a cup and drew a Diet Coke for herself. "Okay, y'all, what's this about?"

Bob's no-color eyes bored into her in an accusing way. "We saw you go to the new owner's trailer."

"Lemme guess. You want to know what we talked about."

"Yes," they said in unison.

She sighed. Of course they were worried, which was the only reason she tolerated their waiting at her front door for a report. "Well, if you must know, Gordon mentioned the guy might close down the trailer park, which would leave poor Gordon in a pretty bad spot. So that's what we talked about. The man said he would leave the RV park alone temporarily and he won't can Gordon."

At least not right away, she didn't say.

"That is all?" the East Indian asked, suspicion evident in his tone.

Though she liked Mandan Patel's wife and his two daughters, his evident distrust of everything and everyone annoyed her. In fact, he irritated her so much, she didn't feel comfortable calling him by his first name. "Yes, Mr. Patel, that's all. What did you think, that I'm plotting against you somehow?"

"We don't know how to approach him," Bob Nichols said in his usual soft voice, which served to apologize for Mr. Patel's sharpness. "He hasn't spoken to us at all. I know his name only because he stayed in the motel."

For the first time Marisa realized she didn't know the new owner's name, either. How had she had two encounters with a sexy guy and not even learned his name? "What *is* his name?"

"Terry W. Ledger is what was on his credit card. It was a MasterCard, as I recall."

"Hunh," Marisa said, the name jingling a distant bell in her mind. She pictured a serene landscape on a billboard advertising ANOTHER LEGENDARY COMMUNITY BY TERRY LEDGER. *Oh, Jesus. Does he intend to subdivide Agua Dulce?* "Did you say he's from Fort Worth?"

"He doesn't own my motel or Mandan's service station," Bob continued as if he hadn't heard her question, "but what he plans will affect us. We just want to know what he's going to do."

"It is only fair that he buy my business," Mr. Patel said. "If he will take away my income, then he should pay. I have already been cheated."

Marisa had no idea if that was true. Mr. Patel had bought his service station and the squatty stucco house behind it from Harvey Skillern the year Marisa graduated from high school, sixteen years back. Marisa only vaguely remembered Harvey, but talk had always swirled among Agua Dulcians about his shady deals.

"I hate to bust your bubble, Man-dan," Ben said, "but you ain't been cheated. You took your own risk when you bought that service station. And this Legend fella don't have to pay you jack. That's the American way, buddy." Ben followed that pronouncement with a long glug from his drink.

"If he's congenial," Bob said, ever the peacenik, "perhaps he wouldn't object to all of us inviting him to a meeting. He might share his plans with us. Perhaps you could arrange a forum, Marisa."

Marisa grunted and opened her palms, not enthusiastic about another encounter with Mr. Ledger. This morning's meeting had left her with a funny feeling in her stomach. "Look, y'all, I don't know him any better than you do. But he won't bite you. Just go knock on his door and ask him your questions."

Bob and Mr. Patel shook their heads. They had a lot to lose, she supposed, but they were in no worse position than her mother—or for that matter, than herself. Now she berated herself for not taking up her own problem with the new owner when she had had the chance.

Ben drained his glass, then reached into a pocket of his khaki cargo shorts, pulled out a silver flask and poured himself another drink. "Well, I don't give a rat's ass what he does. If I have to, I'll just pack up my shit and toodle my sorry ass back to Tennessee." He sipped another drink, then frowned and set the glass on the counter with a *clunk*. "I wouldn't like that much, but I could do it."

Ben had stayed put in Agua Dulce ever since Marisa had returned to take care of Mama, unlike his lifestyle in the past when he had yo-yoed between here and Nashville.

They all sat in silence, sipping. She could almost see the wheels turning behind Bob's eyes, just as she could almost see steam rising from Mr. Patel's scalp.

"You could discuss our issues with him," Bob said. "Perhaps voice our concerns and ask him his plans."

Marisa felt her eyes widen. "Me?"

"It's what your mother would do."

"Guys, I know Mama did stuff like that, but I'm not my mother. I have no influence with this man. What do you expect me to tell him? I'm sure he bought this place for a reason. Do you think anything I say is going to make a difference in what he does with it?"

"You should discuss," Mr. Patel said.

"You made a difference for Gordon," Bob said. "And you used to live in Dallas."

"Gotcha," Ben said, giving her a reptilian grin.

"Listen, you three. I've got all I can do figuring out what me and Mama are facing. I see no point—"

Abruptly Mr. Patel rose and stalked through the flea market, out the front door. They all stared after him.

"Well, lah-de-dah," Ben said, pulling a crushed pack of Camels from his T-shirt pocket.

"You can't blame him for being upset." Bob's gaze swerved back to Marisa. "He has a family. This is a serious problem for them. Every penny he has is tied up in his service station."

"But I'll bet that ain't true of you and that hodge-podge you call a motel, is it, Bob?" Ben's mouth flattened into another evil grin. "It ain't the money that bothers you, is it?"

Marisa's attention shot from Ben to Bob, her curiosity renewed as she awaited Bob's reply.

The motel owner's shoulders squared, his chin lifted. "It's true, money isn't what interests me. I'm on the brink of profound discovery. I don't want to see all my work destroyed."

"Jesus Christ, I knew it," Ben growled. "You've been talking to little green men again."

The front door opened and Tanya came in. She sauntered toward them, six feet tall in high-heeled sandals. She was wearing low-rider khaki pants and a knit shirt, its V-neck cut low enough to show half of a blue lizard tattoo and the bottom cropped short enough to show several inches of midriff. But it was the gold diamond-studded navel ring that was the center of attention.

An image flew into Marisa's mind of the hairdresser's long bare legs astraddle Woody's lap in the front seat of his pickup. Forgiving Tanya's breach of loyalty was difficult, even knowing the encounter with Woody was ten years back. Today Marisa was struck in a way she hadn't been before by her neighbor's blatant sexuality and how she moved past the men at the counter with an assurance that was almost feline.

She leaned a hip against the counter's edge, planted a hand on her hip and ordered a Coke. Her breasts shifted and made the lizard tattoo's head seem to crawl out of her neckline. Every man's eyes landed on the tattoo. Marisa had seen the whole thing. Roughly eight inches long, it slithered down the slope of Tanya's right breast, with the long reptile tail curling around her nipple. Marisa had often wondered just how she had managed to have the thing so strategically placed and how painful getting it must have been. In the shirt she wore today, the lizard's tail was hidden, but barely.

Tanya had several tattoos. Marisa couldn't let herself be judgmental about them or the navel ring. She had a navel ring herself and two tattoos—a small yellow rose on one ankle and a quarter-sized happy face at the edge of her pubic hair, but her body adornment paled in comparison to Tanya's.

The hairdresser took the Coke from Marisa and plopped onto a stool beside Ben. "Jeez, Ben, you smell like hell. How long you been drinking?"

"Not long enough," Ben said and belched. He leaned back and looked down at Tanya's back. Marisa knew he was looking at the long tribal scroll tattoo that spanned her back just below her waist. Marisa also knew Tanya didn't mind if he looked. The woman seemed to have no inhibitions about exposing her body.

"I had the weirdest phone call from Raylene." Tanya said. "The phone rang, I picked up and said hello and she said, 'I was going to call you, but I can't find the phone.' I said, 'Why, Raylene, you're talking on it, aren't you?' Then she said, 'I don't know where I put it.'" Tanya shook her head. "I'll tell you, Marisa, you're not gonna be able to leave her all by herself much longer."

Such remarks about Mama had ceased to bring pain. Still, Marisa, along with Bob and Ben, stared at Tanya as if they couldn't believe her callousness. *Oh, well,* Marisa thought at last. No harm done. At least she now knew who her mother was on the phone with earlier.

Bob finished his coffee, set the cup on the counter and stood. "You won't forget us," he said, looking into Marisa's eyes as he dug money from his wallet.

Marisa let out an audible breath. "If I get an opportunity to say anything, I will."

"What was that all about?" Tanya said after Bob disappeared.

"Nothing. Just worry."

"They probably want you to fix everything for them like Raylene used to do."

Marisa didn't answer. Instead she picked up the empty cups and carried them to the kitchen. Ben and Tanya exchanged a few barbs, then Ben left, too. Tanya lit a cigarette. "Ben's hopeless. He is such a drunk."

"I know," Marisa said, preoccupied with all that had transpired in only a few hours.

"Marisa," Tanya said, "do you think we're gonna get kicked outta here?"

Bingo, Marisa thought, but she said, "I don't know. I wouldn't be surprised."

"I heard the dude's here, staying in the new trailer at the back of the park. I'll bet he's a fat old fart that sweats. Have you seen him?"

Before Marisa could answer, the "dude" sauntered through the front doorway and Marisa felt a surge in her pulse. A royal blue crew neck sweater a little brighter in hue than his eyes topped well-washed Levi's that molded around his thighs. A wide black stripe crossed the front of the sweater, emphasizing his broad chest and shoulders. "That's him," she whispered.

Tanya glanced in the new owner's direction and her jaw dropped. "You're shittin' me."

As Terry Ledger weaved his way through the flea

market the hairdresser eyed him up and down. Marisa thought of one of those predatory South American plants that trapped bugs and ate them.

When the victim reached the lunch counter, Tanya stuck out her hand and tilted her head sideways, letting her long hair cascade over one shoulder. Her breast lifted in a way that showed off the blue lizard tattoo to its full advantage. "Hi, I'm Tanya Shepherd. I'm the stylist next door? And I own the museum. Art of the West?"

A blind man could see the hairdresser's interest had little or nothing to do with this stranger being her new landlord. There was no missing Mr. Ledger's assessment of the view of Tanya's phony boobs, either. Marisa crossed her arms over her chest and rolled her eyes. Maybe Tanya should introduce the lizard, too.

The new guy shook Tanya's hand and smiled, which seemed to come so easy. Too easy. "Charisma." That was the word. "A special charm or allure that inspires fascination and devotion." She had seen it in crossword puzzles many times. And he had to be a bastard. Most men with that special quality just were.

"Terry Ledger. I haven't been into your establishment yet. I intend to drop in today."

Tanya smiled back and shrugged, shifting the site of the lizard. "Cool."

She held her cigarette poised between two fingers, her elbow resting on the countertop as her eyes roved down Mr. Ledger's lanky frame. Marisa wanted to pinch her, but she kept her hands and her thoughts to herself, unable to resolve why this guy's unexpected appearance sent a jiggle through her whole system. Well, she might not know the answer to that, but at least she now knew his name.

He turned her way and took a seat beside Tanya at
the lunch counter. "Didn't you say you served breakfast all day? Sometimes I like breakfast for lunch.
How about a couple of eggs, bacon and toast? Maybe
a shot of that coffee."

"You should try one of Marisa's special coffees,"
Tanya piped up, turning her head and blowing out a
cloud of smoke. She turned back and extended such
a blatant invitation to Mr. Ledger with her eyes that
Marisa had to turn away, embarrassed. "She buys all
these special beans and grinds and mixes them up
herself."

Marisa felt a blush crawl up her neck and wished
she handled compliments better. Terry Ledger smiled
again and it came back how his smile had affected her
the day he appeared beside her in the tiny café kitchen.
Yep, charisma. That was the word.

"Really?" he asked. "Why go to the trouble?"

Marisa figured what he didn't say was, *Who cares,
out here in the boondocks?*

"She's one of those gourmet types," Tanya said.
"She went to this fancy cooking school in Dallas."

"Tanya," Marisa said, "stop—"

"Really?" Terry asked again. "Which one?"

What he didn't say was, *If you're such hot stuff,
what are you doing out here in the boondocks?*

"She's only here because she takes care of her sick
mother," Tanya said, as if she, too, had read Terry
Ledger's mind and thought an excuse was in order.

"Oh, sorry to hear that," he said. "Well, I hope she
recovers soon."

Tanya snubbed out her cigarette. "She ain't gonna
recover. She's—"

"Tanya." Marisa drilled the hairdresser with a lethal look. She turned to Terry. "I'll get you that breakfast."

Marisa went to the kitchen, aggravated that the confused zebra, the *married* confused zebra, was sitting at the counter flirting and carrying on with Terry Ledger as if she had no husband and was as free as Marisa. Marisa wouldn't put it past her to take her interest in Mr. Ledger further than just flirting. And that thought got under Marisa's skin in a way nothing had for a very long time.

As the bacon strips she laid on the griddle began to sizzle, she heard Tanya say she had to get back to her shop for an appointment. Then the hussy invited Terry Ledger to come over anytime, even after she closed if it was too inconvenient for him to drop by during the daytime. For an instant Marisa wondered if Woody and Tanya had screwed around because Woody had seduced her or if he had been attacked by her.

When breakfast was done, Marisa carried it out to her customer.

He smiled up at her as she set his plate in front of him. "I heard her call you Marisa. You must not be Raylene Rutherford."

"You must be right." Marisa bent and picked silverware from the bin under the drainboard. "Raylene's my mother." She placed the silverware and a large paper napkin beside his plate. "This place is her business. I'm helping her out."

"While she's sick?"

"She has Alzheimer's disease."

He looked at her for a moment and she was sure

she saw the same expression in his sky-colored eyes that she had seen the day they danced to the jukebox. "I'm sorry to hear that," he said.

Marisa lifted a shoulder in a shrug. "One of those things. When she was . . . when her mind was right, she was sort of the mayor of Agua Dulce."

"I see. And who has that role now? You?"

Marisa gave a sarcastic huff. "Are you kidding? Mama was one of those natural-born leaders. I couldn't lead a flock of ducks." She picked up a ketchup bottle and blindly stared at the label. "No, I'm just . . . I don't have a family to take care of or anything, so I'm sort of passing the time and doing the best I can to . . . to keep things going for her."

Both of them remained silent, him eating, her choking on the question she wanted to ask him. Finally she found her courage. "Tell me something, Mr. Ledger." He looked up and she locked her eyes on his. "Are you going to put us out of business here?"

His gaze dropped to his plate and he picked up his napkin and dabbed his mouth. A muscle worked in his jaw. "It's too soon to say."

He was lying. Marisa could read that much for sure. "That isn't a no, is it?"

He picked up his mug and sipped. "No," he said, carefully placing his mug back on the counter. "No, it isn't."

Though she had known the answer before he said it, the impact was more than she was prepared for. A burning sensation passed behind her eyes and she started to turn away.

"I'm fair," he said, stopping her. "I always try to be fair."

She swallowed the lump in her throat, but she

couldn't look at him. "Hey, don't worry about it. We're not your responsibility."

He stood, his breakfast unfinished, his demeanor no longer relaxed. "Look, put this on my bill, okay? I probably won't go back to Fort Worth 'til next Thursday or Friday. I'll settle up with you then."

Chapter 10

Terry returned to his temporary home in a black mood. After leaving the café he had dropped in at Tanya's Tangles to look over the interior of the space that adjoined Pecos Belle's. Any time he bought a new property, he examined it before deciding to sell it or raze it. During his inspection, Tanya Shepherd with the oddly dyed hair came on to him so openly he had almost run from her shop.

Women. Not a damn one of them could be trusted.

He plopped into a chair at the dining table and called Kim at her home number in Fort Worth. His office was closed on Saturday, but he could call his assistant anytime. Her, he could trust, which was to be expected. He paid her well for her loyalty, along with her ability to keep his multi-pronged business running like a well-oiled machine even in his absence.

When she answered, her excitement came across the phone lines. The first words from her mouth were that a phone call had come yesterday. A couple of property development guys from Larson's had a sudden gap in their schedule and could make it down to Agua Dulce next Tuesday. She had assured them Terry would pick them up at the Midland airport at ten o'clock that morning. Otherwise they might get lost trying to find Agua Dulce in the Big Empty, as some called West Texas.

"Great," Terry said, but what he thought was, *Shit*. He was hardly ready for representatives from Larson's. He hadn't prepared a sales pitch, and he hadn't had enough time to make up his mind if he wanted to try to place Larson's where Pecos Belle's and Tanya's Tangles were located, or if he wanted to present them with another location a few feet away where no building existed. They had told him they wouldn't have the time to peruse a site in West Texas for three weeks to a month. His mind shifted to a vision of a Larson's Truck & Travel Stop sitting on the site now occupied by Pecos Belle's and Tanya's Tangles. "That means we can get things rolling sooner."

"Yup," Kim said. "And Brad called. He and his crew will get there in a couple of days. I told him about the Larson's folks and he said he'd try to wrap up the survey before they show up. I called the motel and made reservations for them. Is that motel owner weird or what?"

"Hm. He must have told you a flying saucer story."

Thinking of his new town's residents brought Gordon Tubbs to Terry's mind. He had started the day with a visit to the park manager and had seen with his own eyes the condition of the man's health. The guy was only fifty-five years old, but he looked seventy. He had no wife, no children, no extended family. He had lived in Agua Dulce and managed the Sweet Water RV & Mobile Home Village for fifteen years.

"I want to add a new employee to Legendary Development's payroll and enroll him in Blue Cross," he told his assistant. "His name's Gordon Tubbs. You'll have to call him and get more information from him." He gave her the manager's phone number.

"Got it," Kim said, "but who is he?"

"He's the RV park manager here."

"But you're closing the RV park."

"Not yet. The thing makes a profit, so Tubbs pays his way."

Kim didn't ask, but Terry knew she was wondering what Legendary Development was going to do with the manager once Terry closed and dismantled the RV park. LD was a tight operation that carried little fat. Gordon would inevitably become an employee that could only be labeled as "fat."

They finished their conversation and Terry hung up feeling the pressure of Larson's showing up three weeks early. Just one more glitch in an entire day filled with glitches.

"God," Marisa mumbled, standing in the middle of the flea market. Her eyes scanned, her brain inventoried the massive amount of stuff, something she had been doing ever since Terry Ledger left earlier in the afternoon.

Stuff. That was all you could call it. Just "stuff." Some items were genuine antiques; most were junk. Some had been in the flea market for twenty years and would never sell.

How in God's name would she ever get back the money her mother had paid for all of it somewhere back in time? What would she do with a damn stuffed and mounted rattlesnake more than fifteen feet long or a giant papier-mâché gorilla? Then there were the heavier-than-granite plaster reproductions of dinosaur footprints. And two dozen lava lamps of varying configurations. Only the full-size covered wagon might find a home in some Old West museum somewhere. She made a mental note to contact the one up the highway, in Lincoln County, New Mexico.

For Clyde Campbell's widow, eBay had been a solution. Was it a solution for Pecos Belle's? Should she learn how to use the Internet auction site? And how long would *that* take?

She looked around the café at the ten square tables and the long lunch counter with its eight padded vinyl stools. The café would comfortably seat fifty, though she couldn't recall that many customers ever being present at one time. The tables and chairs were from the fifties and sixties—mismatched, Formica-covered kitchen sets with chrome trim and legs. The chrome-legged lunch counter stools had come out of an old drugstore in El Paso. The tables and chairs and the stools would bring fair prices as antiques, but how would she ever get even half the value back from seventy or eighty thousand dollars' worth of restaurant equipment?

And even if she succeeded in selling all of it for a decent price, then what?

She dragged herself back to a stool at the lunch counter and sank down.

Well, she had to do *something* . . .

She would start tomorrow—calling auctioneers, calling antique dealers and ferreting out a broker of used restaurant equipment. There had to be one in Odessa or Midland.

She had to sell the mobile home, but what was a

twelve-year-old singlewide mobile home worth and where was the title? No telling where Mama had put it.

A list. She needed a list to remember all that had to be done. She plucked a napkin from its holder, dug a pen from her pocket and wrote the number "1" on the napkin, but nothing followed. She couldn't think of which absolute necessity was most important.

Suddenly all of it was too much for her small brain. She laid her head on her arms on the lunch counter and cried.

At ten o'clock, when she finally fell into bed exhausted, even with all that vied for her attention, Marisa's thoughts centered on Terry Ledger. Lean and mean. If asked, that's how she would describe him. He had that quality she hadn't often seen but had always been able to recognize. An edge, an air that he instinctively knew what to do about everything and anything. Including women. The type had always appealed to her. And had always been as dangerous as appealing.

He had been attracted, too. She just knew it. She had felt his eyes touch every part of her—hair, face and body. He had *looked* at her, even with Tanya showing off her lizard tattoo and enhanced cleavage.

Well, there were worse things than having a rich, good-looking man ogle you.

She shoved that fantasy to a distant place and focused on Item One on her list of priorities. Mama hadn't had a bath in two days. Events outside the singlewide mobile home had overtaken all available time, but Mama's bath would come first tomorrow morning. Marisa sent a silent prayer heavenward that her charge would awaken in better shape mentally.

Turning to her side, she punched up her pillow and tucked her hand under her cheek. Ben drifted into her mind, which he had been doing sporadically since the day before yesterday. From the looks of him, he had been on a bender for at least two weeks. Lord, someone had to do something about him. He was over sixty now and he hadn't taken very good care of himself.

In a pathetic way, Ben was the father she had never had. She had known him her entire life, could remember being a kid and him bringing her records and eight-tracks from Nashville, autographed by country music stars. In those days, he always had poems to recite and lyrics to sing that he had written for some artist. In one animated drunken recitation, he had introduced her to "The Walrus and the Carpenter." He had made her weep with a dramatic presentation of "The Face on the Barroom Floor." Somewhere among items she had saved from childhood, she had a few poems Ben himself had authored.

Ben had been the first to alert her when Mama had started doing peculiar things.

As much as Marisa detested interfering in other people's lives, she would have to go over to Ben's trailer and try to help him. If she didn't, who would? If he had living family members, no one had ever seen them or heard him mention a name, other than Rachel. Marisa didn't know Rachel's identity, but she knew from the softness that came into Ben's voice when he talked of her that she was someone special. Since coming back to Agua Dulce this time, Marisa hadn't heard him mention Rachel once.

At some point, she slept.

She awoke at daylight.

Now, after a mind-clearing morning jog, followed

by helping Mama bathe, she was in Pecos Belle's kitchen. The breakfast rush had ended and she was bracing the phone receiver between her chin and shoulder, holding a conversation with an Odessa auctioneer. She felt energetic, unwarranted considering the night she had spent. It was probably adrenaline.

She disconnected more confused than before she and the auctioneer talked. She scanned through the pages of notes and phone numbers she had written on a yellow pad. She had to start making decisions.

From the radio, Brad Paisley and Alison Krauss broke into "Whiskey Lullaby," a ballad about lost love and the ravages of liquor. She stopped and listened and thought of Ben.

The door opened and Bob Nichols and Mr. Patel came in. She gave a mental groan. Their being together could mean only one thing. They were ganging up on her again about approaching Terry Ledger.

They sat down side by side at the lunch counter and stared up at her with long faces. Tweedledum and Tweedledee.

"Y'all eating or drinking?" she asked.

"We've come to make a formal request," Bob said, his voice so low she scarcely heard him.

She closed her eyes and hung her head. "Y'all, listen—"

"Please, Marisa," Mr. Patel said. "We are here to say we will pay you."

She gave him an arch look. The only money she expected from her friends and neighbors was payment for the food they ate in the café.

"What Mandan means," Bob said, "is we discussed it and we know your time is worth something. We know you have much to do. All we want is for you to meet with him and tell him how we feel. Perhaps he will share his plans with you."

It was so clear that this was a continuation of yesterday's conversation, they didn't even have to refer to Terry Ledger by name. "And why can't *you* meet with him?"

"I do not speak English so good to argue," Mr. Patel said.

"There's no argument to this, Mr. Patel. He's in the driver's seat. He's bought the town. He can do what he wants to. I imagine if you tell him your honest concerns, he'll be candid about the future."

"But, Marisa," Bob said, "if Mr. Ledger is planning a large gasoline station and truck stop, he must know he will destroy us. He's very rich. We won't be on an equal footing."

Marisa sighed. They were so right. No one in Agua Dulce would be untouched by Mr. Ledger's plans, whatever they were. "I don't know what I would say to him," she said.

"You are very articulate, Marisa," Bob said, "and you are a good businesswoman, like your mother. She always knew what to say. You can talk to him."

Marisa remembered how as a child she had witnessed meetings similar to this one between her mother and these same people. Why did these grown men find it so difficult to simply ask the guy a few questions? She sighed again.

"The water," Mr. Patel said. "He owns the water."

So true. The conversation she had already had with him about the well rushed into her memory. She rubbed her temples with her fingers, wanting to rant about her own problems, but what would be the point? If these two couldn't even bring themselves to knock on Mr. Ledger's door and express their concerns, how could they possibly help *her*? "Y'all are making me crazy."

They both started to speak, but she raised a palm like a traffic cop. "Okay, dammit. I'll talk to him. But just this once. And I still don't know what the hell I'm gonna say."

They left together, both of them appearing happier.

By noon, she had seen no customers. Sometimes Sunday was that slow; sometimes it was the busiest day of the week. She locked Pecos Belle's front door and walked to Ben Seagrave's trailer.

Ben lived in a ten-by-forty-foot singlewide that had to be more than thirty years old. Even from a distance, she could see rust stains trailing down the mottled gray siding from steel riveted seams. She passed a rusting barbecue grill hunkered on the ground and headed up the set of four rusted wrought-iron steps that led to a tiny, similarly rusted iron porch. A skewed and faded canvas awning haphazardly protected the porch and the front door from the relentless sun.

She clomped up the steps to the screen door and found it open, giving access to the solid front door. She pounded with the flat of her hand, an echoless *whack-whack-whack*. A muffled roar came in response and then words she couldn't make out.

"Ben," she called, "it's me, Marisa. You okay in there? Open up. Say hello."

Another roar and a few thumps. Finally the door flew open, almost knocking her backward, and Ben filled the doorway. He looked awful enough with his greasy gray hair and days of whisker growth, but worse than his appearance was his sour odor. He wore the same clothing he had been wearing when she had seen him two days back and he smelled to high heaven.

"Marisssa," he slurred.

"Hey, I was worried about you. Can I come in?"

"Ahhh . . . the place ain't fit"—he belched—"ferrr comp'ny."

"That's okay. It's just me." She stepped forward and he stepped back, allowing her to enter. The stench of close quarters, stale cigarette smoke and bourbon made her catch a quick breath. "You need some air in here," she said and left the door open.

A small living room lay to the right. Its brown-paneled walls encompassed a short blue plaid sofa. An empty fifth lay on its side on the seat. A beat-up Naugahyde recliner stood in front of a small TV, which rested on a leggy stand. On a side table beside the brown recliner sat an ashtray heaped with ciga-rette butts. A guitar lay on the sofa seat and two more stood against the wall, lined up beside an assortment of speakers, stereo equipment and a cabinet holding more CDs than any one individual could possibly play in a lifetime.

She turned her eyes left toward a round dining table with four chairs crowded against it. Another full ash-tray sat in the center along with some scattered pages of notebook paper, the kind school kids used. Beyond the table was a kitchen no bigger than Pecos Belle's. Glancing around, she saw no sign of food, confirming her suspicion that he hadn't been eating. But he had certainly been drinking, if two empty fifths and a half-empty gallon jug of Jack Daniel's sitting on the For-mica counter were any indication. At least Ben didn't drink rotgut whiskey.

"Want a li'l drink?" he asked, running a leathery-looking hand through his thinning hair and leaving strands standing in spikes. A worn Masonic ring encircled his ring finger. Marisa had often wondered where and at what point in his life he had been a Mason.

"No, thanks," she said. "Got work to do."

He shuffled barefooted to the kitchen and picked up a quart-sized tumbler from the cluttered counter beside the sink. He turned to the refrigerator and pulled out an ice tray. For the shape he was in he was amazingly adept at cracking out the ice cubes. He methodically dropped three into the tumbler, which boasted a Golden Nugget casino logo. *Clink . . . clink . . . clink.*

His true condition revealed itself when he tried to heft the gallon jug by its glass loop and it slipped off his finger.

"Here, let me," Marisa said, fearing he would spill whiskey all over the counter or drop the jug on the floor. She took it from him and poured what she estimated to be a shot over the ice cubes.

"More," he said and listed backward.

She grabbed his elbow with one hand and steadied him. "Come over to the café and let me fix you something to eat." She set the jug on the counter. "Some scrambled eggs, maybe."

He scrunched up his face and squinted one eye, then dug a pack of Camels and a plastic lighter from his T-shirt pocket.

"No kidding," she said, "you'll feel better if you eat."

"I always liked you, Marisssa," he said. "Do you 'member . . . when you were li'l?" He plugged a cigarette into the corner of his mouth and lit up with a shaky hand.

She smiled, tucking back her chin to avoid the cigarette smoke. "I do. Now, come on. Let's get some food."

He shook his head.

"I could cook something and bring it over here."

He shook his head again.

"Look, that's what I'm going to do. You get cleaned up a little. Wash some of the stink off. You'll feel better. And I'll be able to stand being around you." She plucked the cigarette from his hand and laid it on the edge of the ashtray on his dining table, then turned him and pointed him toward the narrow hallway that led to the bathroom. "I'm gonna go make you some eggs and toast. I'll bring it back in a few minutes, so get ready."

She started for the door, but remembered what Bob had said last night about weaning Ben off whiskey with beer. As water began to run in the bathroom, she walked over to the kitchen counter, dumped the contents of the tumbler into the sink and secreted the whiskey jug in the cabinet underneath. Opening the refrigerator door, she saw a case of Lone Star beer taking up one wire shelf. She pulled out a can and popped it open, took it to the bathroom and tapped on the door.

"Whaaat?" he bellowed and yanked open the door. He was still dressed, thank God.

She handed him the can of beer. "Here, drink this while I cook breakfast, okay?"

He took the beer, lifted the can to his lips and gurgled half of it in one long swig.

Unable to keep from staring as his throat muscles flexed, she muttered, "Lord, Ben, you're killing yourself." She turned away as he began to undress. "Look, stay on the beer 'til I get back, okay?" She shut the bathroom door.

Making her way back through the kitchen, she saw a trail of smoke rising from the ashtray on the dining table where she had put his cigarette. She stopped and snubbed out the cigarette before it set the whole ashtray on fire.

She couldn't keep from looking at the writing in pencil on the pages of notebook paper. Lines of words, some scratched out or marked through and replaced by others. Poetry. Had Ben been writing song lyrics?

"And I'm warning you," she called out as she sank into one of the chairs and picked up the top page. "I won't be gone long. Don't forget to brush your teeth."

> *It's not you, it's me, you said.*
> *As the words filled my head*
> *Tears filled up my eyes.*
> *Was this our last good-bye?*

It was a love song. A ballad. The words without music didn't mean much to Marisa, but if it had Ben's name on it and if a famous artist recorded it, it was sure to be a hit. She was prying, but she couldn't make herself stop.

> *You said I was too attached*
> *You weren't ready for that*
> *If I just gave you half?*
> *Would that have made it last?*

> *What I thought we had was perfect*
> *The future I had dreamed*

Would have brought me everything
But it wasn't what it seemed.

Now here I stand
Head in my hands
I'm on the outside looking in
To everything I wanted us to be.

The house on the hill
The cat on the windowsill
The picket fence, the memories and still . . .
He's got you.

Half the remaining words were scratched out, some
so violently the paper was torn. Even through the
roughness of the composition, she could tell the song
would be a tearjerker, the kind that had always caught
her ear and the ears of most country music fans. In
her head she could hear the whine of a lonesome fid-
dle, the twang of a steel guitar, the voice of a singer
like Alan Jackson or George Strait or Travis Tritt.

Was this a song about the mysterious Rachel? And
what did it mean? "Damn," she mumbled under her
breath, attempting to put the pages back the way she
had found them. Ben was an intelligent, talented man.
But he was a mess. A tragic alcoholic mess. She cared
about him. Not only did she not want to lose him, she
didn't want the world to lose him.

Mumbling to herself, she stepped out onto Ben's
rickety porch, then had a second thought. She
marched back into the trailer, yanked the half-empty
gallon jug of Jack Daniel's from where she had put it
under the sink and took it with her.

Outside, she could see the new owner's mobile

home at the back of the park. No time like the present to approach him with Bob's and Mr. Patel's latest concerns. She detoured from her trek back to Pecos Belle's. Ben's breakfast would be a few minutes late.

Chapter 11

That jitter returned to her insides as she neared the back corner of the RV park where the new owner had taken up residence. His small mobile home was just that—a mobile home, whereas Ben's abode was a trailer. Terry Ledger's place was years newer than Ben's and looked neat and clean, with tan siding that simulated painted wood, powder blue shutters neatly framing the windows and a redwood deck out front. The solid door was open and through the screen door's haze, she saw a silhouette moving inside. As she climbed the three steps onto the deck, a roadrunner sitting on the rail watched her and she smiled. She liked the roadrunners that hopped and darted everywhere.

The form inside turned her way before she knocked, came to the door and opened it, a pencil in one hand. "Morning," he said. If he harbored anger or antipathy about the way they had parted yesterday, she didn't hear it in his voice.

Freshly shaved, wearing Levi's and a black OC Choppers T-shirt, Lord, he was sex personified. She snuck a glance at ropy forearms showing below long sleeves pushed up and almost forgot why she had come. "Uh, hi . . ." She nodded toward the roadrunner. "Uh, I see you've got a guard out front."

He chuckled, well-shaped lips turning up at the corners. "I named him Hercules."

"Hercules? I hope you left it up to your wife to name your kids."

"I don't have any kids. Or a wife. It was just a name that came to mind."

Hearing he was unmarried sent another little frisson through her. She had suspected he might be single the very first day she saw him, but she hadn't been certain.

The roadrunner cocked its head as if it knew it was being discussed, and Marisa smiled again. "They're so funny. Sometimes they act like they're tame."

"I swatted a beetle yesterday and gave it to him. He's been hanging out ever since. Now he's my buddy."

"Naturally. Uh, may I come in?"

"Sure." He stood back, holding the door open. As she passed in front of him, she caught a whiff of his cologne. Safari, that was it. Hmm. Nothing smelled quite as luscious as an all-male man wearing Safari. And if she had ever seen an all-male man, Mr. Ledger filled the bill. The anxiety that had retreated briefly with the roadrunner talk returned.

His eyes targeted her left hand. "I hope that's not breakfast you're delivering."

She drew a blank at first, then remembered she was carrying a half-empty gallon jug of Jack Daniel's. "Oh, my gosh," she said, looking down at the bottle hooked onto her finger and feeling her cheeks warm. "No, I just—well, I don't know. I just took it away from someone." She gave a breathy heh-heh and brushed back a sheaf of hair. "If you were hungry, you should've come to the café. I made biscuits this morning, and cream gravy."

"Heck. Wish I'd known. But that's okay. I usually eat light after I run." He pointed his pencil at the whiskey jug in her hand. "You want to set that on the counter or would you like a glass?" He laughed.

She laughed, too. "No, uh, no. But yeah, sure. Just let me set it down." She did that, glad to get rid of it.

As she stepped back from the counter, she saw maps and drawings spread over the dining table. They were the only clutter in the place. Everything else was just as spotlessly clean as it had been the first day she came here, a blessing after the few minutes she had spent in Ben's trailer.

He laid his pencil on the table and carried his cup to the kitchen, picked up the coffeepot and gestured toward her. "Coffee?"

"No, thanks." While he poured some for himself, she crossed her wrists behind her back and from the corner of her eye, tried to peek at the maps and drawings. "You run, huh?"

"Cross-country. I try to do five miles if I have the time."

Without an ounce of body fat, he looked like a runner, and she envisioned him in full stride, not even breathing hard, while she panted and staggered at two miles. "I ran this morning, too. I didn't see you, but then, I usually stick to Lanny Winegardner's road. Not as many snakes."

His head cocked to the side and his eyes widened. "You know Winegardner?"

The alert response aroused her curiosity. She thought of what Mr. Patel had told her and what she suspected was Mr. Ledger's grand plan. How would the cattle rancher react to the expansion of Agua Dulce into a huge service station? "Everyone knows Lanny. He's one of the good guys."

She openly looked at the maps on the table, saw the names of Agua Dulce's businesses printed in tiny, neat letters. Mr. Ledger set down his mug, came to the table and began rolling the top map into a tube. Okay, so she was being nosy. She could accept that he didn't want her to see his maps and drawings. "Uh, I don't want to take up your time, but I need to speak to you about something."

He grinned as his agile fingers stretched a rubber band around the map. "Who're you interceding for this time?"

She let out a great breath, his reading her so well making her visit easier. "It's Mr. Patel and Bob Nichols. They're terrified, you know."

He appeared unfazed by that information as he stood the roll against the wall. He didn't say anything, so assuming she had been given the floor, she charged ahead. "Mr. Patel's service station is all he has. He's owned it since I was in high school. He works really hard. For that matter, his whole family works in the station and they all work hard. He has a wife and two kids. Bright, good kids, I might add. And Bob, well, he's lived here for over twenty years. He's built the motel little by little. I think he's in the same position as Mr. Patel. The motel's all he has."

Mr. Ledger took a seat on the sofa arm, his left elbow resting on his thigh. His brown hair, obviously skillfully cut, curled at his collar. "These two are like Gordon Tubbs? Friends of yours?"

"We've all lived together for a very long time, Mr. Ledger. When there's so few of us, we *have* to be friends. There isn't much we don't know about each other."

"Hey, call me Terry. 'Mr. Ledger' sounds old."

Except for a few laugh lines at the corners of his eyes and silver at his temples, he didn't look old. She guessed him to be her age or only a few years older. "Okay. I know what you mean."

"Since you know everyone here so well, you must be aware that Patel could be closed down by the state and it has nothing to do with anything I might or might not do in Agua Dulce."

"Well, we know each other, but he doesn't discuss his business with me. Why would they close him down?"

"Violations of EPA standards. I'd be surprised if he hasn't already gotten warning letters."

The gossip about the station's aged storage tanks leaped into her mind. Even before the emergence of environmental militants, the concern was that the station's underground gasoline storage tanks could deteriorate with age, seep fuel into the surrounding soil, leach into the aquifer and contaminate the town's only source of drinking water. "You mean they'd just arbitrarily close him down?"

"Sooner or later. He's in a no-win position. The legislation requires all the vintage stations to replace their old storage tanks. When the owners dig up the tanks, if they find there's been leakage, the surrounding soil is supposed to be hauled off and replaced with new, clean soil. So far, leaks have been found in almost every case where the old tanks have been uncovered. The deadline's long past, but I've seen no evidence that Patel's even done any testing."

She vaguely remembered hearing something about

the issue, but at the time she hadn't thought she knew anyone directly affected. "So? What, they just force him out of business?"

"The cleanup's expensive. Most mom-and-pops can't afford to do it, so they choose not to. A lot of them have just walked off from their stations."

"I can't believe that. What about the money they've—"

"They leave it up to the state, the taxpayers, to do the cleanup. All too often, it ends up costing more than the property's worth."

Marisa swallowed. She hadn't heard Mr. Patel say one word about being required by the state to replace his gasoline tanks or clean up after them. But as secretive as she knew him to be, perhaps he wouldn't have mentioned something as incriminating as warning letters from the state.

"And Nichols," Mr. Ledger went on, "could go out of business tomorrow and not suffer financially if that's what's worrying you. He comes from old Eastern money. Pennsylvania utilities, I think it is. He lives off a trust fund. A very nice trust fund. He's about half a bubble off of plumb. I suspect his family pays him to stay away."

She didn't totally disbelieve this. Bob Nichols had always been strange and, in his own way, as secretive as Mr. Patel. Hadn't she wondered a hundred times where he got so much money to waste on something as foolish as a UFO landing pad? She sank into a chair at the table, a considerable amount of wind taken out of her sails. "How do you know all this? You just spy on everyone, pry into their lives?"

"It's information that's easy to get. It isn't spying or prying, either. It's prudence. If I don't know what

I'm facing when I start a new development, I can't protect my investment. Besides that, my bankers expect me to be on top of what's going on. If they ask me questions, I have to be able to answer them."

"Development." The word sent a shiver down her spine. Her hunch had been right.

At the same time she worried about *development,* she couldn't keep from worrying over what he might have learned about her and her mother. Not that she had anything to hide, but now she felt naked. And vulnerable. "None of that means the people who live here suffer any less if you tear down the whole place. This isn't like a city, where we can just pick up and move to another part of town. All of us have heard rumors ever since you bought Agua Dulce, but you haven't told us what you're planning. That's all we want to know. You think it's important to make your bankers happy? Well, our whole lives are invested here. *We* think it's important to know what's happening so we can plan for our own futures."

He shook his head. "I'm sorry, but I don't discuss my projects. Everything's in the very early stages. I'll tell you this. When I know something for sure, I'll let you and your friends know. I said the other day, I'm fair."

All at once she was out of words. He had shut her down completely. Why the hell had she ever agreed to come and see him anyway? "Well, I guess that's that." She stood, willing herself not to run from the room.

He stood, too. "Look, I'm being as honest as I can. I'll give everyone's circumstances fair consideration, including Patel and Nichols. I always do."

And what about Pecos Belle's? she wanted to ask,

but didn't, for fear of hearing his answer. After all, he *owned* the Pecos Belle's building.

As she approached the door, he came up behind her. "I'm gonna be here a few more days. Maybe we'll run into each other some morning on the trail."

"I—I don't run cross-country." Not looking at him, she reached for the screen door latch. "It's an accomplishment to get up and down Lanny's gravel road. Besides, I never know what morning's going to hand me, so I don't have a schedule. I just run when I can swing it." She pushed on the latch, but it didn't open the door.

He reached around her and did it for her, his chest and face so close she could feel his body heat. "Then maybe I'll catch up with you on the road some morning when you're out."

She looked into his eyes, her face inches from his. "S-sure. Maybe so."

She left his mobile home, frustration hammering her, and headed home to check on Mama. All she could do was berate herself. Her visit had accomplished nothing. Other than his being a cross-country runner, she knew little more about him now than she had known before. In fact, she had gleaned more new information about the friends and neighbors she had known for years than about him.

She had never felt—or been—so powerless.

Then it dawned on her that she had left Ben's jug of Jack Daniel's on Terry Ledger's counter.

Seeing Marisa's distress left Terry with a kind of anxiety about the project that was unfamiliar. It felt almost like guilt.

Lord knew, his business had placed him in conflict

and controversy many times. Real estate development changed lives as much as it changed landscapes. Opposition from some quarter came with every project— uneasy neighbors, greedy politicians, litigious special-interest groups. Dealing with one or all of those factions was as common as tying his shoes. But this uprising from Marisa, speaking for a handful of people, was different. As he watched her image grow smaller, he had a compelling urge to run after her and reassure her that his plans for change weren't directed at her personally.

Don't be nuts, he told himself. When it came to his projects, he kept his relationships on a professional level, never interjecting himself into anyone's personal life. Or their personal problems. Mixing with the natives in that way could affect his judgment or compromise his forward movement, either of which could cause him a serious financial loss.

He had to get over it. Why should he feel guilt? All he had done was pay a small fortune for this little piece of dirt that had been legitimately on the market. He had every right to do with it as he wished. The people who lived here had to have known from the get-go that building businesses in a privately owned town was a risk.

His company was well known for producing highly desirable living sites. Wherever a Legendary Development subdivision evolved, contiguous real estate values rose. Sometimes they even skyrocketed. Larson's Truck & Travel Stop and Legend Ranches would be a boon to a part of the state heretofore passed over by all but drilling companies, roadrunners and rattlesnakes.

Marisa Rutherford had given him this edgy feeling.

Her penetrating eyes seemed to look inside him; her frank manner made him question himself. Well, in truth, there was more to it than that. He disliked even the idea of a woman with such delicious-looking lips, not to mention a killer body, being angry with him. She had an earthiness about her and an exotic appearance that made him think of Gypsy campfires and dancing girls and, for some reason, set his juices stewing. *Damn.* How could he be drawn in that way to a woman so opposite from the cool, sleek kittens with whom he played in Fort Worth and Dallas?

He knew the answer. Mentally, he called it what he wouldn't say aloud—lust.

But identifying the appeal didn't mean he had to act on it. She was allied with the locals against him. If there was anyone in Agua Dulce, indeed all of Cabell County, who was most likely to bring him trouble—like lawsuits and injunctions to delay or halt his whole project—that someone was Marisa. Yep, he had to do two things. Number one, play it cool in his interaction with her, and number two, keep a healthy distance.

He turned from watching her through his screen door and saw the jug of Jack Daniel's she had left on his counter. His first impulse was to call to her, but he thought better of it. He would take it to her the next time he went to the café to eat. That is, if he ever went there again.

On Wednesday, the arrival of Brad England's surveying crew enabled Terry to divert his attention from the carnal temptation Marisa presented. He had made up his mind the less he saw of her, the better, but the surveying crew's eating three meals a day at Pecos Belle's put forth a challenge. Because he worked with the surveyors during the day, he felt obligated to tag along when they went to lunch in the café, but he could tactfully avoid having breakfast and dinner with them. Where the devil-woman was concerned, dining in his mobile home made maintaining his intention to give her a wide berth easier.

Thunderstorms delayed the surveyors for two days and they made a plan to work through the weekend, but on Friday, Terry left them and headed east. He needed to check on work in progress in and around Fort Worth, and he needed a break if he expected to be at the top of his game for the meeting with Larson's people on Tuesday. It would take a superb selling effort to convince them that a location in the middle of nowhere was a good place to build a multimillion-dollar plant.

He planned to spend the weekend in Fort Worth doing something that allowed him to clear his head. He planned to spend two days skydiving.

The phone was ringing as he entered his condo. Caller ID told him the call came from his mother's office in Odessa. When he picked up she didn't say hello, though he hadn't seen her or heard from her in weeks. She opened with, "Darling, I ran into Herb on the golf course and he told me you're borrowing millions again."

He had never borrowed millions, at least not all in one lump sum. "Hi, Mom. When'd you get back?"

"Oh, days ago. Things didn't go that well, I'll tell you. I'm already wondering if I've made a mistake."

Terry knew without asking that she was referring to her honeymoon and her new husband. He closed his eyes, trying to calculate the number of weeks she had been married to husband number four.

"I don't know why I couldn't see it before," she

said. "I think he has a drinking problem. I don't have time to take care of a man with problems."

Or anyone else but yourself, Terry couldn't keep from thinking. He held a sour memory of childhood and Mom's climb up the ladder of success in an Odessa law firm. He hadn't forgotten how often he had heard her say she didn't have time to spend with him for this or that or to cook a meal or even to wash his clothes. With his dad constantly traveling and/or living overseas for months at a time, at a young age Terry had learned to do laundry and had eaten a lot of hot dogs. These days his mother had a housekeeper, but in his youth, more often than not, there had been no one at home but him.

Out of the blue he thought of how Marisa had given up her freedom and a more stimulating life in an urban environment to run her mother's café and flea market and take care of her. The errant thought made no sense in the context of a conversation with his mother because the woman he called Mom wouldn't even understand something so unselfish, much less do it.

"Well, Mom," he said, "when you meet a guy in a bar, even a fancy bar, and spend all your free time in a bar, I guess it's safe to assume he drinks."

He heard a gasp and pictured her in a designer suit, a manicured hand on her hip, her perfectly made-up blue eyes bugging with indignation. "Don't be tacky. You know I met him at the country club. I'll have you know, young man—"

"Mom, we haven't even seen each other in weeks. Let's don't get into a fight. What's up?"

"I'm concerned over your borrowing so much money. And for a real estate development in some godforsaken ghost town? My God, son, have you lost your mind? A misstep like this could destroy you. Everyone we know is talking about it."

And therein lay his mother's real concern. Terry felt his jaw clench in spite of his determination not to quarrel with her. "It's not a ghost town and it's not a misstep."

"You don't listen, Terry. How many times do I have to tell you, things happen? Things you can't anticipate. Herb says—"

"I'm good at anticipating. Don't worry about it." Terry didn't know who Herb was, but his mother's words brought to mind what he had already failed to anticipate in Agua Dulce, like Gordon Tubbs, Bob Nichols and Mandan Patel. And Marisa Rutherford. "Listen, Mom, I'm only gonna be here a couple more days before I go back. I've got a lot to do. If you don't need anything, I should get going."

"Well, I'm only your mother. By all means, don't let me take up your valuable time."

"Mom, please. I'm sure I'll get to Odessa in the next few weeks and I'll pop in to see you."

She hung up in his ear. Not unusual. His mother was one of the most willful human beings he had ever known. He sighed and pushed the PLAY MESSAGES button.

It seemed that everyone in Fort Worth had called him and left messages, including Michelle. Before the recordings finished he picked up the receiver to return her call and set up a get-together for later, after his return from the airport. Evidently she had moved past being disappointed that he had no interest in marriage. Now they were back to "just sex."

Then, before he keyed her number on speed dial,

he was stopped by a memory—Marisa Rutherford with her shining black hair, her whiskey-colored eyes and her firm ass in tight jeans that gave him ideas he had no business having. An unexpected truth stunned him. He didn't want to be with Michelle while Marisa traipsed through his head. He didn't want to face Marisa after he had been with Michelle.

Just like that, he knew he wouldn't spend time with Michelle this weekend. Perhaps he would never spend time with her again. Marisa was the woman he wanted to know better—in all of the ways he knew Michelle. But he wanted more. For some damn reason, he wanted Marisa's approval.

Shocked and distracted by the thought, he carefully placed the receiver back in its cradle. *It's only because she's the leader of that bunch of kooks in Agua Dulce,* he told himself. As such, she could help make his whole project happen more smoothly.

Whatever the reason, he couldn't wait for the weekend to end so he could return to Agua Dulce.

Chapter 12

Agua Dulce was targeted for a real estate development of some kind. Recalling the little she knew of Terry Ledger and his activities in the Fort Worth/Dallas Metroplex and considering the maps at which she had sneaked a look on his dining table, Marisa had drawn that conclusion days back. Now, to confirm her deduction, pink surveyor's flags on skinny wires were stuck in the ground all around Agua Dulce. Seeing them came as a jolt, but not a surprise.

For a few brief seconds, she tried to imagine a maze of paved streets fronted by homes and lawns—well, forget the lawns—spread over Agua Dulce's acres like a giant spiderweb, but the visual wouldn't mesh in her mind.

Her thoughts veered to the building occupied by Pecos Belle's and Tanya's Tangles. It was centered on the eastern border of the town of Agua Dulce and took up more than two hundred feet of highway frontage. She didn't have to be a genius to know it sat in a prime spot.

The old brick relic had been her only home for the first eighteen years of her life. Soon it would be torn down and replaced with a service station, just like Mr. Patel said. She should feel some kind of emotion over that, but all she could think of was the fact that she and Mama were on the brink of homelessness.

Exactly when, she couldn't guess. Weeks from now? Months? Could she be lucky enough to have a year to plan and make intelligent decisions? Even if the latter held true, she had no time to waste. Monday, she would return to making calls to learn the costs and complications of moving everything Mama owned.

She told Tanya her suspicions about the building. The only response that came from the hairdresser/ artist/jewelrymaker was, "Shit."

Mobilized by the surveyor's flags, Bob Nichols organized a town meeting. On Saturday afternoon, Bob, Ben, Mr. Patel, Tanya, and Lanny Winegardner all trooped into the café. Marisa tried to lift the heavy atmosphere by serving coffee and passing out free sugar cookies. As the group sat at the tables and speculated, all talking at once, she got everyone's attention by telling them she concurred with what Mr. Patel had said days back—a monster gas station would replace Pecos Belle's and Tanya's Tangles.

The information prompted Lanny to report that someone had put out feelers with a Realtor in Odessa about purchasing the XO. A brief silence stole through the room while that bit of information and its meaning sank in.

"We didn't know you wanted to sell," Bob said at last. "I didn't think you would ever do that."

"Well, I wasn't exactly looking to, but for the right price . . . " The XO's owner arched his brow, bit down on a cookie, then sipped his coffee.

That Lanny might sell out hit Marisa like a lightning bolt. The potential buyer putting out feelers had to be Terry Ledger. To buy the XO's thousands of acres, he must be even richer than she had suspected. His plans must be for something larger than she or anyone else had imagined. The word "subdivision" flashed in her mind. She stayed behind the lunch counter, keeping her thoughts to herself, lest she say something that would send everyone into hysterics.

Mr. Patel, Bob and even Lanny expressed concern for what might happen to the availability of the water from the town's well. The discussion ended with Bob asking Marisa to again speak to Mr. Ledger on their behalf about the well and the water supply.

Lanny spoke up. "Fellas, it ain't her responsibility to worry about your water. We shouldn't jump to conclusions, but if it comes to it, I'll drill a new well for my house and the hands. You should do the same."

"But you may never get good water," Bob said. "No one's hit a good water well in years."

Indeed. There were drilled water wells around, impudently inserting themselves among pump jacks that sucked the black gold from the bowels of the earth, but most of the water that came from them was what West Texans called gyp, full of minerals and not fit for human consumption. It corroded plumbing, ate holes in washing machine tubs and killed domestic grass. A manicured lawn in this desolate part of the world was only for those with hearts stout enough to withstand a multitude of disappointments. God knew what the gyp water would do to the insides of a human, but livestock had no trouble drinking it. That detail had always made Marisa wonder why it was okay for animals, but not people.

Lanny arched his brow and tilted his head, acknowledging the facts about the water. Then he took another sip of coffee.

"My family does not use so much water," Mr. Patel put in. "Marisa, you should speak for us. Make Mr. Ledger understand."

"My business doesn't require much water, either," Bob said. "I'd be willing to shut down my swimming pool."

Ben clunked his beer can on the table. "Ain't it a bitch? I don't even like water and looks like I'm the only one who's gonna be left with some to drink." He guffawed, which turned into a coughing fit.

Everyone in the room leveled a flat look at him.

"Perhaps we could pay him for water," Bob suggested.

Mr. Patel and Lanny echoed murmurs of agreement with the idea.

"You have his ear, Marisa," Bob continued. "Perhaps you could approach him and make the suggestion."

"Guys," she said, "that water well's the least of my worries. Besides, Mr. Ledger left and I have no idea when he's coming back."

"I'll talk to him," Lanny said. "We're rounding up for branding, but soon as he gets back I'll try to find the time to catch up with him."

Marisa looked at Lanny, who was always unselfish and willing to take action for the greater good. As important as branding his calves was to him, she knew he would take the time and make a special effort to have a conversation with Terry Ledger and attempt to work out everyone's problems with the water. A little pang of guilt for her own self-centered attitude pinched her. "You don't have to, Lanny. If he's in town, he comes in to eat almost every day. It's not a big deal for me talk to him."

"Oh, thank you, Marisa," Bob gushed. "Thank you so much."

"Darlin', I don't like seeing you shoved into such a bad spot," Lanny said.

"Humph. The bad spot came a long time ago, Lanny. Compared to everything else, a little talk about water's just plain easy." She dredged up a smile. "I'll let you know how it turns out."

The remaining discussion went nowhere. Where could it go, with no one knowing what the town's new owner would do next?

Solemn-faced and silent, everyone but Ben Seagrave left the café. Marisa watched until the last of them, the willowy Tanya, closed the front door and disappeared from sight. The hairdresser had remained uncharacteristically quiet through the meeting. Knowing her, Marisa was sure there was much more going on in her multicolored head than where she might relocate her beauty salon and gift shop.

"She usually has an opinion," Marisa said to Ben. "If Lanny sold out, Jake Shepherd could be out of a job."

"And I imagine that gal might move on to pastures greener than poor ol' Jake. It don't impress me that stickability in a rough patch is one of her strong suits."

Marisa withheld her opinion. Tanya had already stuck with Jake a long time. "I'm pretty sure Mama and I are going to have to move," she said. "I'm going to look into having Mama's trailer hauled to Odessa or Midland. We have to live where I can get a job."

"Why, darlin', you can't move that trailer. It don't belong to your mama."

"What do you mean? Sure it does."

Ben's shaggy head slowly shook. "Clyde bought it

and put her in it. A few years after you went off to Dallas."

That possibility was too preposterous to even be considered. "You must be wrong, Ben. Mama never told me that. I haven't written a check for rent since I've been back here."

Ben's head shook again as the cigarette butt he dropped into his empty beer can produced a sharp hiss. "That may be. But Raylene don't own that trailer. If Clyde hadn't croaked, he might've eventually let her have it to keep, but my guess is his estate ain't about to give Raylene Rutherford *anything*."

Marisa barely managed to stay calm until Ben departed. It couldn't be true that Mama didn't own the mobile home where they lived, for god's sake. Clyde Campbell had been dead several years. If Mama didn't own the trailer, why hadn't his estate kicked her out of it already?

Marisa had become aware years back that if Ben was drinking, one couldn't necessarily believe every word he said. She locked the café's doors and hightailed it home, intent on finding the title to Mama's mobile home. Her first stop was the foot-square safe hidden in the back of Mama's bedroom closet. She didn't know how a title to a mobile home looked, but she believed she would recognize it if she saw it.

Not finding it there, she went to the kitchen drawers, where odds and ends of everything from grocery store receipts to assorted recipes had been stashed over the years. So that her searching the place didn't upset Mama, Marisa turned the TV to the Country Music Channel. While Marisa pored over every scrap of paper, piece by piece, her mother sang along with the music videos and even left her chair to dance once or twice.

After Marisa exhausted the possibilities in the kitchen, she moved to Mama's dresser in the bedroom. Finally, while Mama watched Jerry Springer, Marisa returned to the café and rummaged through the various records kept in the apartment behind the kitchen. She found nothing that even resembled the object of her quest.

Dejected and worn out, she dropped to the sofa in the apartment living room. Homelessness was no longer an abstraction that loomed in the future; it was now a blaring reality.

In fact, it was a five-hundred-pound bomb so overwhelming that Marisa hyperventilated and had to rush outside, where she could draw a breath. Despair threatened to crush her. Disposal of the flea market inventory and the café equipment had to begin at once. Without delay she had to put together a résumé and start the hunt for a job. *Somewhere.* She had to find a place for her and Mama to live. *Somewhere.* And after she found a job, while she worked, *someone* had to stay with Mama.

Did Terry Ledger know about the mobile home? He must. Why hadn't the jerk said something? Anger began to seethe within her, at her mother for allowing this mess to exist and at the man holding their fate in his hands.

Terry drove into Agua Dulce Sunday evening, locked and loaded for his meeting with Larson's site development team. He had brought with him dozens of maps, pages of statistics and piles of traffic and demographic studies. He wanted to tell no one of Larson's impending visit, but he had promised Marisa he would keep her aware of the progress and he was a man of his word.

Knowing he was on the verge of upending the lives of every citizen in Agua Dulce still pecked at him. He hadn't reached the pinnacle of success in the risky world of real estate development and speculative home building without being able to size up a problem and read people. The easiest way to salve his conscience and accomplish what he wanted was to get everyone's cooperation. To do that, the first person he needed to win over to his side was Marisa. In her, he saw a quiet strength and a fair share of horse sense.

Beyond that, hunger was gnawing at his gut. He'd had nothing to eat since breakfast and knew he would find no food in his mobile home. As he neared Pecos Belle's, the lone sixties-era neon sign shouted out in the twilight. Well, in reality, encircled by only partially burning pink neon, the metal oval was more a sputter than a shout.

He debated whether he should stop in and order supper and perhaps tell Marisa about Larson's now, but his saner side, having acknowledged the truth of his attraction to her, sent out an alarm warning him away from her. Nearing the café, he couldn't make up his mind how he should behave.

Hunger won out and he angle-parked his truck in front of Pecos Belle's. As he entered the flea market, the whole place smelled of something good and his hunger intensified. He heard voices.

When he reached the café area in the back of the building, he saw Bob Nichols sitting at one end of the lunch counter, talking to Marisa. With his wild white hair that looked as if he had combed it with an egg-beater, his white beard, khaki pants and bush coat he looked as if he might have come off an African safari. Marisa was wearing tight jeans and a white T-shirt with an eagle and an American flag splashed across the front. Oh, man, she looked as good in a T-shirt as she did in jeans, and he felt a tiny pull low in his belly. *Damn.*

With his footsteps muffled by the mass of displayed merchandise in the crowded flea market, apparently neither she nor Nichols had heard him enter. They had their heads together in low conversation. "Hey," he said, approaching the lunch counter.

She and Nichols both looked up, surprised. Nichols stood up immediately, pulled his wallet from his pants pocket and handed her several bills. He ducked around Terry's side and headed for the front door so quickly Terry didn't get out another word.

"Bob, don't worry. Everything will be okay," Marisa called after him.

"What was that about?" Terry asked, his gaze following the bushy-haired eccentric all the way to the door.

Marisa moved to a spot behind the lunch counter and crossed her arms over her chest, a dish towel dangling from one hand. "You intimidate him."

Terry opened his palms. "What'd I do?"

"You don't have to do much to intimidate Bob. He's cowed by even the roadrunners." She sidled to where Nichols had been sitting, stacked his dishes and began to wipe the lunch counter. "I hope you didn't come to eat. I'm almost ready to close. I've already turned off the griddle and cleaned up."

So much for abating his hunger pangs. "Uh, no. I just dropped by to let you know I'm back."

"Okay. You're back."

Was that reply bristly? Was she mad? And if so, about what? He took a seat at the lunch counter near the glass dome that always protected a freshly baked pie. Beneath it he saw one thick slab of something fruity. Apple, maybe. "Pie looks good. You bake it?"

"Who else would bake it? It's not like I can just run to Albertson's and get one."

"Yeah, I see—"

"You want that last slice?"

"Well, I—"

"I charge three-fifty for a slice of fruit pie with a scoop of vanilla ice cream." She walked over, lifted the dome, deftly scooped the slice onto a serving plate, then slid it into the microwave. She gathered the pie tin and the domed plate, added them to Bob's dishes and whisked them off to the kitchen. Returning, she took the slice of pie from the microwave, dug a scoop of ice cream out of the freezer and set the whole thing on the counter in front of him. A fork and napkin beside his plate followed. Then she returned to wiping the lunch counter, all without a word.

In the face of her obvious annoyance, the only thing Terry could think to do was eat. The first bite of pie— apple it was—was so scrumptious his tongue wanted to cheer. He devoured the pie to the last crumb.

"Good grief," she said, looking at his plate, then at him. "You must be really hungry."

He met her eyes and was sure he saw genuine concern. "I haven't eaten all day," he said. "Homemade pie's something I don't get real often. It's one of my favorite things."

She looked at him a few beats, as if she were studying him. "I could make you a lunch-meat sandwich," she said finally. "I just don't want to heat up the griddle again."

That was the way she was. Caring enough to prepare him a meal, even though he was pretty sure she was mad at him for some reason. "I don't want you to go to the trouble—"

But she was already dragging out ham and cheese, lettuce and tomatoes. In a matter of minutes, she placed a thick sandwich in front of him. He felt sheepish as hell, but he also still felt hungry, so he picked up the sandwich. "Sit with me a minute?"

She stood there, looking at the cold-drink dispenser, lips pursed, jaw tight. At a loss how to react to her sharp attitude, he said, "I just came back from Fort Worth." He felt like a dumb turd.

She picked up two Styrofoam cups, drew two Cokes and set one beside his plate. She came around the end of the counter carrying the other and took a seat beside him. She peeled the paper from a straw, poked it through a scored hole in the lid and sucked up a long swallow. Something to do with him was on her mind or she wouldn't have sat down.

"Long drive," he said and bit into the sandwich.

"I know. I used to live in the Metroplex. Ever eat in the IHOP on I-30 between Fort Worth and Dallas?"

He wiped his mouth with his napkin and couldn't hold back a smile, glad she now seemed to be less angry. "I don't think so."

Her finger made a circle from a drop of moisture on the countertop. "I used to be the chief cook and bottle washer there."

"The manager?"

"Nah. I'm not worth a damn at giving people orders. But I'm a really good cook. Anyway, it was

awful. Everything's fried. Everything but the pan-
cakes, that is."

No way was any of that what was on her mind, but
he was pretty sure it was best to wait her out and not
push. "I don't get out that way much. I live in Fort
Worth. Downtown." He gave her a cautious look from
the corner of his eye and took another bite.

"How nice. Guess that's where I'd expect a guy rich
enough to buy half of West Texas to live."

Okay, enough was enough. He put down his sandwich and turned to face her. "If you're mad at me for
some reason, I'd like to know why."

She stabbed her straw into the ice in her Styrofoam
cup and glowered at him across her shoulder. "Okay,
I'll tell you. It's not bad enough you own this building
where I make my living and you're going to tear it
down around my ears. You haven't even had the cour-
tesy to inform me you own the roof over my head.
And my mother's."

So *that* was it. "I thought you knew."

"Not until Ben told me."

"The drunk."

"Stop calling him that. Just because he has a few
shortcomings doesn't mean you should call him
names." She began to tear a paper napkin into strips.
"He's one of my best friends."

"I wonder if he appreciates your loyalty. I wonder
if he's able to appreciate *anyone's* loyalty. He's a total
alcoholic, Marisa. He's written some of the coolest
songs in country music. He's made a fortune, but he's
squandered most of it."

She lifted her chin and those mysterious eyes bored
into him. "Are you without flaws, Mr. Ledger?"

He didn't dare duck her gaze. "I've got plenty of

flaws, but drowning myself in booze isn't one of them."

She looked away. "Well, good for you, I guess." She began to tear the napkin strips into tiny squares. "For your information we had a town meeting yesterday."

A caution light clicked on in his head. "Who had a meeting?"

"Us peons who live here and try to make a living here. Your ears must have been burning like hell. You were the main topic."

"Don't tell me y'all decided to lynch me."

"No, *they* didn't. I'm the only one here who's capable of violence."

He already knew her well enough to know that retort was hyperbole. She was tough, but at the same time she was a softie. "I'm not going to kick you out of your home, Marisa. I do have something to tell you, though. I said I'd be as up front and honest as I can. Are you familiar with Larson's Truck and Travel Stops?"

"I knew it was something like that."

He stared into her eyes, willing her not to look away. "My plan is to tear down this building and put a Larson's here, in this spot." He tapped a finger on the counter—*tap-tap-tap*.

The mole at the corner of her delectable mouth twitched, but otherwise she didn't flinch. "Then I guess it's a lie that you ain't gonna kick us out of our happy home, isn't it?"

"I understand your situation. I'm trying to come up with a solution."

"Forget it. I'll find my own solutions." She started to rise, but he grasped her forearm. "Marisa, the reason I'm telling you this is because two representatives from Larson's will be here Tuesday. I'd rather you hear who they are from me than to get hit with it unexpectedly."

A haunted look came into her eyes and he thought he saw a sudden rush of tears, but she didn't break down. She freed her arm. "That soon, huh? I was hoping we had a little time."

"All they're doing is coming for a look-see. I don't know exactly what will develop after that. Or when."

She glared at him, near tears replaced by fury. "Dammit, can't you see how lost these people here will be when you put them out on the street?"

"That's a little dramatic, don't you think?"

She gave a sarcastic huff. "If Mr. Patel is put out of business, whether it's by the State of Texas or by your new station, everything he has will be gone. He won't have an income or even a place to live. And Bob and Ben. I don't know how either of them would adjust to living somewhere else. This tiny community is all they have. Why do you think Bob's stayed here? Why do you think Ben doesn't live in Nashville?"

"Marisa, I've spent a lot of money on this place. *My* money. And I'm spending more every day. I don't have an angel. I can't afford to turn this into a charity for mis—into a charity."

"Go ahead and say it. For misfits. You think all of us should be locked up on the funny farm."

"That's harsh. I don't mean that."

"Yes, you do," she grumbled. "And just for the record, I don't think an angel is looking out for me, either."

"I meant I don't have a financial backer. I meant

I'm spending my own money here and my bank account isn't bottomless."

The corner of her mouth twitched again and her head turned toward the flea market. "You need to go. I'm late checking on my mother."

She left the stool and vanished into the kitchen. Seconds later, the lights went out. Neon advertising on the walls cast the whole place in an eerie red aura. He still had half a sandwich on his plate. She returned to the dining area, keys jangling in her hand, and marched toward the front door. He had no choice but to follow.

"Okay, dammit, I'm outta here," he said when they reached the front door. "I'm trying to do the right thing, but you—"

"The right thing, Mr. Ledger, was for *you* to have stayed in Fort Worth and kept *your* money with you. But it's too late for that, isn't it?"

Chapter 13

Monday morning took Marisa to Terry Ledger's front door. Again. Last night, she had been so put out with the man, she had forgotten to mention the well water. Now, as she stood on his deck banging on his door, she could think of two hundred places she would rather be.

The solid door opened and she found herself looking at him through the screen door. He was wearing Levi's and a red polo shirt. He opened the screen door.

"They're worried about the water," she said. "They have no other place to get it. There's a village in this county that has water hauled in from Pecos. It costs a fortune. Those guys can't afford that."

There. She had presented the case. She braced herself for the counterattack. He had to be angry after their exchange last night.

He tucked back his chin and looked puzzled for a few seconds. He probably thought she was crazy, the way she stormed around and blurted out righteous declarations. Then dawning came into his expression. "You mean Patel and Nichols."

"Lanny, too."

He hesitated, just looking at her. For a moment she

feared he might ask her to leave. Finally he stood back. "Come in," he said.

She stepped inside, struggling to ignore his tanned skin and stark blue eyes, the narrowness of his waist compared to his shoulders and just how delectable he looked in red muscle-hugging knit. *S-E-X* scrolled through her mind like streaming video.

Disgusted with herself for allowing him to make her nervous, she swerved her gaze from him to her surroundings. The place was still neat and as spotless as it had been a few days earlier, which surprised her. In her past observations of men living alone, his place should be a wreck by now. Someone must be doing his housekeeping, but if that were true, in Agua Dulce, why hadn't she heard of it? Very little occurred here that she failed to learn about.

Only the dining table and the breakfast bar where papers and file folders were scattered showed disorder. He extended his hand, urging her toward the sofa. She sank onto one end. He sat down on the opposite end, a palm braced on one knee and an elbow on the other, a totally male pose. His eyes looked straight into hers. "These men need to be thinking about drilling another well."

"But that'll cost a lot of money."

"They can afford it."

She opened her mouth to fire back, but discovered she had no argument. In all the years she had known Bob, Lanny and Mr. Patel, she had always been aware how much better off financially each of them was than her and Mama. Even so, she rarely thought of it. Right now, their having more financial security than her and her mother made no difference. She had promised to stand up for them.

"It's a matter of practicality," he added. "I may not have enough water for my project. I may have to drill another well myself. I repeat, these guys can afford to drill their own well. Or wells."

Common sense told her he was right, yet she shook her head, determined not to give up, determined to put forth a diligent effort, as promised. "You probably don't know much about this part of the country. The chances of their hitting good water in a new well are slim to none. And what happens if no one hits water?"

"You've just made my point. And you're wrong about me not knowing the country. I grew up in Odessa. Went to Permian High School. I used to kayak the Pecos."

Okay, so he wasn't a greenhorn outsider. Nor was he a sissy. Taking a kayak down the Pecos during the spring high water wasn't for the faint of heart. Big deal. A lot of crazy people did it. They came to Agua Dulce in the spring for just that purpose. "I still don't see how it would hurt you to let them use the water. If it's money, they're willing to pay you, like you're a water company or something."

"By the time I bring the water system up to state standards, I *will* be a water company."

"Well, there you go," she said, flinging a hand in the air. "All you have to do is send them a bill."

His eyes drilled her, he shook his head slowly and she knew she had lost the battle. *Shit.* She had been effective in presenting Gordon Tubbs' dilemma, but was zero for two for Bob, Lanny and Mr. Patel. She had to get out of here. Damned if she would ever have another meeting with Terry Ledger on someone else's behalf. She had her own problems to worry about. All at once, her breakfast of toast and coffee churned in her stomach. She stood up abruptly. "I have to go home."

He stood, too. "I'll go with you. I want to meet—"

"No! You can't."

"Marisa, I need to meet your mother. She owns a business operating in the middle of what I'm doing."

"If you have business with my mother, you'll have to deal with me."

He tilted his head and looked into her eyes. "Do you have her power of attorney? Or some other kind of legal permission to speak for her?"

Naturally he remembered what she had told him about Mama. Marisa felt as if he had punched her. Another reality check. She had meant to take care of that small matter of power of attorney, but had never made the time. Or found the money to pay a lawyer. Her mouth opened and closed like some damn goldfish. "No," she finally answered.

Hands planted at his waistband, he looked at her from beneath an arched brow.

Frustration threatened to unhinge her. She didn't know her mother's rights or her own rights. As she mentally floundered for more words, an idea came instead. Dammit, he *should* see who it was that he would soon make homeless. She lifted her chin and gave him a narrow-lidded look. "You want to meet my mother? . . . Then by all means, Mr. Ledger, let me introduce you."

She sailed from his living room, across his deck and down his steps, without once looking to see if he followed. He caught up with her at the back door of her mother's singlewide. She said nothing as she entered the mobile home and led him up the narrow hall that opened to the kitchen and living room.

When they reached the kitchen, they saw Mama shuffling backward across the living room in tiny, scuffing steps. Mama's face was beet red and she was perspiring profusely. An alarm went off in Marisa's brain. "Mama? What're you doing, Mama?"

"It's these shoes, Marisa. Tanya said they're backless."

Marisa shot a look at her mother's feet. She was wearing a new pair of mules Tanya had brought from Ruidoso a few days back.

Mama reached the sofa, turned around and began scuffing backward in the opposite direction. "It's really hard, Marisa, going backward."

Marisa walked over and put an arm around her mother's shoulders, stopping her movement. "No, Mama, I didn't mean for you to walk backward. You could hurt yourself."

Mama spotted Terry. Her eyes squinted with suspicion. "Clyde?"

"This is Mr. Ledger. He's a guest in the RV park." Marisa led her mother to a chair at the dining table. "Let's put on different shoes, okay?" Mama sat down obediently, thank God. "Just sit right here, now. Don't move. I'm going to find your tennis shoes." She shifted her attention to Terry, piercing him with her eyes and pointing her finger at him. "Don't say anything, don't do anything. I'll be back in a minute."

On the way to the bedroom she felt the sharp sting of tears, embarrassed for Mama that a stranger was witnessing her on a bad day and annoyed at herself because she had more or less dared Terry to accompany her to the trailer.

In the bedroom closet, she found a pair of canvas Keds. When she returned to the dining room, Terry was standing over Mama and she was drinking a glass of water.

"She looked so hot," he said. "I, uh, thought she might be thirsty."

Perhaps she was. On a sigh, Marisa went to the sink and dampened a sheet of paper towel, then knelt in front of her mother and wiped her overheated face. She smiled up at her, hoping to relieve some of Mama's agitation. "Feeling better?"

"It's hard work. I'm so tired, Marisa."

"I know." Marisa slipped the Keds onto Mama's feet and tied the laces in neat bows. "It'll be easier to walk now that you're wearing your tennis shoes." Marisa made a forward motion with her hand. "These shoes go forward. Okay?"

Her mother pushed her hand away. "You shouldn't treat me this way."

Marisa didn't reply. She had heard such remarks before. The petulance was part of the illness, she assumed. She helped her mother to her feet and walked her to her reclining chair in front of the TV. She eased her down, turned on the set and surfed to the soap she liked to watch. "Just rest. Want some iced tea, some Kool-Aid?"

Her mother's head shook. Marisa angled a look at Terry, who stood there, arms dangling as if he didn't know what to do next. She turned back to her mother. "Okay, then, take a nap, okay?" Marisa smoothed back the disheveled white hair and spoke softly until her mother's eyelids fluttered closed. When she felt assured that Mama slept, she gestured for Terry to precede her out the front door.

Once outside, she marched past him, toward the café, but he caught up. "Don't say a word to me," she told him, tears of anger threatening. "Don't say one word."

When they reached the café's back door, his hand reached out and circled her wrist, stopping her.

She glared at him, tightened her fist and jerked against his grip. "You've seen what you wanted to see. You're in control. Just do whatever it is you're going to and leave us the hell alone." She unlocked the door and went inside.

He followed. "I want to talk to you, Marisa."

The café's back door opened into the apartment's postage stamp–sized living room. It held an outdated sofa and two chairs and a lamp that had once been someone else's junk. She stopped in the living room, not wanting to take their conflict out into the café. "I'm trying to get organized so we can move out of here if that's what's on your mind. But you're going to have to have a little patience. Surely you can see I can't do it overnight."

"I'm not saying I want you to move."

"Then what *are* you saying?"

He dropped into a nearby armchair and looked up at her, his elbows resting on his thighs. "Let's settle down for a minute."

As her temper cooled, Marisa felt her heartbeat slow. She sank to the sofa, but she couldn't bear to look her oppressor in the eye.

"The way she is," he said, "is this a normal day for her?"

For Mama, abnormal had been normal in many ways even before the Alzheimer's disease had taken over, but how could Marisa describe that to Terry Ledger? She crossed her arms over her chest and looked away. The only person with whom she had

ever had an eye-to-eye conversation about Mama was
Ben. "Sometimes."

"Shouldn't she be in some kind of therapy or under
some kind of professional care?"

Now came the do-gooder questions. She had heard
them all more times than she could count, had even
asked them herself. She leveled a glare at him. "She
has doctors. What are you suggesting, a nursing
home?"

"Maybe. I don't know. It just seems like there
should be places where she could be cared for."

"You mean a human warehouse. This is my *mother,*
for god's sake." Did he not know that such places that
were decent cost more per month than she made now
or had ever made? "Even if I could bear seeing
her . . . there, it isn't free."

"Your family? Do they help you?"

"Why are you asking me these questions? Mama
has two sisters, one older, one younger. My aunt Rosemary shows up once a year whether she's needed or
not. My aunt Radonna's . . . well, busy." Marisa
frowned, resenting the third degree from someone
who didn't even know her and Mama. With the flat
of her hand, she brushed away the idea of help from
her aunts. "They've got their own lives. In a different
way, they're as goofy as Mama. I'm glad they don't
come around."

Terry interlocked his fingers, turned his head and
stared at the floor. She could see he didn't know what
to say. No one ever did when confronted with Mama's
illness. Marisa had already asked and argued all of the
questions she knew were going through his mind. As
they sat through beats of silence, she almost felt sorry
for him.

"How much time does she have left?" he finally asked.

Of course a man like him would want to know the bottom line. "No one knows. She's been the way she is for a quite a few months. No worse, no better."

She saw a muscle clench in his jaw. "I admit," he said, "I don't know much about this illness."

She let out a great breath and leaned forward, bracing her elbows on her knees. "Terry, listen. You strike me as someone who thinks he can fix things. Trust me, this can't be fixed. I assume the drugs she takes help, but I don't know that. Some days she thinks better than others. We talk and actually have fun. She still has some long-term memory, still has a sense of humor sometimes and a sense of who she is. She still knows me and most of the people around here. When all of us go our separate ways, I don't know for sure, but I think she'll miss everyone."

She felt a stinging rush to her eyes as she thought of how seeing Mama struggling to walk backward had blindsided her. "I have to say, I can usually see a bad day coming. This morning, I missed all the signs. If I had spotted them, I wouldn't have allowed you to come into the trailer. If Mama knew what she's doing, she'd be mortified at anyone seeing her acting so foolishly. I try to spare her dignity."

"But you're almost a prisoner here."

"Sometimes I think that. But most of the time I don't. I'm okay with it." Marisa made a sweeping motion toward the café with her arm. "All of it. There have been rewards. After all, until you came along, I was doing something I love to do. No boss, no pre-set menu prepared by someone else, no teenage manager who knows nothing about food telling me how to cook."

"You must have a plan. For the future, I mean."

She blurted out a bitter laugh. Every time she thought of her future, all she could see was a blank page. "Plan? That's a joke." She rubbed a temple with her fingers. "Sometimes I lay awake all night thinking about just how long forever is. Some mornings I get out of bed telling myself, 'I cannot do this another day.' But you know what? Every day, I do do it. And that pretty much covers my plan. In other words, Mr. Ledger, my *plan* is and always has been to take one day at a time. And try to stay sane."

He rose, came to the sofa and sat down beside her. "These people who live here, Nichols, Patel, Seagrave, they put a lot of pressure on you. It looks to me like you end up taking care of them, too."

Marisa shrugged, looking down at her neatly trimmed nails. Short, well-kept nails were important in the world of cooking. "That's what friends are for. I've known them all my life. They may be the crazy uncle you lock in the closet when company comes, but they're my support group."

"They're grown people. They shouldn't be looking to you to solve their problems."

She aimed a long, serious look into his eyes and saw something she hadn't noticed earlier. The eyes that looked back at her were gentle and caring. The tough businessman image was a facade. Instantly she knew he worked hard at protecting a kind heart. "Don't you see they can't do it? They've never been able to take on the world and everyday life like most people do. That's why they live in this isolated place.

Mama used to be their wits and their security, but—" She shook her head. "Obviously that's no longer the case."

He picked up her hand and enclosed it in his. She again felt the warmth and reassurance she had experienced that day they danced to the jukebox in the café.

"You take too much responsibility on yourself," he said.

She took back her hand and, with her fingertips, wiped away the tear that had almost fallen. "Everyone has responsibility."

"But not everyone meets it quite as head-on as you seem to. And not everyone worries about everyone else before he worries about himself."

"Head-on Marisa. That's me. One of my better-known weaknesses."

He took her hand again and his thumb moved back and forth on the top of it. This time, she didn't move it, even though a little shiver rippled through her. That was probably exactly what he intended. Men were so dumb. Give them a shock or a crisis and they think of sex.

She released a deep sigh. "Look, we could whip this dead horse all day, but I need to get the café open. No telling how much business I've missed by being closed all morning."

He nodded. "Tell you what. I want you to quit worrying. I've got to move ahead, but I'll work around you as long as I can. I'll try to come up with a solution you can live with. I know a lot of people."

"Don't you dare feel sorry for me. Or send anyone else around to feel sorry for me, either. I'm—we, Mama and me, we aren't sops for your or anyone's else's conscience. It's always been just her and me. We'll manage."

He straightened, frowning and blinking as if she had insulted him. "I wouldn't think of feeling sorry for you. It has nothing to do with my conscience. Business. We're talking a business arrangement. I just have to figure out what it is."

For the first time in days she felt safe, which was insane considering the present circumstances. What was it about him that threw her off her good sense and gave her that feeling of security?

"You're an admirable woman, Marisa."

She gave him a humorless chuckle. "Yep, that's me. Head-on, admirable Marisa."

It was after noon when Terry reached his mobile home, shaken by meeting Raylene Rutherford. He had never known anyone with Alzheimer's disease. Not since his days in the army and his experiences in Iraq had he seen another human being who had affected him more deeply. He meant it when he told Marisa he admired her. Who wouldn't admire the patience and the care she showed for not just her mother but every person in Agua Dulce? He doubted he could contend half as well with all that confronted her every day. How could any man with ethics even consider uprooting her and her mother?

Unfortunately, the building that housed Pecos Belle's sat dead center where he planned to locate Larson's. He thought of presenting Larson's with another Agua Dulce site. After all, there were two hundred acres from which to choose.

But his twelve years of experience in the commercial real estate profession argued that even the thought was a waste of time and he knew he wouldn't make the suggestion in a face-to-face meeting with

Larson's people. Pecos Belle's had the prime highway frontage, the number one selling point in his arsenal. To suggest a different site was a certain deal-breaker.

Sure, he could get along with moving the mobile home where Marisa and her mother lived to another site in the RV park—the expense would be small—but all that did was ensure them a roof over their heads. Relocating their home wouldn't provide them with an income after the flea market and café were gone.

As ideas raced through his head, none of which stuck, he perused the disarray of documents and maps scattered over his dining room table and breakfast bar. He had pissed away more than half a day, was nowhere near being prepared for a big customer and he had to leave before eight tomorrow morning to be at the Midland airport by ten o'clock. He had only hours to accomplish what needed to be done. With a million dollars invested, he couldn't afford to back off now. He called on the discipline he had learned in the military. *Just focus on the mission.*

She and Mama had been given a reprieve. Of sorts.

As Marisa cooked hamburgers for seventeen—some class returning from a field trip to Carlsbad Caverns—and listened to laughter and thumps and bumps as kids crawled over and through the covered wagon, she fantasized about walking out and asking the teachers if they wanted to buy the damn thing. *It would make a great addition to a playground,* she would say. *Oh, you're right*, the head honcho would say. *Let me get my checkbook.*

Fantasy.

"Crap," she mumbled and lifted a basket full of

golden French fries from the oil. She spread them on a parchment-lined cookie sheet and quickly salted them while the hot oil still showed as tiny bubbles on the fries. The secret to great French fries was soaking them in ice water before cooking, then salting them the instant they were out of the hot oil. She added a sprinkling of her own secret "house seasoning," which was nothing more than a mix of paprika, cayenne pepper, chili powder and a smidgen of brown sugar. And sometimes something else, depending on her mood.

As soon as her customers left, stuffed with hamburgers, French fries and chocolate brownies, she turned on the radio. Alan Jackson and Jimmy Buffett sang out "It's Five O'clock Somewhere," which triggered a fantasy about quaffing margaritas and lying on a beach in Cancún. She had done that once. It had been fun until she drank too much tequila and got sick.

All day she had felt a small lift in her spirits, which she owed to the conversation with Terry Ledger. She even felt like she had a few moments she could call her own. She walked back to the closet of a room that had been her bedroom when she and Mama lived in the apartment—now it served as an office of sorts—and dug her secret project out of the closet.

In a cardboard file box she had accumulated hundreds, maybe thousands, of recipes, some of which would end up in the cookbook she would publish someday. *Recipes That Work,* she called it. These days, she believed, folks knew so little about basic cooking, they couldn't look at a recipe and tell if it resulted in something fit to eat. Her cookbook would solve that problem, would address hundreds of questions typical of wanna-be cooks. And God willing, it would make her a pile of money.

She sat down at the computer, logged on to her cookbook program and started with the bread pudding recipe she had recently made and burned.

Chapter 14

Instead of waking up Tuesday morning with his pitch to Larson's site development team on his mind, Terry awoke thinking of Marisa and the possibility of bringing her into his camp. If someone asked him why, the explanation would be so complex and confusing he wouldn't attempt to make it. He wasn't sure he understood the reason himself. He only knew he felt a need to take her into his confidence and share his vision with her. Would doing that give her a stake in the project and win her over to his side? The question diminished in his thoughts as he drove toward the Midland airport to pick up Larson's people, but the idea didn't totally go away.

The closer he got to Midland, the more excited he became to meet with Larson's team. The travel center was the linchpin of his project. He wasn't comfortable moving ahead with the rest of his plans without a firm commitment from them. Bottom line, he needed the money from the sale.

The site inspection by Larson's two representatives took less time than the trip to the airport. They listened to Terry's presentation and looked over his exhibits, but made little comment. They filled their briefcases with the documents and maps he supplied and he drove them back to their company plane. They told him they would be in touch and flew off to Oklahoma City uncommitted. Not a brushoff, but not a rip-roaring display of keen interest, either. Even as good as he was at zeroing in on the crux of most issues, this time he hadn't a clue about the Larson's team's true opinion.

Their lack of enthusiasm was a tear in his parachute, but he hadn't hit the ground yet. Self-confidence was the keystone of his success. As long as they hadn't said no, he could still pull a deal together. "It's my own damn fault," he mumbled. He hadn't shown enough enthusiasm himself. Throughout the meeting he had been preoccupied with how he would tell Marisa and her mother, and even Bob Nichols and Mandan Patel, if Larson's said, "It's a deal."

Leaving Midland with Marisa and Raylene Rutherford still on his mind, he spotted a Wal-Mart up ahead on his right. Almost as if his truck were being steered by one of Bob Nichols' aliens, he turned into the parking lot. He came out of the giant retail store with watercolors, brushes and art paper. Sitting alone all day in a singlewide mobile home with nothing to do was no life for even a woman whose brain was out of order.

With a good feeling he couldn't quite define or justify, he put Larson's Truck & Travel Stop on the back burner and began to think about the second phase of his plan, Ledger Ranches retirement community. Phase I didn't necessarily have to depend on Phase II and vice versa. He hadn't yet met Lanny Winegardner, but there was no time like the present. When he came to the XO Ranch's caliche road that intersected the highway, he made a right turn.

Two hours later, he came away from a meeting with Lanny Winegardner with more than a little hope and excitement. No question that Winegardner would sell. They only had to come to a meeting of the minds on a price and hammer out an agreement on mineral rights.

And he only had to figure out how to get the money to make the buy. His bankers had always had confidence in his developments, but he feared their reaction to this one. To quote one of Larson's team members, "This place is pretty far off the beaten path." For the first time ever, Terry wondered if his moneyman would go along with him. In the loneliness of his crew cab, traveling the long, empty highway from Midland to Agua Dulce, doubt he didn't normally feel at the beginning of a new development crept in.

At last he saw Pecos Belle's beat-up sign. He was starved. He pulled into the place where he ate most of his meals lately. A dozen people sat at the tables and the counter eating. He took a stool at one end of the counter and set his Wal-Mart package on the floor.

Marisa spoke to him as if he were a friend rather than just another customer and took his order for a chicken salad sandwich. She was dressed as usual— tight jeans and boots, a belt with a big buckle and a bright yellow T-shirt with a black and white Cruel Girl logo across the front. Typically, he didn't pay close attention to the color of clothing women wore, but the bright yellow shirt seemed to set off Marisa's olive skin, black hair and light brown eyes. She looked beautiful.

On closer observation he saw weariness in her eyes, but her mouth smiled at her customers and at him. Something new hummed between them, a connection resulting from their meeting yesterday. He ate slowly, enjoying the excellent sandwich, watching her and waiting out the departure of the last straggling customer.

After clearing off the tables, she came to him. "Dessert? Devil's food cake with fudge frosting. I made it fresh this morning." She threw her dish towel across her shoulder and grinned. "It's full of real butter and heavy cream. Guaranteed to clog your arteries."

"Sounds great. Might as well live dangerous."

He watched as she lifted the glass dome off the dessert plate and sliced a thick wedge off a tall, three-layer cake. Her hands looked delicate, but fragile hands didn't construct scrumptious pies and cakes and the delicious meals Marisa served in the café. Her outward appearance only served to remind him she had stores of inner strength.

"Something tells me living dangerous isn't new to you," she said, amusement lighting up her eyes as she looked him in the face and set the dessert and silverware on the counter in front of him.

Topaz. Mexican topaz. That was the color of her eyes. "How's your mom today?" he asked.

"Better than yesterday." She poured a mug of coffee and set it beside his plate. "Can't have cake without coffee."

He sliced a bite off the cake and savored it. The texture was moist and fudgy and the frosting melted in his mouth. Marisa Rutherford was wasting her talent in a café in Agua Dulce.

Excited to show her the art supplies, even before he finished his cake he picked up the Wal-Mart sack. "I brought something for your mom."

"Oh?" She set the coffee carafe on its burner and returned to where he sat.

He pulled out his purchases—a tin of more than a dozen dry watercolors in little round trays, four brushes and two pads of watercolor paper. Like some kid seeking a pat on the head, he spread the items on the counter. "What do you think?"

She didn't say anything at first, just picked up the brushes and stroked the bristles. "Wow. This is for Mama?" She looked up, her eyes bright. Tears?

Oh, hell. He hadn't meant to make her cry. "I just thought it would give her something to do."

She smiled and blinked away the wetness in her eyes. "It might be good for her, at that. Hey, thanks. I'll ask Tanya to show her how to use them. She likes Tanya."

Terry smiled back, thrilled in a silly way to have pleased her. "If you've got some time, can I show you something?"

"Show away. I'm here, captured, you might say."

"I mean, in my trailer."

A grin tipped one corner of her mouth as she began to return the art supplies to the sack. "This wouldn't be one of those old-fashioned come-ons, would it? Like, 'let me show you my etchings'?"

He chuckled. Women flirted with him, they chased him, once or twice they had even stalked him, but women never teased him. "Well, truthfully, I *would* like to show you my drawings, but they're bluelines, not etchings."

"What's bluelines?"

"Blueprints. Of my plans for Agua Dulce."

"You're kidding." Her hand splayed against her chest. "You're going to show those to li'l ol' me?"

He lifted a shoulder in a shrug. "Why not?"

"You said you don't discuss your plans."

"Change of heart. Since you're the mayor, I figure you should know more details."

"I'm not the mayor, but I'd like to see what's going on. Maybe after I close. I have to make supper for Mama and help her with a bath, but after she goes to sleep, I can walk over."

"After dark?"

"It'll be that late before I finish."

"You shouldn't be walking around the desert in the dark. There isn't even a moon tonight." He wrote his land-line number and his cell phone number on a napkin and handed it to her. "Just call me when you're ready. I'll come get you."

The corner of her mouth quirked. "Okay, I guess. But I walk around after dark all the time."

"Not tonight."

Terry returned to his mobile home, elated in spite of the disappointing outcome of his meeting with Larson's. He tidied up the place, washed the few dishes he had left in the sink and wiped away the ever-present sand on the flat surfaces. Then he shuffled through his CDs. He had brought a CD player from Fort Worth to take the edge off the nighttime silence. She probably liked country, so he picked one by George Strait. All women liked George Strait.

He had bought a bottle of white wine in Midland. He stuck it in the fridge to chill, then showered, shaved and put on a pullover sweater against the coming cool of the evening. When dusk faded to dark, he began to worry that she wouldn't call, but just after nine, the phone warbled.

Lightning flashed on the horizon and the air smelled of rain as he pulled up at the Rutherford mobile home. Marisa was waiting outside. She climbed into his pickup, filling the cab with clean feminine fragrance. She was wearing a pure white sweater made of something fuzzy that made her look soft and cuddly.

Her first words when she settled into the passenger seat were, "You've bought the XO, haven't you?"

Was she psychic along with all of her other attributes? "Okay, Sherlock, you got me. Not yet, but I'm trying to."

She turned her head and stared into the night. "I had a hunch. I can't believe it. Do you know the history of the XO Ranch?"

"No. Do you?"

"I know a little. I know a Winegardner has owned it since 1920, before the oil boom. Lanny himself has operated it for over twenty years. It's always had really good cattle."

He heard gloom in her tone and felt a need to reassure her. He forced a smile. "Nothing stays the same. Have you ever thought about it becoming something better?"

"No. I guess I don't adapt well to change."

Back at his mobile home, they stepped into the soft light provided by the one lamp in the living room and the light over the kitchen sink. George Strait was singing about all his exes living in Texas.

"You like George Strait?" he asked her.

"Sure. Who doesn't?"

"There's more CDs." He pointed to a storage box shoved against the wall at the end of the breakfast bar. "Take a look. Pick one."

She shuffled the plastic cases. "Oh," she said, selecting one. "I love this guy. He has a great voice. He sang in Arlington all the time. I saw him a couple of times." She handed over a CD and Terry put it on to play. Steve Holy's rich voice filled the room with a ballad, "The Hunger." She watched the CD player and Terry watched her. She looked up at him as the song ended and smiled. "You must like him, too, if you have his CD."

"I like all good music. . . . Listen, I've got a bottle of wine in the fridge."

"Gosh, I haven't had wine in ages. I guess I could have some."

He poured the wine into two tumblers and they laughed about his lack of proper serving glasses.

"So, show me," she said, ambling over to the dining table where the blueprints lay.

With some pride, he spread his blueprints and architect's renderings of Ledger Ranches retirement community over the table and the breakfast bar for her to peruse, determined to convince her that his ideas for Agua Dulce were constructive.

As she studied them, he explained over her shoulder, "There'll be five different-style houses homeowners can choose from, all in keeping with the architecture typical of the Southwest desert. The colors will blend into the landscape. There'll be a clubhouse and a pool and a rec room. Tennis courts adjacent to the clubhouse." He pointed to a blank area near the clubhouse. "This is where I'll eventually build a small strip center with spaces for shops, maybe even a theater. I'm undecided about a golf course. Depends on how much good water we come up with."

"Wow," she murmured and looked up at him. She didn't need to say anything at all. The light in her eyes told him she was impressed.

A deep sense of satisfaction rippled through him. Weird. He had never required the validation of another person for any of his developments. "I'm thinking of changing the name from Ledger Ranches to Agua Dulce. It seems a shame not to keep such a poetic name."

She smiled at him again, nearly melting his heart. "It is poetic. Mama would love that. She used to introduce herself as the mayor of Agua Dulce because she liked the rhythm in the words. It's Spanish. It means 'sweet water.' "

"I know."

She began to shuffle through the renderings. "Everything's so pretty. I wish—I wish Mama could see and know what's happening. Agua Dulce has always been her little world."

An emotion curiously like envy passed through him, a sense of something he had missed long ago. He could recall nothing he had ever wished his own mother could see, doubted if she would have bothered to look even if he had laid out his every dream in a blueprint. Obviously Marisa's mother was different. To have earned so much loyalty from her daughter, Raylene Rutherford must have been a strong, special woman. Since he still didn't know what to say about her, he only gave a nod. "Your mother must have been quite a person before . . . well, before."

Marisa's perfect lips tipped into a wistful smile and something inside him longed to be the inspiration for that smile every day. "If you only knew," she said. "My mama had an answer for every question, a solution for every problem."

She took a baby sip and he suspected she had only accepted the wine to be polite. Suddenly he remembered the jug of Jack Daniel's he had shoved onto the top shelf of his cupboard. "I've still got that bottle of Jack Daniel's you left. Would you rather have a mixed drink?"

She smiled. "I figured you drank that."

"I'm not much of a drinker of the hard stuff. Even if I was, I'd choose something with a little less bite than Jack Daniel's."

"I'm not a drinker, either. That jug belongs to Ben, but he sure doesn't need it. You can just keep it. Maybe you'll have company who'll like it."

He nodded at her glass. "If you don't want that, you don't have to drink it."

"That's okay. It's just that it doesn't take much for me to get silly."

"So, finish about your mom."

Her head inclined and she continued to study the renderings. "What can I tell you? What's really sad is she used to know so much. She read a lot, all kinds of books. I grew up surrounded by books. As you can see, we don't have much in the way of outside entertainment around here. When I was a little kid, she would assign me reading projects. She used to say, 'You must learn to read well, Marisa. As long as you're a good reader, you can learn anything, do anything.' "

She inhaled and let out a deep breath. As much as he wanted to be an honorable man, he couldn't keep from seeing the shift beneath her sweater. "Yep, Mama was a free spirit, comfortable with who she was and curious about everything. Seeing her now, you can't keep from thinking of how she used to be."

She looked up at him again, her eyes bright in the low light. "It was nice of you to think of her, Terry. I appreciate it."

The depths in her eyes left him tongue-tied. Lord

God, she was a beautiful woman. He shrugged and almost croaked, "No problem."

The soft thrum of rain that began to resound against the roof took her attention. "We need that," she said. As the shower escalated into a downpour, she turned her attention back to the drawings. "So, how're you going to build houses in the middle of the XO's many oil wells?"

"The XO's a big place. Plenty of the land doesn't have wells. The mineral rights are the biggest obstacle in our negotiations at this point. I suspect the oil profits have already been tapped, but I can't develop a subdivision if I don't own the mineral rights under it. I can't risk having Lanny or some of his kin lease their rights to a wildcatter, then have a homeowner wake up and see a drilling rig set up in his backyard. In Texas the mineral rights override the surface rights."

"Hunh. I didn't know that. That wouldn't be too cool, would it?" Her eyes angled at him in a sly look. "You met with those people today, didn't you? Your deal really will wipe out Mr. Patel, won't it?"

"You'll be happy to know Larson's team wasn't that excited about this location."

"Good for Mr. Patel. Bad for you, right?"

"Well, it's not great. I was halfway counting on the money from selling to them to kick off my subdivision. They haven't said no, but they're gonna take some coaxing. It'll work out."

The beep of the pager on his belt interrupted. He stopped himself from swearing aloud at the lateness of the call. He recognized the number as that of the Mexican from Kermit to whom he had offered a job as a landscaper and groundskeeper last week. He returned the call and arranged for the man to come to work tomorrow. When he disconnected, Marisa was looking at him with a question in her eyes.

"Since I'm keeping the RV park open a while longer than I planned," he explained, "I'm hiring a professional to spiff up the grounds."

"That's good. That'll make Gordon happy."

"Income's income," he said, plumping the maps lying on the breakfast bar into a neat stack. "Might as well attract all the tourist business I can. I agree with what you first told me about the RV park and about Tubbs. The park's profitable and Tubbs does a good job."

"I'm glad I won't have to worry about Gordon."

He braced a hand on the breakfast bar, only feet away from her. "He's not part of your family, is he?"

"No. Why do you ask?"

"I don't get why you've been so worried about him."

"I worry about all the people here."

"But why?"

"Oh . . ." She looked past him but remained silent for seconds. "If you knew them you'd understand," she said at last. "It's too hard to explain."

End of subject. He took the hint and steered the conversation in a new direction. "I talked to the landscaper I just hired about doing some things around the mobile where you and your mother live. Plant some flowers, do some landscaping. Maybe put up a fence. We could—" *We?* When had he started thinking of himself and Marisa as *we*?—"Uh, I could pour a sidewalk between the mobile and the café's back door. Concrete would be a smoother path than the stone walkway that's there now."

Her hand touched his forearm, a frown creasing her

brow as he fell into her whiskey-colored eyes. "You don't have to do all of that for us. We'll be leaving soon."

No, he almost blurted out. "But I'm not pushing you to move." *What* had he said? She and her mother *had* to move. They *had* to get out of his way.

"I've sent out some résumés," she said. "I expect to hear something soon. In days, hopefully, rather than weeks."

They were standing shoulder to shoulder, their faces inches apart. He leaned in closer, wanting to assure himself that a woman as honest and unselfish as she was real. She didn't back away, so he settled his lips on hers. Sweet. Delicious. He placed an arm around her shoulder and gently urged her lips open with his. She gave him entrance and returned a kiss that made him dizzy. As the room spun around him, his baser instincts pushed him to haul her body against his and kiss her silly, but he controlled himself.

When he lifted his mouth from hers, she looked up at him, lips parted, eyes wide. "Oh," she said softly.

"Oh, yes," he whispered, cupping her nape with one hand and pressing his forehead against hers. "Do you know how long I've wanted to do that?"

He could smell her perfume, her body, her mouth, all of it an aphrodisiac. His own body's response was hard and immediate. Now or later, it was going to happen between them. He knew it. In the background, Steve Holy softly sang "Good Morning Beautiful." The romantic words penetrated Terry's psyche and he thought about waking up with Marisa beside him.

He took the glass from her hand and set it on the breakfast bar, then risked placing his hands on her waist and pulling her close. He was certain she could feel his erection as he placed another open-mouthed kiss on her lips. "More," he whispered into her mouth. "I want so much more."

"I—I can't, Terry."

He dragged his mouth to her ear. "But you want to." He continued down the sweet, fragrant trail of her silky neck, his pulse pounding in his dick. "I can feel that you want to."

Instead of wrapping her arms around him, her hands came to rest on his forearms, like she might push him away. "It's a bad idea, Terry. I've given up men."

Her belly felt hot against him. His eyes landed at the hollow of her throat and he could see that her heart was pounding. "Liar." He opened his mouth against her throat and flicked the pulse beat with his tongue, her fuzzy sweater tickling his face. "You're fibbing to me, lady."

"I need to go." Her voice came out quavery, which only made him hotter. "Honest," she said. "I try not to be away from the trailer for long spans at a time. Mama's out cold, but you never know what might happen."

He was hard and hot and ready. In the worst way, he wanted to lead her to his bed and ravage her, let her ravage him. He groaned mentally. "I understand." He ducked in to nuzzle her neck and her sweater tickled his nose. Smiling into her eyes, he tugged at the neck of it. "That thing has to go."

She pushed away, giving him a Mona Lisa smile and putting space between their bodies. "*I'm* what has to go. And I mean right now."

Shit. Of course she had to go. She shouldn't leave her mother alone. What was he doing, anyway? Marisa Rutherford was a woman he shouldn't even consider fucking. With a great sigh, he dropped his hands. "Okay. I'll take you home."

Chapter 15

Marisa had never kissed a millionaire and that was why she had kissed him back.

Liar.

The accusation echoed in her mind as she stared up at her bedroom's dark ceiling. Outside, thunder crashed. Lightning flashed and brightened her bedroom. Rain thrummed like kettledrums on the singlewide's roof. She couldn't sleep though she was exhausted.

In reality, the fact that she had never kissed a millionaire was *not* why she had kissed him back. The real reason was because she had thought of it a thousand times since she met him. The guy was just plain kissable. Lord, Tanya had almost creamed in her jeans just talking to him.

And he wanted sex. Well, most men wanted sex. And a man who looked like him and was rich to boot probably got it whenever and wherever he wanted it. A secret smile quirked her lips because she had been strong and had resisted him.

But who was she kidding? She didn't want to resist him. She liked everything about him—the way he looked, talked, smelled, his wise blue eyes, the no-nonsense way he conducted himself. In fact, she liked him so much she couldn't remember when she had last thought of Woody.

But what did she have in common with him? Their social strata were separated by a million levels as well as a million dollars. No doubt he had fifty girlfriends back in Fort Worth or Dallas, high-maintenance women who were sophisticated and smart, who had soft hands and manicured nails, who never smelled like a kitchen.

Or maybe he had just *one* girlfriend, which would be worse.

Even if she—unsophisticated, ordinary Marisa—succumbed to his desires and her own, she would be nothing more than his "Agua Dulce sleepover." Temporary sex while he worked on this project.

Not that she was such a Goody Two-shoes that she was averse to temporary sex. She had learned years back that good sex and romance didn't necessarily go together. In retrospect, perhaps good sex rather than romance was what defined her trysts with Woody.

But with Terry Ledger, things would be dangerous. She had tasted lust on the lips of men numerous times, but she hadn't sensed so deep a connection—not with Woody or any other man she could recall. Though more profound, the feeling was similar to that weirdness that had come over her the first time she had seen Terry in the café and they had danced to Frank Sinatra singing from the old Seeburg jukebox.

Stop wasting your time, she scolded herself. Good-looking millionaires didn't just drop in and take up with the Marisa Rutherfords of the world. Any kind of relationship other than an arm's-length one with Mr. Terry Ledger could only have a bad outcome for her.

She rose on her elbow, punched her pillow into a

ball and flopped onto her stomach. Beyond her own
rotten experiences with men, she had witnessed a bad
one firsthand for more than thirty years. In more ways
than one, a man and sex had imprisoned Mama. First
the sperm donor, Hector Espinosa, had left her pregnant in the middle of nowhere; then a married man,
Clyde Campbell, with his money and his empty promises of security, had held her captive in Agua Dulce
for all of Marisa's life.

No damn way would she end up like Mama.

Terry Ledger could plant all the flowers, build all
the fences and pour all the concrete sidewalks he
wanted to, but Marisa wouldn't allow herself to be
tempted by carnal desires and flawed assumptions of
security—and thus be entrapped by a man who couldn't
possibly care about her.

Furthermore, she had to stop thinking about him
and squandering the precious time that she needed to
use to plan for her and Mama's future.

The rain became a deafening deluge. Tomorrow
there would be flash-flood warnings.

"Be strong, Marisa," she muttered into the storm.

An uneventful week passed in Agua Dulce. The sun
baked the landscape. The spring heat, usually bear-
able, had been made uncomfortable by the humidity
that came with May's thunderstorms. The café's swamp
cooler struggled, but failed in its purpose.

Another week passed. Other than an intense calm
shrouding everything in sight and the temperature
climbing into the nineties, nothing changed in a dis-
cernible way. No town meetings occurred, none of the
citizens came to Marisa expecting her to do something
for them and Ben stayed sober except for a six-pack

of Coors a day. Only Ben and a few strangers came into Pecos Belle's to eat.

Terry Ledger had been gone from his mobile home the whole time. In an odd way, Marisa had started to feel as if she had imagined him.

After a surprisingly good weekend with Mama, on Monday morning, Marisa found Lanny waiting at the café's front door when she opened. He looked better than she had seen him in months, if ever. His clothes—a white Western shirt and Wranglers—were clean and starched and ironed, he had on new boots and a new pearl gray hat. And he smelled like a perfume counter in Dillard's.

"How's it going?" she asked as she led him through the flea market toward the café.

"Fine," he said to her back.

"It'll take me a few minutes to get the coffee on." She detoured behind the lunch counter toward the Bunn.

"That's just fine."

"Breaking your old habit and eating breakfast with me this morning?" Everyone knew Lanny usually ate with his cowhands. With no one in his house but him, he liked having his meals in the bunkhouse where his hands lived.

"I could, if it's not too much trouble."

Marisa chuckled as she busied herself setting up the coffeemaker. "Lanny, this is a café. The day I find fixing breakfast for a customer too much trouble is the day I'd better close the doors."

He chuckled, too. "Guess so."

Marisa had known Lanny all her life. He was a man of few words. His wife had died of breast cancer at forty-one and he had remained a widower for fourteen years. He had three kids, all of whom Marisa knew, but they never came around. His oldest, a daughter, was the same age as Marisa and had been in the same grade in school in Wink. His only son lived in New York, where he studied, of all things, music, and sang in various plays and operas. The two daughters lived in Austin, but for all the attention they paid to their father, they may as well have lived on Mars. It was common knowledge that all three of them had enviable incomes from trust funds set up years back and fed by oil royalties.

With the coffee on to drip, she walked back to the kitchen and lit the burners under the griddle, then returned to the lunch counter, where Lanny had taken a seat. "You're all dressed up today. Going to town?"

He shot a glance over one shoulder, then the other.

A frown tugged at her brow. Was he worried someone would hear what he said? "There's no one in here but us," she told him.

He looked up at her from beneath his hat brim. "I think I've got the place sold," he said quietly, as if he were afraid to utter the words.

As her pulse rate surged, Marisa caught a quick breath. "Really?"

He nodded. "It'll be final in two or three months. The new guy made me a deal I couldn't turn down."

"You mean Terry Ledger." Unnecessary to make the words a question.

She glanced at the coffee carafe and saw it was full. After her conversation with Terry, this news was no surprise, but that didn't prevent it from calling for a strong jolt of caffeine. She dragged two mugs off the shelf and poured coffee for them both.

He lifted his mug to his lips and blew across the hot liquid's surface.

When Terry told her he was attempting to buy the XO she had only half believed him. She didn't know exactly how much land the ranch encompassed. It took up more than half the county, so it had to be thousands of acres. A working ranch that big would surely go for millions. Now awe and a little bit of something that felt like fear almost left her dumbfounded. "Wow, Lanny, no more punching cows for you."

"I like the cows. I'll miss 'em. They're all I've ever known. All I've ever had, to tell the truth."

Lanny was far removed from the stereotypical loud and brassy Texas rancher and oilman. Born on the XO, he had scarcely left it except to go to college, where, no doubt, he studied something to do with cows.

"But now you won't be tied down. You'll be able to travel the world. Do anything you want to."

"Won't be any fun all by myself."

All at once she wondered why some woman hadn't latched on to him. He was a nice man, almost handsome all cleaned up, and he was definitely rich. She gave him an encouraging smile. "Something tells me you won't have any trouble getting someone to go with you."

He took a long swallow of coffee, then set his mug on the counter and gave her a solemn look through his silver-rimmed glasses. "Come with me, 'Rissy," he said softly.

Marisa felt her jaw drop. Was he kidding?

He took off his hat and set it on the counter, exposing short salt-and-pepper hair. "I know it's sudden and we haven't gone a-courtin' or anything, but we've known each other for thirty-odd years. I've always thought a lot of you, Rissy. I've always been able to see that you're a good woman. And you grew up to be a pretty woman."

He *wasn't* kidding. And he was old enough to be her father. She had an insane urge to laugh like a madwoman, but couldn't. "Well, I, uh . . . I, uh, don't know what to say, Lanny. Thanks, I guess."

"Before you say no, hear me out. I've thought it through. We could get married. I'd give you some money up front. You know, to seal the deal. It'd be yours, to do anything you wanted to with it. I'd buy you a pretty diamond ring. I'd take care of you and Raylene, get her some professional help. Or whatever she needs."

Marisa's throat began to work; her eyes teared. It was the most sincere—and the only honest—proposal of marriage she had ever received. "Gosh, Lanny, I'm flattered, but—"

"I didn't expect you to just jump in and say yes." His mouth turned up in a sweet smile she had never noticed he had. His teeth were even and white, not false, something else she hadn't noticed about him. Seeing his good teeth reminded her he didn't smoke or chew snoose, which was a plus.

"I know you're a practical woman," he went on. "I knew you'd have to think about things."

"But Lanny, I can't honestly say I love you. I mean, I like you a lot. You're a wonderful, honest person. I'd trust you with my last dime and I admire you, but—"

"Rissy, me and my first wife didn't have half that much going for us."

Marisa had never heard Lanny's marriage was unhappy. She stared down at the mug of coffee from which she hadn't even taken a drink. "I just don't know, Lanny."

His expression became more earnest, his deep brown eyes more intense. "You're in a lot of trouble here, Rissy. I know for a fact Raylene couldn't find much money to put back. You're not gonna be able to sell all this stuff for much, either. If at all."

Dammit, it was hard having him—or anyone—know that. That bastard reality had just slapped her again. Marisa couldn't hold back her anguish. Tears sneaked down her cheeks. "I know," she said, feeling a hitch in her throat.

Lanny stood up and came around the end of the lunch counter, pulled a handkerchief from his pocket and dabbed at her eyes. He placed the crisp white thing over her nose. "Blow," he said, as if she were six years old.

She pushed his hand away and wiped her nose on the back of her wrist. "You're right about one thing, Lanny. Mama and I are in deep trouble."

His thick arms folded around her, he pulled her against his chest and began to rub her back. He felt warm and wide and secure. Even with her nose plugged by tears, she could smell his cologne, but couldn't identify the fragrance.

"Shh-shh," he murmured. "Don't cry, now. I didn't mean to make you cry." She felt his big hand petting her hair and the vibration of his deep voice in his chest. "I'd take care of you, Rissy. You'd never want for anything."

Rissy. The name she had been called as a child. "Oh, Lanny, I appreciate it, but it's crazy to even think about—"

"Rissy, I don't want just anybody for a wife. I want somebody I know and care about. I think, in time, you could care about me a little, too, and you damn sure know me. I admit it's not like in the storybooks, but what goes on in storybooks ain't the way life is. Sometimes folks just have to forget all that and do the best they can with what's in front of 'em."

She stepped away. "Where's that damn handkerchief?"

His eyes smiled as he handed it to her.

She wiped her nose. "You know what, Lanny? I'm not gonna just say no. I'm gonna think about it for a few days. I'm gonna honestly think about it." A nervous titter burst out. "Like you say, I'm in trouble. I can't afford not to think about it, right?"

His mouth tipped into a smile that matched the one in his eyes. "That's good enough for me. Tell you the truth, it's more'n I expected."

"Okay, then, that's the deal. I'm gonna think about it."

He nodded. Awkward moments passed while they stood there. Then his hands came up to her shoulders. "Could I kiss you? I mean, while you're thinking about it, I guess we could say we're a-courtin'."

"Okay," she said.

His mouth tasted of mint, sweet and sterile, and she had no trouble kissing him back. To her surprise, he was a good kisser. When he lifted his mouth from hers, she looked up at him and smiled. "How about that breakfast, cowboy?"

She cooked him breakfast—bacon, eggs and hash browns—and sat beside him at the lunch counter, drinking coffee while he ate. He shared snippets of his deal with Terry, though he didn't tell her the price he got for the XO. "He told me I could have a house in his subdivision," he said on a deep chuckle. "But I said no thanks. I can't see me living in a subdivision."

"Where *do* you see yourself living, Lanny?"

"Colorado, maybe. In the mountains." Another sweet smile came her way. "What do *you* think? About the mountains, I mean."

She had never been to Colorado, but the idea of living in the mountains had some appeal. She had seen them in the far, far distance all of her growing-up years. "I don't know. I never really thought about it."

"They build those log houses up there. They got trees. Real pretty."

"I've seen pictures. It sounds nice."

She got another huge smile from him.

After breakfast, he said he had to get to Midland on business. She walked with him to the front door. He leaned down to kiss her good-bye and his glasses bumped her temple. He tried again and their noses bumped. He gave her a shy grin. "We'll get better at it. It's not the most important thing anyway." His whole head turned red in a blush and he cast his eyes downward, toward the floor. "I mean, it's important and I like it and everything, but there hasn't been anybody since—"

"No, really, it's okay, Lanny. I know what you mean."

He nodded without looking at her. "I'm fifty-five, but I'm pretty sure I can still—well, never mind. We'll work it out."

If life gets any more bizarre, I can't handle it, Marisa thought.

She plunged into making crusts for pecan pies, her

mind darting all over the place as she measured equal portions of lard and butter. Though lard made the best crust, not many cooks used it these days. Too unhealthy. But to her way of thinking, pie was already unhealthy, so what difference did a little lard make?

The emotions churning inside her felt like a kaleidoscope, like none of what was happening around her was real, the same disconnect she had experienced the day a neurologist in Midland sat down with her and told her the cold, hard truth about Mama. Until that moment, Mama had been Wonder Woman.

As she draped the crust into four pie tins and began to crimp the edges, her mind finally stopped on this morning's event.

Now she had kissed two millionaires in her life.

And one of them wanted a wife and companionship more than he wanted sex. And the other? Well, who could guess what he wanted, really?

More importantly, what did *she* want?

A marriage of convenience? Was that phrase even used these days?

After being a part of the singles scene for so long, when it came to men, she no longer expected fireworks and bells ringing. She had long ago given up on ever seeing that knight ride up on his white horse.

Men had used her badly over the years. Mike in Midland, who had lied to her about who he was; Eric in Arlington, who had taken her money; Woody, who had cheated on her. Of course, all of it was her own fault. Much of the time she felt sorry for men and their weaknesses, which opened the door for losers to take advantage of her.

What of Terry Ledger and the energy that passed between them? His bad-boy looks and take-no-prisoners attitude touched a slutty chord within her, to be sure. Him, she didn't feel sorry for. What he aroused was a little earthier than sympathy.

Forget it, her practical side told her. Sex with him might be fun and maybe wild, but there would be no such thing as a relationship. He would end up hurting her worse than Woody had.

Lanny, however, was a different kind of man. Solid as granite. She had never heard a bad word about him. He was gentle and kind. If anything, he was too kind. Gossip had it that the distance between him and his children was a result of his having given them everything and expected nothing in return.

He had to be intelligent—he had graduated from Texas Tech. Yet, a college education hadn't changed him. He was still the old-fashioned cowboy he had always been. To talk to him or see him dressed in his Wranglers and the snap-button shirts he made no secret of buying at Wal-Mart, one would never guess the immensity of his wealth.

He did wear expensive boots and hats, Marisa had always noticed. It was an odd thing about real cowboys. Most of them spent more on their boots and hats than on the rest of their clothing combined, including wristwatches. Lanny could afford a Rolex for each wrist, but he wore a Timex. "What difference does it make?" he said when she teased him about it once. "All it's for is to tell the time of day."

And now that he had sold the XO, he was a whole lot richer.

I'm fifty-five, but I'm pretty sure I can still—

His deep blush and stumbling words came back to her. Sex. Did everything in the whole damn world, sooner or later, come down to sex?

Fifty-five. Twenty-one years older than her, only eleven years younger than Mama. Marisa had never had sex with a fifty-five-year-old man. Though his not having been with a woman since before his wife's death would be incredible to some, she had no trouble believing it. He was that loyal.

I'd take care of you and Raylene, get her some professional help. Or whatever she needs.

Oh, yeah. He could pay for the best of care for Mama and never notice so much as a dent in his checkbook. She had been managing Mama's care on a day-to-day basis, but hadn't a clue how long that would last. She had always known in the back of her mind that the time would come when Mama would need full-time attention, 24/7. There, Marisa's thought process stalled. How could she quit work and stay home with Mama? How could she pay for institutionalizing her? She doubted that even working two jobs would cover the cost.

As Mama used to say, a bird in the hand, et cetera, et cetera . . .

She thought about the coming weeks, the uncertain future and the triple-digit temperatures. Could she take Mama and live as Lanny Winegardner's wife, in a house in the mountains of Colorado?

Sure she could.

Chapter 16

Two days later Marisa was still weighing the pros and cons of Lanny's proposal when Tanya strode into the café, her striped hair pinned up in a bed-head do that could seriously tarnish her professional reputation. She plopped onto a stool at the lunch counter and slapped down on the countertop a crushed pack of Virginia Slims, a Bic plastic lighter and handful of change. Marisa picked up the coffee carafe and poured the obviously upset hairdresser a mug of Cowboy Breakfast Blend.

On closer inspection, Marisa saw Tanya's mascara smudged in dark half-moons under her eyes, her nose and eyes red. Had she been crying? In the year Marisa had known her, she had never seen her cry.

"Did you know Lanny sold his ranch?" The voice came across quivery.

As far as Marisa was concerned, if Lanny wanted someone to know he had sold his ranch, he should be the one to announce it. Even if she hadn't had that feeling, these days, Tanya was the last person in whom she would confide. She had chosen to not tell she had slept with Woody. Even if it had occurred years before Tanya knew Jake or Marisa, either, the fact still chafed. Marisa shrugged as she returned the coffee carafe to its element. "I heard."

"That dude, Ledger."

When Marisa turned back, Tanya had lit a cigarette. She blew out a plume of smoke. *Like steam,* Marisa thought. The two fingers that held the cigarette were trembling. Marisa leaned a hip against the back counter, crossing her arms under her breasts, and prepared to listen to her neighbor rant.

Tanya reached down the counter and dragged over the bowl filled with packets of artificial sweeteners. In the low-necked knit shirt that she wore, the slope of her breasts shifted with each arm movement, showing off her lizard tattoo.

The hairdresser's lips pulled into a sneer. "He's not gonna have a ranch. He's gonna have a fucking town for old people." Her teeth clenched as she tore open a pink packet of artificial sweetener and dumped it into her coffee, followed by a dollop of cream. She stirred with vigor, splashing coffee over the rim, then slammed the spoon onto the counter. "I don't know what the hell he expects me and Jake to do. Jake doesn't know how to do anything but cowboy." She lifted the mug to her lips.

The dilemma the sale of the XO presented for Jake Shepherd and Lanny's ranch hands hadn't yet crossed Marisa's radar, but now it blipped like a jumbo jet on final approach. Lanny's cowboys kept to themselves, rarely came into Pecos Belle's. If they needed a trip somewhere, they went to Odessa, where they could combine the acquisition of necessities with a visit to the honky-tonks. Jake was the only one of them with whom Marisa was acquainted and she knew him only because he lived in the RV park and was married to Tanya.

Neither the XO cowboys nor Jake and Tanya had ever asked Marisa to fight one of their battles for them. But then, Jake wouldn't. He was too proud. "If I know Jake, he'll come up with something," Marisa said. "Maybe he has a talent you don't know about."

"If he does, he's kept it hidden. He's a forty-five-year-old loser, Marisa. A high school dropout. Hell, he probably dropped out before that." She drew another deep drag from her cigarette. "Shit. Whatever. I'm not looking for him to start a whole new career."

Jake might not be Einstein, but as far as Marisa was concerned, he was a good person. From his point of view, even rattlesnakes had something good to contribute. She didn't like hearing his wife bad-mouth him. "There's other ranches besides the XO. He could—"

"We've already been through that. He's called everybody he knows. He's been talking to a foreman at some hellhole in Arizona about working as a cowhand. Shit, he wouldn't even be foreman. Fucking *Arizona*, for god's sake. Who the hell wants to live in fucking Arizona?"

Someone had to come to Jake's defense. "Some people like Arizona," Marisa said. "Tanya, look. If it's all he can find—"

"I don't know what I'm gonna do. One thing I'm not doing is moving to some damn desert—"

"But you live in a desert now," Marisa couldn't keep from pointing out. Granted, West Texas wasn't the same *type* of desert as Arizona, but it was arid and hot all the same.

"I'm thinking about Dallas," Tanya said as if Marisa hadn't spoken, squinting toward the sandwich poster on the wall above the back counter. "If I could get a chair in a good salon in Dallas, I might make some real money. And I could work at getting my paintings into a gallery."

"What would Jake do in Dallas? I wonder if he's ever even been to Dallas."

Tanya's cocked head bobbed, her eyes blinking rapidly. "Well, you know what? That's *his* problem. I just know *I'm* not moving to *fucking* Arizona."

Marisa sighed. From what she could tell, Tanya had always been number one on Tanya's list of whom to please. "So what're you saying? You're gonna leave him?"

"I don't know. All I know is I'm not moving to Arizona." The confused zebra picked up her mug and took a swallow. She seemed calmer now.

"If you're of a mind to leave him, Tanya, you'd better give it a second thought. People who really care about you are few and far between. He does everything he can for you. It'd hurt him something awful if you just up and pulled out."

"He should've thought about that before he became a fucking cowboy."

Little shards of anger burst within Marisa. The woman seemed to have loyalty, if it could be called that, only as long as a person could do something for her. Like Jake had probably done when he married her. "He was a cowboy when you met him. You're the one who should have thought about who he is."

"All I know is I'm not moving to *fucking* Arizona." Her green eyes, glistening with unshed tears, zeroed in on Marisa. "What are *you* gonna do, Marisa? I mean, you've got Raylene and all. You might as well be chained to a bowling ball."

Marisa cringed. "Mama would be hurt if she knew you said that. I don't know what I'm gonna do. I haven't made any decisions."

And she wouldn't tell them to Tanya if she had.

"Well, at least you aren't moving to fucking Arizona."

Tanya stood up without another word, stamped through the flea market and yanked open the front door.

Marisa stared after her a few beats, stunned but not very surprised at her hissy fit. Tanya's personality puzzled her more every day. Marisa shook her head to clear it. She had too much to think about to dwell on Tanya. She veered back to Lanny and his plan to move to Colorado.

The late-day sun was casting long golden fingers and deep purple shadows across the desert when Terry arrived in Agua Dulce. He had been away for three weeks.

At the Sweet Water RV & Mobile Home Village, the first person he saw was Ben Seagrave, sitting on the top step of the three-step stair that led onto his porch. He was dressed as usual—faded T-shirt, khaki shorts and sandals. His hair stood on end; his face glistened with perspiration. He was strumming a guitar. For some reason, Terry was glad to see the cranky old fart.

Terry braked and stuck his head out the crew cab's window. After riding all day in the comfort of air-conditioning, he felt the burst of desert heat that hit him like a flamethrower and sweat broke out on his body at once. "How's it going?"

"Heeeeyyy, long time no see. Where ya been?"

The songwriter sounded half drunk. Beside him sat a partial six-pack. Terry had never seen him without something alcoholic at hand or in his hand. Terry propped an elbow on the windowsill. "Had some things to take care of in Fort Worth."

"Get out. Sit a spell. Have a beer." Seagrave continued to strum the guitar strings.

As the musician ran through some complicated fret work, Terry could tell the guy knew his way around a guitar. But then he should. He had been a professional musician for years and had awards, trophies and a substantial amount of money that spoke for his talent.

After the five-hundred-mile drive from Fort Worth, Terry was tired. A cold beer sounded good. Besides that, he wanted to avoid thinking about the three weeks he had just spent. Three weeks of constant negotiating, troubleshooting and nonstop effort to pull the Larson's deal out of the fire. He had saved it, but only by a hair and only by doing something he hadn't planned quite yet. For all his effort, the project still hung by a thread.

He slid out of his truck, shut the door with a soft *clack* and ambled over to Ben's steps, at the same time throwing a casual look toward Pecos Belle's. He glanced at his watch. Marisa would be cleaning up.

Though his days in Fort Worth had been long and busy, his nights had been stressful. Too many nights, Marisa and her future, her tight jeans and the kiss they had shared in his mobile home had traipsed through his dreams. She had been such a presence in his thoughts, he hadn't been able to generate an interest in spending his off-hours with Michelle. Several quarrels had resulted, and finally Michelle told him to take a hike. On that score, he had no real regrets.

Instead of spending what little free time he'd had in Fort Worth with a female, he had spent it skydiving. Even taking part in one of his favorite activities, he found himself wondering if Marisa would take to floating through the air beneath a parachute.

He had helped his friend Chick exercise his horses a few times, then gone with him and his eight-year-old son, Clay, on a two-day trail ride. As they camped out on the Brazos River and fished for catfish with a trotline, he wondered if Marisa liked fishing.

The woman had occupied a place in his head so often she may as well have been with him physically.

Last weekend he and Chick took Clay to a rodeo in Mesquite, where they'd had great fun and a lot of laughs. Seeing the relationship between Chick and his boy, Terry envied Chick and wondered if he himself could be as good a father as his best friend was. Or if he would ever get the chance. The questions left him uncharacteristically down in the dumps.

Ten years ago he would have never given fatherhood a second thought. Then a few years back, he awakened one morning and realized most of his peers had wives and children and were talking about family vacations and Little League baseball and how little Joey was doing in 4-H. Some even had second wives and a second set of kids to talk about. Suddenly, he was the guy on the outside looking in.

All through the long drive from Fort Worth, dissatisfaction with his present lifestyle pecked at him. The only explanation was the fact that he would soon celebrate his thirty-seventh birthday, yet another reminder of time passing and him with nothing but money and real estate to show for it.

Nearing the steps, he could see great wear and tear on the face of Ben's guitar and a strip of duct tape that had been wrapped around the wide end.

As Ben plucked at the strings, Terry sank wearily

to the bottom step and cracked a beer, letting the sound of the guitar drive out all else. There was something soothing in music from strings, especially if it was the only sound in the quiet end of a day in the desert. Limb by limb, cell by cell, in spite of the heat, he felt himself relaxing. Fort Worth, big-city bankers, destructive bureaucrats, demanding customers—all seemed to live on another planet.

"Heard tell you bought out the XO," Ben said as he picked a one-two rhythm in a tune reminiscent of Johnny Cash.

Shit. Winegardner must have told. "Hm," Terry replied, and took a swig of beer.

"Won't be the same without Lanny 'round here."

The rancher had mentioned leaving Agua Dulce, but Terry hadn't heard with certainty that he planned on doing it. Terry had hoped he would change his mind and take him up on the offer of becoming a resident of Ledger Ranches retirement community. "He's leaving?"

"Colorado, I think he's going."

Ben did a run on the guitar strings. "Here's a new one I'm fiddling with." He struck a low chord and began to sing in a nasal but sonorous voice.

> *I walk up to your door*
> *And draw a deep breath in.*
> *I've reached my journey's end*
> *But where did I begin?*
>
> *Been miles and miles from home*
> *To get where I've been*
> *No matter where I've gone*
> *I'm back to you again.*

Terry had no technical knowledge of music to brag about. He knew how to dance to country and sometimes went out in Fort Worth to Billy Bob's or the Stagecoach Inn to see and hear the big-name country performers. Ben's voice, deep and gravelly and on key, floated to his ear and he closed his eyes and listened to the words of the poet.

> *I've seen mountains and valleys,*
> *Been through sunshine and storms,*
> *When all I ever needed*
> *Was to have you in my arms.*

The singer paused, picked a melancholy melody, then took up the words again.

> *I've swum oceans of tears,*
> *Walked deserts full of sand,*
> *Trying to convince myself*
> *You're not what I had planned.*

> *Now, standing at your door,*
> *There's no place I'd rather land.*
> *My heart is in your hands.*
> *Say you'll love me, too.*
> *Again.*

As the song ended on a soft note and a chord that died away, Terry felt the hairs on his neck stand up, hearing some of his feelings put into lyrics Ben had written.

"Just worked that little ditty out this week," the musician said. "Calling it 'The Journey.' How'd you like it?"

"Sounds okay. Who's gonna sing it?" Terry didn't care who sang it. He had asked Ben the question to distract himself from the pointed words.

"Don't know yet. Coupla fellers lookin' at it."

Am I trying to convince myself Marisa isn't what I had planned? Terry asked himself.

Nah. That was bullshit. What he felt was frustration. He was drawn to her because, with her prickly personality, she never seemed to be in sync with him. He had a deeply ingrained desire to see everyone happy and agreeable.

Being the control freak that he readily acknowledged he was, he couldn't keep from picking at a situation where someone wasn't playing on his court. He likened the quirk to worrying an unhealed sore.

Before he could get into a conversation with Ben about the song, Bob Nichols approached from behind Ben's singlewide, walking as if he were barefoot on a carpet of broken glass. "Good afternoon," he said, almost whispering.

"Hi, Bob," Terry said, his own voice involuntarily lowering. Agua Dulce's water well leaped into his mind. While in Fort Worth, he'd had several conversations with the state regulatory agencies regarding the well. After learning he wouldn't have to drill a new well right away, he had made a decision to allow Nichols and Mr. Patel to continue to use the water, a move that should make Marisa happy. He was eager to tell her about it.

"Hey, Spaceman. Who you talkin' to today?" Ben gave a deep heh-heh-heh. His voice didn't grow softer. "Lemme guess. Somebody on Venus?"

"Oh, much farther than Venus," Bob answered, glaring at his tormentor with an offended look. "I've recorded some very interesting thumps. A mathematical rhythm, if you will, similar to your music."

Ben cocked his head and arched his brow. "No shit? You don't suppose that was my bass string you heard?" He plucked a thick string and produced a loud growling sound.

Bob Nichols' face contorted into a wince, his brows tented in a hurt expression. Though Terry suspected these two might play this verbal ping-pong every day, he still felt sorry for Nichols. He had seen and heard enough of the little guy to be convinced that he believed his fantasies about aliens and space travelers.

From his perch on the top step, Ben looked down at Terry. "You gonna be around for the weddin'?"

"Who's getting married?"

"Why, Lanny and Marisa. After he inked the deal to sell out to you, he asked her. She's taking Raylene and going to Colorado with him."

Terry's mind reeled. A fist to the gut couldn't have been more shocking.

"Now that you've bought Lanny's ranch, will you be asking me to tear out my spaceport?"

Nichols' whispery voice brought Terry back to earth and he turned to see Bob Nichols' eyes staring him down. He must not yet know that Winegardner had refused to sell the chunk of land where the UFO landing pad was located. Land that had valuable highway frontage, too. Terry had tried to talk the rancher into including it in the XO sale, but he wouldn't budge. "I've known Bob Nichols for over twenty years," he said. "He's never harmed even a ladybug. I'm gonna let him keep using that little piece of land."

At that statement, Terry had ceased to debate with Lanny. Getting control of the mineral rights where he had mentally mapped out his subdivision had been far more important than acquiring the small parcel of ground Nichols happened to be using for his space traveler experiments.

"Uh, no, Bob, don't worry about it. Lanny will be deeding that ground to you when we close on the deal."

The squinty eyes that showed between Nichols' mop of white hair and beard grew wide. "Oh, my gosh. I can't believe it." The eyes teared and Nichols clasped his stubby hands in front of his chest. "Oh, my gosh. I'm so grateful. He won't be sorry. When *They* come, you'll see. Everyone will see."

"Well, I'll be goddamned," Ben said. "I knew ol' Lanny was a generous guy, but that's just too much."

"Why would you say that?" Nichols asked indignantly. His voice raised a note louder than Terry had ever heard him speak. "Maybe he has an interest in science."

Here they go again, Terry thought, his thoughts still jumbled and disorganized after what he had heard about Marisa. *Fuck*. Were things going to start going to hell again? Winegardner might be a nice guy, but he was old enough to be Marisa's father. "I'm not making any changes in the RV park for now." He stood, restless. "When's she getting married?"

"I'm not certain she is," Nichols said. "She hasn't said so for sure."

"Well, she might as well," Ben argued. "Hell, Spaceman, she ain't got a choice when you get down to cases."

"Everyone always has a choice, Ben." Nichols squared his shoulders as he looked at Seagrave. "People always do what they want to do, Ben. That's something I've learned. People always do exactly what they want to."

The statement came eerily close to expressing one of Terry's own beliefs. In fact, he had *said* something similar many times. It was unnerving, having a philosophical tenet in common with someone as crazy as Bob Nichols.

As he looked at the motel owner, he was reminded of the work his assistant, Kim, was doing back in Fort Worth, nailing down a motel franchise. Only his promise to Larson's development team that he would build a franchise motel had brought them back on board. He didn't yet know which franchise he would settle on, but any project that had the Terry Ledger signature on it would be modern and efficient. And it would, coincidentally, wipe out the Starlight Inn's business. The trade-off of Bob using Agua Dulce's well water compared to losing his motel business didn't strike Terry as being fair, but he hadn't figured out what to do about that yet.

In truth, one of the reasons he hadn't ardently pursued a motel franchise before now was because he had few complaints about the Starlight Inn as it existed. It might look like a cluster of cereal boxes on the exterior, but inside it was clean and neat and Nichols seemed to be effective at running it. The dichotomy of a man who had spent thousands building a UFO landing field being able to operate an efficient business was mind-boggling.

But at this moment, more worrisome was what was going on with Marisa. What was wrong with her? Was it money?

It had to be money. A flurry of disappointment overtook the jealousy Terry felt. He had elevated

Marisa above all of the women he knew, and it was off-putting to learn she would marry someone for money. He glanced toward Pecos Belle's. "Café open? I haven't eaten since breakfast."

Ben rubbed his bare belly with a gnarled hand. "Yep. I had chicken and dumplin's over there earlier. That Marisa's a helluva cook. I'll probably starve to death when she leaves."

"Yeah, could be," Terry said absently, distressed because the thought of her leaving just when he had found her caused a knot in his stomach that had nothing to do with hunger. "Guess I'll go over and get a bite to eat."

He started for his truck.

"Better get a move on," Ben called from behind him. "She'd prob'ly like to close up."

Chapter 17

And closing up was what Terry found her doing when he reached the café. Standing on her tiptoes, cleaning the top of the Coke dispenser, she was wearing boots, faded Levi's and a silky green tank top. "Hey," he said, hesitating where the flea market ended and the café's small dining area began. The cool, damp air from the café's swamp cooler touched his skin and gave him a momentary shiver.

She turned her head his way and smiled, but went right on with her cleaning. "Hey, yourself," she said.

Was she glad to see him? He couldn't tell.

Her cropped tank top showed a narrow slice of bare skin at her waist . . . and a gold belly ring. Sensation shot to Terry's groin. Christ, what was wrong with him? He knew women who wore navel rings. But on her tan skin and barely peeking from beneath her shirt bottom it seemed erotic.

Sitting down on one of the padded vinyl stools, he adjusted his crotch in the privacy under the lunch counter.

"When'd you get back?"

He propped his elbows on the cool counter and clasped his hands. "Hour or so ago. You all buttoned up for the night?"

She put down her bottle of cleaner and her towels. "Not yet. Want something?"

Oh, boy. Was that a loaded question. His sex life had been screwed up and nonexistent ever since he bought this damn town. *And met this woman.* "Whatcha got?"

"Chicken and dumplings and some coleslaw. I baked yeast rolls today. Three left."

"Sounds great."

She went back to the kitchen, then returned with a plate of steaming food and the three rolls. He waited for her to ask him where he had been. If she did, he would tell her. He would also like to tell her that he had passed up several opportunities for casual sex and broken up with a girlfriend because of her. When she didn't ask the question, he said, "I just saw Ben."

She smiled again. "Was he sober?"

"Partially." The food smelled delicious. He sliced into a tender piece of chicken.

She picked up her towel again and started wiping the far end of the back counter. "Poor Ben. I can't remember the last time I saw him completely sober."

"He was working on a new song. Didn't sound too bad, either. Have you heard it?" He liked being able to join in the gossip the Agua Dulcians shared with each other. It gave him an odd sense of family. He slipped a bite of dumpling and creamy sauce into his mouth and his taste buds rejoiced.

"No, but that's good he's working on something. I don't think he has for a long time."

She had been methodically cleaning the back counter and now had reached the end, near where he sat. She turned around, giving him a pointed look and planting a fist on her hip. Her breast shifted and the impression of her nipple showed under the silky top. The gold navel ring peeped from between her shirt hem and the waistband of her jeans. "I don't know what will happen to Ben when you close the RV park and he has to move away from here. Far as I know, he has absolutely no one to care about him but us here in Agua Dulce."

In the whole three weeks Terry had been in Fort Worth, he had heard no criticism of his actions or derision of his motives. Most people with whom he interacted agreed with him and approved of whatever he wanted. Now he wondered if they were phony and if it was Marisa and her critical attitude that were real. "I may not close down the RV park. I may dress it up a little and continue with it."

There was no "may" about it. He "had" to make improvements and keep it going if he wanted to see a sale to Larson's Truck & Travel Stops materialize. That had been another of the provisions the Oklahoma company had tacked on to agreeing to buy his site and build their trademark truck and travel stop.

"Really? That's good news for all of us." She stepped across the narrow space between the back counter and the lunch counter and placed her palms on the counter's edge, her breasts level with his eyes. "Did you know the real name for chicken and dumplings is fricassee? But in Texas it always has been and always will be chicken and dumplings."

Terry forced his eyes up to hers and held her gaze for a few seconds. He was almost close enough to kiss her and his mouth yearned to do just that. "You're really into food, aren't you?"

"Some people paint pictures, study UFOs. . . . Uproot entire towns. I do food. Want dessert? All I've got is ice cream."

A visual of a scoop of ice cream slowly melting on her warm, tan belly and him licking it off around that gold belly ring formed in his mind, and he could tell by the sly look in her eye she had read his thoughts. "I'm okay," he said.

Her eyes held his for a few seconds. It was bothersome having her know everything going on in his head. And in his pants. He glanced up at the Coca-Cola clock above the soda machine, saw it was seven o'clock. "Uh, if you're ready to lock up, I'll take you home."

She frowned. "I don't need to be taken home. It's two hundred feet away."

An urge to compete with Winegardner seized him, yet he hesitated, unsure exactly why and for what he was fighting. "Then, would you *allow* me to take you home? I'd like to talk to you."

"Well, I don't know." Looking past him, she let out a great breath. "You should know something. I'm going out with Lanny. Sort of. We can't do what we . . . We can't have a repeat of that night in your trailer."

Terry willed himself not to react, but with her statement, the action going on inside his shorts began to shrivel. "Going steady, huh?"

"You don't have to be sarcastic. Lanny and I are thinking about getting married. Ben must have said something about it."

"I wasn't being sarcastic. I guess that's good for you and Lanny both." Terry forced himself to smile, but she didn't smile back. Emotion showed in her eyes, but it wasn't the mindless joy of a prospective bride.

She began straightening the clustered menu, napkin holder, sugar dispenser and salt and pepper shakers. The long muscles in her arms worked as her hands moved efficiently, and he thought about those able hands touching his intimate places.

Finally gathering his nerve, he put down his fork and settled his gaze on her profile. "You don't have to, you know."

Her motion stopped, but she didn't look his way. After a few seconds, she resumed her task. "You don't know what I have to do. You don't know me and aside from what your spies have come up with, you don't know much about me."

"I haven't spied on you, Marisa. I was thinking all the way from Forth Worth. I was hoping to change things. With us. You and me."

She gave him one of her direct looks that always left him a little speechless, and he did his damnedest to hide the longing that must be glowing like neon on his face.

"To what end?" she asked.

"What do you mean?"

A slim shoulder lifted in a shrug. "Every trail has an end. No point in starting out if you don't have somewhere to go."

He couldn't keep from squinting in puzzlement. Was she so old-fashioned it would take commitment to get close to her? . . . Or to get her into his bed? Was she talking about *commitment*? . . . From *him*?

Sure she was.

So if she wanted commitment, what the hell did *he* want? He didn't even know. Christ, his whole personal life had gotten fucked up since he came to Agua Dulce. "I'm still not sure what you mean."

A wise smile—or maybe it was a smirk—tipped one corner of her mouth and the little mole at the corner of her lip moved. "That's exactly what I thought."

Terry spent a miserable night, his brain racing like a mouse in a maze. After Marisa locked up, he had driven her around the corner of the building to the singlewide where she lived, but the conversation they'd had was about her mother's paintings. Not what he had intended at all. She hadn't said she was or wasn't marrying Lanny.

As he lay staring into the dark, though he hadn't seen her naked, his imagination had no trouble painting that picture and before long, his brain began forming an even more disturbing picture of her naked body in the arms of a naked Lanny Winegardner. He thrashed in bed until he awoke at daylight and set out on a run through the desert.

The morning sky began to turn pink and he identified the silhouette of an ocotillo ahead. The smell of sulphur gas floated on the cool morning air. Ah, West Texas. No other place like it. "Why was I so damn stupid?" he mumbled as his rhythmic footfalls on the rocky ground echoed in his ears. Sweat ran in rivulets down his face.

Why had he thought clearing his life of other women would allow him to take up with Marisa like snapping his fingers? He had never had control of even a conversation with her, much less anything beyond that. From the day she learned who he was, she had kept him off balance and on the defensive.

At the end of five miles, he had reached a conclusion and made a decision. Even if he succeeded in "getting somewhere" with Marisa, then what? She was

complicated and had many problems. Though Terry
Wilson Ledger had never given up on anything in his
life, he had to give up on Marisa. Everything he had
working was at stake.

Pissed off at himself for being a sucker, he showered
and shaved, threw his gear into his truck and drove
up to Ruidoso for some gambling, but he was back
by Monday morning. Casino gambling wasn't his type
of risk taking.

Spending Monday on the phone arguing with state
and county agencies about septic tanks and drain fields
in Rancho Casero did nothing to improve his irritable
state of mind. Normally, he never argued with bureaucrats. Normally he cajoled and persuaded them to a
point of view closer to his own. Today, he didn't have
the patience.

Through Kim on his cell phone, he negotiated a new
contract to build a five-thousand-square-foot house in
a country club subdivision in Fort Worth. Something
for Chick to do when his crews weren't buried by
construction in Rancho Casero.

He ate his meals in his mobile home.

The next day, Kim called and told him they had a
deal for a Days Inn motel franchise, and a weight
lifted from his shoulders. She faxed him a pile of documents to review.

Later Brad England called and reported that his
preliminary design for Ledger Ranches was ready for
inspection. He needed Terry back in Fort Worth.

Terry threw his gear together again and left early
the next morning, but not before Marisa had opened
the café. Since he didn't know when he would return,
he stopped in to pay his tab.

She was sitting at a table when he entered, shuffling

some papers. An aroma of cooking fruit and spices filled the large room. He stepped into her line of sight. "Baking something good, huh?"

She looked up, her head cocked, fresh lipstick glistening on her heart-shaped lips. "Apple pies."

He walked over to her table, pulled out a chair and helped himself to a seat. Her musky perfume threaded through the food smells. "Sorry I'll miss getting a slice. I'm leaving town. I stopped off to pay my bill."

"You've only eaten here once since you got back." She returned to reading the piece of paper in her hand.

"I know." He had no trouble detecting a bristly tone. She probably wanted to give him a piece of her mind about something. Too bad. Despite how much he had come to like her commonsense opinions, the days when he listened to her were over. She would soon be a married woman, which considerably lessened her influence. "Something's come up. You happen to know what I owe or do you need to look it up?"

"Six dollars," she answered curtly. "Forget the cents."

"Great." He stood up and dug his money clip from his jeans pocket, peeled off a ten and handed it to her. "Keep the change."

"No." She grabbed the ten, got to her feet and quickstepped to the cash register.

He sighed mentally and waited for her to make change. This was *not* how he meant this meeting to go. "You didn't say the other day. When's the wedding?"

She slammed the cash register drawer and handed him four dollars. "We haven't decided."

The answer he wished he could hear was, *It isn't*

happening, but that was a silly notion. "Well, good luck," he said, folding the bills into his money clip. He turned and made for the front door. "See ya," he called, refusing to look back.

Outside, he jerked his truck door open and climbed in, fired the engine, then sat there a minute staring at the junk in the display windows and thinking of how much effort it took to keep those two giant windows clean. A visual came to him of Marisa standing on a ladder washing those windows, her arms lifted, her midriff and that belly button ring visible. He thought of lifting her off the ladder and her body sliding down his, her smiling that bright white smile with those full lips as he held her and—

Fuck! "Okay, dammit," he grumbled, "just go ahead and marry an old man for his money."

He pulled out onto the highway and pointed his truck toward Pecos. His next thought was he didn't notice any reduction in the inventory in the Pecos Belle's flea market. Curious. And problematic. That mountain of junk would have to be liquidated and in this part of Texas that would be a monumental task, hardly one a single woman caring for a sick person could easily handle.

Well, surely those aunts would help when the time came.

At Pecos, he connected with I-20. As the interstate stretched out ahead of him, almost empty but for truck traffic, his mind began to put together his plans. On this trip to Fort Worth, he would accomplish what had languished while he had floundered and worried about Agua Dulce's odd population. He wouldn't return to West Texas until he and Brad had settled on a final plan for Ledger Ranches retirement community, until he had designed a marketing strategy with which Kim could move forward and until he and Chick had selected half a dozen home designs.

He would be too busy to think about Marisa. In a way, her being tied to Lanny was a good thing. It hardened his attitude toward both her and the Agua Dulcians and he no longer felt guilty or obligated.

When's the wedding?
For a few seconds Marisa totally gave herself over to the fear those words set off, fear that had chomped at her like a hungry wolf ever since Lanny proposed and she had failed to tell him the idea of their getting married was too outrageous to consider.

For a few more seconds in the empty café's silence, she let herself imagine how it might be if it had been Terry who had proposed to her. Terry Ledger of the quick smile, the sun-streaked brown hair, the agile-looking hands. . . . The soft lips and the sturdy, *young* body.

Well, not entirely young, but younger than fifty-five. *Shit, shit, shit.* Everything about him appealed to her, though her good sense told her it was too ridiculous for a grown woman to be swooning over the unattainable.

Better to focus on the doable, right? In the two weeks since Lanny proposed, he had proved to be an even gentler, nicer man than she had first thought. The perfect suitor. He had been to visit her in the café often, had been to visit Mama. He had taken her to dinner in Odessa and Midland several times, hiring a nurse out of Kermit to watch over Mama for the few hours they were gone. He hadn't shown up yet with the promised diamond ring, but every time he came into the café, she wondered if he had it in his pocket. She had no doubt he would bring one. No man had ever spoiled her like she believed Lanny might.

She had discovered in him a sense of humor she hadn't known he had. He could dance. He was a news junkie, so he knew every current event and was interested in politics. He could quote every daily cattle price in Texas. A life different from the one she had imagined when he first proposed began to unfold in her mind's eye and she had begun to think living with him as a companion could be interesting and even a joy.

Not once had he pressured her for sex. She hadn't offered it, either. Even as positive as her thoughts about him had become, she still hadn't reconciled herself to crawling into bed with him.

The whole damn thing was insane. Just insane.

The kitchen timer dinged and jolted her from her woolgathering. She stuffed the bills she had been sorting into a file folder and went to the kitchen, where the cinnamon-laced apple pies were baking. She was removing them from the oven when the front door chimed. She glanced toward it and saw two tall women. It was early for tourists unless they had spent the night at the Starlight Inn.

Chapter 18

When the pair came closer and sat down at the lunch counter Marisa recognized the older one, though she hadn't seen her more than once or twice since high school. Lanny's older daughter. She had been dark-haired in school; now she was blond.

Marisa gave them a quick head-to-toe, not failing to note that they weren't wearing rags. Nor were they poorly shod or lacking in flashy jewelry. An uneasy feeling niggled at Marisa. Pecos Belle's wasn't a likely hangout for Lanny's well-to-do kids.

She set the pies on trivets to cool and, wiping her hands on a towel, walked out of the kitchen and greeted the two women. The three of them went through the inane high-school-reunion-how's-your-mother conversation. Old home reunion week. Phony. Marisa offered them coffee.

"I'd rather have iced tea," the younger one said. She was also blond. The older one said she, too, preferred tea.

While Marisa filled plastic glasses with ice and tea, she prodded her memory. She knew from gossip that Lisa Winegardner, the daughter who was the same age as Marisa, had left home for college in Austin, but later flunked out. While there, she had met and married some kind of computer wizard and remained in Austin permanently. The younger daughter, Kristy, had soon followed her sister, but hadn't married. She now held a part-time token job in a retail store and spent her free time playing golf and taking class after class at the University of Texas. Everyone knew neither of them had ever seriously worked for a living and never would.

Marisa had been back in Agua Dulce over a year now and couldn't recall seeing or hearing of either daughter coming to visit Dad even once before now. Her sixth sense told her why they had come as a team today, but she refused to believe the worst unless she heard it from their mouths. "Just passing through town?" she couldn't resist asking.

"We came to visit our father," Lisa said, hooking wispy strands of blond hair behind her ear with two elegantly manicured fingers.

"It's been a while since you were up."

"I'll get right to the point, Miss Rutherford—"

"Miss Rutherford?" *Oh, hell,* Marisa thought. Her instinct was right again. "Gosh, when we were on the volleyball team in Wink, you called me Marisa."

Lisa stiffened, a near snarl crossing her perfectly outlined lips. "Marisa, then. I'm saying it right out. I want you to leave my father alone."

The younger sister didn't speak, but holding her glass of tea with fingers tipped by talonlike red nails, she sipped and turned her head away.

The words "my father" didn't fit the Lanny Marisa had come to know. "Dad," maybe, or "Daddy," but not "father." She placed a fist on her hip and gave her future stepdaughter a direct look. "Maybe he's the one you should be talking to. I haven't bothered him. He came to me."

"I doubt that. I know how it goes. A younger available woman, an old man—"

"I beg your pardon. I'm not an *available* woman and your dad isn't an old man. And I didn't—"

"He's twenty-one years older than I am, Marisa. That means he's twenty-one years older than you." Her brown eyes turned almost black. "My God. My mother would turn over in her grave if she could see what's going on."

The memory of Lanny's negative remarks about his marriage flew into Marisa's mind. She couldn't keep from narrowing her eyes. "And what do you think is going on, Lisa?"

"Oh, get real. You're not fooling anyone. Your mother . . . everyone knows about her and Clyde Campbell." A smile Marisa could describe only as malicious quirked the corners of Lisa's mouth. "But in the end, putting out for an old man didn't do her any good, did it? She didn't wind up with a penny of Clyde's money, did she? I'd think that would be a lesson—"

"Just stop right there." Marisa could feel the very blood in her veins flaming. She just might punch Lisa Winegardner's face. "Who do you think you are, coming into my business and spouting insults? My mother never wanted Clyde Campbell's money. God knows, that lying bastard lost her more than she gained."

Lisa's eyes shot daggers. "I know a gold digger when I see one. Like mother, like daughter." She set her glass on the counter with a *thunk*. "My brother'll be here today and we're going to have this out once

and for all. You might as well know right now you're
not getting your hands on a penny of our family's
money. The estate's been set up for years and no one's
touching it. I'm telling you again. You leave him
alone."

She started to rise, but Marisa rounded the end of
the lunch counter, her fist clenched at her side. Lisa's
eyes bugged. She sank back to the stool and clutched
an oversized handbag to her chest like a shield. Kristy
stood up and backed away. Lisa scooted backward off
her stool and stood up, too. In her high heels she was
at least a head taller than Marisa.

Marisa lashed out. "You know something, Lisa? If
you'd show up once in a while and be a daughter to
your dad, you might see how lonely he is."

Before she punched the dumb blonde's lights out,
Marisa breezed past her and started for the back exit.
Then she stopped. Why should she flee? She hadn't
done anything wrong. She turned back to her antagonist. "On the other hand, a visit from you would probably be a waste of Lanny's time. You're too damn
selfish to care about him and too damn dense to see
how bleak his life is. Come to think of it, you always
were dense as a fence post. I remember what a hard
time you had graduating from Wink High School."
Marisa thrust out her hand and pointed toward the
front door. "Just get out of here. And take your accu-
sations with you. If you've got an axe to grind, take
it up with him."

Marisa stomped out of the café into the apartment
and slammed the door. She was shaking all over as
she sank to the sofa in the living room. What had
she done?

Told off her future husband's oldest kid, that's what.

And the kid had been afraid Marisa might hit her. "I've got to learn to control my temper," Marisa muttered to the empty living room.

Early in the afternoon, Marisa returned to the singlewide to check on Mama and get her lunch together. She found artwork thumbtacked to the walls all over the mobile. Marisa couldn't have found a thumbtack in that mobile home if the alternative meant being on the wrong end of a firing squad, but Mama had found some somewhere. Amazing. For a moment she worried about the holes the tacks made in the walls, but on second thought, Mama didn't own the mobile and Terry was probably going to get rid of the thing anyway.

To her astonishment and Tanya's, Mama was producing some interesting watercolor art. Abstract, but interesting. Jake did the framing for Tanya's oils, so she'd had him frame a couple of Mama's watercolors and hung them in her museum. One of them had actually sold.

Where the ability came from Marisa didn't know, but Mama appeared to have some knowledge of which colors went together and how. She and Tanya had conversations about how violet contrasted so nicely with gold and how mixing red and green made brown and Mama seemed to understand what Tanya told her.

She no longer spent her days in front of TV. Now she painted for hours. Sometimes she missed the paper and painted the tabletop, but most of the time, Marisa could wash off the damage. Though she was happy Mama had something to do, she was annoyed that the person who had presented the watercolors had been Terry.

Terry, the will-o'-the-wisp. He was probably getting close to Fort Worth about now.

Something's come up.

I'll bet, Marisa thought. What had come up was probably in his shorts and he probably had a big date with some hot blonde.

"Hey, good job," she told the artist, looking at a conglomeration of colors that could be a flower bed or a garden.

Her mother went into a long explanation, pointing out details with color-stained fingers.

The tension of the earlier confrontation with Lanny's daughters began to melt away as an unavoidable truth came to rest within Marisa. This, here and now in this mobile home, was her real world, shared with a gentle woman incapable of the kind of selfish meanness demonstrated by Lisa Winegardner. Marrying Lanny would be thrusting Mama into an environment Lanny's vicious daughters would be a part of. She couldn't do it.

Morning came with the blue skies and bright glory of a summer day in the desert. And all the heat. Ben met Marisa as she opened the café. She hadn't seen him so early in the morning in weeks. He was shaved and his shaggy hair was combed. He had on a faded but clean tan T-shirt and clean khaki cargo shorts and she could tell he had bathed. He might be more sober than usual, but she still detected the faint odor of alcohol. "What are you doing out so early?" she asked him.

"Just checking to see how the world turns at seven o'clock."

Ben always spoke with a drawl, but this morning he

didn't have the alcohol-induced slur she had become accustomed to hearing from him. She led him through the flea market back to the café.

"How's Raylene this mornin'?" he asked, following her like a puppy.

She put coffee on to drip, drew water for fresh tea, then moved into the kitchen and turned on the flame under the griddle. "She was at the table painting when I left."

The aroma of brewing coffee filled the air. Ben leaned a shoulder on the doorjamb and watched as she set up the kitchen for the day. Salt and pepper, a shaker of her own special blend of seasonings, olive oil—"Et cetera, et cetera," she mumbled to herself as she worked.

"Ain't that somethin' she can paint pictures?"

"I'm blown away by it. So is Tanya." The coffeemaker gurgled, signaling the brew was ready. "Get us a cup of coffee, will you?"

She flicked a few droplets of water on the griddle, testing the temperature. The drops bounced and transformed into steam, so she pulled two sausage patties from the freezer and placed them on the griddle. "Since you're here, you're having breakfast," she declared. "Sausage and eggs."

"Lord, girl, you're always trying to feed me. What makes you think I want to eat?"

"Don't argue," she scolded. "Do it to please me. And start off with a cup of coffee."

He backed out of the doorway and sauntered to the coffeepot. "Guess you heard about the ruckus out at Winegardner's."

Aha! The real reason Ben had come to the café so early. A riffle of uneasiness slid through Marisa. All night she had imagined Lanny's kids swooping down on him like vultures. *Turkey* vultures. "What happened?"

"It was all about you, darlin'."

Twenty-four hours hadn't passed since yesterday's appearance by Lisa and Kristy. Marisa had never figured out how Ben seemed to be the first to know every crumb of gossip. "I'm not surprised. Lisa was in here giving me hell yesterday."

Ben returned to the doorway, handed her a cup of black coffee with a trembling hand. "Poor ol' Lanny. Guess he had it out with his kids." He set his mug on the counter and fished a crushed pack of Camels from his T-shirt pocket. "I hear they left the ranch late last night, worried about where their next new Jag's comin' from."

Marisa gasped and frowned. "You can't smoke in my kitchen."

Ben growled and mumbled as he returned the cigarettes to his pocket.

Marisa continued to frown as guilt for her role in upsetting Lanny's family pinched her. "I thought they had trust funds. I thought they could buy anything they wanted forever."

"Well, darlin', what Daddy giveth, Daddy can taketh away."

"Shit," Marisa muttered.

Ben sighed. "There ain't nothing Lanny ain't done for those kids, but not a one of them gives a shit about him." He picked up his mug and took a long swig of coffee. "They never were Lanny's kids anyway. They were always just Joyce's. That woman spent most of her time on this earth turning those kids against their daddy."

Joyce. Lanny's deceased wife.

Marisa's memory spun backward, but Joyce Wine-gardner was no more than a gauzy, if well-dressed, image. Marisa had already left Agua Dulce by the time she passed on. Ben, on the other hand, probably knew her as well as he knew Lanny. Marisa had to ask, "Why would she do that?"

"She was as unhappy a human being as I ever seen. A fish out of water, for sure. She hated everything about Agua Dulce, hated the ranchin' business." He pronounced it "bid-ness."

With so much distance between her and Lanny's ages, Marisa had never been interested in knowing the history of Lanny's marriage. Tanya's tantrum over moving to Arizona with Jake waltzed through her mind. Marisa was weary of people who refused to step up and handle the consequences of their decisions. She couldn't remember ever having that luxury herself. "If that's how she felt, why did she marry him and come here?"

Marisa the Cynic.

Ben gave a deep heh-heh-heh. "Ain't that obvious?"

"Yeah, it is," she said, aware her own reasoning might not be any different from that of Lanny's deceased wife. Financial security was a potent motivator. She flipped the sausage patties and placed the cast-iron press on top of them, then broke two eggs onto the hot griddle.

"Think you'll go through with it, darlin'?"

She hesitated before answering. "Go through with what?"

"Don't get coy with your ol' Ben, sweet girl. My thinking may be a little cloudy, but yours ain't. You know damn well what I'm talkin' 'bout."

Marisa set her jaw. Her decision was nobody's business. "Do you think you'll quit drinking this year?"

"I'll prob'ly quit drinkin' before you marry Lanny."

A lump swelling in her throat threatened to stop her flurry of activity, but she pushed on. "That's probably right. I doubt it'll ever happen."

"Too friggin' bad," Ben said, running a hand through his combed hair and ruining the neatness. "Just too friggin' bad to let ungrateful kids run your life. Glad I ain't got any snot-nosed brats trying to tell me what to do."

She looked over her shoulder at him and smiled. "But you've got me."

He was studying the surface of his coffee. "You'd be good for ol' Lanny, Marisa."

"Oh, I don't know about that." A tear escaped and trailed down beside her nose, the delayed reaction to Lisa's attack. "It's too hard, Ben."

She turned the eggs too carelessly and broke both yolks. She looked up at him.

His gaze quickly veered from her face to the semi-liquid yolks leaking yellow beyond the edges of the whites. "Hey, it don't make no never-mind to me. It's all going to the same place."

She managed a sniffly chuckle as she scooped the breakfast onto a plate and passed it to him. "It'd be too hard for me and Lanny both. My life's already complicated enough. What's the point in doing something that can only cause trouble for him? No, I'm pretty sure I'm going back to Plan A. I feel bad for Lanny, but he'll have to soothe his soul and spend his money with someone else."

Carrying the plate, Ben shuffled around the end of the lunch counter to a stool. "Just too friggin' bad," he mumbled. He reached for the salt and pepper shakers, sprinkled salt on his eggs, then covered them with a blanket of pepper.

"Do you ever wonder what's going to happen to all of us, Ben?"

"Nah. I don't give a shit." He picked up his knife and fork and whacked his eggs into a hundred pieces.

"You do, too. You just don't want to admit it." She sipped her coffee. "Trying to figure all of it out is driving me crazy."

"You know something, baby girl? Half the time, I think Raylene's better off than any of us. Look at her. She's happy all the time, don't have a clue what's happening and she's got you to take care of her. I might wish for a deal like that m'self." He dug into his breakfast.

Marisa refilled his coffee mug. "Don't ever wish Alzheimer's disease on yourself, Ben."

"Maybe I've already got it. Rachel used to say I was drowning brain cells faster than they could recover." He sopped a piece of toast in his eggs and shoved it into his mouth. " 'Course it was her fault most of the time that I was doing it."

Rachel. The song lyrics Marisa had seen on Ben's table flashed in her mind. She hadn't heard him so much as say Rachel's name in months, maybe years. She rounded the end of the lunch counter and sat down beside him. "You haven't mentioned her in ages."

He didn't reply at first, just concentrated on his breakfast. Marisa didn't push. He had always kept his relationship with the mysterious Rachel private. He pushed his plate away and drew his mug closer. "Nothin' to mention. That song's come to an end on a pitiful sour note. She's out o' the picture for good this time and I'm recoverin'." He pulled his cigarettes out of his shirt pocket again.

Marisa sighed. At least he wasn't in her kitchen.

"She was somethin', that woman," he went on, lighting up. He inhaled deeply and exhaled a stream of smoke. Marisa reached up the counter and dragged an ashtray to him.

"Yessir, my sun, my moon, the evenin' star. Had hair black as yours and eyes the color o' coal. Yessir, one look and she could turn my knees to jelly. . . . And one word and she could make me want to do murder."

"What happened to her?"

"Nothin', I guess. She's doin' all the things most married women do."

Marisa felt her eyes pop wide and didn't try to hide her shock. "Rachel got married?"

"She always was married, darlin'. Always was."

A frown tugged at Marisa's brow. Mama had never told her that. "Ben, that's awful."

Big sigh. "I hung on for years. I used to think it'd all work out with her and me. Maybe I'd bring her out here, maybe build her a nice house around Pecos or Kermit or somewhere, but she never stuck with me long enough at one time for me to do it."

He lifted his mug and gulped a drink of coffee. "She played me, always setting me up against her husband. Calling me up at two in the morning, sayin' she'd had it, wantin' me to come get her. I always did. Then she'd go back to him to end it and they'd kiss and make up." He drew such a deep drag his cigarette that the tip lit up like a beacon. "It took me a lot o' years, but I finally told her I couldn't keep showing up in Nashville ever' time they had a breakup, then leavin' town ever' time they had a reconsh-rec-on-shiliation. After that, I just left for good."

Now Marisa knew why Ben had seemed so restless for so many years. He had been in love with a married woman his whole life. Indeed, he had moved back and forth between Agua Dulce and Nashville uncountable times.

And now that he had come here to settle down, he was soon to be uprooted again.

"God, Ben," she said softly. "That's so sad."

Ben raked ash off the end of his cigarette into the ashtray Marisa had given him. "Nah. It was sad a long time ago, but . . ." His words trailed off. "You know, baby girl, there ain't much that's fun about gettin' old, but one thing that's nice is stuff you used to think was important stops matterin' so much."

Marisa couldn't resist the opportunity to learn something significant about Ben's life.

"Did Mama know about her?"

"Oh, sure. Your mama was one o' the few people I ever told my secrets to. Tight-lipped, your ma was. You could tell her anything and she'd die before she'd ever breathe a word of it."

"Did she know Rachel?"

"Nope. Nobody around here knew her." He took another drag off his cigarette, squinting from the smoke.

"Where is she now?"

"Why, Nashville, o'course."

"Is she the reason you haven't been back there?"

"I don't want to chance running into her, Marisa. I just don't trust m'self. You ever hear that song 'North Dakota Boy' by them Canada boys?"

"It's been a while. It's a good song."

"Well, that's ol' Ben Seagraves in that song. If anybody hauls me back to Nashville, it'll be after I'm dead."

"Did you sell your place there?"

"Yep. Put the money in the stock market. It's bringing me a hell of a lot more return than that house ever did. Now I can buy enough Jack to drown m'self if I want to."

"When we all have to leave here, where will you go, Ben?"

"Don't know. Fer now, I'm staying put. Terry told me he ain't touchin' the trailer park. He's even gonna make it better."

"One thing's for sure. That isn't true of Pecos Belle's or the beauty shop." Quiet fell between them. She looked away, down the counter at the kitchen doorway, the tiny sanctum where she spent so much of her time. What would she do when she could no longer retreat to it?

"I've got some replies back on the résumés I sent out," she said. "I'm going to follow up on them. One place that contacted me is in Midland. With Mama's doctor there, that wouldn't be too bad."

Ben tamped out his cigarette in the ashtray Marisa had given him. "Lord, Marisa. I can't imagine this place without you and your ma." Suddenly his eyes teared and he wiped them with his fingers. "Even if she does crazy stuff, I still like seeing her around."

His hand went to his pants pocket and came out with a flask. He didn't even bother to pour a shot into his coffee. He drank straight from the flask. "I gotta go, baby girl," he said hoarsely. He got to his feet and dug into his pocket again, came up with a handful of money and laid it on the counter. "Once," he said, "when I's real pissed off, I wrote a song about Rachel. One o' these days when I'm drunk enough, I'll play it for you."

Unable to think of a better response, Marisa smiled. "Sure. I can't wait to hear it."

As he cleared her line of sight, Marisa couldn't keep from being amazed at all she had learned just in the past few weeks about the people around her. Ben was an emotional cripple. He had wasted his entire life being in love with a woman he couldn't have and who had no loyalty. Was that the common basis for his and Mama's long friendship—being in love with someone neither of them could ever have? Living like a hermit, Ben had numbed his pain with Jack Daniel's. Mama had numbed hers with hard work.

Terry Ledger and his plans had been a catalyst for all sorts of skeletons to come out of closets.

Marisa rose and went to her kitchen. She had a lot to do. Today's lunch special was chicken-fried steak, real mashed potatoes and cream gravy.

As she peeled potatoes, she thought of Lanny and the controversy swirling around the two of them. Had she lost her mind, thinking she could marry him and they would live on an island known as the mountains in Colorado, with no thought to his family and what they might think? Or no contact? His three kids might be shits, but they were still his offspring and he supported them. Financially, anyway. She couldn't, *wouldn't*, be the one who created a bigger rift between him and his kids.

Nope. Not happening.

But there was more. How could she marry Lanny, or any man, when her heart and mind were bound up with Terry Ledger? She thought of him day and night, how easy it had been to kiss him, the sweetness of his lips, how comfortable and secure she felt in his arms. She thought of his intense eyes, which said so much more than his mouth, and of the emotion she sensed in him. How was it possible she had these feelings if he didn't have them, too?

Something deep within her told her she had to let this "thing" with Terry, whatever it was, play itself out. Even if it had a bad outcome, she had to give it a chance.

She called the XO. When one of the hands answered she left a message for Lanny to drop by the café.

Chapter 19

At noon, Lanny did just that, wearing a hangdog expression. He sat down at the far end of the lunch counter, right outside the kitchen doorway. A dozen customers were scattered around the dining room. Besides fruit pies, Marisa had made enchilada casserole and black bean salad for the daily special, a labor-intensive recipe that worked off some of her nervous energy. Since she was well known for the dish, posting the menu on the sandwich board out front brought in the locals traveling the highway and made a larger than usual lunch crowd.

"I'm sorry, Rissy," Lanny said softly, as she prepared three plates of casserole and salad. "She shouldn't have come in here. She's too much like her mother."

"There's nothing for you to be sorry for, Lanny." Marisa kept her voice low and out of hearing range of customers. "Believe it or not, I see her point."

She positioned the three plates—one on her wrist, one in her left hand and one in her right—and started out to deliver the food. Having learned to wait tables as a child, she was an expert. "I'll be back in a minute," she told Lanny. After taking the plates to a table of women who had come from Tanya's salon, she returned to her post behind the lunch counter.

"Rissy," Lanny said, "these past weeks have been real good. For me, anyway. I'd sorta forgot how it felt to have the company of a lady and have a good time. I thought you were having a good time, too."

"I was, Lanny, but we can't just blow off your kids. They're your family."

A customer caught her eye and pointed to his empty glass. She picked up a pitcher of tea, scurried to his table and filled his glass, then made the rounds filling other empty glasses. Every customer gave her raves on the food. When she returned to the lunch counter, while she had the tea pitcher in hand, she poured a glass for Lanny.

He wrapped a wide, work-scarred hand around the glass. "They don't act like family. Or at least, not like my idea of family. All they want from me is money. And they've got that." He lifted the glass and drank.

"I know, Lanny, and I wish it wasn't that way. You've done so much for them."

His shoulder lifted in a shrug. "Some tell me I've done too much. They say I've ruined 'em. Maybe so. But what good is it having all this damn money if you can't share it with the ones you love? . . . They don't have anything to do with what goes on between you and me, Rissy."

She set the pitcher on the back counter so she could face him and speak quietly. "Don't you see how hard everything would be if we got married? It doesn't matter so much that your family would hate me. I'm used to people being pissed off at me. But they'd resent Mama, too, and she's helpless to defend herself."

He looked up at her with solemn eyes. "Rissy, if

you're not gonna say yes, don't let it be because Lisa jumped on you. If you don't like me and don't think we could get along, that's one thing, but don't let people who won't be part of our lives scare you off."

Looking into his deep brown eyes all she could think was that both of his hateful daughters had his eyes. Blood ties that couldn't be denied or swept under the rug. "Lanny, the only way to remove your kids from your life is to do something meaner than you're capable of. And I'm not sure you *should* do it, even if you could. Bottom line, there's just no way a man like you can divorce himself from his kids. Besides, I don't want to live in a family quarrel. I remember how it used to be when Mama and Aunt Rosemary were always fighting."

"I'm getting old, Rissy. I'm lonesome. Seeing what's happened to Raylene has taught me a lesson. When she was my age, she was still okay. A little funny-acting, but still okay. Not that many years have passed, and now look at her. I want a shot at being happy while I still know what's going on."

"Oh, Lanny, I want you to be happy, too," Marisa said, gliding past the reminder that just a short eleven years ago, Alzheimer's disease was something that happened to someone else and Mama had still been in good shape. "If I've ever met someone who deserves to be happy, you do. But I'm not your answer. Your kids think I'm a gold digger. Maybe they'd feel less threatened if you found someone a little older. I *am* the same age as Lisa, you know. You *could* be my dad."

His head slowly shook. "You're the one I picked out to spend the rest of my life with. Don't say no just yet. Let's let things alone a while."

She sighed. "Oh, Lanny, really—"

"Just let things go along," he said. "Time passing makes a lot of difference. Sometimes a problem has a way of working itself out with no help from anybody."

She didn't raise a protest again, but she knew the fragile bond that had evolved between them, whatever its definition and origin, was broken. Lisa and Kristy's visit hadn't scared her off, but it had brought her to her senses, which, maybe, was the same thing. That, and the gossip from half-drunk Ben.

Lanny gave her a hug and left the café. She had no idea if he would ever be back.

As Lanny's pickup pulled away, Tanya came in. She had been at the singlewide helping Mama paint. She stopped at the display windows and watched Lanny's pickup disappear on the horizon, then came back to the café. She was wearing jeans and flat-heeled sandals. Unusual attire for her.

"You tell him you're gonna marry him?" she asked.

"No. How was art class?"

"Okay. I can't get over how Raylene takes to it. It's so weird." She pulled a bent pack of Virginia Slims out of her bra and lit up. "Raylene's calling me Tina today."

Marisa couldn't keep from chuckling. It seemed that lately Mama called Tanya a different name every time she saw her. "You want something?"

"Thank God I don't have any customers this afternoon," she added as Marisa drew a Coke into a Styrofoam cup. "I'm not up to listening to people's troubles."

Setting the Coke and a straw in front of her neighbor, Marisa took a second look and saw that she was still wearing yesterday's makeup. "Are you sick?"

Tanya looked up at her, tears glistening in her mascara-smudged eyes. "Jake told me to get out." A tear leaked from one eye and trailed down the side of her nose. "I've got to get home and get packed."

"You're kidding," Marisa said, but she could see that Tanya's statement was no joke.

She knew little of Tanya and Jake's history. The most she had ever heard Tanya say was they met in a honky-tonk on Friday night, got married on Saturday and Jake moved her to Agua Dulce on Sunday. Still, Jake throwing her out was the last thing Marisa would have ever expected. And Tanya's reaction was even more surprising. Marisa had thought it was Jake who needed Tanya, not vice versa. Had she been wrong all along about their marriage? Had that pesky but usually accurate intuition failed her? "Wait a second. Where do you think you're going?"

"I don't know. But I've gotta be gone before he gets home."

As far as Marisa knew, for family, Tanya had one brother. He was in the army, stationed in Alaska. Her mother was deceased and her estranged father had remarried and moved to Florida. Marisa rounded the end of the lunch counter and took a seat beside the hairdresser. "What's going on with you two? And what about your shops?"

Tanya used the end of her cigarette to light another.

"You shouldn't do that," Marisa scolded. "It's bad for you."

"BFD." Tanya looked up and blew a stream of smoke at the ceiling. "Jake doesn't really love me, you know."

"I thought it was the opposite. I thought you didn't love him."

She shook her head and made a deep sniff. "I don't know if I do, but I did think we were used to each other."

"Look, Jake's a good guy. I'll bet y'all could make up and put things back together and—"

"Marisa," she said, her lips tightly drawn, "he doesn't need me. He's like every other fucking cowboy I've ever met. They don't need a damn living, breathing, thing but their horses and their dogs."

Marisa's eyes squinted involuntarily. She couldn't remember seeing a dog other than a stray around Agua Dulce. "When did y'all get a dog?"

"We didn't get a dog. That's what I mean. Jake's even worse than most. He doesn't even need a dog."

Marisa cocked her head and arched her brow. Good assessment of most of the cowboys she knew. She had never doubted that men who chose cowboying for a living had to have done so for deep, mysterious reasons, because a cowboy's life was far from easy and the pay was awful. "You've been together a long time. That has to count for something."

Tanya stared at the posters pinned on the wall behind the back counter. "Yeah, we have. Nearly ten years. It hasn't exactly been heaven, though. I mean, look at this place. It'd be hard enough living here if you were hooked up with somebody who liked to talk and who liked to do something once in a while. Hell, before you came here, me and your mother were the only women in town. When she started losing it, I didn't have *anybody* to talk to."

Marisa stared out the display windows at the sun-drenched emptiness that ran on until it crashed into a bunch of purple mountains that were probably in New

Mexico. She remembered what Ben had said about the lack of coping skills in Lanny's deceased wife. Marisa survived life in Agua Dulce herself because her every waking moment was filled with something that demanded doing.

"I might as well be living by myself," Tanya said. "I still like fucking, but Jake doesn't even like that anymore."

There it was. Tanya's ever-present bluntness about something most people kept private. Marisa felt the corner of her mouth quirk. "Well, there's that."

"I've never cheated on him."

"I didn't say you did."

"No, but you think it. Everybody thinks it."

"Why does he want you out?"

"He thinks 'cause I don't want to go to Arizona I've just used him all these years. He thinks I married him just to get out of that topless joint in Odessa."

"What topless joint? I thought he met you in a honky—in a nightclub in Odessa." When Tanya didn't reply, Marisa's suspicion mushroomed. "I thought you were a hairdresser out for the evening."

Tanya glanced over her shoulder and her green eyes zeroed in on Marisa's. "I am, now. But I wasn't."

Marisa picked up her cup and swallowed a large gulp of Coke. "Okay, so you were a dancer. What's wrong with that?"

"I wasn't just a dancer, either."

"Okay, so you were a—a . . . well, what the hell were you?"

For the first time since she came in, Tanya laughed, but it reminded Marisa of one of those clowns whose face is painted in a big grin but who's crying inside.

Tanya's head shook. "Oh, Marisa, you are so naive. That's what I've always liked about you. You take everything to be just like you see it."

Tanya couldn't be more wrong about that. Marisa didn't take *anything* to be as it appeared on the surface. It was the underlying layers that left her either stunned and dismayed or thrilled and overjoyed. She sat staring at Tanya for a few minutes. Now a lot about her made more sense—her enviable ease with men, her great body, her total lack of modesty, her frankness about most things sexual.

Tanya sighed, put down her mug and stood up. "Ben told me I could crash at his place. Maybe I'll take him up on that 'til I can figure some things out."

"But you don't like Ben."

"I know. But I'm liking him better since he took up for me."

"Ben? Our cantankerous Ben? What did he do?"

"He heard me and Jake yelling. Jake called me some real bad names. Ben came over to our trailer and told Jake a man shouldn't ever call a woman names like that. Jake told him I was nothing but a damn whore and Ben said it didn't matter what I was. What was important was that I had been loyal to him and I loved him."

Shocked that Ben would insert himself into an argument between Tanya and her husband, and even more shocked that Ben would step up in Tanya's defense, Marisa sat there speechless. But then, even snockered, Ben had always respected women.

"Do you think Ben's too old for me?" Tanya asked.

Horror was Marisa's first reaction. Then her thoughts flew to Lanny. "Tanya, after all that's happened in the last few weeks, I don't have opinions on questions like that."

"Do you think he can still do anything? I mean, some men his age can and some can't. 'Course, even if he wasn't an old guy, he drinks so much he probably can't get it up."

I'm fifty-five, but I think I can still . . .

Marisa stopped her wandering thoughts before they took her into even darker territory. She braced her elbows on the counter and rubbed her temples, wishing she could erase the present conversation. "Who knows?"

Tanya smiled a sweet smile. "He was awful nice to me last night."

Marisa forced herself to her feet before Tanya could go any further along this track. A conversation about a budding affair between Ben and Tanya was more than any woman with as many problems as Marisa had should have to analyze, much less endure. She got to her feet. "I have to clean up the kitchen. In case someone comes in to eat supper."

Tanya gathered her cigarettes and lighter. "I'm going to Ben's."

Chapter 20

Tanya's story left Marisa saddened. All around her, lives were falling apart. A serious case of the blues assailed her, so after she started the dishwasher, she took her feather duster and tackled the wares in the flea market, keeping her hands busy with making everything shine.

But her mind stewed. She should have known better than to put stock in marrying a man she didn't love for the sake of security. Hadn't she learned that compromising your principles caused more problems than it solved? Instead of relying on someone else to take care of her, she had to figure out how to take care of herself. And Mama.

Her foot might be nailed to the floor for the present, but she had an opportunity to direct her own future. She could finish her cookbook, maybe get it published. Someday Mama would pass on—Marisa had already faced the fact. Then she could go back to Dallas and finish school, really *get* that job as a sous-chef.

Late in the afternoon, several men came in for supper. She recognized them as the Fort Worth surveying crew working for Terry Ledger. Having been in before, they were friendly and joked and told her how much they had thought about her home-cooked meals

while they had been away. From them she learned
Terry had returned and now things were going to start
moving faster.

After hearing that tidbit of news, she felt panic set
in again, accompanied by even deeper depression.

She fed Mama and put her to bed, then sauntered
outside, her mind darting from the Odessa auctioneer
with whom she'd had half a dozen conversations to
the reply to her résumé from the Midland country
club that needed a cook.

That the country club referred to the job as "cook"
disturbed her. She might not be a bona fide "chef,"
but she was no mere "cook," either. She had been
cooking and selling the results for as long as she could
remember. She was a food artist, a baker, with a little
formal training and a lifetime of experience and self-
education. She could write books on food and cooking, even on nutrition.

Returning to Agua Dulce, where she had a free
hand in how and what she cooked every day, had
spoiled her. She could no longer see herself slopping
out a daily ration of frozen, pre-prepared entrées and
maintaining a steam table of canned foods cooked to
the point of being mush. She had done that enough
already. If the country club's attitude was that all they
needed was a "cook," perhaps she would be just as
well off waiting for another opportunity where her
ability might be more appreciated.

Yeah, right.

Sitting in the low light of day turning to night, an
old Tammy Wynette broken-heart song playing in the
background and a home behind her that not only
didn't belong to Mama but could be hooked onto the
back of a truck and hauled away, the truth bore down

on her. Refusing to consider the job in Midland wasn't an option.

Restless and troubled by the melee going on in her head, she returned to the café. In the farthest back corner of the refrigerator was a six-pack of Budweiser. She had bought it once for Ben, but had never told him it was there. She cracked a beer and took a long, bitter swallow. "Teetotaler Marisa falls off the wagon," she mumbled to the quiet room.

She turned up the volume on the radio, listening to Toby Keith singing about a couple falling in love on the dance floor. She closed her eyes and swayed to the music in the empty café's dim light, taken in by the romance in the song's story. When the music ended, she kicked herself for indulging in self-pity and marched to the kitchen.

She opened a second beer, then dragged out ingredients—sugar, flour, oatmeal, butter—and set about making chocolate chip cookies from the supposedly stolen Neiman Marcus recipe. One of those urban legends. She had never really believed it was stolen from the famous department store's bistro.

As she mixed up a triple batch of cookies, she finished the beer and opened another. Baking and drinking, she thought about making a living from selling cookies, like Mrs. Fields. "Mrs. Rutherford's Famous Stolen Chocolate Chip Cookies," she muttered.

Well, the Mrs. part was a ruse, but who knew? Maybe Mrs. Fields wasn't married, either.

Married. Well, she had come close for a few days. And to a man as good as he was rich. She could be proud of that much and she would always be grateful to Lanny for asking her.

The cookies multiplied from a dozen to golden piles

heaped on three plates. As the last tray baked she sat down at the lunch counter with a fourth beer and a book of crossword puzzles. As she struggled to focus her vision on the black and white squares on the page and pondered a word for "a German sea goddess," she heard tapping on the front door.

A tiny ping of anxiety darted through her. In the back of her mind, she was constantly aware of the isolation of her location and the fact that the nearest law enforcement was at least thirty minutes away. At night she didn't open the front door to anyone, usually didn't even acknowledge a knock. She left the lunch counter stool and eased back to the kitchen, where she could peek out without being seen.

Terry Ledger. What could he want at this time of night?

Leaning against the refrigerator, uncertain if he had seen her, she bit down on her lower lip and debated not going to the door. In the end, she wiped her hands on her greasy apron, then pulled it over her head and flung it on the lunch counter.

Key in hand, she made her way to the front door, stumbling and banging only one table and knocking its contents to the floor.

When she opened up, he said, "Hi."

She felt a grin tip one side of her mouth as a happy dance went on inside her. "Hey, stranger. Long time no see. It's ten o'clock. Does your mama know you're out?" Her voice sounded too loud.

He frowned and tucked back his chin, then shot a glance at the locomotive clock. "I was hoping you had some pie left over." He stuffed his hands into his jeans pockets, the muscles in his forearms flexing. "To go, of course."

She glanced over her shoulder at the plates of cookies sitting on the end of the lunch counter. "How
about a chocolate chip cookie? They're stolen."

"Stolen?"

"Well, I mean the reshi"—she rolled her eyes and
licked her lips—"the rec-i-pe's stolen."

"You stole a recipe?"

"Never mind."

"Still got some coffee?" He grinned and dug a wad
of bills from his pocket. "I've got cash."

She couldn't keep from grinning, too. The fool was
just too fucking charming, as Tanya would say. "I can
probably make some."

He came inside and clumped along behind her in
cowboy boots, back to the lunch counter. She assem-
bled the small coffeepot she used to make the exotic
stuff and threw in some of Tanya's favorite, Cowboy
Breakfast Blend. Then she took the tray of cookies
from the oven and placed a dozen hot cookies on
a plate.

He made an exaggerated show of inhaling. "Man,
do those smell good. Is it safe to eat 'em?"

She cocked her head and stared into his eyes. "Why
not? I'm a really good baker."

"But you said they're stolen."

"Just eat." She set the plate on the counter in front
of him with a clack, then picked up her nearby beer
can and took a long swig. As a non-drinker, she was
more than slightly light-headed after four beers.

His eyes, his gorgeous, sexy, laser blue, Mel Gibson
eyes narrowed to a squint. "You're drinking?"

"I drink." She leveled a hard, if unfocused, look
at him.

He chuckled and chomped down on half a cookie. "How many beers have you had?"

"Who cares?" She glared at him through a squint. "Did anyone ever tell you you look like Mel Gibson?"

He grinned, reaching for another cookie. "Once or twice. But I'm bigger. And younger. Who's taking care of your mom?"

"She's asleep. Out cold." She finished off the beer with one long swallow. Turning her back on him, she opened the trash can's lid just a crack with the foot pedal and slipped the empty can inside. No way did she want him to see the three cans she had already emptied.

"So who's gonna eat all these cookies?" he asked.

"I might feed them to the roadrunners. Wildlife needs cookies, too."

"If this is a party, we need some music." He sauntered over to the old jukebox and plugged it in. She heard the clatter of dropping coins, and Patsy Cline's clear voice filled the room with "Sweet Dreams." He walked back to where she stood by the lunch counter and motioned to her with his finger. "C'mon."

She stayed glued in place, determined not to be ordered around by the man who had made her heart ache for weeks now.

He grasped her wrist and pulled her forward. "Let's dance."

Her boot toe caught on the edge of the lunch counter and she fell forward. He caught her with one strong arm and pressed her body against his. He grinned again and closed her right hand into his left. Heat. The desert temperature was hot enough. She didn't need additional heat. She pushed against him a little. "I don't want to dance."

He resisted her push and turned her in a circle. "I think we've done this before. You must be having man trouble again. So tell me what it's all about this time. Lanny's family?"

What right did he have to pry? "No," she said sharply as the room tipped to the left.

"Ben told me what happened."

"You know, he really should mind his own damn business. He's worse than any old maid I ever saw."

"Shh-shh. It wouldn't work, Marisa."

"How the hell do *you* know?"

"Because I know you. You're one of those honest women."

"Well, so what? You say that like it's a bad thing. . . . And you don't know me."

"I know you better than you think. Reading people's part of my trade. Honesty's the thing I admire most about you." She looked up, into his face, and he smiled. "That is, besides you being so pretty and having a great body."

She smiled, too. A girl couldn't afford to turn down a compliment. "Oh, yeah?"

"Yeah. You feel good, too." He kept looking at her intently as they moved around the tile floor, as if he were seeing inside her and she kept looking back, glad he was holding on to her. She felt vulnerable and naked and didn't even care. Finally she ducked his gaze and placed her cheek against his neck, felt a quick intake of his breath.

As if the scent of warm man and Safari were Gilead's balm, the knot inside her seemed to untie and the tension of the past weeks and her many dark thoughts drifted away. She turned to butter in his arms.

The next thing she knew, Patsy Cline was singing

"So Wrong," Terry Ledger's left hand was cupping her jaw and they were kissing and it was slow and sweet in all the ways she liked and as familiar as if they had done it a thousand times. Not one thing about it felt "so wrong." Yet it was different from the first time, perhaps because, being slightly drunk, she was less inhibited.

He lifted his mouth from hers and their gazes locked. They kissed again, deeply, with hands everywhere and panting breath. Beyond the lust on his lips she tasted something she hadn't expected—loneliness. A yearning for home. Until now, he hadn't quite captured her heart. There had always been an open door for her to escape, for until this moment he hadn't convinced her he was real.

When their lips parted again, she was his.

She slid her hands up his arms and around his shoulders. His head lowered and his open mouth pressed soft and warm on the curve where her neck met her shoulder as he moved her to the music. She thought of the apartment behind the café and the bed she had shared with Woody many times, the one with the mattress now bare of sheets. After Woody's confession, in a fit, she had ripped off the old sheets, stuffed them in the burn barrel and never remade the bed. Now, desire heightened by Budweiser, she hooked the fingers of one hand behind his belt buckle and gave a little tug.

He caught her hand and moved it, but didn't stop teasing her neck with his lips. "Don't you need to go home and check on your mom?"

"Hmm," she murmured and tilted her head for more of his mouth.

He complied, his lips traveling over her shoulders,

the slope of her breasts. His tongue touched sensitive places and sent shivers from her nose to her toes.

As if they had minds of their own, her fingers went back to his belt and tugged the end from its loop. A deep hum came from his throat and he gripped her hand again. "You're playing with fire."

"I hope so," she said softly. She wrapped her arms around his waist, hooked her hands on his shoulders and pressed herself against his fly. His erection felt like an iron rod pushing against her belly. She reached down and undid the top button of his jeans, found his zipper.

He stopped abruptly and set her away. "Not while you're drunk."

"I'm not drunk."

"Let's cool it. I'll help you close this place up. Then I'll take you home."

The first thing that struck Marisa when she reached the café the next morning was how wide open Pecos Belle's was, how huge the display windows were. Huge enough for anyone passing by to get an eyeful of her dancing and making out with Terry. She walked to the front door and gazed back across the flea market to the café, trying to determine if anyone who might have seen them could tell where he had his hands. Unable to decide, she dragged herself back to the kitchen, ate a slice of bread and swallowed two aspirin.

She got through lunch without a "special" and no one seemed to notice or mind. By late afternoon, the physical agony of a beer hangover had diminished and she felt better. Now total mortification sneaked in. What had she been thinking, getting drunk in the kitchen, then behaving like a sex-starved twit? Lord, she had even tried to unzip his pants.

And what would *he* be thinking today? She had a nagging suspicion she knew and if she knew men, he would show up before the day ended. She had given him a green light. No stud worth his manhood would let that go unpursued. Then again, he might be so embarrassed by her being drunk and forward he would never want to see her again.

With those upsetting thoughts in mind, she returned to the singlewide to check on things there. Mama was asleep in her recliner. Marisa went back to Pecos Belle's and busied herself preparing for the evening's diners, all the while telling herself she *wasn't* waiting for Terry. But as every hour passed and he didn't put in an appearance, her mood darkened.

She had already wiped down the tables and chairs and was working on the lunch counter when he came through the front door. She stopped her task and looked at him. He hesitated just inside the doorway. Even from across the room, she saw the look in his eyes, that predatory hunger. So he was as transparent as most of the other men she had known. Instead of being repelled by that discovery, she had an odd feeling of relief and self-satisfaction. He did want sex with her as much as she wanted sex with him.

He twisted the dead bolt with a heavy metallic *snick* and turned the OPEN sign to CLOSED. The sane, sensible part of her, the part that stood watch over her virtue, told her to protest, to proclaim that she hadn't yet decided to close the café, but sane, sensible and virtuous were weak defenses against the iniquitous woman inside her that had spent the day anticipating fantastic sex with a hunky guy.

Fearing he could read her mind, she returned to wiping down the lunch counter, though as he ambled through the flea market, she sneaked peeks from the corner of her eye. In tight Levi's and a bright blue T-shirt, he looked more delicious than her best cream pie. And just as edible.

Then, in what seemed like seconds, he was standing at the end of the lunch counter. That aura of S-E-X was glowing around him like neon and her heart was trying to leap out of her chest.

"Hey," he said softly, then came to her side and placed a possessive hand on her back, his palm hot against her thin tank top. Enveloped by the smell of him, the feel of him so close, the very idea of him, she didn't know what to say. She felt her face flame at the wanton behavior that had overtaken her last night. "I'm still open," she managed.

"No, you're not. I just locked the door. I'll get the lights if you tell me how." He turned her to face him, cupped her jaw with a large hand and kissed her, long and slow, with a tantalizing hint of tongue. God help her, she kissed him back, like for like.

In time, their mouths parted, but his eyes held hers. "I thought about you all night," he said huskily.

She placed her forearms between them. "I was drunk last night."

"But you're not tonight." His eyes still locked on hers, he grasped her dish towel, pulled it from her hand and dropped it on the counter. He bent to kiss her again, but she turned her head to the side.

His hot mouth found her neck instead of her lips. "And after you spent the night inside my head, I woke up this morning with a blue-steel hard-on. All I could think about all day was kissing you all over, teasing that belly ring with my tongue."

A shiver raced down her spine. *Eek!*

"Terry, please. Someone could see us." She freed herself from his arms and as if by rote, picked up the dish towel and sashayed to the kitchen. Big mistake, because he followed to where her only escape was through the kitchen's back door, into the apartment. Her heart pounded harder. She turned on the water in the sink. A cloud of steam rose in the tight space and dampened her face as she thrust the towel under the stream of hot water. "Honestly, Terry, this is such a mistake." She twisted the towel, wrung out water. "And I've got to finish cleaning."

"I'll help you later," he said, standing behind her, running his fingers along her upper arm. Heat from his body against her back combined with the steam from the water, making the room feel like a humid cocoon.

Preparing to close the café, she had turned off the overhead kitchen light before he came in. Now in the subdued light from the under-cabinet fixture, his arms came around her waist. His hand slipped under her tank top and bra. He deftly undid it and she went soft all over at the release of her breasts into his hands. The room began to spin, and her eyelids fluttered closed.

His open mouth landed on her shoulder. His hands caressed; his fingers teased and plucked at her nipples until they became hard and eager and her deepest vaginal muscles began to flex. His mouth moved up to her ear. "You feel it inside you when I do that, don't you?"

"Yes," she answered in a tiny voice.

What she also felt was chaos. Her nerves seemed to be strung along the very surface of her skin and the words whispered in his deep voice played them like guitar strings. *Godohgod.*

He knows too much about women. And about sex, the protector of her virtue warned her.

A hum came from his throat as his tongue flicked against her neck, and all she could think of was those shameless flicks in other places. She gave up, dropped the towel into the sink and leaned back against him. She could be a good girl tomorrow.

He got the message. In one quick move, he reached around her with his left hand and turned off the water. At the same time his right hand slid inside her elastic waistband and down into her bikini panties. Without a second thought she spread her legs. His fingers combed into her pubic hair and began to stroke her where she felt swollen and hot. After her imagination had worked overtime all day, she felt instantly wet. He took advantage. *Oh. God.* She hated having him know. "Terry—"

"Shhh. Just let me in," he murmured, his fingers parting her and probing.

On a soft moan, she gripped the edge of the sink, bent her knees and felt herself open.

His fingers easily slid into her wetness and she felt herself flex around them. "That's it," he whispered. "Just pretend this is my eight inches sliding all the way to your heart."

She squeezed her eyes shut, the visual all too vivid. Her breathing grew shallow. Every rational thought left her mind, replaced by the utter bliss of being tormented in all the right places by a man who knew where they were. He played at will until she was almost crazy with desire and frustration. She was so ready.

When she thought she couldn't wait another minute, his fingers moved to the throbbing heart of the issue. The instant he touched her clitoris her brain turned to red mush and she began to spasm hard. She bit down on her lower lip, stifling the outcry that rushed to her throat, but she was helpless to stop the animal grunts that escaped instead.

When she finished, her dignity as well as her strength decimated, his hand cupped her between her legs and pulled her back against him. With the other hand, he brought her face around to his and kissed her, his tongue sweeping into her mouth and stroking with an erotic rhythm. When they broke to breathe, he whispered against her lips, "I knew you'd be easy. I just knew it."

"I'm not easy," she said weakly, struggling for the strength to stand straight.

"Trust me. It's a good thing."

He was the devil in person. "Let me go," she said, doing her best to be insulted, and giving him an elbow in the midriff.

He relaxed his grip and removed his hand from inside her pants, allowing the scent of her moisture to escape in the tight, steamy room. He splayed his hand across her stomach and continued to hold her against him, fitting the cleft of her backside against an erection that felt like steel.

"What are we gonna do about this?" he murmured against her ear. "Turnabout's fair play."

Embarrassed now at being *easy,* she couldn't look him in the face, but that didn't mean she didn't want that eight inches right where he had promised it. Her knees still felt like jelly and she drew a shuddery breath. "I have to make Mama's supper and put her to bed. If you want to stay in the apartment and wait for me, I can come back afterward. . . . There's, uh . . . a, uh, bedroom—"

"Can't you just come to my place?"

"I don't want the phone to ring and me not be where I can answer it. Mama usually goes to bed by eight thirty or nine."

He turned her in his arms and smiled down at her. "I'll be here." He kissed her, so soft and so sweet and so impossible to resist.

On shaky legs and smelling like sex, she left Pecos Belle's with good-looking, rich and horny Terry Ledger waiting in the apartment behind the café. This was the stuff fairy tales were made of. Or porno movies.

She had just reached the singlewide when Ben's pickup pulled up outside.

Oh, crap.

Soon she heard his footsteps on the deck and rapping on the door. "I brought some barbecue from Freeman's in Midland," he said when she opened the door. "I got Raylene a CD and I'm in a dancin' mood."

Oh, hell. From the sound of him, he was back on the Jack. And Marisa knew better than to leave her mother in his care when he was in such sorry shape.

He came in, dropped a greasy sack on the dining table and went straight to the CD player. Along with the smoky, pungent smell of barbecue, something loud and country filled the small living room.

Mama had already risen from her chair. "Get yourself over here, Clyde, and swing me around this floor."

Goddamnit! Great. Just great.

Chapter 21

A man shouldn't raise his expectations when it came to women. Terry had lived by that axiom all his life and it hadn't been proven wrong yet. He told himself this as he shaved.

Last night, he had waited like a dumbass in the café apartment until Marisa came and told him her mom and Ben were dancing and she had to stay with them. Terry had come home with a case of blue balls like he hadn't suffered since he was a teenager.

He stepped into the shower muttering a string of oaths.

Hadn't he already lectured himself a dozen times on the stupidity of getting involved with Marisa? Hadn't he matured past letting his libido drive his behavior? What he needed to do was make sure he had food in his kitchen so he didn't even have to go to that café to eat. Ever again.

Besides, the damn thing would soon be gone. He had already gotten bids from a couple of construction companies out of Odessa for the cost of razing the whole building. And if the café was gone, Marisa and her mother would be gone, too. On that alarming thought, he turned off the water and stepped out of the shower.

Fuck. He didn't want Marisa to be gone. He didn't want her mother to be gone. Her nearly marrying Lanny had been a close enough call. *Fuck*. He didn't know what the hell he wanted. He should stall before accepting one of the demolition bids on the Pecos Belle's building.

But this morning he didn't have time to stew over Marisa and her business. This morning he had to catch up with the surveying crew, to whom he was paying a hefty sum to lay out lots and streets for Ledger Ranches. No doubt they had started at the crack of dawn to get in a few hours of work before the heat wiped them out.

In his fridge he found a package of hot dogs. Good enough. Since when did he think he needed eggs over easy, cooked to perfection, sugar-cured bacon or buttered biscuits that melted in his mouth? He tore open the package of wieners and placed four in the microwave. He made two sandwiches by folding a slice of bread around two hot dogs and washed them down with a quart of orange juice. The breakfast of champions. A meal he had eaten a thousand times as a kid.

Leaning a hip against the counter and chewing, he reviewed his behavior toward Marisa. Last night he had gone at her like a horny teenager, an approach that was all wrong. He had watched guys put the old full-court press on women, but until Marisa, he had never done it. His style had always been subtler—lunch, dinner, good wine, good entertainment, conversation. And things had always evolved in a positive way toward the bedroom and in the bedroom. Testimony to the fact was that even when he and a woman parted, they usually remained friends.

He might as well face it. What he wanted just as much as he wanted her body was to get to know her. Sex would naturally follow, but for now, he wanted to know what made her tick, what made her happy or sad. He didn't know her likes and dislikes, didn't know how it must have been for an only child growing up in the isolation of an outpost like Agua Dulce. True, he was an only child himself—they had that in common—but he, at least, had grown up in a real town around ordinary people.

He had heard from Ben that she and Lanny had gone out on dates several times, with Lanny hiring a sitter for her mother. Terry could do the same. If he could get Marisa out of Agua Dulce, they could at least have a conversation without something in the café interrupting or one of the town's citizens showing up with a new problem.

He picked up the phone and punched the café's number, which he now had on speed dial. When she answered in her soft alto, words refused to form on his tongue. "Hi," was the best he could think of.

"What's up?" she asked. He heard wariness in her tone, yet he couldn't keep from chuckling at the double entendre. "You really wanna know?"

A pause. He suspected she rolled her eyes as he had seen her do a dozen times. "Well, you know what I mean," she said in a I'm-in-no-mood-for-jokes voice. "What's going on?"

"I was just thinking, why don't we go out?"

"Out where?"

"Ben told me you went out with Lanny. We could go over to Odessa or Midland for dinner."

Another pause. He imagined her cussing Ben for

gossiping. "I don't know," she said. "It's a hundred miles and it was a hassle. Finding someone to stay with Mama isn't that easy."

"What if I take care of it? What if I find someone? You won't have to do anything but dress up and look pretty." He couldn't believe his ears. He was *negotiating* taking a woman out to dinner.

He heard shuffling noises in the background, muffled voices. "Be with you in just a minute," Marisa said. She obviously wasn't talking to him.

"Listen," he said in frustration, "I've got to catch up with my surveying crew, but I'll work on it. I'll let you know what I come up with."

"Sure. I gotta go." She hung up.

He stood there staring at the phone, thrown off balance by what had just happened. The positive thinker in him wanted to feel good because she hadn't said no, but he couldn't get past the distinct feeling he had been brushed off anyway. *Fuck.*

"Women," he mumbled.

Then he sighed. No, not *women—Marisa.*

Marisa stood in the café's tiny kitchen, breaking eggs onto the griddle's hot surface, appreciating each one's sizzle not rising above a whisper. How many eggs had she cooked on this griddle, she wondered as she lifted the bacon press and checked the strips of bacon. The familiarity of doing it day after day gave her roots in a rootless world.

She had half expected she might not hear from Terry again. He had been mad last night. He didn't say so, hadn't thrown a tantrum, but she had seen anger in his eyes, in his tightly controlled body language as he left the apartment.

She hadn't been in the best of spirits herself and the night had been forty hours long. And to compound her distress, today she had awakened from her few hours of sleep mortified beyond words by what had happened in the café kitchen. A matter of seconds and she had gone off like some damn rocket. He must think her a sex maniac. He had even called her "easy."

And now he was asking her for a date? What was up with that? An old saying she had heard all her life came to her about a man not taking the cow when he could get the milk for free. She sighed and scooped breakfasts onto four plates. She wanted to cry, but she didn't have time.

He must be serious about a date if he had volunteered to find a sitter for Mama. It was true that the woman from Pecos whom Lanny had hired to stay with Mama was available on almost any evening. Her day job was working as a home health nurse, so she was fully qualified to contend with a patient like Mama. Marisa could make Terry's life easier by giving him her name. But a crotchety part of her didn't want to make his life easier. Besides, he could also get the woman's name from Ben. He seemed to get all sorts of other information from Ben.

She grabbed a couple of biscuits she had baked earlier and slid them into the microwave. She hated rewarming her light-as-a-feather biscuits in the microwave and turning them heavy as lead, but it was the best she could do with the equipment she had. Customers didn't complain.

Besides being disgruntled with herself, she was unhappier than usual this morning with Ben. He and Mama had played music and danced for hours.

Marisa felt a nagging annoyance at Terry, too. Yet, where he was concerned, an even deeper conflict roiled within her. A tiny, traitorous part of her supported his development and wanted him to succeed. In fact, she had come to worry over the financial risk he had taken in this desolate part of the world almost as much as she worried about her own future.

He came in at noon, took a seat at the lunch counter and ordered a hamburger. She had no time to sit, but managed to talk to him as she flitted back and forth cooking and waiting on customers. And overshadowing her every activity and even her conversation with total strangers ordering food was the picture of herself hanging on to the edge of the kitchen sink, lost in an incredible orgasm.

"I found someone," he said on one of her passes to the kitchen. "Ben gave me the phone number and the woman's name who stayed with your mom before."

She stopped and looked at him.

"She says she can stay from six to midnight," he said. "That gives us enough time to drive to Odessa for dinner. Or we could skip dinner and see a movie if you like."

Why was he doing this? Hadn't she already proved that with her being "easy," wining and dining were unnecessary? "Look, Terry—"

"This isn't about just wanting a hot body, Marisa. I want to start over. I want to do this right."

"And you think going out to dinner somehow changes something?" The response was a *gotcha*, for sure.

He sat there looking at her, his hamburger poised above his plate. She didn't have to be a genius to decipher what she saw in his eyes. Nor was it necessary to give him a speech on raw animal attraction.

He shook his head once, then turned back to his burger. He bit out a chunk and chewed. "Okay, think about this. I want us to get acquainted, build some history."

Ha. That was a new one. Men were so dumb. But bless his heart for trying to be gallant and trying to put a puritanical face on what they both wanted. She couldn't keep from chuckling. "Okay, so we spend an evening lying to each other about our life stories. *Then* we fall into bed. Or the backseat. Or something."

"No backseat. I don't have a car and the crew cab's too small."

She chuckled again. "Haven't you ever heard where there's a will, there's a way?"

He grinned. "C'mon. Stop giving me a hard time. I'm trying to be a gentleman here."

Now that her daydreams about him loomed as a reality, in truth, she felt confused and not up to acting out the fantasy. "Honestly, I'm not trying to be difficult. I just feel like I need to say, 'Why me?' You must know a bunch of glamorous chicks who've got a lot more to offer than I do."

"It's true I know some glamorous chicks, but that's all they are. It is *not* true that they've got more to offer than you. You're one of the few women I've ever met that I trust."

So who had broken his heart? She felt a frown tug at her brow. "You must have been keeping some pretty bad company."

"I'm trying to change that. Let's go to dinner tonight and enjoy an evening out. No strings, no obligations."

After he had touched her intimately and driven her to fall apart in his arms, she didn't believe the last part, but what did she have to lose by going to dinner? She lifted a shoulder. "Okay. But only if it's somewhere the food is decent. I don't want to see you pay good money for bad food."

Marisa closed Pecos Belle's early. Before dressing for her date with Terry, she carried clean bed linen to the apartment and made up the bed. Just in case one of her aunts showed up to spend the night, she told herself.

Then she showered and shampooed and debated if she should just wear clean jeans and a shirt or one of her few dresses. She had shaved her legs in the shower, just in case it became important, and as she creamed them, she checked the yellow rose showing on her left ankle, wondering how many women Terry had dated who had tattoos. On her olive skin, the tattoo wasn't as obvious as the ones on Tanya's pale skin, but it still could be easily seen.

Men had told her they thought her yellow rose sexy. In her own opinion it didn't compare to the happy face at the edge of her pubic hair. She shared the story of how and when she had acquired the happy face with no one.

She put on a yellow cotton sundress with white daisies around the hem. Very girly and un-Marisa. She pinned up her thick, straight hair with a plastic claw clip, from which tendrils escaped immediately and hung down her neck. She considered her only pair of high heels, but she hadn't worn them in more than a year. She could break an ankle. She slipped her feet into tan sandals.

The sitter came, bringing a crochet project to pass the time.

Terry soon followed, wearing khakis and a peacock blue button-down and drenched in Safari, the whole package as luscious as a rich lava cake. Hmm. Blue was definitely his color. Those fantastic sky-colored eyes roamed over her appreciatively, making her glad she had decided to wear the dress.

On the drive to Odessa, he talked about his years as an Army Ranger and living in Europe and Italy and the Middle East. He talked about the joy of sky-diving and hang gliding. He had to be nuts.

She had no such adventures to relate; nevertheless, she told him about her half-assed efforts to become a chef and the years she had spent turning out rubber food in the better-known family restaurants in Midland and Arlington.

They dined on filet mignon broiled to a perfect medium rare. Perhaps she could have done it better; then again, maybe not. They talked, they laughed, they looked into each other's eyes and found no time for being distracted by a movie. They even danced. The tension mounted between them. Some things were just inevitable.

Toward the end of the evening, he pulled a brochure from his shirt pocket and slid it across the table to her. On its cover was a colorful array of hot-air balloons. "Breakfast in heaven," he said. "Anytime you say."

"I don't get it." She opened the brochure, read about a champagne breakfast package with a hot-air-balloon company in Albuquerque. "Wow. I know people who've done this, but—"

"Two or three days. I'll find someone to stay with your mom."

"Terry, it isn't necessary for you—"

"It is necessary, Marisa. C'mon. Say yes. You aren't afraid, are you?"

She studied him across the table. It seemed logical that a man who would skydive and hang glide for fun would just naturally invite a date to go soaring in a hot-air balloon. Of course they would sleep together during the two or three days. All that had prevented it before now was a lack of convenience. "Not of riding in a hot-air balloon."

"What, then? Is it me? You're afraid of me?"

"I have to be. There's nowhere for you and me to go. You're already wiping out mine and Mama's livelihood, but you could wipe out more than that." She pressed her palm against her chest. "You could wipe out *me,* Terry. It wasn't as scary when I thought we were just going to sneak a little recreational sex."

"You're not the recreational-sex type."

You don't know everything, she thought, but she laughed. "Oh, right. What was it you said? I'm one of those *honest* women? I'm also easy, remember?"

"Facts are facts, pretty lady. I happen to believe you're not nearly as hard-assed as you try to make everyone think. In Agua Dulce, you mother-hen the whole damn place, but as far as I can tell, no one looks after you. . . . And something tells me no one ever has."

His last statement jolted her and left her feeling starkly exposed. It was true. Marisa had always known it, but never acknowledged it aloud. Mama had never been June Cleaver. The two of them had been more like friends looking out for each other than mother taking care of daughter. Even as a child, Marisa had frequently been the decision maker in their two-female household.

Marisa had accepted long ago that her mother marched to a different drummer. Born the year Hitler invaded Poland, Mama had turned twenty-one in 1960, which meant she had a foot in each of two drastically different social camps—the generation of responsible, dedicated Americans who fought and won World War II and the if-it-feels-good-do-it movement of the sixties and seventies. Indeed, the clutch of eccentrics around whom Marisa had grown up included her mother.

An unexpected burn flashed behind her eyes. Some truths were just too hard to face. "I don't need looking after."

"Everyone does, Marisa, at some point."

"That may be true for some, but I'm perfectly capable of taking care of myself. And I'm the only person I know who's one hundred percent reliable."

"Try me," he said, his eyes holding hers. "I'm reliable. I promise I won't wipe you out. I've already said I'm after more than fun and games. I didn't used to be, but I am now."

Was that a warning or a promise? Her pulse surged. "Is this a new urge or something you've been thinking about for a while?"

"All I know is I want to see where we can go. If you're as gutsy as I think you are, you'll stick with me."

Without a doubt, Terry Ledger was the most exciting and interesting man she had ever met. And now he had shown an insight and depth of understanding that was almost overwhelming. She, too, wanted to see where they could go, though she didn't trust either him or her own emotions. Looking into his beautiful, gentle eyes, she couldn't keep a smile from sneaking across her lips. "I guess we could start with Albuquerque."

He grinned like an elated little boy and she imagined him jumping from his chair, pumping his fist and yelling, "Yes!" He took back the brochure. "Okay, then. It's done. I'll put it together."

And she had no doubt he would. Just like that, she had a date to spend a day or two with a millionaire. Mere months ago, such a possibility was more remote than a trip to China. She wanted to be flattered and thrilled, because he aroused emotions totally new. Unfortunately, they were as frightening as they were new.

They held hands all the way home and he continued to talk—about his high school years in Odessa. He had played quarterback at Permian High School, had received several college scholarship offers, but to spite his parents, for whom he harbored anger to this day, he passed up college, joined the army and had never been sorry.

He dragged information from her about her life. She told him about dropping out of culinary school in Dallas because she felt guilty taking money from her mother, but when she couldn't make enough at a part-time job to sustain both school and herself, it was school she sacrificed.

He smiled at her across the cab and squeezed her hand. "That would be like you."

After Mama's sitter departed, they stood wrapped in each other's arms at her front door and smooched like kids for what seemed like far too short a time. Only supreme will kept her from hauling him inside the mobile to her bedroom. He was right in that Mama probably would never know, but something inside her wouldn't allow her to take the risk.

Long after she went to bed, she found herself staring into the darkness, thinking. In her whole history with men, what guy had ever been better company than Terry? The answer: none. What guy had been more honest? Again, the answer: none. He had made her no promises, just openly and honestly asked her to step out onto a tall building's ledge. With him. Was she the daredevil he was?

They did have something in common. Their childhoods had been hauntingly similar—each filled with lonely hours and insecurity and a powerful instinct to survive. She dared to let herself fantasize how a future could be with a man like him.

Her thoughts drifted to Albuquerque. Since moving back to Agua Dulce, she hadn't left Mama for more than a few hours at a time. Terry had said he would locate someone to stay with her, but she could think of no one acceptable. Unless . . .

Unless one of her aunts would be willing to come and stay a couple of days. Of course—that was the answer. Neither of them had been to see Mama in months. Aunt Rosemary and Aunt Radonna—they were the solution.

Chapter 22

"I know you're busy." Marisa raised her voice to be heard over loud laughter coming through the receiver and a female voice belting out "Redneck Woman" in the background. Marisa's aunt Radonna had managed a raunchy bar in Odessa for several years. "I tried to reach Aunt Rosemary, but Uncle Duane said she's in Missouri."

"Yeah," Aunt Radonna yelled. Marisa was forced to hold the receiver a few inches from her ear. "The woman burns up the highway visiting her kids and their rug rats. She'll do anything to get away from that asshole she married. I'll bet those poor kids hate to see her coming."

Aunt Rosemary's three daughters and a bevy of grandchildren lived in three different states. The aunt had a reputation for starting trouble wherever she went and quarreling with her daughters and sons-in-law. Just as she did with Mama and Aunt Radonna. Marisa laughed at her aunt's quip, though she suspected it was no joke.

Marisa had never understood the three Rutherford sisters' relationship. They didn't see each other often and rarely had good things to say about each other, yet they considered themselves a fiercely loyal family.

Growing up listening to the back-biting and spite-fulness among them, Marisa had often thought that if she had been lucky enough to have a sister, she would have made certain they got along and were pals. To Aunt Radonna's credit, though she didn't frequently come to Agua Dulce to visit Mama, she did call occasionally.

While her aunt Rosemary had been unhappily married to her first and only husband for years, Aunt Radonna had been married several times. She had no children and at present was between husbands.

Marisa knew only surface facts about her mother's family, but she surmised something had gone badly awry for all three of the sisters to have such screwed-up relationships with men. Maybe it was in the genes. Maybe a genetic component explained her own failures with the opposite sex. "So how about it, then, Aunt Donna? Can you stay with Mama a couple of days?"

"Sure, darlin'. I need to come see her anyway. How is she?"

"Probably worse than when you saw her last. To be honest, I don't know if she'll know who you are. She still mentions Aunt Rosemary sometimes, but—"

"But not me, eh? . . . Well, we were never close. Nearly ten years difference in our ages, you know. But that doesn't mean I don't love her. Hold on, darlin', while I close this door. Damn drunks." The background noise shut down and Radonna came back on, speaking in a normal voice. "So my little niece is going off to shack up with some guy, huh? I hope he's a good lay." She cackled.

Marisa winced. "It's not like that. He's just a friend who—"

"Baby doll, you won't get any criticism from your ol' auntie. Life's what you make it. I say take every interesting chance you get. I can't come over there on a weekend, sugar. Weekends are when these booze-hounds sow their wildest oats. It'll be Tuesday before I can get some help in here to corral 'em."

Marisa agreed to Tuesday and they disconnected. Afterward she hesitated before calling Terry to tell him she had found a sitter. Even at this late date, she had misgivings about a two- or three-day trip with him. Wild and crazy sex for a few hours was different from spending days and nights with someone. Sharing the morning after was a new—and possibly dangerous— threshold.

Terry didn't come into the café all day, which was just as well, Marisa reasoned. She had more customers than usual and thus was extremely busy. Still, all through her evening closing procedure, she speculated on why he hadn't come. All through getting Mama's supper, she worried.

Mama was in bed by nine. After a hot, busy day, Marisa longed for a lengthy bath herself, so she filled the tub, added two different kinds of water softener and finally, some of Mama's bubble bath. She loved West Texas, but sometimes something as simple as a bubble bath was a major undertaking. As she soaked, she continued to debate if or when she should call Terry and tell him about her aunt Radonna agreeing to come.

Or should she wait until she saw him again?

Or should she call him and back out of the trip altogether?

A yes answer to the latter question would be the safest. Of that she had no doubt.

After her bath she pulled on some lighweight pants and a T-shirt and sat down in front of the TV with her magazine of crossword puzzles. This was how she spent many evenings, but tonight the clock hands seemed to be stuck. If she went to bed before ten, she would be wide awake at three.

On TV, a meteorologist reported that Cabell County was experiencing its fifth-driest year in history. Who cared? Cabell County was a desert. Only a scientist would be able to tell one dry year from another. The difference between a dry year and a wet year, the meteorologist reported, was eight inches.

Just pretend this is my eight inches sliding all the way to your heart.

She huffed. Eight inches. He wished.

Well, thanks to the TV weatherman, at least she had now owned up to the reason for her restlessness. She had to find something to think about besides sex with Terry Ledger. Disgusted, she slipped her feet into flip-flops, her arms into a sweat jacket and walked outside. There, she turned on the radio and dropped into one of the rocking chairs on the deck.

Terry paced in his kitchen. All day he had waited for Marisa's call confirming that one of her aunts was willing to stay with Raylene while he and Marisa went to Albuquerque.

Nine thirty. By now, she would have put her mother to bed. The day's unrelenting heat had begun to give way to evening's temperature drop, so he slipped on a nylon windbreaker and headed on foot for the Rutherford singlewide.

As he walked, far on the distant horizon he spotted a flare, a lone fire used like a giant candle to burn gas off oil wells or drilling sites and prevent wildfires and explosions. When he was a kid, before the collapse of the oil industry, the nighttime West Texas landscape had been peppered with burning flares as numerous as city lights. Now, with oil exploration curtailed, flares were few, but most of the ones he could see probably had some attachment to Lanny Winegardner's oil kingdom.

The ever-constant zephyr from the west touched his face, the night's silence filled his ears. Smells—sage and sulphur gas—seemed pronounced in the darkness.

Above the crunch of his footsteps, music floated through the air, something with a sad note. At first he thought it came from Ben's mobile, but then he realized it drifted from Marisa's direction. Recognizing "It's Getting Better All the Time," he stopped and listened. The song was a slow one by Brooks and Dunn, about recovering from a broken heart. For some damn reason, Terry thought of the day he met Marisa and the asshole who had two-timed her. He had never done that to a woman. But then, he had never really had a *committed* relationship, either. Sex for the hell of it wasn't commitment.

Drawing nearer to the singlewide, he saw her on the deck slumped in one of the rocking chairs, one foot propped on the deck rail, her hair falling behind the chair back.

You could wipe out me, Terry.

A warning charged from somewhere deep within him, a mysterious consciousness telling him to be careful of her feelings and to protect her. From what, exactly, he didn't know. He didn't want to hurt her. But he didn't want to give up being with her, either. The scolding from his psyche rattled him, but he shook off the sensation and moved on.

He didn't typically have protective feelings about women. Most of the ones he met were in the business world and were often tougher than he. They didn't display the sweetness and feminine vulnerability he sensed in Marisa.

"Nice night," he said before he reached the deck, not wanting to startle her.

She startled despite his warning, and stood up.

As he stepped onto the deck, though she had on a jacket, it was open and he saw that she was braless in a thin T-shirt. The tension that instantly coiled in his belly nearly took his breath. Coupled with the mysterious protectiveness that had fallen on him just seconds earlier, a million words rushed into his head. None seemed to find their way to his mouth, probably because all the blood had drained from his brain to his groin. "I didn't scare you, did I?"

Marisa heard the tenderness in his baritone voice and was moved by it, though not surprised. He had already shown himself as being more gentle-natured than the ruthless businessman she had started out believing him to be. "A little," she said and smiled. "I didn't recognize your voice at first."

His walking up on her had left her a little shaky, so when he came forward a few steps and, without a word, wrapped her in his arms, she leaned into him, snuggled against his shoulder and breathed in the scent of him. He smelled clean and musky and she slipped her arms under his jacket, around his waist, and caressed the firm muscles of his back, just like they were old and familiar lovers. The scene at the kitchen sink filled her mind and she couldn't deny the desire just touching him aroused. She even felt wetness between her thighs.

"Hmm," he said. "You feel good. And you smell good. Like flowers."

"Lavender bubble bath. I borrowed some of Mama's."

Vince Gill's breathy voice came on the radio singing of the power and pain of being found by love. In Terry Ledger's arms she had no problem relating to the song's message, though her sense of self-preservation warned her against being sucked into a fantasy.

He began to move her around the deck in a slow dance. "We do this pretty well," he murmured.

She drew in a deep breath, willed herself to ignore the poetic words of Vince's song. Through the thin fabric of her pants she could feel the firmness at his fly. "Something tells me you didn't come here to dance."

"I don't know why I came." His hands slid to her bottom. "It's just that you've been on my mind all day. I wanted to see you."

She looked into his eyes and believed his words. "Me, too," she said softly, loving the tenderness in his strong hands. She freed her arms from beneath his jacket, slid them up to his neck, rose to her tiptoes and pasted her lips to his. He tightened his hold on her bottom and began to kiss her with long, slow kisses that tasted like peppermint. She sensed an urgency in him and pushed her tongue into his mouth, deepening the kiss. He met her with equal passion and soon they were devouring each other's mouths like hungry coyotes.

"I don't want to wait 'til Albuquerque," he said hoarsely.

She pushed away and stepped back, fighting for breath. He stood there, his eyes homed in on hers. There was no mistaking the desire she saw in him. Oh, hell. Sex tonight, sex in Albuquerque. What difference did it make? "Wait a minute," she said. "I have to get a key."

She went into the mobile, stole up the hall and checked on Mama, then lifted the apartment keys off a hook in the kitchen, glad she had put clean sheets on the bed. Outside, she grabbed his hand and said, "Come on. I don't have that much time."

The minute they closed themselves inside the apartment behind the café, they began tearing at each other's clothing. "You first," she said, helping him shed his windbreaker in the living room. "You're wearing more clothes."

He dropped to the sofa and pried off his boots.

The apartment felt tight and hot, so she switched on the swamp cooler that filled half the window in the living room. When she turned back to him, he had removed his shirt, reavealing a tanned, muscled chest and well-defined biceps. She scanned the line of dark hair that trailed down his flat stomach and disappeared into his waistband. A bulge showed in his jeans and he made no attempt to hide it. An effort to swallow the tennis ball–sized lump in her throat brought nothing but a dry click. Nothing was left to do but lead him to the bedroom.

In the pitch-black bedroom, she groped for the switch on the lamp beside the bed. The tiny space came alive with soft, low light. He was already shucking his Levi's and boxers. Of course he felt no awkwardness at getting naked. The session in the café kitchen had already shown he was an aggressive lover.

For a few beats, her gaze traveled the smooth ridges of muscle that ran from each hip bone down the sides of his belly. Efficient. That was the word that described his body. No fat. Every part had a purpose, including the erection rising as thick and rigid as marble from a nest of dark curls. The very thought of the thing inside her sent a shiver of anticipation through her body. "Oh, you're so—"

"Yours for the taking," he said, his velvet voice rumbly and deep.

She forced herself to look up into his beautiful blue eyes, now dark and stormy with passion. For her. A thrill like she had never known coursed through her and she began to tremble.

She had on no underwear, had to dispose of only three garments. In a matter of two heartbeats, she peeled off her jacket, pulled her T-shirt over her head and dropped her pants. She felt his eyes. They burned her skin from her forehead to her toes.

"You're beautiful," he murmured.

A thank-you didn't seem necessary. Before she could turn back the bed, he came to her, enclosed her in an embrace and kissed her again. His hands moved down and gripped the backs of her thighs. As if she weighed no more than a feather, he lifted her off her feet. Her back hit the comforter that covered the bed. He followed her down, stretching his nakedness alongside hers, rubbing against her, pushing his knee between her thighs, kissing and kissing her all over—her mouth, her neck, her breasts, even her fingertips. She kissed him, too, and stroked him everywhere her hands and mouth could reach.

He stopped abruptly, his breath rasping, his chest heaving. "Can you feel me shaking?"

She did feel the tremor in his body, which only added to the tumult in her own. "Sort of," she replied weakly.

"I haven't been in this bad a shape since I was seventeen."

He resumed where he left off. His hand gathered her breast and his mouth covered one nipple. As his tongue played, delight danced through her, all the way to her sex. Heat began to sizzle through her veins. She clasped his head with one hand and ran the other down the valley of his spine all the way to his taut, sleek buttocks. He felt as good as he looked and she had to have more of him.

She sat up and pushed him to his back. "Let me," she said and suckled his nipples, dragging a little grunt from him. She began licking and kissing her way down his chest and midsection, savoring the salty taste of his skin, inhaling the musky smell of his body. She dipped the tip of her tongue into his navel, slid her hand down between his legs and stroked his hairy scrotum.

"Aw, damn," he ground out.

She teased him more, taking his firm penis into her mouth. A strangled sound came from deep in his throat and his fingers dug into her buttocks.

He let her taste him for only a few seconds before he gripped her shoulders and pulled her back up to his mouth. Then they were kissing again, his hands buried in her hair and holding her still while his tongue delved into her mouth.

She couldn't let go of his erection, relishing how the thick thing filled her hand, loving how his whole body responded when she brushed the tip of him with her thumb.

"You're killing me," he growled, wresting control from her and turning her to her back. His mouth traveled down her neck, over her breasts and lower, sucking in little patches of flesh. So delicious and so arousing, as if she needed to be aroused any more. "Everything," he murmured against her skin. "I want everything."

So did she. And she no longer felt playful. The self she had always held back at such moments demanded to be free. She arched her body and offered him her stomach. "Then take it," she said.

He scooted backward and sank to the floor between her knees, his hands dragging her hips to the edge of the bed. A little burst of axiety skittered around in her chest, but his hands held her like a vise. Even if she had wanted to do something about them, she couldn't think what. It had been so long since a man had loved her in this way.

Like a wanton, she bent her knees and opened herself. His hands slid up the backs of her thighs and pushed her knees high and wide, leaving her totally vulnerable. For a nanosecond she felt panic, but then his warm breath touched her, his late-day stubble rasped her delicate flesh, and his tongue was there, pushing into her. Her breath caught and her neck arched as pure pleasure washed through her like warm May rain.

He French-kissed her in a maddening rhythm. It was wicked and erotic and her hidden places rejoiced. In no time, a throb began deep in her sex. Her hips wanted to move, but couldn't. "Terry—" She grabbed both fists full of his hair and tried to steer his mouth to where she frantically needed it. "Terry, please . . ."

He didn't abandon his mission. Instead, he draped

her legs across his shoulders, grasped her wrists and pinned them to the mattress, his tongue not missing a beat. The need consumed her. White noise roared inside her head, and she began to shake. "Please," she whimpered.

He stopped and pulled back, his eyes burning black as they locked on her sex. She could feel herself convulsing in quick little beats, her deep vaginal muscles begging to receive him. She didn't care if he saw. She wanted him to look at her, wanted him to know he made her hot enough to catch fire. And she wanted the thick hard thing she'd had in her hands and mouth just moments ago inside her body "Hurry," she said.

A corner of his mouth, red and wet from loving her, tipped up.

"No way. This should last a good long time." He leaned into her and began to trail his mouth and tongue along the inside of her thigh. "I love the way you taste. . . ." He moved to the other thigh. "I love the way you smell."

She squirmed and tried to lift herself to him. "Terry . . ."

At last his fingers pushed into her, his tongue touched her clitoris, and fireworks exploded behind her eyes. She sobbed out. His fingers worked inside her, his tongue flicked, his mouth suckled. She sobbed and whimpered as she came again and again. When she could no longer endure the exquisite agony, she begged him to stop.

He stretched and reached for his jeans off the floor. With shaking hands, he found his wallet and a condom. They scrabbled through climbing beneath the covers and together fumbled with rolling on the latex sheath. He seated himself inside her with a thrust so powerful they both gasped, and in that dazzling instant, every male she had ever know vanished. "Oh, God," she whispered almost forgetting to breathe.

"Look at me," he ground out.

She opened her eyes and saw him holding himself motionless above her, his expression intense. Their gazes held as his hips began to rock.

Then, pumping, pumping, hard and fast. Matching his rhythm, the power and force of him filling her, surrounding her, shattering every conscious thought. Sometimes their gazes held each other's; sometimes not. Sometimes they kissed fiercely; sometimes they didn't. But the rhythm and the friction never faltered. The old iron headboard hammered the wall as he flailed into her, rasping, pressuring, driving her to the edge again.

"Come again," he growled.

She did, helpless not to give him all that she was. Panting openmouthed, she fell into a purple void, her deepest muscles milking him.

His jaw clenched. A vein throbbed in his neck and she knew his climax was near. She gripped the stiles in the headboard and dug her heels into the backs of his thighs, pressed against him, her body taut and arched like a drawn bow, urging him, wanting him to know ecstasy equal to hers. His moment came, violent and powerful. His fingers dug into her buttocks. He bucked hard, pounding into her deeply once, twice, three times. She hung on until his body stiffened and a cry tore from him.

Even after he collapsed on top of her she hung on, unable to bear letting him go. They were both sweating and shaking and still he held her tightly, at considerable physical cost, she suspected, after the release he'd just had.

"Awww, God," he gasped at last, rolling to her side and pulling her with him.

They were drenched in sweat, but that wasn't her concern. She was filled with anxiety. Something profound had happened. She just didn't know what.

"That was wild," he whispered, his eyes serious, his chest still heaving.

"I know."

He stroked her hair back from her face, his hand trembling. "You okay?"

No, she was not. He had touched a frightening place no one else had ever found. She had abandoned herself in a way she never had with any man. She opened her mouth to tell him, but she could see in his eyes that he knew. Some kind of line had been crossed and he knew as well as she did that neither of them would ever be able to go back to the safe haven they occupied just an hour before. Still, she managed a tiny nervous laugh. "I think so."

"God, Marisa." He placed a wet kiss on her lips and she tasted her own essence. "You're so—you're just so good."

"You, too," was all she could say.

"Stay here," he said and left the bed for the bathroom in the hall. When he returned and slid back into bed, he maneuvered both of them until they lay belly to belly, then enveloped her in a nest of furry limbs. The heavy scent of fresh sex filled the tiny room. His knee pushed between hers and she slung her leg across his hip. His hand found hers and entwined their fingers. His eyes, always intense, but now even more so, looked into hers. "Do you believe in fate?"

Not confident of her answer, she hesitated. "Sometimes . . . Do—do you?"

"I'm starting to."

If she had ever met anyone who wouldn't believe in fate or karma or any kind of mystical explanation for feelings, it was Terry. "I do believe in a special chemistry," she said softly. "I've read about it. I think I can see it in Tanya and Jake."

"Yeah?" He cradled the back of her head with his hand and kissed the tip of her nose. "How come you're so smart?"

"I'm not. But sometimes there's no other explanation for why two people are together."

"Us? Do we have chemistry?"

"I—I don't know. It feels like it."

He smiled and kissed the corner of her mouth. "I think so, too." He hugged her closer. He was so good at hugging. "When do you have to go?"

She smiled back and ran her instep up his calf, loving the idea that she could, and took their joined hands to her lips. "Soon. An hour maybe."

He buried his nose against her neck. "I don't want you to go. I wish we could stay right here."

She wished the same. She knew of nothing that compared to feeling as small and protected as she did lying against his big solid body. To drop off to sleep in his arms was an even greater temptation than making love with him in the first place. She snuggled closer, pressed her face to his armpit, wanting to permanently mark her senses with his every scent.

They lay in silence, their breathing audible, him holding her like she might bolt and escape. She wanted to say, *A penny for your thoughts,* but didn't dare. He might ask her the same question and she could no more define her emotions at this moment than she could fly.

Just when she thought he had dropped off to sleep, he rolled on top of her and gazed into her eyes.

She laughed softly. "What? I thought you went to sleep."

"If I've got just an hour, I'm gonna make the most of it."

She gave a low chuckle. "Go ahead. You'll get no complaints from me."

He chuckled, too, and trailed his mouth down her body until he reached her gold navel ring. "All I really wanted, you know, was to get at this thing. It's been driving me crazy ever since I first saw it. It was you who insisted on more."

"Guilty," she admitted, chuckling with him again. She liked laughing after sex.

He closed his mouth over the tiny gold orb and gently tugged, flicked her navel with his tongue and moved on down. "Whoa!" he said, sitting back on his heels, and she knew he had spotted her happy face tattoo.

He put his finger on it, his eyes drawn into a squint. "Where'd you get that?"

She lolled there, smiling up at him, feeling soft as a kitten, helpless as a lamb. "Dallas. A long time ago."

"How? . . . and why?"

"July Fourth. Too much catfish. And maybe too much beer."

"And after that, you quit what? Catfish or drinking beer?"

"Both."

"I don't like some tattoo character seeing you there." He covered her mound with his hand.

She laid her hand on top of his. "He didn't see me. I had on a bikini. Those guys are like doctors anyway. They put tattoos everywhere. He wasn't turned on."

"I still don't like it. He saw a private part of you. He's made a mark on you. That little part will be his forever."

She gasped and laughed. "You're jealous?"

He fell forward, braced on his hands, and kissed her hard. "You don't know the half of it. Now that I've found you, I don't want to share any part of you."

A thrill coursed through her. She could think of worse things than having Terry Ledger feel possessive. She slid her hand up his arm and found his nape. "You're my man," she said softly, gazing into his eyes. "Make love to me again. Give me something to dream about. As if you hadn't already."

They parted at midnight. Almost as an afterthought she told him Aunt Radonna would be coming on Tuesday.

Chapter 23

Terry knew no word to describe the euphoric state of mind in which he began his day. His steps felt more solid during his morning run. The sunrise seemed more golden. Even his coffee tasted better.

He had known instinctively that sex with Marisa would be good; he had not known it would be off the chart. He couldn't stop thinking about how her body had responded to his every touch, how she had given him so much more than he expected. He had known they had a connection; he had not known it was so strong that he wouldn't be able to put her out of his mind even to conduct his business.

He called the balloon company and made arrangements for a "romantic breakfast ride" on the coming Tuesday, then set Kim to finding a great place to stay in Albuquerque. When "Good Morning Beautiful," came on the radio, he stopped studying blueprints, listened to the words and remembered the first time he had kissed Marisa. He thought again about how waking with her every morning would indeed make his days beautiful.

He willed himself to work. He discussed some changes in the home designs with Chick in Fort Worth. He discussed the test results on the water well with an engineer in Austin. The contractor who had given him a bid for demolishing Pecos Belle's building called, seeking a commitment, but Terry put him off, unable to bring himself to cause Marisa or her mother any more hardship than they already faced.

At noon he found himself on his deck wasting time talking to the roadrunner as if it were a person. Ben shuffled over in sandals, wagging his guitar. "Don't tell me you're talking to spacemen, too," he growled.

Terry looked at the musician's rumpled clothes, his spikey hair, his unshaven jaw and concluded that he had already been enjoying his favorite beverage.

"Just visiting with Hercules, here," Terry said. The roadrunner cocked his head.

Ben coughed, cleared his throat and spit on the ground. The bird jumped off the deck rail and hopped away. Ben dug a crumpled pack of cigarettes from his pocket and lit up. "I was afraid Bob had converted you. O'course, it may be even crazier talking to birds than it is talking to spacemen."

Terry laughed, braced his hands on the deck rail and looked down at the musician. "What's going on?"

Ben propped his guitar against the deck steps, pulled a flask from the waistband of his khaki shorts and took a long swallow. He looked up, a squinty glare coming from his rheumy eyes. "It ain't none o' my business, but I seen your truck over at the café late. I seen lights in that apartment bedroom."

There was no mistaking the edge in Ben's voice. Terry felt his cheeks warm, felt himself withdraw, surprised at being confronted by the musician. He gave him a squint-eyed look right back. "You're right, buddy, about it being none of your business."

"I'm a friend of Marisa's," he said.

"So am I."

"I wonder."

"What's that supposed to mean?"

"That girl ain't never had a daddy. She ain't never had nothing or nobody, but she's never taken a thing off o' anybody. She mostly gives more than she gits. I love her mother like a sister, but she didn't win no prizes in the parentin' department."

"I figured that out. Your point is?"

"I don't wanna see anything hurtful happening to Marisa."

Terry had come to like Ben Seagrave, but he resented his prying and resented being challenged. He was willing to tolerate Ben's drinking and commentary only up to a point. "Are you threatening me with something, Ben?"

"I'm a lover, not a fighter. Ain't ever been a threat to nobody. But I'm telling you. I'll look out for Marisa if it takes my last breath or my last dime."

Terry doubted if Ben was capable of looking out for anyone, but he admired the man's loyalty. Being a true friend to all of the citizens of Agua Dulce, Marisa naturally inspired loyalty. Embarrassed that his private evening with Marisa wasn't private anymore, Terry cleared his throat. "Get a grip, buddy. I don't intend any harm to Marisa."

Ben cocked his head, his eyes still boring in. "Yeah? . . . I spent my whole life 'round you slick types. The music bidness is full of 'em. You don't mean her any harm 'less it gits to be nesses . . . ness-a-sary. . . . 'Less she gits in your way."

"Go home, Ben. Marisa's in no danger."

His euphoria punctured, Terry turned and walked

into his mobile and slammed the door, leaving his antagonist outside.

Fuck. All of a sudden, he had that feeling of everything spinning out of control again. His Larson's project had stalled, waiting for a decision from the top, progress on his subdivision suffered from lack of attention and he couldn't keep his mind on work and off Marisa. Even his buddy Chick, in this morning's phone conversation had remarked about his absentmindedness.

He had thought that once he had sex with Marisa, the tension within him would settle, but he had been wrong. Now it was worse. She was under his skin in a way no woman ever had been. Holding her, feeling her loving and giving, was like finding his way home after being lost in the desert. Sinking into her sweet body was like stepping out of a plane at ten thousand feet, roaring balls-out across a lake on his Jet Ski, hang gliding off Oahu's North Shore. All he could think about was getting back into her bed again, of spending his every waking and sleeping moment with her.

He watched Ben shuffle across the RV park yard, headed for the café. Marisa serving lunch sprang into Terry's mind.

You could wipe out me, Terry.

Not true. He would jump without a chute before he would hurt her.

You're my man. . . . Give me something to dream about.

If a woman had said that to him eight months ago, he would have run in the opposite direction. Today he *wanted* to give her every dream she had ever had.

He *wanted* her blessing for everything—his plans, his projects, the very clothes he wore. He wanted to take her out of that café, wanted to see her work less and enjoy some of the luxuries of life, material things he could provide. He wanted the feel of her in his arms, in his bed every night.

As the music from the radio died away, he ran a hand through his hair. Christ, was this the big *it*? Was he in love with Marisa?

Terry's failure to appear in the café the next day caused a niggling worry within Marisa. The hours of lovemaking in the apartment bedroom burned in her memory and would every time she saw him from now on. As she left the café, disappointed, she peered toward the back corner of the RV park, but her view of his mobile was blocked by several campers.

Ben came in after lunch and she fed him coffee. He was drunk, but not as far gone as she had seen him before. He was irritable and restless to the point of pacing. She tried to talk to him, but he smoked and drank his coffee and responded to her attempts with growls and sharp remarks. He had a burr under his saddle, but she couldn't guess the reason.

Later, she spent a restless night wondering why Terry hadn't come to the café or even called her. The next day at noon he brought her a bouquet of flowers from the grocery store in Odessa and she reacted like a silly kid. He told her the trip to Albuquerque was all arranged. They kept a discreet distance. She appreciated that. She even put the flowers in the kitchen out of sight. No sense arousing the busybodies in Agua Dulce. She suspected something was going on with his plans for Pecos Belle's, but didn't ask, not wanting to taint the fun she was having or the happiness that filled her heart for the first time in years.

Marisa was in the café when Aunt Radonna arrived Tuesday, her fifty-seven-year-old body covered by tight red capris and a black T-shirt that declared in glittering rhinestones across her ample chest I'M HERE FOR THE PARTY. She had red spike heels on her feet, bands of clicking bracelets on her wrists and a cloud of fragrance surrounding her. To Marisa's astonishment, when they left the café and walked back to the singlewide, Mama called Aunt Radonna by name and asked her who she was dating now. Instantly Marisa had a better feeling about leaving Mama in her care.

In the evening, Marisa walked through getting Mama ready for bed with her aunt. Afterward, when she went to her room to pack, her aunt followed.

As Marisa stuffed toiletries in a small duffel, Aunt Radonna rummaged through the closet. "Honey, you don't have any clothes. All I see is jeans." She held up one of Marisa's cowgirl shirts and scowled at it. "And these tacky shirts."

"In the café, I dress Western, you know." Marisa glanced down at her aunt's long, sculpted nails. "Are you sure you're going to be able to get along in the café?"

"Hamburgers in the microwave. Frozen pizza in the toaster oven. If I haven't learned anything else in the bar business, I've learned that much." Radonna rehung the shirt and plucked a plain black dress from the closet. "Well, at least you've got a little black dress."

"I don't think this is going to be a dress-up trip,"

Marisa said, suddenly intimidated by her lack of wardrobe.

"You'll go out to dinner, won't you?" Aunt Radonna bobbed her eyebrows and gave Marisa a conspiratorial look. "You'll need food for energy, you know."

Marisa had forgotten how much fun her aunt was. No doubt Terry *would* plan a dinner, and maybe at a fancy place. He struck Marisa as being that kind of guy.

"Now, your mama used to have some nice turquoise jewelry. Put that with this little black dress and—" Aunt Radonna leveled a hard look at her. "Raylene still has that turquoise squash blossom, doesn't she? The one I wanted for myself for about twenty years? As old as it is, it must be worth a fortune by now."

Marisa had sold the coveted handmade Zuni piece long ago—along with Mama's old Dodge pickup and numerous other personal treasures—to pay for Mama's medicine. She sank to the edge of the bed and shook her head.

"My God, Marisa. That was a one-of-a-kind. And the Indian who made it's dead."

A rush of tears flew to Marisa's eyes. "It's been hard, Aunt Donna. We needed the money."

On a sigh, her aunt came and sat down beside her and embraced her, nearly smothering her in cloying fragrance. "Well, you had to do what you had to do. I hope you got what it was worth. I wish I could help you more."

Marisa quelled the sarcasm that flitted through her mind. Her aunts could help more. If nothing else, they could put in an appearance every once in a while and give Marisa a few hours' respite. "Mama had an appraisal. A big shot from Midland bought it for his wife."

"It doesn't matter. It was just a bunch of blue rocks." She released Marisa and returned to the closet, came up with a plain red knit top. "Darlin', this is pathetic. You have no clothes. . . . So who's this guy? Somebody just passing through town? Or something more permanent? I hope he's not a cowboy."

"He's half permanent. He's the one who bought Agua Dulce and the XO."

Aunt Radonna's eyes flared and she gasped. "Why, my God, Rissy. He's rich." Her manicured fingers wrapped around Marisa's wrists, her blue eyes wide with a fierce intensity. "This calls for a whole new strategy."

She whisked out of the room and returned with a handful of clothing. Bracelets clicking, she flapped out a hot-orange low-cut top with spaghetti straps and a diagonal ruffle across the front. Why her aunt had brought something like that to wear in Agua Dulce, Marisa couldn't guess.

"Now, this is sexy," Aunt Radonna said. "If you're going off with a guy, especially a rich guy, you want to look sexy. And it shows just a little cleavage. Not too much, just enough to tease."

Marisa fondled the top's fabric. It felt soft and slithery.

"Silk knit," Aunt Radonna said, then clasped the top close to her breast, closed her eyes and drew a deep breath. "Heavenly."

She pulled Marisa to her feet and pushed her to the dresser mirror. "On you this color will be great." She wrapped her arms around her and held the top in front of her. "See?"

Marisa tilted her head and studied her reflection. The orange color did look pretty good. She could see how the top might show cleavage.

Radonna stuffed the garment into Marisa's hands, turned away and picked up a drapey skirt that would strike Marisa above the knee. "You wear that top to dinner with this little black skirt. Take my word for it, he'll have his eyes on your boobs all through dinner. He won't even notice what he's eating." She gave a giggle. "Or the prices on the menu."

Marisa laughed. Mama had always called her younger sister a glamour puss who spent all her money on clothes and considered herself an expert on men. And maybe she was. No telling how many lived in her past. Marisa had to agree about the outfit. "Okay," she said. "I'll be careful with it."

Aunt Radonna flopped a wrist, her bracelets jangling. "Don't worry about it. You won't have any fun being careful." She began to sort through other pieces of clothing she had brought into the room. She held up a plain emerald green knit dress that Marisa could tell fit like a glove. "Deep colors, baby doll. With your coloring, deep colors for you. I wore this to a party at the Midland Country Club once." A dreamy expression passed over Aunt Radonna's face.

Marisa had expected her aunt's clothes to be on the trashy side, but while her taste in colors was bold, the styles were subdued, which suited Marisa. The green dress was beautiful and Marisa found herself wanting to wear it.

"Try it on," Aunt Radonna said, a gleam in her eye.

Reluctantly Marisa disrobed and wriggled into the

green knit. Radonna was right. The dress looked great. Finally Marisa had to ask. "Aunt Donna, this is Agua Dulce and we're talking a couple of days. Where did you think you were going to wear clothes like these?"

Radonna tilted back her head and gave a deep, rich laugh. "Baby doll, my motto is be prepared, like a damn Girl Scout. You never know what"—she winked—"or *who* will crop up. Sean Connery might pass through."

Marisa laughed again. "Haven't seen Sean in ages." She looked down at the clothing scattered on the bed. "I can't wear this stuff. I don't have shoes—"

"What's your size?"

"Nine."

Aunt Radonna darted from the room and returned with a pair of black patent high-heeled sandals with ankle straps. Fuck-me shoes if Marisa had ever seen a pair.

"These are eight and a half, but since they're sandals, you can get by with them."

Marisa slipped one foot into a shoe and found the fit passable. "I'll borrow the skirt and the top and the shoes, but I don't think I'll need the green dress."

"Oh, nonsense. Take it anyway. Now, nightclothes. What are you sleeping in?"

"Shorts and a T-shirt."

Aunt Radonna's lips twisted into a sneer. "Yuck. And I didn't bring a thing with me." She shook her head and stared at the floor. "Oh, well, don't wear anything. Naked works better anyway. That way, when things heat up, nothing gets in the way."

Marisa felt her face flush. "Aunt Donna—"

Her aunt came to her. Her hands gripped Marisa's

upper arms, her eyes held a serious expression. "Rissy, look at me."

Marisa couldn't keep from looking at her. "I know you're thirtysomething," her aunt said, "but you've never been married. You do know what it's all about, don't you? I mean, what happens?"

Good Lord. Was Aunt Radonna intending to deliver a lecture about the birds and the bees? "I'm afraid I do, Auntie."

Aunt Radonna scrunched up her shoulders. "This is so exciting. My little niece sleeping with a millionaire. Now, take my advice and don't be shy. Don't hold back. You're not a kid. He'll expect you to know a little something about . . . well, you know, about . . . things. I know you read a lot. I don't suppose you've got a good book around on sex."

Chapter 24

And wouldn't it be so Terry Ledger to rent a whole airplane? Having traveled on any kind of aircraft only three times in her life, Marisa had been giddy with excitement when she saw the small jet he had chartered. As she boarded carrying a duffel that held her borrowed dresses and shoes, Marisa felt like Cinderella boarding a pumpkin carriage.

They flew off, leaving behind pages of lists and instructions for Aunt Radonna on how to take care of Mama and how to run the café and flea market. Marisa hoped for the best, but she had her concerns.

Terry held her hand as they climbed into the clouds and the barren landscape beneath them telescoped. She glanced at his strong profile, admitting to herself that her knowledge of him was as scarce as trees in the desert. Doubt, as if it had been waiting in hiding behind a vast cloud, slithered in, filling the plane with its hot breath of mistrust and disbelief.

Don't forget he's only temporary, the protector inside her head reminded her. *Don't imagine common ground where none exists.*

I won't, she promised with conviction.

But no matter what she promised herself, there was no forgetting how sure of him she had been a few nights ago, sharing the bed in the Pecos Belle's apartment. When he told her he hadn't felt like this since he was seventeen, she had believed him.

A pre-arranged rental car waited for them at the airport. Terry drove them to Tamaya Resort and from Marisa's perspective, into another world. The hotel's architecture harked back centuries to the pueblo-style buildings and courtyards of old New Mexico, possibly to her own ancestors. The luxurious appointments reflected the colors and decor of the Santa Ana Pueblo. When Marisa opened the heavy draperies on the window wall of their room, she discovered a private balcony and a breathtaking view of the mountains. The aroma of bread baking in ovens reproduced from those of ancient Indians wafted through the air and she made a mental note to investigate later.

The ambience captivated her. At her disposal were hiking trails and a museum, swimming pools and a full-service spa—more amenities than she could possibly take advantage of in two or three days. She didn't tell Terry she couldn't swim. She hadn't learned as a child because the only body of water in Agua Dulce large enough for swimming was the Starlight Inn's bedroom-size swimming pool.

She could get used to this life, she dared let herself think. That is, if she didn't worry about the cost.

And the cost had nothing to do with money.

All I know is I want to see where we can go.

And that was the million-dollar question, the protector in her head put forth. Her protector was such a punster.

Except for holding hands on the plane, somehow, she and Terry hadn't touched since making love in the apartment bedroom. The tension of mutual desire simmered between them like a kettle of delicious stew. They didn't even unpack before they fell into the king-sized bed and stayed there the rest of the day. Oh, the luxury. There must have been a time when she'd spent an entire afternoon in bed with a man who was all male and attuned to her every need, but she couldn't recall it. This must be what honeymoons were made of, she couldn't keep from thinking. Lord, she was drunk on happiness.

"Do you like kids?" The question came from out of nowhere, his rumbly baritone voice low in the room's dim silence. Spent and sated, in the gauzy afternoon light filtering through the draperies, they lay spoonlike. His hand caressed her breast and he kissed her shoulder.

She smiled and wriggled for a better fit, savoring his warm skin and his crisp chest hair against her back. "If they're in cages," she answered and tempered the sarcasm with a two-syllable chuckle.

He gathered her closer still. "Seriously. Do you?"

"I'm never around kids. Why do you ask? Do you think we've made one?" She chuckled again at her own joke.

"No. I'm careful about that."

He had proved that. Nothing unplanned for Terry Ledger. "I always thought I'd have some kids," she said. "But the truth is, I've never been in a relationship where children were a good idea. In that way, I'm as much a misfit as Bob or Ben."

"You're so warm and giving. You'd make a great mom."

I don't have any kids. Or a wife. His words from one of the first conversations she'd had with him. She had played them over and over in her mind. Later, from Ben, she had learned Terry had never even been engaged. The question about kids aroused a new curiosity and added yet another dimension to their fledgling romance. She turned her head toward him. "How old are you?"

She couldn't resist asking. She had pegged him at thirty-five. Most men she knew already had families by that age.

"Thirty-seven in August," he said. "You think I look older?"

She turned, pressing her front against his, but leaning back to look into his face. She touched his thick brown brow with her fingertip, cupped his square jaw with her palm and smiled into his eyes, now as blue and peaceful and placid as a mountain lake. "You look just fine, Mister Ledger. Eye candy, I'd call you."

"Yeah?" He smiled like a little boy pleased with her answer. His fingers moved down her ribs until his hand rested on her hipbone. "I don't know if anyone's ever called me eye candy."

"Maybe not to your face." She smoothed a palm over his muscled shoulder. Having a naked man at her disposal in a king-sized bed was too decadent. "How have you escaped a wedding and a houseful of kids for so long?"

A shrug. "How have you? You aren't much younger than I am."

How had she, come to think of it? She'd had a couple of serious crushes, like with Woody, whose black eyes and sexy smile had turned her sappy from the beginning. In Arlington, she had even lived with someone for a time. "I don't think I've ever been in love."

"What about that cop character the first time I saw you?"

Thinking of Woody and Terry in the same sentence was hard enough, but thinking of her ex-lover while lying in bed with Terry was almost impossible. Her eyes narrowed as she taxed her brain, made muzzy by outrageous sex and total absorption with the being that had her surrounded, body and soul. "Um, we'd sort of hung out together for a year."

Well, actually, what they had done for a year was have sex. She had never been able to get away from the café or Mama long enough to hang out anywhere. "I thought I cared about him, but I was wrong."

"So it was just sex?"

That she didn't want to admit, at least not to Terry. She smiled at the simplicity of the question, when in truth getting together with Woody hadn't been simple at all. Still, looking back, she realized it had been *just sex*. She grinned. "Could be."

He laughed.

"Have you ever been in love?" she asked him.

She felt his body stiffen a little. His hold on her hip relaxed and his eyelids lowered. "No."

Uh-oh. Dangerous territory. Still, "no" seemed like the logical answer. Since he was ambitious, driven and disciplined, emotional entanglements would always have been at the bottom of his agenda. Maybe she was pushing too much, but she had to delve deeper, since a mountain of fear of her own emotions was building within her and her heart was in serious danger. "Not even a teeny-weeny bit?"

"I'm a coward. If things looked like they were headed in that direction, I usually called a halt."

"Everything on your terms, eh?"

He shrugged.

She had known the answer before she heard it. That

instinct again. She bolstered her courage and looked into his expressive eyes. "Are you afraid now?"

Those eyes held hers for a few seconds. "Scared shitless."

Her heart swelled and she kissed him with every emotion she had. He wrapped her in his arms and rolled on top of her.

Later, as dusk darkened the bedroom, he asked if she preferred going to the hotel restaurant for dinner or going to a restaurant downtown. "But we'll have to get out of bed," he said on a laugh.

For only a brief moment, she thought of the clothes her aunt Radonna had insisted she borrow for wearing out to dinner. "Well, now. A place this fancy must have room service."

"Room service? C'mon now. You don't want to stay in the room the whole time we're—"

"We won't. Tomorrow we're going riding in a balloon, right?"

The fact was, she already felt as if she were floating on air.

The balloon ride was just as fantastic as Terry had promised. Thrilling and indescribably beautiful as, standing within the circle of his embrace, for an hour and a half she floated with him through the gold and mauve sunrise, along the foothills of the Sandia Mountains, over the exquisite and colorful patchwork of the Rio Grande River and its valley.

When they touched down, a ground crew waited with what looked like an armload of red roses, but was, in fact, only two dozen. In the cool of the summer mountain morning they breakfasted in the open air on sweet breads and fruit and champagne, at a table cov-

ered with white damask and set with delicate china
and silverware. They crossed wrists and toasted and
she leaned in and kissed him, letting all that was in
her heart rise to her lips and transfer to his.

She was dizzy on more than champagne by the time
they embarked on the return trip to the hotel. The
fragrance from the roses filled the car and she found
herself touching the velvet petals and frequently putting a bloom to her nose. If she had ever had a better
time with any man in her whole life, she couldn't recall
when it had occurred.

Back at the hotel, when they entered their room,
they saw the message light blinking on the phone. "I'll
get it," Terry said. She let him, since he was the one
most likely to receive a phone call.

He retrieved the message, took down the number
and placed a call. "Terry Ledger here," he said into
the receiver. As he listened, his expression changed
from relaxed to tight. "When?" he said, low and serious. He glanced at his watch. A sense of misgiving
rose within her.

"No, I understand." he said. "It'll take us a few to
get in the air, but . . . I'll take care of it." He hung up.

She lifted her chin, giving him a cautious look.
"Why do I feel like I should ask who that was?"

His expression remained solemn. "Bob Nichols. We
have to get back. Your mother's missing."

Marisa's stomach dropped to her shoes. "What?"

"Let's go." He began gathering their things and
stuffing them into their duffels.

"Wait a minute. What do you mean, missing? As
in out of touch, disappeared? What?"

He stopped packing and looked right at her. "Apparently she left the mobile home. No one saw her go. They have no idea where she is."

Since returning to Agua Dulce to care for her mother, one of Marisa's greatest fears had been that Mama would escape her custody and get lost. She stared at him, her heart beating so hard in her chest she thought she might faint. Groping for her scattered emotions, she charged to the bathroom and swept her toiletries off the counter into her bag. "How soon can we get back?"

"Three hours max," Terry said from the bedroom. "I'll make sure the plane's squared away."

Two and a half hours later, thanks to a tailwind, they landed at the Midland airport where Terry had left his crew cab parked. In record time, he drove the hundred miles to Agua Dulce. Her muscles tied in knots, Marisa could scarcely talk.

Chapter 25

Agua Dulce looked like an encampment. A dozen cars and trucks were parked at and around Pecos Belle's, including a fire truck and an ambulance. She saw saddled horses and recognized several XO pickups and horse trailers. Lanny had brought his cowboys. Marisa didn't even know their names.

As she scooted out of Terry's pickup, Bob Nichols came to them in quick little steps, his face red and blotchy, patches of perspiration visible on his shirt. "We've been everywhere, Marisa. But don't worry. We'll find her." His brow furrowed and his gaze veered off toward the horizon. "If only I had a satellite hookup . . ."

Marisa couldn't fathom the benefit of a satellite hookup. Looking at the shirt he had sweated through, all she could think of was the temperature. It had probably hovered around a hundred all day and there wasn't a tree in sight. "Do you know how she got lost?"

"Not for sure. It appears your aunt got involved with Ben. He's drinking again."

Before Marisa could reply, Aunt Radonna, her hair hanging loose and damp with sweat, came from somewhere, weeping and smelling of liquor. Marisa couldn't find the generosity to forgive her irresponsibility. What scrolled through her mind was where the hell had the woman been while Mama ran away?

"Rosemary's coming," Aunt Radonna said, her voice breaking. "When she gets here, she'll know what to do. Everything will be okay."

Marisa found no comfort in that expectation. "Forget it. I don't care if she comes or not. As for you, Radonna, just stay out of everyone's way."

The person most likely to know what to do was Terry. He had told her he had been an Army Ranger. He knew about survival and rescue. He had lived in the Middle East. He, for sure, knew about surviving, or not surviving, in the desert. Marisa became aware of his absence from her side, and when she looked for him, she saw him in conversation with the sheriff. She walked toward them.

"If she's been out in the sun all day, she's suffering from dehydration by now," Terry was saying to the sheriff as Marisa approached. "She may well be—" He stopped in midsentence as she neared and looked at her.

Dead? Was that the word he had stopped short of saying?

She could see concern in his eyes. He turned his attention back to the sheriff. "Be sure the search teams are outfitted with extra bottles of water. I hope those cowboys have been riding the arroyos. What about a chopper?"

"Got one coming out of Midland," the sheriff said.

"I know a private outfit. I'll see if I can get one, too. Time is of the essence. Hot as it is, she won't last another day."

The sheriff nodded again.

Relief at Terry's taking charge eased some of Marisa's tension. The very first time she had seen him she had sensed that he was a man who knew what to do. His hand came up to her shoulder and he guided her away from the sheriff. "They first noticed her absence around ten o'clock this morning," he said gently. "When Bob saw your aunt drinking at Ben's so early in the morning, he went straight to your mobile. When he didn't find your mom, he got the hotel's phone number from your aunt."

Marisa stared at the sandy, rocky ground as her mother's helplessness and visions of scorpions and rattlesnakes filled her head. And heat.

"There's still a lot of daylight left," Terry added. "They've already covered all the area north of the motel and around Patel's place. Do you have a suggestion where to go from here?"

She shook her head. Since no one knew how Mama's foggy brain functioned, where she might trek unsupervised was anyone's guess. "When we walked for exercise, we went up Lanny's road toward his ranch house."

"Then we'll start from there next. You okay?"

What choice did she have? She had to be okay. She nodded and they walked back to the sheriff. Terry and the sheriff laid out a grid on either side of the XO's long driveway and assigned sections to the searchers.

"I'm gonna go back to my place and change clothes," Terry said to her. "Why don't you wait in the café?"

"No. I'd go crazy just waiting. I just need to get some different shoes."

Fifteen minutes later the group fanned out and began moving in side-by-side lines across the desert, the merciless afternoon sun giving no reprieve. Tanya, her streaked hair banded into a ponytail and Nikes on her feet, walked beside Marisa, her eyes scanning the landscape as they went. "You know what happened, don't you?"

"I can guess."

"Your aunt's something else, I'll tell you. She can outdrink Ben. I can't believe you went off and left Raylene with her. You didn't know she's a drunk?"

Marisa hadn't known. Over the years, Mama had had plenty of criticism for Aunt Rosemary, but had rarely said anything negative about Aunt Radonna. "Not really. I knew she was always up for a good time, but I thought she was responsible. Where *is* Ben anyway?"

"Passed out. He's drunk enough Jack to flood the Pecos. He may not get up for three days."

Marisa snorted, keeping her sight glued to the desert surroundings.

"Dumb assholes," Tanya bit out. "I'd like to kill him and your aunt both."

Marisa might have been into a little righteous vengeance herself, except that she was too busy blaming herself for having gone away in the first place.

Just before dusk, Mama's prostrate form was spotted by a combination of a chopper and one of Lanny's mounted cowboys. Marisa and Terry rushed to her side and found her unconscious but alive. She was covered with bruises and lacerations, and was badly sunburned and ant-bitten. Marisa fought back tears, what her sixty-six-year-old mother had endured looming huge in her mind. EMTs administered emergency hydration with IVs, and the ambulance blared up the road toward Odessa with Mama as its passenger.

Terry estimated she was ten miles and half a dozen arroyos from Agua Dulce. Astonishing facts. To cover that much ground, she had to have been walking in the blistering sun for almost the entire time she had been out of touch and out of sight.

Marisa and Terry followed the ambulance. So did most of Agua Dulce—Tanya and Jake, Bob, Mr. Patel, his wife and his two children. Lanny had been good enough to offer Aunt Radonna a ride. The only Agua Dulce resident missing was Ben.

The bedraggled entourage filled the hospital's small waiting room, stark in its plainness, as the last rays of daylight crept away and dark slithered in. Bob and Mr. Patel and his family stood guard over a humming cold drink machine. Mrs. Patel, dressed in a red sari and a ton of gold bracelets, and the two Patel children, dressed in shorts, T-shirts and flip-flops, took seats away from everyone else. Tanya and Jake sat side by side in armchairs, holding hands. Lanny sat in the corner out of the way with Aunt Radonna, who continued to weep and sniffle.

Since the incident with his daughters, Lanny had kept his distance from the café, and Marisa assumed his children had won the battle for sovereignty over the Winegardner millions. Lanny was still friendly enough when she saw him, just distant. By now he surely must have heard about Marisa's affair with Terry.

Terry left her side to find a men's room and Tanya came and plopped down beside her. "Were you and Terry really in a hotel in Albuquerque?" Marisa looked at her, unwilling to share.

"Why didn't you tell me you were sleeping with him?"

"I'm not sleeping with him," Marisa lied, unable to label the way she felt in his arms as *sleeping with him*.

The hairdresser frowned and made a noise in her throat. "Whatever. I'm not criticizing. He's a cool guy. Why wouldn't you screw him?"

Stung again by Tanya's bluntness, Marisa grunted. "Cut it out, Tanya. The whole place might hear you. Besides, I'm in no mood for this."

"I saw how he looked at you the very first time I met him in the café. You should hang on and run with it. See where it goes."

All I know is I want to see where we can go.

His words scrolled through Marisa's memory. The whole damn world wanted to see where they could go. To her dismay, where they could go was becoming muddier by the minute. "Have you and Jake made up?"

The hairdresser smiled. "Things are pretty good. It's kind of been like it used to be, when we first got together."

"Does he know you had a thing with Ben?"

"I didn't do that. I just said I might 'cause I was so pissed off at Jake."

"You should be careful what you say. Someone might believe you."

"Whatever. I wouldn't leave Jake to hook up with a drunk. Been there, done that. Jakes's treated me good. He's the best guy I've ever been with. He ain't Superman in bed, but he cares about things, you know? And I owe him."

Marisa read Jake Shepherd as being a salt-of-the-earth kind of individual. If he didn't care about things, would he have married a prostitute? "What do you owe him?"

"He saved me. And it couldn't have been easy on him. I'd been using for a long time."

Somehow, learning Tanya had been a drug user came as no surprise. Marisa didn't bother to ask how long or what, but the good opinion she already held of Jake Shepherd climbed several notches. "You've decided to go with him to Arizona, then?"

"I don't know. He's still looking for something closer to here. A guy at the Four Sixes told him their horse wrangler needs a hand. Jake's real good with horses."

A doctor in blue scrubs came into the waiting room and asked for Marisa. Except for Aunt Radonna and Lanny, every Agua Dulcian in the waiting room gathered in a half circle around Marisa. The doctor gave the disparate group a quick once-over before going into his report. He had installed Mama in the ICU, suffering from dehydration, exhaustion and exposure. He asked for the name of her neurologist. Before he finished, Terry had returned and stood at Marisa's back, his palms resting on her shoulders.

Again, the doctor's puzzled gaze roved over the group. "Are these folks all relatives?"

"Uh, no. And yes."

Her answer evidently didn't convince him. He gave permission for only Marisa to see Mama and only for five minutes, which the nurse let stretch to ten. If Mama knew she was there, she didn't acknowledge it.

When Marisa returned to the waiting room, Terry had marshaled the group and all were in various stages of leaving. Only he and Aunt Radonna stayed behind. He had told Lanny he would give Aunt Radonna a ride back to Agua Dulce.

They claimed three uncomfortable seats in the drab

waiting room, prepared for a vigil. Radonna remained quieter than Marisa had ever seen her, seemingly lost in her own thoughts. She had on a wrinkled T-shirt, dirty jeans and rubber shower shoes that showed her red toenails and chipped polish. In the too-bright overhead light, her face looked puffy, not just from crying but, Marisa suspected, from the alcohol binge that had gone on for at least a day and a half. With her makeup gone, furrows of wrinkles showing on her cheeks and neck, mascara smudged beneath her eyes, she looked like what she was—an aging barroom babe. No longer a party queen. She looked pathetic and even older than Mama. Marisa's anger at her began to seep away.

She couldn't say as much about the guilt that had been steadily growing within her from the moment Bob's phone call came to the hotel in Albuquerque.

She got to her feet and paced in a circle around the waiting room, the soles of her running shoes squeaking in sharp little clips against the tiled floor. During the afternoon she had sweated through every garment she was wearing. The clothing had dried and felt stiff on her body, and smelly. Only now did she notice the room temperature must be close to that of a meat cooler. "I hate this," she muttered, flipping a glance at Terry, who sat slumped in a chair, his elbows resting on the plastic arms, one ankle cocked across his knee.

He looked calm and cool. No worse for the wear, even after tramping through the desert for hours along with the other searchers. His naturally wavy hair was only slightly out of place and he needed a shave. Still, he looked civilized.

She couldn't keep from thinking of herself compared to him. She had grown up living behind a store and café, had moved from there to a cheap closet of

an apartment in Dallas. And had never lived in anything different before she returned to Agua Dulce and
a singlewide mobile home. He had lived on a farm
and in a nice house in Odessa.

Her mother had made a meager living selling simple
food and souvenirs. He had grown up with well-
educated, well-to-do parents.

Marisa thought about the tawdriness of her tattoos
and the fact that she didn't even have a decent dress
and shoes to wear out to dinner in a good restaurant,
the kind of restaurant where she would feel more at
home in the kitchen than in the dining room.

No matter what words came from his mouth or what
he did to help her, Marisa had been kidding herself,
believing that someone like him could ever have a
true, special, enduring interest in someone like her.

The devil jumped up on her shoulder and reminded
her he was no novice in the bedroom, either. No doubt
his past included a long string of women and, for all
she knew, so did his present.

She felt shame, for giving in to the erotic episode
in the café kitchen when her mother was in such a
desperate place, for stealing time in the Pecos Belle's
apartment and leaving Mama alone in the mobile
home. If she were honest, on what grounds could she
condemn Aunt Radonna?

She felt like a hypocrite looking askance at Tanya
when she could have stopped all that had happened
between herself and Terry if she had simply said no
that very first night in the café. And now her carnal
desire for him had put Mama's life in jeopardy.

His eyes pinned her and he patted the empty seat
beside him. She trudged to the chair. He placed a
warm hand on her back. "You haven't done anything

wrong," he said, as if he knew the reason for her agitation.

She didn't like having him—or anyone—read her mind. She had done plenty that was wrong. Number one, she had put herself ahead of a helpless person who depended solely on her for care and sustenance.

"I know she's your mother, but you don't owe her your every waking minute. Her illness isn't your fault."

Marisa heard the words, but they had no impact. She stared at the room's metal and gray plastic furniture, its painted metal doors, its battered phony wood sofa table, its empty blue Formica-clad receptionist's desk—all hard planes and cold surfaces, just like her life had always been. Here, she was witnessing her future. Empty hours in hospital waiting rooms like this one for an unknown number of days, months, years. Her own blood relatives had no more than a token amount of time for their dying sister.

All of the softness and happiness of just twenty-four hours ago began to blur. How could she expect Terry or any man who was a stranger to sustain an interest over the long haul? The whole damn situation was unfair, but there it was.

Marisa knew what she had to do. She had to whip herself back on track, had to forget fun and games with Terry, had to return her focus to getting all the money she could raise out of the contents of Pecos Belle's. She looked away, a knot in her stomach. A few seconds passed before she could speak. "Mama's all I have, you know." She didn't look at him, wondering if those words might hurt him.

He didn't reply.

"I'm going to stay here," she went on, deliberately

focusing her eyes on the double doors that led to the hospital corridor. "If you don't mind, you should take Aunt Donna back to Agua Dulce. She needs to get her car and get home."

"And what about you? You can't stay here. There isn't even a sofa. You can't sleep in one of these chairs."

"I'm staying. Please. Take my aunt back to Agua Dulce."

Chapter 26

The waiting room's glass entry doors opened with a swoosh and all three of them startled. Aunt Rosemary strode in, followed by her husband, and charged straight to Marisa. "What the hell happened?" she demanded, her eyes sparking, her dyed-to-maroon hair protecting her head like a football helmet.

Breaking into sobs, Aunt Radonna met her sister. "Oh, Rosemary. It's all my fault. I should've—"

"You were drinking, weren't you?" Aunt Rosemary gripped Aunt Radonna's shoulders and gave her a little shake. Her blue glare snapped from Aunt Radonna to Marisa. All three of the Rutherford sisters had similar blue eyes. "If you needed someone to stay with Raylene, you should've called *me*. Radonna doesn't know how to take care of anyone. She can't even take care of herself."

Uncle Duane spoke up. "Rosemary—"

Her head jerked toward her husband, not a hair moving on her red lacquered do. "Shut up, Duane. This doesn't concern you."

Aunt Rosemary's husband shoved his hands into his pockets and rolled his eyes.

Marisa hadn't heard from Mama's older sister in

months. Without rising from her seat, she looked up at her aunt and opened her palms. "Who knew where you were?"

"What kind of remark is that? Somebody always knows where I am."

"Well, you haven't exactly been attentive to Mama or me, either."

"I've been busy, I'll have you know. But I'm here now." Aunt Rosemary's hand went to her hip and she walked over to the double doors that opened out into the hospital corridor. "Where's that doctor? I'll talk to him, then we'll make decisions about Raylene and—"

"We will not!" Anger, heretofore suppressed, drove Marisa to her feet. "In the first place, there's no decisions to be made. And in the second, even if there was, I wouldn't consult someone who hasn't even called to ask about her sister in over six months."

"Why, who do you think you're talking to, young lady—"

"Ladies, ladies." Now Terry was on his feet, patting the air with his palms. "This is a hospital and the patient's in bad shape. Let's just cool it, okay?"

Aunt Radonna, now crying again, dropped back into her chair.

Marisa shifted her gaze between the two women. "You two don't seem to get it. This isn't the damn measles we're talking here. Your sister, my mother, is dying. An inch at a time." Hot tears sprang to her eyes as all that had happened through the day landed on her again. "Doesn't that mean anything? Can't you stop fighting long enough to—"

"Oh, don't say that, Rissy." Aunt Radonna blew her nose on Lanny's monogrammed handkerchief. "I can't bear to think about Raylene . . . leaving. She used to take care of me, when I was just a little girl."

"*I* took care of you," Aunt Rosemary barked, tapping her collarbone with her thumb. "Raylene couldn't take care of a house cat. Look at how she raised her daughter."

Marisa sank back to her chair seat, wiping her eyes with her fingertips and breathing in great gulps of the chilled waiting room air. Had these two women come in on one of Bob Nichols' spaceships? And now that they were here, what was to be done with them?

Terry remained speechless, but she felt his hand on her waist. He had probably never seen anything like Mama's two sisters. Rosemary turned to him. "And who are you, I might ask?"

Ever the gentleman, Terry put out his hand. "Terry Ledger. Friend of the family."

Aunt Rosemary shook his hand, never taking her laser gaze off his face. Finally, she turned away. "I still want to talk to that doctor. I want to know his qualifications." She plopped into a chair, picked up a magazine from the coffee table and snapped it open. Uncle Duane dropped change into the Coke machine and the sound of the falling quarters clanked through the mechanism, followed by the crash of a soda can in the exit compartment. When everyone stared at him as if he had done something wrong, he ducked his head, retrieved his can of soda and seated himself beside Radonna.

Marisa studied the two women, remembering that they weren't behaving any differently from the way they always had. Neither of them had ever been someone she or Mama could rely on. She walked over and sat down on the other side of the weeping Aunt Radonna. "Look, Terry's gonna take you back to Agua Dulce. I know you need to get your things and go home."

Uncle Duane leaned forward, hanging on to his soda can. "Rissy, we can—"

She gave him a look and shook her head, then turned back to her aunt. "After you get your car and your things, when you feel better, you can come and see Mama."

Aunt Radonna looked up from her handkerchief with wet, bloodshot eyes. "But if I leave, what if . . . what if something happens, Rissy? She's the only family we've got left. . . . What if—what if she doesn't make it?"

Thanks a lot, Marisa wanted to say, but what she said instead was, "Mama's on a steady path toward the end, Aunt Donna. It's a fact you have to learn to live with, just as I have. That's just the way it is."

Marisa had to stop and draw a deep breath to fight off another sudden burn in her eyes. She didn't often put her thoughts about Mama's prognosis into words and she had never said aloud the words "Mama" and "death" in the same sentence. "Anyway, you don't need to worry this time," she continued, her voice shaky. "You heard the doctor. He thinks she'll pull through. Just go on home and I'll let you know when everything settles down. You live here. When she gets better, you can come spend some time with her. Maybe I can come over to your place and relax or take a bath."

"You know you're welcome to do that, Rissy. Will they let me see her before I go? I want to tell her good-bye. . . . Just in case—"

On a sigh, Marisa glanced up at the wall clock. "You can take my five minutes the next hour."

It was after midnight when Marisa finally convinced Terry to take her aunt back to Agua Dulce. She sensed his reluctance to leave, but he didn't argue. Leaving Aunt Rosemary and Uncle Duane in the waiting room, she walked with him and Aunt Radonna to his crew cab and stood on the hospital steps, watching him help her aunt get seated and belted in. He was a good man, a responsible man. A caring man. Yet Marisa had an inexplicable feeling of being alone. In fact, she had never felt so alone.

He came back to where she stood. "I'll go home and get cleaned up, maybe get a nap, then come back."

Marisa shook her head. "I don't want you to come back, Terry. Really. I don't want you to."

He cocked his head and his eyes locked on hers. "Why not?"

She swallowed to keep from breaking into tears. "We can't do this, Terry. I'm not *able* to do this. You use up too much of me. And I've already got both hands full with Mama and getting us out of Agua Dulce. I have to find a job. Those are the things I need to think of. That's where I need to be spending my time."

"I'll help you, Marisa. You're not alone."

She gave him a damp smile and wiped a tear away with her fingertip. "Terry, we have to be realistic. Or at least, I have to be. There's no upside here. Things are only going to go downhill for Mama, and for who knows how long. Even if I had faith that you and me could become a couple, I wouldn't impose such a huge a burden on you or anyone."

His head turned away from her, as if he were thinking about what she said.

"Besides all that, I don't have time for it," she added, giving him an even easier out. "After all that's happened this past year, I don't know if I have anything left inside me. Or I should say, anything I'm willing to risk on a long shot."

He drew himself up. "You're calling me a long shot?"

"To be honest, I wish I hadn't let things go so far between us. It's just made this conversation that much harder."

The man who had made love to her, who had whispered the most tender words of affection in her ear, who had driven her to heights of passion she had never known before, changed personalities right in front of her. His eyes turned hard, one corner of his mouth tipped up, but it wasn't a humorous expression. "Funny, but I didn't guess you to be chickenhearted."

"Please, Terry. I know you're mad and I don't blame you. But stop and think about it. Once I get me and Mama out of your hair, your life will be so much easier."

"I'm not looking for easier."

She pressed on as if he hadn't spoken. "Without me in the picture you'll have an easier time dealing with the others. Without me, they won't argue with you about what you're doing. You can focus on your development. I know it's going to be a huge success—"

"I thought what was going on between us meant something, Marisa. What you're handing me is lily-livered excuses, not reasons."

"Terry, please—"

"I'll tell you this much. I can be back here in a few hours. But if you have no faith, if you won't let me be with you when things are hard, then I guess you're right. This can't work. You won't let it. If you really mean for me not to come back, you can believe I won't."

She stood there, dying inside and watching a fantasy slide through her fingers like the West Texas sands. "Don't come back," she said.

Terry stared out the window at Hercules pacing the deck rail in the morning sunshine, as if he waited for Terry to come out and play. Terry couldn't find amusement or even the usual modicum of entertainment in watching a fucking bird. He hadn't slept since yesterday morning when he and Marisa had awakened together in Albuquerque. Nor had he showered. He had sweated through his clothes yesterday and still had them on. He smelled worse than a weeklong survival mission in a swamp.

He felt hollow inside, as if everything in him had been ripped out and a gaping hole left. How could things have gone so sour in a matter of hours? How could Marisa take the bond that had grown between them and just throw it away? But that was what she had done. Cut and run, ending everything without even allowing him the opportunity to share her problems or help her solve them.

The day away from Agua Dulce with Marisa had been more than he had imagined it could be. He had known attractive women, but never one who was as beautiful inside as outside. With his own eyes, he had watched her forgive her flaky aunt, who had damn near killed Raylene. Who else did he know who would do that? Yet Marisa had taken the aunt under her wing like a mother hen and moved on. Just as she did with everyone she met, including him.

Well, what had happened now was his own fault. He had put his heart out there for her to pummel, had almost told her his feelings. Would have, given a little more time.

What had he been thinking, giving her a role in his contentment? He had never allowed a woman that much power over any part of his life.

From out of nowhere a deeply secreted memory rushed at him. Him, at age six, his mom packed and loading suitcases into her car, all the while telling him a boy should be with his father. He could still remember the feel of his small hand buried inside his dad's big one as his mom drove away. He had crawled under his bed and cried all night, terrified at her being gone and worried what he had done to drive her away.

He stopped his stroll through the surreal halls of his memory. What the hell was he doing, thinking of his mother? His mom and Marisa were nothing alike.

He left his seat at the dining table and moved to the kitchen, reached into the cupboard for a glass. On the top shelf sat the partial gallon of Jack Daniel's Marisa had left there the day she came to talk about the water well. He dragged it off the shelf and studied the label. He wasn't one to dwell on the past or feel sorry for himself. Nor was he one to douse his anguish with alcohol, but today he just wanted to take the edge off the pain.

Childhood intruded again, as if he didn't have the discipline to will it away. Though he lived in uncertainty and guilt for months after his mother left, her departure hadn't been the end of his relationship with her, after all. The following year his dad hired on with an oil company and moved to Saudi Arabia. A debate followed as to whether Terry should live with his widowed grandmother or his mom and her new husband.

Given no choice, he ended up with his grandmother on her farm for two years, where they spent summers gardening and canning her vegetables. They fed and cared for her small herd of cattle, visited with the neighbors and watched soap operas on snowy TV. He was happy at his grandmother's, but by fourth grade he had been yanked out of school in the small town where she lived and planted in the home of his mom and her husband in Odessa. In terms of trusting relationships with women, things had gone downhill from there.

He reached for a glass and poured himself two fingers of whiskey. The first sip burned the length of his gullet. The second went down easier and smoothed out his mood. One more drink might actually touch the crimp in his gut. Bottle and glass in hand, he returned to the dining table and the stacks of blueprints and file folders. He swept the whole lot onto the floor, clearing a spot for his bottle and his glass.

By dusk, it seemed like every whiskey-drinking, love-gone-wrong song he had ever heard had played on the radio. Bad business, drinking to the company of country musicians. Making his way to the bathroom, he stumbled over a dining room chair and almost fell. After he finished in the bathroom, making the trip back to the dining table seemed to take too much energy, so he staggered to the bedroom and fell across the bed. As the room spun around him, he closed his eyes. Sleep. He needed sleep.

The cell phone at his belt awoke him. He squinted against the brilliant sunlight that filled the room. He was hot. A drum was beating between his temples. His feet ached. He sat up and glanced down, saw he was still wearing boots. He fumbled the bleating phone to his ear. "Talk to me. And it better be good."

"Terry?"

Fuck. Walt Grayson, his CPA in Fort Worth. Terry leaned an elbow on his thigh and dropped his forehead into his palm. "Hey, Walt. What's new?"

Nervous laugh from Walt. If Terry had more strength and if his brain worked better, he would be alarmed. "Not much, with me," the CPA said. "I've been calling your office in Fort Worth. Didn't you get my messages?"

At least a dozen. At this moment, Terry couldn't come up with an excuse why he hadn't returned the calls. "Uh, yeah, I think so. I've been busy, Walt."

"When you headed back this way? We need a sit-down."

"Why? Am I broke?"

"Not yet. But you could get there if you don't see some income soon off that development in West Texas."

"The RV park's got income. Campers every night. Rancho Casero is still selling."

"I'm talking real income. Terry, you've spent a pile of money. You've gone deeper into hock than I've ever seen you. You're maxed out everywhere, man. Debt service on that big-ass bank loan is just around the corner and the RV park and Rancho Casero together don't produce a revenue stream that'll cover it."

On an intellectual level, Terry knew all of that, but

somehow there had been a disconnect between his brain and his activities on the ground. "You must have something in mind. What do I need to do?"

"Chick's on the final leg of that big fancy house in Fort Worth, the one you're building for that baseball player. That's a substantial amount of cash outstanding. If you come back here and push it a little you could probably close it this month and pump up your operating account."

Terry rubbed his stubbled jaw. The baseball player under discussion owed Terry Ledger Homes over a million dollars. Chick was a great construction foreman, a super engineer, but he was a plodder. Not a mover and shaker. The CPA was probably right. Left on his own, Chick would get the mansion built, but he probably wouldn't get the payment for it collected by the end of the month.

"Other than that," Walt went on, "for right now, you need to get Larson's off their dime and close that deal. Either that or move on to another idea."

Another problem that called for Terry's personal attention. He had left too much of the Larson deal up to his assistant, Kim. No way could she wrap it up. Even if she had the capability, she didn't have the authority.

"Uugg," Terry mumbled.

"Bills from West Texas are coming in faster than the money to pay them. I don't want to see you get boxed in."

The life of a speculator. This wasn't the first time Terry had been backed against a wall, but he had never been boxed in.

"I'll work on it," Terry said. "I'll get back to you."

They disconnected and Terry fell back on the mat-

tress and closed his eyes. It had been years since he
had awakened wiped out this severely by a hangover.
And it had been years since he had received a call
like the one he had just gotten from his accountant.

He took no small amount of pride in being the legendary wealthy and successful "self-made man." OC,
he had been called many times. Uptight. Control
freak. A psychiatrist for whom he had built a four-
thousand-square-foot house told him it came from his
childhood, when he'd had control of nothing, when
his life had been in a constant state of upheaval due
to his mother's ups and downs with husbands, or boy-
friends, or her career.

Well, Walt had his attention. That hard-won Ledger
success was at stake. Even if he wanted to torture
himself, he no longer had the luxury of fooling with
Marisa and the crackpot citizens of Agua Dulce. He
had reached that conclusion before, but this time it
couldn't be ignored.

He opened his eyes and stared at the ceiling. Hung-
over or not, he was a problem solver, accustomed to
hammering at a thing until it fit his need or his idea.
His attention to detail, his drive for perfection, his
concentration on the prize were all unique abilities
that taken him to a plateau beyond most men's
wildest dreams.

His thoughts began to come together in his mushy
brain. One trip to Oklahoma City and he could pin
down Larson's and come away with a signed contract.
He had already figured out that they *wanted* to move
on the Pecos Belle's property. The axiom he had in
common with Bob Nichols came to mind. People always do what they *want* to do. Stalling on signing a
final contract was just Larson's way of playing hard-

ball, hoping Terry would weaken and sweeten their deal. Distracted by Marisa and the Agua Dulce odd-balls, instead of maintaining control in the travel-stop deal, he had let Larson's bully Kim and call the shots. If he got his shit together and acted now, the mega travel stop could be doing business in Agua Dulce in six months.

Marisa and her mother had to go. *Fuck*.

As far as Ledger Ranches was concerned, for all practical purposes, a few more details and street construction could begin. The cash from the sale to Larson's would be set aside for that purpose.

But to get his hands on that money, Marisa and her mother had to go.

And so did Tanya.

Visualizing a grand opening of a Larson's Truck & Travel Stop took his thoughts to Mandan Patel and his cute kids. Terry didn't especially like Patel, but he recognized hard work when he saw it. Patel and every member of his family slaved in that service station and convenience store. Terry continued to salve his conscience where Patel was concerned by reminding himself that even if Larson's didn't put the guy out of business, sooner or later, the State of Texas would.

Then there was Bob and his motel. Terry had the Days Inn franchise in hand, had assured Larson's he would build it to open in conjunction with the travel stop. It would sit next door to the travel stop, on the opposite side from the Starlight Inn. Bob Nichols' days in the motel business were numbered.

Tanya and Jake Shepherd. Tanya was a surprisingly talented artist. After he razed the building where she showed her work, what would she do? She probably didn't have the contacts to get into a good gallery.

And once he closed on the deal to buy out the XO, her husband would be out of a job.

By Terry's calculations, only Ben and Gordon Tubbs had a secure existence in the future. Gordon, because Terry had promised Larson's the Sweet Water RV & Mobile Home Village would remain open year-round, and Ben, because he didn't own anything in Agua Dulce. He only rented a tumbledown mobile in the RV park.

He stopped himself. Hell. He was doing it again. Instead of making decisions about his development and his future, he was stewing over the Agua Dulce residents. He had to quit it.

And he had to get to Fort Worth and sit down with his accountant for a strategy session and at the same time check on the houses under construction by Terry Ledger Homes.

He sat up and pried off his boots, then got to his feet. His stomach roiled. Hanging on to the walls, he made it to the bathroom. For the first time since he had come to Agua Dulce, he wished for a TV, driven by a sudden urge to hear the news and weather reports and learn what was happening in the rest of the world. He took the radio to the bathroom to listen while he shaved. Besides country music, all he was able to tune in to was a farm and ranch report from somewhere in New Mexico.

Chapter 27

Marisa returned to Agua Dulce several days later, exhausted and nursing an upset stomach. She blamed it on a weeklong diet of junk food. Mama had been moved from the ICU to a hospital room and would be coming home in a few days. Her neurologist had prescribed a newly developed drug to slow the deterioration of her memory. Unfortunately, it would do nothing to restore what was already gone.

Pecos Belle's had been and was being maintained by a sober Ben. The kitchen was a mess, but the café doors had evidently remained open and Ben had sold food to a few customers brave enough to try his cooking. He had even sold some items from the flea market.

Self-imposed penance on his part. Marisa accepted the gesture as his way of apologizing for his role in what had happened to Mama.

Instead of confronting him with the sad result of his drinking and co-opting Aunt Radonna as his partner, Marisa left him to handle the café a little longer and went to the singlewide, where she sank into a hot bath in Mama's bathroom. Bubbles would have been nice, but suds in the hard water were too much trouble. She closed her eyes and gave each taut muscle the opportunity to unkink and dedicated her overworked brain cells to rehashing and compartmentalizing the past week of her life.

During the stint at Mama's bedside, with Aunt Radonna living in Odessa, Marisa had had an opportunity to take an occasional break and bathe. But unwinding at Aunt Radonna's place was a pipe dream. A parade of people—mostly men, mostly losers— passed through her small singlewide mobile home at all hours, even if her aunt wasn't at home. Marisa had never been certain while bathing that company wouldn't show up at any minute.

Aunt Radonna had dropped by the hospital daily, bringing toaster-oven pizza from the bar where she worked or fast-food hamburgers—the cause, Marisa believed, of her upset stomach.

Though Aunt Rosemary lived a distance away, in Tahoka, she had come a couple of times, too, giving unrequested advice or delivering a dose of criticism to everyone in sight. Or venting her spleen at Aunt Radonna if the younger aunt happened to be present. A demon must surely live inside Aunt Rosemary, Marisa concluded, and she found herself happy that her older aunt hadn't come to Agua Dulce to visit Mama all these past months.

Through it all, inside a dark closet in Marisa's head, the image of Terry Ledger stood at the forefront of her thoughts.

If you really mean for me not to come back, you can believe I won't.

He would follow through with that pronouncement. If ever she had met a man with the will and discipline to stand by a hard promise, he was that man.

On a practical side, what that knowledge meant to

her at this moment was that if she didn't get in gear and get moved out of Pecos Belle's and out of the singlewide owned by Terry, she might wake up some morning soon confronted by a bulldozer. So she had her work cut out for her in the coming days, to be sure.

She took her time dressing in clean clothes, then returned to the café with solid resolve. She had plans to make and execute. No more time for pussyfooting around.

Ben must have passed the word that she was back— Bob, Mr. Patel and Tanya were waiting for her. Bob took one of her hands in both of his. "We're so glad you're back."

"We have missed you, Marisa," Mr. Patel said. "The coffee has not been good."

"You need your hair trimmed," Tanya said, touching the ends with her fingertips. "Come over and let me do it."

Marisa managed to smile at all of them and say thanks.

After she reported on Mama and they departed, she looked over the kitchen and checked the contents of the cupboards, the refrigerator and freezer, preparing to resume business. She refused to ask Ben if he had seen Terry. Her short-term lover was history. A thing of the past.

Ben gladly turned the kitchen over to her, sat down at the lunch counter with a cup of coffee and lit a cigarette. "He left a couple of days after they found Raylene," Ben said.

He was speaking of Terry, of course. News of his leaving was almost a blessing. "Who?" she asked.

"Terry. He went back to Fort Worth."

"Guess that's a good place for him."

"Said he ain't coming back 'til he's ready to start construction."

Could she expect anything less? Or more? Well, at least words like "construction" and "development" and "subdivision" no longer elevated her blood pressure. She had come a long way.

She stopped her activity for a few seconds and glanced at the auctioneer's phone number she had written on a Post-it and stuck on the wall beside the phone. Another Post-it note in alien handwriting was stuck beside it, bearing a Midland phone number.

Ben's voice got her attention. "What're you gonna do, Marisa?"

"Haul everything to the auction in Odessa," she answered, having just at this moment made the firm decision in her head.

"There's a guy been calling you from Midland. Says he's got a job. I wrote his number down on one o' them sticky notes."

Ah. The Midland Country Club. Now she knew where the additional Post-it had come from. All at once everything was moving at warp speed. The auction, a job, making a move to Midland. All she had to do was make the phone calls and catch up with the process that already seemed to be moving forward.

Terry was ready to return to Agua Dulce. He'd had the most productive month he had known since he won the eBay bid for the town. Dozens of faxes and phone calls had passed back and forth between himself and the Cabell County officials and they were satisfied with the retirement community project. He and the state were on the same page about a water and sewer system. He had loans in place and was ready to sign closing papers on his purchase of the XO.

The deal with Larson's had closed, giving him the cash to move forward with Ledger Ranches.

Gordon Tubbs had told him Marisa and her mother were gone. A moving van had picked up most of the valuable items from the flea market and hauled them to an auction yard in Odessa. What Marisa had deemed junk had been trashed and burned. Marisa and her mother had moved to Midland. She had been hired by Midland Country Club as the cook, the caterer and the food manager.

A flicker of sadness passed through Terry, but he stopped it before it pierced the wall he had built around his heart. It had taken the whole month to construct that wall and he wasn't about to let anything erode it. The fling with Marisa was just that. A fling. Not his first, not his last.

Despite his regret over all that had happened and not happened with her, the old excitement that always came with the launch of a new project drummed inside him. He intended to head to Agua Dulce as soon as he finished a meeting with Chick. On the periphery of the plans in his head he had been thinking of some things he wanted to hash over with his construction foreman that had nothing to do with home building, but everything to do with Agua Dulce. They met for lunch at Uncle Julio's on the west side of Fort Worth.

"I've been trying to figure out how to turn the existing situation and people in Agua Dulce into assets," he told Chick. He handed his menu up to the waitress, along with an order for beef fajitas.

"That whole area could be a tourist mecca. With Carlsbad Caverns just up the road and casino gambling in Ruidoso, Agua Dulce is a natural for a stop-over, overnight or over several days. I'm already committed to Larson's to improve the RV park and keep it open, so I'm thinking of turning it into one of those super campgrounds. Once I get under way with Ledger Ranches, I'll have the sewer system and the water to accommodate it."

Chick dumped sugar into a glass of iced tea. "Logical. What assets are you talking about?"

"Bob Nichols, for one. After we build that motel, he won't have anything to do. He's a little nutty, but he's a good manager of his motel. Why couldn't he manage a space museum? Or some kind of UFO exhibit?"

"You're kidding." Chick's eyes popped wide as he dipped a tortilla chip into salsa. "You mean all that little-green-men-with-big-eyes shit?"

"Why not? Roswell's right up the road a ways with that Area 51 crap. They've even got a UFO museum. And the Marfa lights are not too far to the south. A lot of people believe in that outer space stuff. Seems like a perfect spot for tourists who want to take it all in."

Chick laughed and sat back in his chair so the waitress could place a sizzling plate of fajita fixings in front of him. Terry was undaunted by Chick's laugh. Everyone who had ever lived in West Texas, including Chick, knew about the space alien stories out of Roswell, New Mexico, and the eerie lights that appeared around Marfa, Texas, which had never been explained by science.

"Next you'll be telling me you've got a job for that hillbilly poet," Chick said, laying steaming strips of beef across a tortilla.

Terry began the construction of his own fajita. "I've

been thinking about him, too. He's a great musician and poet. If I could keep him sober, he would be good entertainment in the rec center I'm going to build in Ledger Ranches." He topped his stack of beef strips off with grilled onions and green peppers and a heap of shredded cheese.

"Why you worrying about that bunch of people? All of 'em sound like they need keepers."

One by one, the Agua Dulce citizens flitted through Terry's mind, as they had done a hundred times through the summer. He couldn't keep from laughing at Chick's opinion. "In a way they do. They're like one big family. They're all from different places, but they've found community in that out-of-the way spot. I worry what's gonna happen to them when they separate."

"They've nearly cost you your ass, buddy. If you hadn't come back here and dealt with everything, you could've been in a heap of trouble."

"But I did come back, and most of the problems are taken care of. I'm moving on."

Chick sighed. "That's one of the things I've always admired about you, Terry. You never stop moving ahead. You don't even get distracted for very long. You could be standing in a mudhole in the middle of a cloudburst and still think it was a pretty day."

"Life's short, Chick, and good opportunities are few. You gotta take advantage when you see them."

"Speaking of opportunities, you can't possibly use all that land you got from Winegardner in a subdivision. You oughtta figure out a way to stay in the ranching business. You could get a break on taxes if you kept on raising cows." Chick bit into his thick fajita.

"You mean the property tax thing for agricultural use."

"Yep. I just filed it on my place in Weatherford. Makes a helluva difference in property taxes. Who doesn't need a break on taxes?"

"It's a thought," Terry said, as Jake Shepherd and his ding-dong wife, Tanya, sprang into his mind. "I don't think Lanny's sold all his cows yet." An image grew in Terry's mind of white-collar corporate dudes on ranch work weekends. Retreats of that nature were growing in popularity.

"What're you gonna do about the woman?"

"What woman?"

"The one you've been drooling over all summer. I'd like to meet this dame. I didn't think I'd ever see one that would turn you lovesick."

Terry sat back in his chair, not wanting to believe his feeling for Marisa had been so obvious. "Who's lovesick?"

Chick chortled. "You, buddy. You've had it worse than I ever saw you. Worse than I did over either one of the women I married. Kim and I had a bet when you'd finally surrender. She won, because I said 'never.' "

Terry felt his cheeks warm. He never discussed his liaisons with Chick and certainly not with Kim. "I'm not surrendering anything. We were just friends for a while," he said, shocked at how difficult the words were to say. "She's gone now," he barely managed to add without making a fool of himself.

"Too bad. Kim thought it was for real. You're not getting any younger, you know. I'm a firm believer you gotta try it at least once. It's one of those gambles you just gotta take."

"What is?"

"Getting hooked up with a woman. And I don't mean just in the sack. If you find the right one and make it last, it could be the best thing ever, like it was with me and Amy when we first got married."

Chick's first wife, the mother of his son. Years had gone by since Terry had heard him make such a positive statement about her. He gave his old pal the squint-eye. "What, you and her are talking again?"

"Yeah, a little. Seems like the spark's still there. Since we got the kid together, it's worth taking a second look."

Terry laughed and shook his head, but in his heart he felt envy.

He and Chick parted and Terry pointed his truck west. As he left the outskirts of Fort Worth and put on the cruise control, his thoughts drifted to Marisa and Agua Dulce. Standing in the hospital waiting room, when the doctor asked if all of the Agua Dulcians were family, Marisa had answered "yes." That was how she viewed that odd little knot of people. Maintaining them all together in one unit like one big happy family was the way to her heart.

Maybe his own heart would like that, too.

Mandan Patel and the old service station flashed in his mind—the only piece of the Agua Dulce puzzle he hadn't figured yet. An idea had been simmering in the back of his thoughts, but with the outcome being an unknown and possibly expensive, he had been reluctant to pursue it.

But some things just had to be done. On a sigh, he picked up his cell phone and called his Fort Worth office. He instructed Kim to dig out the research on the service station property, including what Patel had paid for it and when. He also told her get a current appraisal on it and to find out from the state what would be required for a cleanup to meet EPA standards. And the cost.

"There's a jerk out here who wants biscuits and gravy," the waiter told Marisa.

"Tell him we don't serve biscuits and gravy for lunch," she said, her attention on her list of needs from a purveyor. She had been in charge of this country club kitchen for three weeks and was just now getting it into a shape that suited her.

With the freedom to do whatever she wanted in the kitchen, her new job had turned out to be better than she had expected. She had rented a small house for her and Mama and found a middle-aged woman to stay with Mama through the day. Eventually she would have to make different arrangements, but for now, they were making do.

The contents of Pecos Belle's sat with an auctioneer as he prepared publicity for a huge sale. If the sale turned out to be successful, she would be able to buy a house for herself and Mama.

"I already told him that," the waiter said, "but he's being an asshole. He wants to talk to the chef."

She laughed. "Okay. I guess that's me." She pulled her apron over her head and headed for the dining room. The Midland Country Club not only didn't serve biscuits and gravy for lunch, it didn't serve that menu for breakfast, either. The clientele was too snooty for country fare.

Seeing the back of the recalcitrant customer's head, she recognized him immediately and felt a sharp pang in her stomach. She stopped in her tracks, waiting for her heartbeat to slow. More than a month had passed since he had left her in the Odessa hospital waiting room. She had gone over his words a hundred times, cried into her pillow many nights, kicked herself for being a hardheaded fool.

Now her mind raced for a tactic.

Well, she had to see him. He had done nothing but be supportive and caring. He didn't deserve to be snubbed. She pressed an arm across her midsection, drew a deep breath and walked forward.

He looked up and got to his feet when she approached. He was as gorgeous as ever. Mel Gibson eyes, blue knit shirt that almost matched them in color. Most of his clothing seemed to be blue.

"Hey," he said softly and smiled.

She smiled, too. "Hey, yourself. How'd you get in here? You aren't a member, are you?"

"I bribed the guy at the front door. Can you sit down a minute?"

"Not really." She sank to a chair, her heart galloping up and down her rib cage. He sat down opposite her.

"I'm getting the dinner menu ready," she said. From somewhere, she summoned a cavalier attitude. "So how's it going in Agua Dulce? Torn down our old building yet?"

"I don't own it anymore. I've sold it to Larson's."

To her surprise, the news didn't affect her. She had truly put Agua Dulce behind her. "Oh. Well, that was the plan, right?"

"I need your help with something," he said, leaning to the left. He appeared to be digging into his pants pocket.

"You know me. I'm an easy touch as long as you don't ask to borrow money."

"I've got this and I don't know what to do with it." He came up with a balled-up handkerchief and placed it on the table in front of her.

She stared at it for a heartbeat as an odd feeling passed through her. She pushed the folds open with her fingers. A diamond ring, a solitaire engagement type, lay within the folds. She looked closer. It was a very nice diamond ring that had to be at least three carats. Her throat went dry. She cleared it and sat there blinking at what lay before her and all that it implied. "What makes you think I'd, uh, know what to do with it?"

"Because someone who's been in the flea market business as long as you were has to be an expert on stuff of all kinds. I figured you'd know what it's for."

She looked up and saw his eyes leveled on hers. Her heart was pounding so hard her own vision blurred. "Not much has changed with me. None of my obligations have gone away."

"I didn't think they had." He reached across the table, picked up her left hand and slid the diamond onto her ring finger. It fit perfectly. Had he known it would?

He continued to hold her hand across the table. "What I'm saying to you, Marisa, is I can't get you out of my system. I think that makes your obligations my obligations. And they aren't unmanageable. We can handle them together."

She looked down at the ring and at his hand clasping hers. She shook her head, hope and fear warring in her heart. "Terry, I can't. What I mean is, I don't see how—"

"I love you," he said, voice soft, his gaze solemn.

She blinked and covered her mouth with her fingers. She couldn't think of a response.

His eyes held hers for a few more seconds, then he turned his head and looked away.

She should say something, but what?

His head swung back and he faced her. "Look, humor me, okay? I'm having a generous moment. I'm fixing everybody in Agua Dulce. I just came from a meeting with the whole bunch of them. Bob, Ben, Jake and Tanya. They're all enthusiastic about staying in Agua Dulce. Their roles will be different from what they are now, but hopefully they'll be better."

She couldn't keep from noticing he didn't mention the Patels. A tiny worry niggled at her. "I suppose Mr. Patel and his family will be moving?"

Terry's thumb made a circle on the top of her hand. The diamond ring glinted even in the dining room's indirect lighting.

"I bought Patel's station. But he's going to stay on and run the motel I'm gonna build. He likes living in Agua Dulce and his kids like going to school in Wink. I'm gonna remodel that old station and do the soil cleanup, and Tanya's gonna open her beauty shop and art gallery in it. If I live long enough, maybe I'll get the cost of the cleanup back in rent."

Marisa swallowed. "Oh, my God—"

"So, you see? Everyone's still there. You and Raylene are the only absentees. The town won't be complete without you. All those people. Their lives won't be complete without you and your mom. . . . Marisa, *my* life won't be complete without you."

She tilted her head back and laughed. He was outrageous and she loved him madly. Then it dawned on her—when he had said "I love you," she should have said it back.

"You laugh," he said, "but what I'm telling you is that you, Raylene and I are going to be the first residents of my subdivision. You can pick out which house plan you like. Soon as the utilities are in and there's a street, Chick's coming and he'll start our house. We'll have to travel between there and Fort Worth, because I'm not giving up my business in Fort Worth, but it'll be great. Oh, I forgot to mention, I'm changing the subdivision name to Sweet Water Ranches."

She fondled the ring on her finger, daring to let hope dip its toe into her existence. "We've never talked about things. Never made any plans. Or anything."

"My life is planned only up to a point. Surely you've noticed that. I'll always be a speculator. I'll always be a risk taker. I can't help it. It's who I am."

High roller. She'd heard the word, but Terry was the only one she had ever met.

"Terry, engagement rings and new houses are for people who've made pledges to—"

"Don't you think," he said softly, "that we pledged to each other that night in your bedroom behind the café, when we said we believed in fate? Or when we went to Albuquerque? Did you think I was playing games?"

Yes. No. I don't know.

"This is crazy."

"It isn't crazy. It's great. We've talked about everything and told each other everything that's important. You just haven't noticed."

"I don't know—"

"Marisa, I may be a risk taker, but I'm nothing like

that Woody character. I hope you aren't thinking I am. I'll never betray you. All I want is to make you happy. No matter what's going on, I'll always take care of you. Good God, I've already committed to taking care of the whole damn town of Agua Dulce."

"I don't know what to say."

"Yes, you do. What you say is, 'I love you, Terry.' I want to hear you say it because I believe you do. We're not kids, Marisa. We're both smart people who know what we're doing. We might as well admit what we mean to each other. We can have a good life together. At some point we might even have some kids and be a family."

How could she say no? Why would she even consider denying him? She wanted him more than breath itself. "I don't have to learn to skydive, do I?"

His eyes teased her. "No, but don't you want to?"

She laughed. And cried. And gripped the ring lest it vanish from her finger. "You're a devil," she said. "I do love you. I think I have ever since that first time we danced to the jukebox."

He grinned, the devil. No telling where he would lead her, but she was willing to follow. She had more faith in him than anyone she had ever known. She knew only one thing for sure. Wherever life with him took her, most likely it would be *great*.

The *Love*
of a
Lawman

by

Anna Jeffrey

**"A writer who is bound
for superstardom."**
—Katherin Sutcliffe

In this sexy contemporary romance, the
author of *The Love of a Stranger* takes
readers home to a little town in Idaho,
where old flames reignite.

0-451-21388-2

National Bestselling Author
Lisa Wingate

Texas Cooking

No one is more surprised than Colleen Collins when she's offered a job writing a fluffy magazine article about rural Texas cooking. But after only a few days in the charming little town of San Saline, the big-city reporter is falling for the local residents, and finding it impossible to reisist the frustrating True McKitrick, a local-boy-made-good whose mere presence makes her feel alive—and at home.

0-451-41102-1

"WINGATE WRITES WITH DEPTH AND WARMTH; JOY AND WIT." —DEBBIE MACOMBER

"EVERYTHING ROMANCE SHOULD BE, YET SO MUCH MORE." —CATHERINE ANDERSON

Available wherever books are sold or at
www.penguin.com

O011

All your favorite romance writers are coming together.

SIGNET ECLIPSE